THE WITCH QUEEN'S MATE

THE WITCH QUEEN'S MATE

by

Jennifer Karter

2022

THE WITCH QUEEN'S MATE

ISBN 13: 978-1-63679-202-6

This Trade Paperback Original Is Published By
Bold Strokes Books, Inc.
P.O. Box 249
Valley Falls, NY 12185

First Edition: April 2022

Credits
Editor: Cindy Cresap
Production Design: Susan Ramundo
Cover Design By Jeanine Henning

Acknowledgments

I want to start by thanking my spouse and my dad, who have been alongside me for the whole ride as co-pilots, navigators, passengers, and backseat drivers. They are my fellow world-builders, whose brilliance and creativity are engraved in every page of this book. I could not have written Silvi's father, Ulgar, without having a father just as selfless and loving.

I want to thank my mom. Throughout her life, she taught me love, good communication, values, and her religion: Wicca. Wicca is the basis for the Neamairtese religion, though I took significant artistic license, and this fictional religion is in no way an accurate representation of Wicca.

Thank you to my mentor and friend, Ashley, who taught me how to listen with my heart, how to talk about sex in order to form healthy relationships, and that you don't teach spirituality, you draw out what's already there.

A huge thank you to my early readers who loved me enough to give me their honest feedback and priceless recommendations. This book would not be the same without their generosity and brilliance: Sunaina, Roslyn, Barb, Cathy, and Blair.

I also want to thank Raquel for hours spent discussing my book in Spanish. And to Lauren for sharing her knowledge in all things horses. Thank you to my friends who have always supported me and encouraged my creativity and fun while tempering our mutual workaholism.

A huge thank you to Bold Strokes Books and my fabulous editor, Cindy Cresap, for this amazing opportunity to share my story with likeminded literary adventurers and for making it so much better of a book.

Writing this has been such a pleasure. Thank you to my readers for inspiring me to bring these characters out of my head and onto the page.

Dedication

To my mom.

My mom was a Wiccan, my dad is a Baptist. When I was born people used to ask my mom what they would raise me to be and her answer was always the same: Tolerant.

CHAPTER ONE
THE LADY'S CHOICE

The pain hit Barra like a million stinging nettles on every inch of her body. She had never known pain so great or so thorough. It was as if the pain were sinking into her being rather than simply damaging her flesh. Barra fell to the ground writhing, her body desperately trying to escape the feeling. The shackles around her ankles and the yoke around her neck restricted a great deal of the convulsions, but more to her detriment than her safety. She could feel bruises forming where she slammed against the wood and metal.

Barra's eyes flew open and her seizures stopped as suddenly as they had begun. A million curses stood on her lips but went unuttered. She did not yet have the strength to put them into the world. Several of the Neamairtese around her ran to her side, helping pull her to her feet, pick pieces of dried grass from her deerskin clothing, and smooth her hair back up into place. Unlike the rest of the group, Barra's people understood exactly what was happening and stared at her in panicked realization. This could not have come at a worse time.

The queen of the Neamairtese was dead and the Lady, goddess of the Neamairtese, had chosen Barra to be the next queen. While the queen's death was always a cause for mourning, in most circumstances, to witness the Spirits imbue the next queen was a great honor. The people around Barra did not look honored; they looked scared. They were being escorted to the empire of Victricus to be sold as slaves and there was nothing they could do about it. If they attempted to escape, they would be cut down by the soldiers. The soldiers had made it abundantly clear to everyone who survived their first day, it was forced marching or death.

The fear around Barra paled in comparison to Barra's own pounding heart and the cacophony of voices clamoring in her head. She was having enough trouble making sense of her own thoughts, let alone the others swirling inside. With the Spirits had come all the memories and experiences of the previous queens for thousands of years, and they coexisted in her mind, threatening to overwhelm her own feelings of confusion and dismay. Every thought, those she recognized as her own and those she knew came from women wiser than herself, concluded the same thing: I can't mess this up.

Becoming the new queen meant rituals were required, tradition had to be followed, and the Spirits honored. She needed to ask the Lord and Lady to bless and protect her. If she died before she could complete the necessary rites, the Neamairtese magic could be lost forever.

But her responsibilities went so much deeper than simply not dying. Barra was now the undisputed leader not only of her fellow prisoners, but the hundreds of thousands of Neamairtese spread out across the western lands. It was a burden she would have struggled to accept under normal circumstances. Exhausted, battered, and with no evident future but as a slave, Barra couldn't even begin to comprehend why she of all people had been chosen and what in the Spirits' name she was supposed to do now.

The Victricite soldiers attempted to push everyone to the side and reprimand Barra in a language she couldn't understand for delaying them. Their bronze armor, decorated with brightly dyed leather, tassels, and streamers of red satin, shone in the late-day sun. The forty or so armed men marched in perfect unison, they stared dispassionately forward when not interrupted, and they filled out their armor in the way only well-fed and well-trained men could. If Barra and her people could get moving quickly enough, the soldiers might not remember Barra's face, they might not remember they were ever interrupted. She could only hope.

As the group resumed its slog down a wide, sparsely beaten trail surrounded by dry grasses as far as the eye could see, the divide between the prisoners grew. Just over half of the prisoners were hearty Svekards. Their long blond and light brown hair was the cleanest part of them, but after being forced to march over ten miles today alone, even their hair was reaching a dirtiness that Barra knew was considered disgraceful to them. They all wore their hair in a small collection of braids, even the men's beards were well-trimmed and braided. However, their bodies smelled as if they were rarely cleaned or tended to. They wore thick pelts and woolen clothing that was not designed to march this far from their native mountains in the late summer heat. Much of the general stench came from the collective body odor they profusely produced.

The Svekards were the sworn enemy of the Neamairtese. The two groups had fought and killed each other for as far back as their history went. The only thing that had saved the Neamairtese from being wiped out during the long war with the Svekards was the Svekards' fear of magic and abhorrence of leaving their beloved mountains and foothills.

The Neamairtese were taller and leaner than the Svekards, with a vastly different approach to hygiene. While their bodies had almost as little dirt on them as the soldiers and not a single hair below the neck, at least when they'd first been captured, the hair on top of their heads was another matter. Woven between individual hairs were enough feathers, branches, and leaves to make an eagle's nest. The result had been tied and shaped into a water droplet shape on top of their heads that made them appear even taller. The hair that was visible in the tangle ranged from dark brown to bright red, with most being a mix of the two. They wore tight-fitting deerskin clothing and several necklaces of strung bones and teeth.

The Svekards had already been marching with their own kind since the two groups had combined from separate slave gathering missions—the Neamairtese captives coming from the west while the Svekards came down from the northeast. Now, after witnessing Barra's seizures, they gave her people as much space as was physically achievable to the point of bumping into each other and being hit by the soldiers for marching too far to the edges of the road.

Her people shuffled along as close to Barra as possible, as much to protect her as to try to make a plan. However, every time they attempted to speak to her, the soldiers came over to yell at them in the clipped, throaty Victricite language before breaking up their pack and trying to disperse them. So, as the day grew toward dusk, the two groups simply huddled together with their own kind.

The group reached camp as the sun was beginning to set, lighting the entirety of the large granite outcropping a deep orange hue. The camp was designed in three concentric circles. The innermost was a fenced pen for the captives. Two fire pits were provided, one on either side of the pen, littered with the leavings of previous captives. The second circle contained perfectly spaced campsites consisting of a firepit and a metal chest filled with all of the firewood, tent materials, and rations necessary for the soldiers for the night. The last circle was an area of empty stone and dirt. It would be suicide to attempt to escape during the night from the inner circle through the soldiers' camp and across the open space patrolled by the soldiers.

Barra was released from her shackles along with the rest of her people one at a time and shoved forward into the pen. She had unconsciously begun referring to them as "her people" as all the previous queens had, rather than "the other Neamairtese" as she had done before that day. Once inside, Barra made her way to the few resources that had been left behind for them. There was a lot to do and nowhere near what they would need to do it right. Barra could only hope it would be enough.

None of the captives in this camp were trained as a priest or elder nor had any witnessed the last queen's ritual. They had all been young, strong individuals on a hunt when they were captured, so the majority of them hadn't even been alive when the last queen was imbued by the Spirits. However, no self-respecting Neamairtese over the age of five didn't know how to call the four directions, evoke the Spirits, and ask the Lord and Lady for their blessing. They would make do with what they had and work off a mixture of Barra's memories and legend.

As the last Neamairtese was released from her bonds, the group gathered around Barra expectantly. For a long moment, all Barra could do was stare back at them. She had no idea how to lead or even where to start. In the past, she had always acted on impulse, trusting her gut to know what was right. When she didn't know the answer, she sought help. Neither acting on impulse nor asking for help were the actions of a queen. Before, if she made a wrong choice, only she suffered and she had only herself to blame. The same could not be said now.

Looking around her, trying to keep her expression bland and contemplative, Barra realized she wouldn't even know who to ask. These people were not from her tribe. Though, it might be more accurate to say that she wasn't from their tribe. Since the death of her mother two years earlier, Barra had simply let the winds take her wherever they led, looking for purpose and love. She'd strode into their tribe, everything she owned on her back and in her hair, at the same time the hunting party was headed out. She'd joined for the simple fact that she had nothing better to do and hunting was a way to show her worth to these new people. After one week hunting with them and two weeks marching beside them, they were still relative strangers.

It wasn't just her lack of intimate knowledge about these people that held Barra back. She was the queen and was supposed to know the answers. Her people were already scared and vulnerable, afraid of the burden suddenly placed on their shoulders. The best thing she could do was hide that she was feeling the same way. She couldn't show weakness. She was her people's link to the Spirits; if she looked weak, they would think the whole of their connection to the Spirits was weak. This was her job.

Barra let out a slow breath, drawing up the phrase her mother had always said to her as a child when her rashness got her into trouble and she didn't know how to fix it. "One thing at a time. What's first?"

The ritual. First, they needed to perform the ritual that would solidify the magic in her and, as importantly, identify her mate. To do the ritual, they would need a fire, they would need the right herbs and minerals to throw in the fire, and they would need to cleanse themselves as much as possible. None of those tasks were easy under the current conditions, but at least she had a place to start.

From the crowd, Barra chose the people she knew best, based on weeks of impersonal observation.

"Terenesa," Barra called to the slender, green-eyed woman whose expression showed encouragement in addition to the same expectant look Barra was getting from everyone else. Trying to sound queenly, Barra said, "It would be most helpful for you to gather resources for the ritual as best you can."

Terenesa was what the Neamairtese called a kindler. Kindlers were magic users with the ability to manipulate the manifestations of the Spirits. Unlike Barra and the previous queens, kindlers couldn't communicate directly with the Spirits or use their magic. Instead, they could make a request of a blowing breeze, a flowing stream, a burning flame, or a living plant and cause it to grow, diminish, or change directions. Kindlers could also intensify or help direct the queen's magic, much like they did with the magic of the Spirits. Kindlers didn't create fires, they simply kindled them. Terenesa was renowned amongst the Neamairtese as one of the strongest kindlers outside of the Central

Tribe and would have the best knowledge of the right ritual materials. Terenesa would do a better job of it than Barra, without Barra diving too deeply into the previous queens' memories. However, Barra had no intention of admitting it.

Terenesa smiled warmly and nodded as if she had expected the request. "To the best of my ability, I will do so."

"Daralan." Barra turned to the tallest and oldest man in the group, though he was far from old. "As the oldest, please lead the preparation of the fire and assign people to call the four directions. Unless you choose someone else, I will assume you are leading the ritual."

Unlike Barra, Daralan was immediately identifiable as a leader. She had initially found his quiet, stoic approach annoying as if he were waiting for her to fail their team on the hunt. Over the two weeks of marching, she'd come to see the way people sought out his unassuming advice. She had to assume people wouldn't have sought him out if he was as judgmental as she first thought.

"Yes, my queen." Daralan's smile was humble as he nodded before scanning the group, clearly picking out who he would engage.

Barra looked down at her hands and the disgraceful amount of dirt on them. Short hairs had been growing on her knuckles, arms, and legs since her capture. Were they at home, all participants would be required to fully bathe and shave their bodies, aside from the hair on top of their heads, of course.

Tamping down the frustration that threatened to flare up, Barra repeated in her head in her mother's voice, one thing at a time. She was sure she could find similar sentiments in her inherited memories, but they would not comfort her like the memory of her mother's voice.

Barra turned to the group once more for the final person she would need, at least for the moment. "Aedrican, please assist me. Everyone else, let us begin."

As the group moved into action, Barra breathed a sigh of relief. They showed no signs of having any idea Barra was as clueless as she felt. On the contrary, Aedrican bounced up to her with a smile that contrasted so dramatically with how she felt that she almost found it comical. "Aedrican, for the ritual, we need more water to clean ourselves. When the Victricites give out our rations, trade our meat for more water with the Svekards. As barbarians, they will not miss the chance for more meat, especially if they think it will make us weaker by comparison."

The young man nodded his agreement with her appraisal. He was young and charismatic. She recognized in him the same love of the new and drive to prove his worth that had defined her life. She wondered if he would give her the same look if she weren't queen.

As the fire was built and the herbs gathered, a couple of Victricite soldiers called over Aedrican and a Svekard man, handing each several water skins, hunks of bread, and a handful of dried strips of meat as they had for the past couple of weeks. Barra watched Aedrican turn to the Svekard and offer the trade. After a long pause, the Svekard placed two of his six large water skins on the ground, took the entire portion of Neamairtese dried meat from Aedrican, and hurried back to his people to distribute the improved rations. Clearly proud of himself, Aedrican strode back to his own people and placed the water skins and bread beside the growing mound of ritual materials.

As the preparations continued around Barra, she found it harder and harder to hold still, a task she'd never been good at. To distract herself, she turned her attention to the forthcoming ritual where she would undertake her spirit walk in which her magic would become rooted inside her mortal body for the length of her life. The equally important second piece of the ritual was the choosing of her mate.

Barra would have no part in choosing her mate. While she was on her spirit walk, the Lady would guide Barra's body to her heart's mate. Every soul had a perfect mate, but only the very lucky found their heart's mate each lifetime. Barra would not be a full queen with all of her powers and strength until she and her mate were together. They would guide their people side by side.

Until she returned, her people in the western lands would search for her, desperately afraid they had done something to stop the cycle and lose the queen forever. Before she could do anything to help either her people here or at home, she would need her full power and that would only come with her mate.

Barra reached up into her hair and drew out a small grouping of pine needles, smiling ruefully at the memory they represented. At the time she had put the pine needles in her hair, she had hoped they would represent the beginning of something lasting. She'd pulled them out from under herself and her lover, laughing and kissing all the areas the small tips had stabbed on their naked bodies. But to that particular lover, Barra was just another tryst, all the more exciting for the fact that she had been a stranger the first time they had lain together.

The pine needles were falling apart, and soon they would be lost in the jumble of other items in Barra's hair, each representing a memory. They would fade like the memory. Barra wasn't looking for a tryst. She had moved on.

Rubbing the object between her fingers, she scanned the crowd around her again. There were so few people. The Lady would not have chosen her if her heart's mate were not at hand. She had to trust that fate had led her and her mate to be here together for this moment. It seemed to Barra like a rather terrible moment to choose, but who was she to judge such things.

Barra paused on each of the women around her. She'd have to be very wrong in her understanding of self if her heart led her to a man. As her eyes fell on Terenesa, she lingered.

She was about ten years older than Barra, but Barra had to admit Terenesa was attractive. It wasn't just the cut of her body, but the kindness of her smile and the intelligent gleam of her gorgeous green eyes. "If I had to choose," Barra whispered to herself before cutting herself off. It wasn't her choice. All she'd ever wanted was someone who would truly love her for her. Surely that was who the Lady would pick.

It didn't take long for her people to have a raging bonfire. The Victricites paid them the minimal amount of attention necessary to get everyone from point A to point B. Barra assumed their ritual would simply be ignored.

The Svekards, on the other hand, looked like a colony of frightened rabbits, doing a poor job of digging burrows in the rock to hide from their fear. Barra's people stood in a large circle around the fire preparing their souls for the Spirits as Aedrican walked slowly around washing the hands of each member. With the excess each member was able to capture in their hands, they wiped down their arms and attempted to smear the grime from their faces. They would be thirsty and tired tomorrow, but cleansing themselves was far more important than one day's discomfort.

A light breeze pushed the heat of the fire around the circle, making the smoke dance toward the stars in a broken pattern. The moon was near full, surrounded by a blanket of stars that had looked down for millennia on the ritual the Neamairtese repeated with every new queen. An almost silent rustling in the grasses and trees at the edge of the granite outcropping told of small animals congregating to observe the humans in their midst.

Once the handwashing was complete, the singing was quickly joined by dancing. The group swayed and threw their arms about in unison, stomping their feet to an ancient rhythm that beat inside each of their hearts. The dancing changed cadence and the singing changed tone as the Spirits were called and welcomed into the circle. Each had a way they liked to be welcomed and honored. The people took the time to call each correctly.

The group turned to the east, the direction for the rising sun, for new beginnings, for Air. The leader for that direction, the youngest among them, began to sing, high-pitched with soft coos intermixed with energetic yips like those of a wolf pup. Air was the spirit of infancy, future sight, and the connection between life and the soul. As a group, they called out, "Air, we call you to witness these rites and guard this circle, welcome!"

As one, they turned to the south, where the leader for that direction led them into a lively dance as if they couldn't keep their feet on the ground too long without getting burned. Fire was the spirit of youth, will, energy, and protection. The Neamairtese called out to the sky, arms flung wide, "Fire, we call you to witness these rites and guard this circle, welcome!"

They turned next to the west, their movements losing the jerkiness of the last spirit to take on a beautiful flow, as slow and melodic as their singing. Water was the spirit of healing, purification, and emotion. Terenesa sang out, her voice as beautiful as a bird's with the rest of the group providing soft harmony to her sung words. "Water, we call you to witness these rites and guard this circle, welcome!"

Lastly, the group turned to the north, each participant around the circle planting their feet and settling into a strong stance. Their movements were slow, starting at their hearts and opening, inviting, releasing. Earth was stable, nurturing, and strong. She was the first spirit born and the last spirit called. She would close their circle. Daralan called out, his voice steady yet polite, "Earth, we call you to witness these rites and guard this circle, welcome!"

Their circle completed, the group turned to the central fire and Barra invited in the Lord and Lady, asking them to bless their ritual. They would be the most important guests tonight, and their presence would determine whether Barra and her magic would survive another generation. Herbs and minerals were thrown into the fire causing it to flare a wide diversity of colors and the whole plateau was starting to smell of sweet smoke.

Barra made slow progress around the circle receiving tiny pieces of bread, the only food they had available, from each participant as offering. She ate each crumb-sized piece before placing her thumb to the person's forehead in blessing. She could remember doing this thousands of times as over a hundred previous queens, but the power of each touch, each blessing struck her with renewed intensity.

Barra took a deep breath and returned to the fire. This was her moment of truth, when she would cease being a normal human and become the Neamairtese connection to the divine. She would still be herself, but she would also be so much more. She felt her heart skip a beat not only at the promise of such importance, but at the fear of the leap before her. She knew exactly how it was supposed to go, but what if the Lord and Lady had decided their ad hoc ritual just wasn't sufficient? She'd be stepping to her death and the death of her people's way of life.

"Fire is my element," Barra whispered to herself under the sounds of the continued chanting. Like Fire, she was impulsive, passionate, independent, and creative. Fire would protect her, not harm her. "This is my moment."

Barra closed her eyes and drew up the knowledge she had not possessed that morning. It was all there, the right words of power and of tradition. If she tried hard enough, she could remember them being spoken by all the queens before her. Barra tipped her head back and gave a long, barking howl before the words spilled forth from her in one long breath: a call, a prayer, and a promise, all in one.

As the last ounce of breath left Barra's body, she felt herself leave it as well. She was above the ritual, looking down on the circle of chanting people. She could no longer feel the light touch of the breeze or hear the words of the chants she knew so well. The beating of her own heart had never been a recognizable sensation, but the sudden lack of it gave her an odd sense of calm. She watched herself, or more accurately, the physical body of herself below, step forward into the fire and she could barely feel the warm sensation, like the summer sun licking at her skin. The spirit of Fire would watch over her body.

Barra turned to see the spirit of Air. He would protect her soul up here during her spirit walk. Here, she would gain the advice and wisdom from the Spirits to lead her people, though it would be up to Barra to figure out what it meant and how to use that knowledge to guide her people to safety and prosperity. To the Spirits, time was not so defined and linear. Barra knew from the previous queens' memories that the advice she would receive would be both critical and cryptic. Much of it would not make sense until the moment she needed it.

Silvi gave Clen a smile she hoped was friendly, just not too friendly, before looking back down at the carving beneath her fingers. The rock she was using to dig deeper into the granite outcropping was far too small for the job and it made her fingers ache to grip it. But it was a labor and a pain of love and dedication. Plus, it made an excellent distraction from whatever evil the Neamairtese were undertaking on their side of the pen. Silvi tried not to think of what kind of dark spirits or malevolent creatures they were calling down upon them all.

She and the Svekards around her had been headed west as representatives of their respective clans to the annual Svekard Summer Fish Fry. It was one of the only events that Svekards from almost every clan did together.

At the base of the mountains that made up Svek, was Lake Nauel, named after the Svekard who had discovered the migratory fish that spawned there every summer. The spawning event sent a cartload of freshwater fish home with every participant. Sharing the plenty was the official reason for all Svekard clans to have the opportunity to send representatives.

One unofficial reason for the event, besides decreasing hostilities between clans, was to give young people from around Svek the opportunity to meet other young people outside their clan. This was the reason Silvi's mother had insisted on Silvi's participation that year. According to her mother, Silvi was far too old to be unmarried.

Svekards married for love and tended to marry late, just not typically as late as Silvi would if she didn't find a man she loved soon. Silvi had had many suitors over the last several years but had turned all away. She simply didn't love them and saw no future with them. She wanted a man who cared what she had to say, not just what she looked like, and ideally a man like her who could read. According to Mama, the fish fry would be the perfect opportunity to find such a man.

Silvi had kept Mama's suggestive reasons to herself and asked her clan's chieftain to allow her to be one of their representatives for the purposes of stocking up on the herbs she used in her veterinary practice. Such herbs were rare in Clan Spine Mountain, high in the mountains. The people there lived off the fish they caught in the fjords; raised sheep, oxen, and pigs; and farmed barley, wheat, and oats during the several months of the year when the ground wasn't frozen solid.

Silvi's father hadn't wanted Silvi to go. She remembered Papa standing in the main room of the wood and stone cottage her parents shared with Silvi, Silvi's sister and brother-in-law, and their two children. He'd explained that Svekards weren't safe outside the clan, not with Neamairtese lurking, waiting for any opportunity to pick them off one by one. The Neamairtese hunted Svekards the way emaciated wolves hunted moose, waiting in the shadows and isolating their prey before attacking. The clan was what kept Svekards safe, strong, and protected by the Gods.

Nonetheless, Silvi had gone. Mama had made sure of that.

The group never made it to the festival. The Victricites had ambushed them in the night, killing their watchmen and taking the rest as prisoners. They'd been ferried down river far beyond the reach of their people before being combined with the kidnapped Neamairtese and forced to march south.

In the time since their capture, Silvi had made a few distant friends and caught the eye of several men, Clen included, but none had been of interest to her. It was hard to get close to anyone when she knew at any point the Victricites could choose to end their lives. Then again, Silvi had never been very good at forming close friendships. A few of her turned-down suitors had even accused her of caring more about animals than she did about people. It wasn't a matter of caring about people, in Silvi's opinion. Animals needed her and she could fill that need. A husband ought to be someone who filled a need of hers and whose needs she filled more than the need to call a person spouse.

Clen looked up from his carving, continuing his attempts to flirt with Silvi. He said, "My father's mother always said I had her mother's eyes, that they were the same as Fippa's eyes. She said I didn't just have hero's blood but hero's eyes. I see them in you as well. She always said that the eyes were the most important part...the loveliest part of a person."

"I see," Silvi said, knowing Clen would probably miss the joke. The fact that he wouldn't get it only made her more disinterested in him. At least tonight, the drone of his voice helped to drown out the chanting coming from the Neamairtese fire. Talking of the hero Fippa and their shared connection to her lineage also brought Silvi strength as she knew it was doing for Clen. She liked to see him comforted. It was the carving of Fippa, Neamairtese witch slayer, that Silvi and Clen were helping carve deeper into the rock as Clen wandered from topic to topic.

It took seven generations for Silvi to draw her lineage to Fippa, the hero who had tracked down and killed the witch who stole her child. Fippa's child was already gone, sacrificed to dark powers, but she saved four other children that day and dozens more from clans near the witch's lair that would have fallen victim to the witch's evil. This particular carving of Fippa depicted her triumph over the witch as she kicked her into the boiling caldron that had been meant for her young victims.

The rocky ground and boulders around Silvi were muraled with the drawings of similar heroes, crafted night after night by other Svekards long since turned to slaves or killed on their way to Victricus. They all drew strength and hope from the fortitude of their ancestors and each other, carving the murals deeper into the rock to last the erosion of time. Each camp over the last couple of weeks had possessed such carvings, but never had Silvi and her group turned to them with such vigor.

As one of the Neamairtese on the other side of the pen broke into wild animal noises, Silvi gripped her rock hard enough to puncture her palm and scraped all the harder. "May the Gods protect us," she and Clen whispered in unison.

Silvi looked over to watch through the circle of Neamairtese as a woman stepped out from inside their bonfire. She looked completely unharmed. From around her side of the pen, Silvi heard dozens of people hiss, "Witch!"

They all watched as the witch took first shaky and then confident steps toward the edge of her circle. Even from this distance, Silvi could tell that the witch had her eyes closed, though she didn't seem to need her sight to know where she was going. She placed her hand on one of the women in the circle before pushing her out of the way and leaving the group.

Silvi barely noticed the surprised and confused shouts of the other Neamairtese as the witch strode unquestioningly across the clear line that divided the Neamairtese camp from the Svekard camp. What she did notice was the way they congregated behind the witch like a pack of hungry wolves.

Around their side of the pen, Silvi saw her fellow Svekards take up defensive stances, yelling at the Neamairtese to leave them alone. Silvi knew her clansfolk could beat any of the tall, willowy Neamairtese in direct combat, but Neamairtese never fought fair. All the stories Silvi knew led her to the same conclusion: when Neamairtese acted strangely it was prudent to get as far away as possible, regroup, and attack when the playing field was more even. Fippa had been granted power by Leapora, goddess of protection and the family, to defeat her witch. Without such intervention, Silvi didn't see how her people stood a chance, no matter how strong or determined they were.

"Stay together and stay back," Silvi called out. "You wouldn't fight a berserker in the tavern, you'd get out of his way." It was something her papa would have said. Silvi wished he was there to be the one to say it. Papa was a man of few words, but he always made them count. She sighed with relief as the people around her lost their stalwart stances and began to back away. None would have considered their action cowardly. There was no dishonor in refusing to fight a foe who cheated. Running from a witch was sensible.

The witch paid them no heed but walked toward the center of the group. The Svekards scattered, each trying to avoid whatever witchcraft the Neamairtese were trying to cast on them. The witch turned in Silvi's direction and advanced with an emotionlessness that reminded Silvi of the eerie puppets her neighbor used for plays during festivals. Her face was placid and her steps perfectly even despite the uneven terrain around her.

Silvi broke into a run, trying to seek shelter in numbers with the other Svekards, but the witch kept coming. The faster Silvi moved, the faster the witch seemed to be overtaking her. She moved with a speed and grace that was clearly beyond a simple human and all Silvi could do was try not to trip as she fled.

Silvi let out a rather unSvekard-like shriek as the witch snagged one of her furs and wrenched Silvi toward her, almost toppling her to her knees. The witch closed both hands around the sides of Silvi's head in an iron grip, steadying her before pulling her in, mashing their lips together.

Silvi struggled to escape for half a second before going rigid, all control of her body vanishing. She accepted the kiss for the simple fact that she had no ability to do otherwise.

The witch pulled back and released Silvi's face, her hands falling to her sides, but Silvi was no less restrained. She felt as if she had been thrown into freezing water, her muscles hardened to stone, breathing impossible, and every nerve so cold that it burned. Her head shot back on her shoulders, facing toward the sky, though she could see nothing but a milky darkness. For a long, terrified moment, Silvi was sure the witch had stolen her sight.

"Kill the witch!" Clen yelled from somewhere behind Silvi.

Silvi's vision was a blur as her body moved of its own accord. One moment she'd been rigid and blind and the next she was in an entirely different spot in the pen with Clen barreling toward her. Now, she was the puppet, her muscles moving against her will faster than she could comprehend. She grabbed the front of Clen's furs and effortlessly threw him across the Svekard side of the pen where he slid and rolled to the edge of the fence, a good thirty feet away.

A wave of cold fear rolled over Silvi as she searched the crowd for an explanation as to what had happened to Clen. The crowd stared from Clen's unmoving body to Silvi in disbelief. She raised her hands to look in horror, hoping to see that it wasn't actually her that had just disgraced herself by attacking one of her people.

Several of the Svekard men ran at the witch in unison. Silvi tried to cry out, to tell them to stop attacking, to say she was sorry, to ask the Gods why she was doing any of this. Before she could even open her mouth, she was moving again, bolting forward, and preparing blows that would do the maximum damage in the least amount of time. She barely recognized the crunching of bone beneath her fist as she rounded on the next man and then the next.

CHAPTER TWO

A MARK OF DISGRACE

Completely oblivious to everything that had happened to her body since stepping into the fire, Barra's spirit returned to the Neamairtese fire. She closed her eyes and opened them, once more inside her body.

"What?" Barra gasped as she tried to take in the scene around her. She should be standing next to the fire, her newly chosen mate at her side and her community standing around her singing. She should not be standing in the middle of the Svekard area, her people behind her in apparent shock, with five burly men barreling toward her.

From the side of Barra's vision, a Svekard woman darted into view with inhuman speed. Before Barra could turn her head to look for her mate, the Svekard woman had reached the first man running at Barra, striking him in the jaw hard enough to knock him from his feet. The woman leaned into the punch, bringing her weight onto one foot and mule-kicked the next man. The cracking of ribs was audible, but the woman didn't pause. She spun, racing to the next man closest to Barra, grabbed him, and threw him into another would-be attacker. The last man didn't have time to try to escape. The Svekard woman was suddenly in front of him, her hand around his throat. She lifted him by the neck above her head and screamed at him, "*Ni polit seeteer frie!*"

The woman lowered her head and yelled the same thing at the rest of the crowd. She tossed the squirming man who was beginning to turn a bluish shade of purple into the crowd and watched ambivalently as the people went down in their attempt to catch him.

The look on the Svekard woman's face quickly dissolved into dismay as she stared at the ruin before her. She turned toward Barra, clearly as furious as confused, but could take no action against her.

"Oh no!" Barra whispered, staring at the woman as the truth of her situation took root in her mind. This woman, this barbarian, was her mate. A portion of the Neamairtese magic, the magic of the Lady, now rested inside her unclean chest and Barra would only ever be a piece of the queen she was meant to be.

Any move that either the Svekards or Neamairtese had in mind was cut off by sharp, heavily accented yelling from the fence. The Victricite soldiers had taken notice of the altercation taking place and were pointing their spears around at the crowd threateningly.

Barra felt like her mind was finally catching its breath after being winded. She needed to get her people away from this situation as quickly and peacefully as possible. "Return to the fire," she called to them, turning and leading the way. She hated to leave like this. Everything had gone so wrong and she desperately needed to fix it, but apparently now was not the time.

The Svekards looked more than happy to see the Neamairtese leave and set to tending to their injured. Barra looked over her shoulder to see the woman who had caused the injuries attempting to help, but she was rebuffed each time.

Barra's people returned to the fire. All around her, Barra could hear them whispering the same conclusion, the Svekard woman had received her kiss and thereby her magic. Barra couldn't look at them. If she did, they would see her pain, her fear, her confusion. Instead, she kept her eyes trained on the fire as she rotated around it to each of the cardinal directions and repeated to each spirit, "Thank you. Knowing that you are always welcome, go in peace." With a flick of her wrist, the people to Daralan's right moved right while he and the people to his left moved left. The circle was open and the ceremony closed.

Typically, this would be the time for celebration and feasting. Instead, the Neamairtese sat in their broken circle around Barra and their fire, waiting for her to tell them what to do. More than anything, Barra was pretty sure they just wanted her to tell them whether they had screwed everything up, including the entire future of their people. The problem was, she didn't know.

A bit of a heads up would have been nice, Barra silently whispered to the spirit of Air. He could have at least mentioned it. Instead, she'd received messages and understanding as the Spirits always gave them, vague and broad. Buried in every word were many lifetimes of wisdom that would take more than a lifetime just to unwind. Why couldn't the Lady have just said, "Oh and by the way your mate is a Svekard woman, so allow me to teach you their language." None of her predecessors had ever spoken a word of Svekard. They only knew tales of Svekard backstabbing culture and murderous rampages against the Neamairtese.

The queen is not today, she is yesterday and tomorrow, last year and next year, a century ago and a century to come. Barra closed her eyes and took a deep breath, listening to the first piece of the Spirits' wisdom coming to her in her time of need. The Neamairtese magic was safe for now. Moving forward, they needed three things: hope, freedom, and trust. Hope, she would have to give them now. Freedom, she was going to have to figure out. But trust? They needed to trust the Spirits and the Lord and Lady. They needed to trust her, and they would hopefully one day have to trust her mate, for there was no taking back the way the Spirits had interminably connected them, no matter how much Barra wanted to take it back. Finally, they would have to trust themselves.

"This is not what we expected," Barra said slowly, keeping her eyes shut and trying to tap into the words and ideas of the queens who had come before her. "Clearly, the Spirits have chosen what we would not. It is for that reason that they are the ones who chose. Though the road ahead of us is dire, now we know that the Lord and Lady walk with us. We are all of us together." She opened her eyes and spread one arm out to indicate the people around the circle and the other to wave toward the Svekards. She didn't make eye contact with anyone around the circle as she tried to sound as if she truly believed her next words. "Yes, we face a unique challenge, but my new mate provides a unique advantage we have never had before. As you know, this will take time, but we will do it together. Through our triumph, we will make our people proud. For now, let us build camp. One thing at a time, we will face this together."

Around Barra, the Neamairtese nodded glumly. It hadn't been a stirring speech, but they had enough direction to make it through the present. They left their spots around the fire to establish beds for the night. They would sleep almost naked in just their undergarments as they always did at home when the weather was warm enough. Each person was close enough to their neighbor that they could cuddle for warmth if the temperature dropped.

Daralan approached Barra who had made no move to prepare for sleep. "What are you going to do about her?" he asked with a small bow of his head. His tall lanky body and the darkness of his hair piled on top of his head made it so when he held still, which he did often, he looked more like a tree than a man. His frame was lithe and muscular with a grace and flexibility that belied his years. Barra guessed he was near forty and still in the prime of his life. Despite his looks, he was very clearly an old soul. He took a seat next to her and followed her gaze to the Svekard side of the pen.

If he expected some sort of spiritual wisdom, she had none to give. Instead, she simply gave a long sigh and shook her head, "I don't know. I don't even know where to start." She supposed now was as good a time as any to test that nonjudgmental approach of his.

Barra didn't think she'd ever felt so lost or demoralized. She always knew what to do. Her mother had warned her about being rash, and Barra's decisiveness had gotten her into some rather tight situations. But to have no idea how to proceed when so many people were counting on her terrified her.

"For your mate, this is going to be much harder because she has no idea what just happened, and doesn't understand. None of the Svekards do and they're scared. Starting weeks ago, they've been abducted from their home, marched who knows how far, been stuffed in a pen with people they fear and just been attacked by one of their own. If you don't know where to start, that's where you start." Daralan kept his hazel eyes on the people huddled in small clusters, only their blond hair and fur clothing visible. At the center of each of those groups was an injured man, and all around him anxiety and distress radiated and bred more fear.

Barra turned to look at Daralan with muted awe and wondered why the Spirits hadn't chosen him to be her mate. She didn't feel any sort of attraction to him nor for any man, but certainly more than for the barbarian still wandering around trying to find someone who wouldn't push her away. Svekards were violent, aggressive, stupid, and uncultured. It didn't matter that it was Barra's own magic that had made the woman attack her men so viciously, it only proved that this woman was just like the rest of them.

"You wish to be a counselor?" Barra asked Daralan. She was queen and technically ruled all of the tribes of the Neamairtese, but hers was more of spiritual power. No one would ever question or disobey an order from her, as to do so would be to go against the will of the Spirits, but that also limited her to ruling according to their will. The mundane activities of governance were left to the rule of each tribe's elders. A person became a counselor not through age, but through knowledge, wisdom, and expertise. The greatest hunters made decisions about the tribe's nomadic movements to preserve the food supply for all Neamairtese. The most fair-minded passed judgment on disputes and the wisest created the rules to keep everyone in covenant.

Daralan didn't look over at her as he said, "I wish to serve our people." Barra nodded at the humble answer. She was going to need his guidance and was relieved at just how wrong her first impression had been.

She's scared, Barra told herself as she turned her attention back to watching her mate move progressively slower between groups, lengthening the time between rejections. They were scared of her, but she just wanted to help, Barra realized. She'd never thought of Svekards this way. They were a people who fought constantly and would stab their own brother in the back for a bit of power. Yet, here they were with their attacker in their midst doing nothing more to punish her than keeping her away. Yet, she was trying to come back time and again. She wanted to atone whether they wanted it or not.

The recipe popped into Barra's head. Whether because the Spirits had suggested it or because she'd been searching for it, Barra didn't know, but it was exactly what she needed. Hopefully, she could scrounge the necessary materials. "I know what to do," Barra said, rising to her feet. At least she knew where to start.

"I'm sorry," Silvi muttered as she shuffled away from that particular group for the fourth time. She just wanted to help, to apologize, and most of all to prove that she wasn't going to hurt anyone. She supposed she should take it as a positive sign that they were simply telling her to go away and give them space rather than attacking her in return or casting her from their camp altogether.

She ambled to a space approximately equidistant from each of the groups of worried Svekards and plopped down into a cross-legged sitting position. Clen had terrible scrapes and bumps. Out here, away from home and the plants of the healers, the wounds were likely to turn red and yellow and Clen would die of infection. Hilder, the man she'd punched in the jaw, was still unconscious and it was anyone's guess what his condition would be when he finally woke. Silvi buried her face in her hands and tried not to cry. Svekards cried for victory, not defeat, and this definitely felt like a defeat.

To be cursed to attack her own clansfolk was a black mark on her honor and a shame to her family. Only a few of these people were from her actual clan, but amongst Svekards, shared history and struggle marked a clan far more than geography. Until she returned home, this was almost as much her clan as the home of her family.

She would receive a degree of amnesty for acting under the influence of witchcraft, but no one would ever look at her the same. No one would ever trust her. If this story ever reached her home, the dishonor could travel down for generations.

"Pox on all witches," Silvi muttered, drawing the symbol of Hadrone, god of death. As a veterinarian, a curse of disease was the worst she could imagine. Her curse itself had no power, but in this moment, the sentiment was what mattered.

Witches were evil creatures with a vile hatred of Svekards. They were the worst Neamairtese and that was saying something. Witches gained their powers through pacts with dark spirits who they kept appeased through the sacrifice of Svekard lives, typically children. They were known for sneaking into clan villages in the dark of night when their powers were strongest and stealing young children from their bedrooms, paralyzing or killing anyone in their way. Those few that ever survived the clutches of a witch brought back stories of the dark rituals that gave the witch her or his unnatural abilities.

Children were the most important members of Svekard society besides heroes because they represented Svekard legacy. Targeting children made any witch worthy of the most unspeakable punishment in return.

Svekards knew of witches also for their role in the War of Generations when they fought with dishonor to win unfair victories. In the beginning of the war, Neamairtese had killed as many Svekards by salting their crops and killing their livestock as by actually killing them. Neamairtese, in general, never fought with honor, choosing to use ambushes and attack while hidden in trees before running away. But when Neamairtese savages had a witch, they would maim an entire army without swinging a single blow. Svekard warriors would stumble home, burned, blinded, and with horrible cases of gangrene, shame-faced to admit that they hadn't gotten within a stone's throw of a single enemy. Nothing was more dishonorable to a Svekard as surviving a defeat. The Neamairtese practice of humiliating their enemies made them undeserving of life.

A short, sharp whistle from the Neamairtese side drew Silvi's attention. She raised her head enough to see the witch who had cursed her standing at the edge of the line dividing their tribes, beckoning at her. "Witch," Silvi hissed before dropping her head into her hands once more. She wanted nothing to do with that horrible woman. She could just go off and die somewhere for all Silvi cared...heck, she'd prefer that, then maybe this curse would be over if it wasn't already. That was the worst part, Silvi realized, not knowing if the damage was done or if she would spend the rest of her life as a danger to her people.

The whistle came twice more, but Silvi refused to react. Several seconds passed without anything to distract Silvi from her own morose thoughts besides the vague hope that the witch had given up on summoning her. She was wrong.

A shiver shot from the base of Silvi's spine to the base of her neck, making the hair there stand on end. She was headed toward the witch before she even realized she'd risen to her feet. The witch was holding a sharp rock to her wrist. She planned to injure herself, Silvi was sure of it, and there was no way she could allow that to happen.

Silvi reached the witch with unnatural speed and for a moment wondered if she was going to hurt the woman in her desperation to prevent the potential violence against her. After such speed, the delicacy with which she took the rock from between the witch's fingers seemed to surprise even the witch herself. She tossed the rock aside and turned a hard, hateful glare on the woman whose curse was apparently still not over.

Up close, Silvi took in the young, angular features of the witch. She estimated the woman to be near her age of twenty-four if not a few years younger by the look of her eyes and teeth, though the rest of her features gave her a much younger look. She was shorter than the rest of the Neamairtese by a couple of inches or more, which put her only an inch or so taller than Silvi, who was herself almost as tall as a Svekard man. That was without the giant pile of hair on top of the witch's head. It looked as though she had cleaned the entire forest floor with her head, including picking up a few small antlers and bones along the way.

The witch gave Silvi a placating smile and indicated for her to sit. Silvi only shook her head and bared her teeth at the vile woman. If she didn't think the witch would simply find another way to threaten her own health and safety, Silvi would be marching away and back to her people, though based on their treatment of her so far, she assumed they were oblivious to her departure in the first place. In the meantime, she would refuse this savage anything and everything she could.

The witch sighed and held out a bowl of brown and green muck, probably food by Silvi's estimation. Only the Gods knew what kind of uncivilized sludge those people put in their mouths if their hair was any indication. Silvi shook her head again.

When Silvi's rejection finally sank through the witch's crazy hair to her brain, she nodded as if at a child. Clearly, Silvi simply didn't understand. The witch scrambled to her feet, retrieved a new sharp rock, and returned to stand before Silvi. She placed the sharp edge against her arm again and gave a frustrated harrumph when Silvi's hand closed around her wrist instinctively, preventing her from applying any pressure. She spoke calmly at first to Silvi and then repeated the phrase, frustration lining each word.

"Yeah, well, I'd like to let you. How's that?" Silvi said. She was done with this woman and would be plenty pleased if the woman could simply damage herself and let everyone move on. "What? You just going to keep me here stopping you until I do what you want? No chance."

The frustration on the witch's face drained away as an idea occurred to her. In a single smooth motion, the witch placed the rock in her other hand and sliced out across the arm holding her own.

"Ow! Damn you!" Silvi yelled, pulling her now bleeding arm away to cup it next to her body. A long dirty gash ran from her wrist halfway up her lower arm and was bleeding profusely. "What the—?"

She looked up from her arm to her attacker only to find that the witch was reaching for her damaged arm, her fingers smeared with the brown muck. Silvi tried to pull away, but again found her reaction too slow. She had superhuman speed when it came to protecting the witch, but apparently the same abilities were not available for herself. The witch had spread a good helping of the muck across Silvi's arm before she was able to push the woman's hands away. Her arm was buzzing and tingling with a not unpleasant warmth. The certainty that she had once again been violated by this woman's magic drove Silvi to near desperation. She placed both hands on the witch's shoulders and gave the lightest of pushes, the most her arms could achieve before locking up on her. The witch took several defensive steps backward, nonetheless.

Silvi's hand immediately went to her arm, attempting to banish the slimy material and inspect the wound. But there was no wound. The gash and the stinging pain that had been there only a second before were both gone. All that was left was a murky smear of blood, dirt, and ground up plants over sun-kissed skin. Silvi stared from her arm to the witch who was looking at her expectantly. The woman gave a conciliatory smile and held out the bowl again with one hand and pointed over Silvi's shoulder with her other hand.

Silvi didn't have to look over her shoulder to understand. She shook her head for what felt like the millionth time. "No," she said slowly. It didn't matter that her people weren't going to let her close enough to use this muck on their wounds. "They would rather die than use witchcraft," she said more for herself than the Neamairtese in front of her.

The last word seemed to translate, however. The witch's chin drooped, and her eyes fell to her feet as if this disappointed her greatly. What surprised Silvi wasn't the witch's apparent distress, but the sadness that seemed to be laced throughout it. She mumbled something to herself before locking gazes with Silvi once more and saying what Silvi could only believe was an apology.

A great wave of anger washed over Silvi. How could this woman possibly try to apologize while keeping her trapped? How dare she ask for forgiveness or sympathy? But what made Silvi the angriest was that she did feel sympathy. Whether from the curse or the witch's manipulative personality, she felt a deep desire to believe that the woman was sorry.

As the person who tended to the sick or injured animals of her village, Silvi prided herself on her ability to understand the pain in a hurt animal's eyes. This "woman" was no different, and Silvi cursed her capacity for empathy for such a hateful creature. Yet, a part of her simply wanted to reach out and take the woman into her arms and comfort her.

"Then take it back," Silvi said, her voice containing far more desperation and less anger than she had meant. When the witch looked at her in confusion, Silvi attempted to act it out, pointing first at the witch, then at herself, several twitching magic fingers later, and Silvi was pretending to smile and go back to her people. "Take it back," she repeated.

It was the witch's turn to shake her head.

"Why not?" Silvi demanded, waving her imaginary magic fingers at the witch and at herself. She wanted so badly to reach those fingers out farther and shake the witch until she understood and stopped this horrible curse.

The witch pointed at herself, pointed wriggling fingers at Silvi and then pulled them back as if drawing something out of Silvi. She turned away from Silvi toward her people and acted as if she was giving what she'd taken from Silvi to someone else. Silvi nodded vigorously. "Yes! Give it to someone else, someone who actually wants to protect you, someone who even vaguely likes you."

But the witch was shaking her head again, a look of pure defeat.

A hateful sigh slipped between Silvi's lips as the meaning of it all set in. "You can't take it back." She reached out, grabbed the bowl of magic muck from the witch's hand, and chucked it as far as she could to the Neamairtese side of the pen before turning and stalking away.

Barra fell asleep almost an hour later, tears still streaming down her cheeks. She felt so alone. In her dreams, the Svekard woman was there, but this time she didn't throw the healing salve. Instead, she drew Barra into her arms as the woman's warm brown eyes had said she wanted to. She held her and told her everything was going to be okay until Barra believed it. Maybe, just maybe, everything Barra had read in that look was real. Perhaps somewhere under that violent, grungy, scornful exterior was a woman with the capacity to understand.

However, when morning came and brought with it Victricites yelling at them and brandishing their swords to make it clear what was waiting for anyone who refused to move quickly enough, Barra's fear and guilt were back full force. "Kvichta," the woman had said. It was one of the only Svekard words Barra recognized. It was a derogatory term for magic that as far as Barra understood referred more to fallen kindlers, former Neamairtese with a connection to the divine who had been banished for turning to dark spirits to achieve results the Spirits refused to provide.

Her mind played the same scene over and over again: the Svekard's look of unadulterated hatred before throwing Barra's peace offering and storming away. She couldn't know the physical and spiritual energy that Barra had put into the salve to make it work, and Barra was sure the woman wouldn't have cared.

She had been willing to give the woman a chance. Despite her visceral hatred for Svekards, Barra had trusted the Lady and tried. But the woman, like all Svekards, only had room in her heart for hate.

When the camp had been prepared as much as was possible for the next people who fell victim to the Victricites, the group moved out for another full day of marching, sore feet aching with even the first step.

The sky spread out above them as Barra had never seen before. It was disconcerting to be able to see the horizon on every side rather than seeing trees in every direction as she did at home. The blue of the sky was so pure and deep, like bluebells in summer. The sparse clouds swirled as if they were too weak to hold their shape against the current of the wind or hold their own color against the influence of the sun. It was beautiful, but all Barra could think about was how much she wished for her own sky instead.

The Neamairtese could sense her unease and gave her space. If they needed a morale boost, now was not the time to seek it. Only Daralan marched close enough to hear Barra's whispered admission. "She hates me."

"She doesn't know you," Daralan said.

Barra just shook her head, not even bothering to look up from the dust cloud that her shuffling feet were creating. "You didn't see her last night. If she could, she would have hurt me." That morning, the

Victricites had killed one of the injured men who would have slowed down the group if his tribesfolk had tried to carry him. She could feel the hatred of all of the Svekards directed at her and wasn't so sure she didn't deserve it.

"She is your heart's mate." Daralan attempted to console her. "Though it may take time, she will come to know it too. Trust the Spirits."

Barra gave a small, despondent sigh and whispered so no one else could overhear. "It's me I don't trust. What if I let the Spirits down? If I let our people down? With everything the Spirits told me jumbled and mixed with my own feelings, it's hard to tell what is them and what is just my own fleeting thoughts and opinions."

"We trust you." Daralan provided all of the support Barra needed but none of the concrete advice she wanted.

"You...Thank you," Barra said. She bit the tip of her tongue, trying to figure out how to say what she should not, but what would nag at her until she did. "The queen needs someone like you."

Daralan heard what she had carefully not said and shook his head. "Though I am here for whatever you need, the Lady did not even consider me as your mate. You and I celebrate on opposite ends of Torchane."

Torchane was the Neamairtese fertility festival in early spring. Every willing adult attended the festival to eat and drink, celebrating the end of winter. As the evening turned to night, the Neamairtese turned their celebration to the spirit of Earth, asking for her blessing of fertility to the land through a large orgy.

In every tribe's festival, from the smallest tribes on the eastern edges to the massive central festival that drew representatives from all tribes, the setup was the same. The evoker stood at the center of the festival to guide and start the ritual. At the central festival, the evoker was the queen, while in other tribes, a spiritual leader would fill the role. To the evoker's right were all the men who would participate and to the left all the women. Everyone stood naked in the chilly evening air. Once the directions had been called and the Lord and Lady invited into their ceremony, the orgy began with the evoker's first orgasm, brought on by her or his mate or chosen lover for the task. Men would move left and women right to mix until each person had found their desired balance of male and female partners.

Barra only ever traveled as far right as necessary to satisfy her best friend and favorite lover, Helenda, but accepted only female partners herself. From Daralan's comment, he must have remained on the right with male partners. To the Neamairtese, any location on the field was as valid as any other, as long as consent was requested and received.

The queen and her mate were the only traditionally fully monogamous couple amongst the Neamairtese. The decision to be monogamous or not was a conversation couples had regularly and openly throughout their relationship. Outside of the queen, a person's mate was the person who lived with them, helped them raise their children, and had the primary responsibility for supporting and loving them emotionally and physically. Sex was an important part of being someone's mate, but it was far from the only aspect. As often as not, mates agreed to have partners outside of their pairing to meet their diverse and divergent sexual desires.

The queen and her mate had been told by the Lady herself that they were made for each other, so the decision had been made for them. They were still allowed to bring others into bed with them but were expected to do so as a pair. Barra couldn't imagine Daralan would be excited about joining any of her choices or the other way around.

At Helenda's urging, Barra had tried a man once and determined it was not for her. "It just feels so good to be filled," Helenda had said with a seductive shiver.

"That's what your fingers are for," Barra had countered, "or your tongue." The fun that comment had sparked had been way more enjoyable than her time with Helenda's male friend. She knew she was jaded by jealousy that he had something Helenda wanted that Barra would never have, but she also knew how she felt, and men were not for her.

Barra didn't think she could be happy in the long run with Daralan as her mate, but in that moment, the idea seemed appealing just to have someone with whom she could truly share her fears and vulnerabilities. When Barra drew up the memories of all the queens of the past, the strongest constant was the endless support and love of the queen's mate.

With the full magic of a queen, Barra could have easily incapacitated the Victricites and sent the Svekards running. However, the full magic of the queen required things Barra simply didn't have. A full queen was a well-washed, clean-shaven vessel for magic with the energy that came from constant good sleep, self-care, and intimate sex. She had around her a community of advisors and supporters as well as a bountiful supply of ritual materials. To cast spells, the queens before Barra had called on the Spirits for assistance and pulled on the strength of their mates, neither of which were responding to Barra now. Barra's powers were as dim as her mood and there wasn't anything she could think of to do about it.

Barra wasn't the first queen to feel overwhelmed or inadequate from the immense weight placed upon her shoulders. There had been two queens who received their mantle during pivotal moments in the many wars with the Svekards and a third who had arisen during a famine. Barra was the only queen in memory to take on such a challenge alone.

Unless the Lady decided to literally deny fate, Barra supposed she ought to try to make amends with the woman the Lady had chosen for her. It seemed better than being alone forever.

Throughout their march south that day, through increasingly dry brush and dead grasses, Barra tried numerous times to re-approach the woman she'd taken to calling her Svekard.

Her first problem stemmed from the fact that she found it difficult to tell the Svekards apart. She could tell any of her people apart from across the broadest meadow by the shape of their face, the style of their hair, or the artifacts worn around their necks. The Svekards all seemed to look the same. Their body shape was covered by uniform, dingy furs and their faces were shrouded by their braids—hair and beards.

The second problem was her Svekard's clear desire not to be approached. The moment Barra was sure she'd found the woman, her Svekard would shift into the crowd and be lost. Even with her people's clear avoidance of her, her Svekard was doing an excellent job of blending in.

Barra hadn't expected this reaction of apparent antipathy from the rest of the Svekards toward her Svekard. Sure, they'd pushed her Svekard away last night, but they had all been staring at her during her entire interaction with Barra as if in awe. It was as if they couldn't make up their minds between fear, aversion, and reverence for her Svekard.

It wasn't until they reached the next camp, identical to the one from the night before, that the Svekards were able to completely isolate

Barra's Svekard. They provided her with a share of the tribe's food before casting her out. Barra could barely see the woman sitting by herself at the far edge of the Svekard side, facing a fence post so that her back was to both her own people and Barra's.

The rest of the Svekards sat around the fire, their deep, husky voices just audible from where Barra sat. She could hear the rolling cadence of their storytelling, accented by the popping of their fire, and watched as the group provided hand motions to supplement the story. Barra would not have particularly noticed the physical aspects of the ritual if not for the fact that she could see her Svekard mimicking the motions. During long pauses, the woman would stroke her thumb up her forehead as if by compulsion.

"How am I supposed to love her?" Barra whispered to herself. It was a question she had refused to put into words earlier. Looking across the divide at the woman hopelessly alone, Barra couldn't help but feel frustrated and rather hopeless herself. She had offered her Svekard magic to heal her people. She had offered her comfort. She had given her a great gift in making her the queen's mate even if she hadn't truly meant to do so. But all of it had fallen on deaf ears and closed fists. It wasn't just a language barrier between them, but her Svekard's blatant refusal to try to make things work. Her Svekard's prejudices ran too deep to open her eyes and her heart. How could Barra be expected to win over a woman like that?

Barra was glad for her own chosen isolation as she reached up to flick a tear from her cheek. "How can she be my heart's mate?" It was a slightly different question, with far more implications for her own character and worthiness. To be led by the Lady to a barbarian felt like a disgrace. As far as any queen knew, her people and the Svekards had never harbored anything but hatred for each other. Was she not good enough for a Neamairtese? In her heart was she more like the barbarians across the pen than her own people?

With a sinking heart, Barra looked over her shoulder at her people. She'd provided all the blessings that seemed fitting to her people's food and sleeping area before leaving them to their own socializing and rituals of self-care. Unlike the Svekards, the Neamairtese took care of their people, and a long string of mutual massages was forming to ease the strain of marching and sleeping on stone embankments.

No one would bother Barra as she sat on the line between two very different groups of people, willing her Svekard to come to her. Barra supposed she had the power to summon the woman, but doing so had made her Svekard so angry. It seemed rather counterproductive, at least tonight. For now, she would simply sit here, apart from her own people as well and ask the Spirits to guide her.

CHAPTER THREE
A BROKEN HOME

Silvi's second night as an outcast, she went automatically to her spot by the fence without trying to speak to anyone. The camps along the route south all looked so similar, it was hard to remember that this was a new site and not the one she had sat in twenty-four hours before in exactly the same position.

Evenings in the lowlands were warm enough that Silvi didn't need the shared body heat around the fire. If the temperature kept rising as quickly as it had been for the past two weeks of marching from the foothills to the southern plains, soon her own furs would be uncomfortably warm at night even without the fire.

Tonight, like every night since the beginning of their captivity, once the fire was started and the food distributed, the Svekards sat down in their circle to complete the tradition of legacy. Slade, the best of the storytellers amongst them, would name the lineage of each person in the group until they reached one of Svek's great heroes. One hero would be chosen to have their entire story recounted. The tradition reminded each Svekard that they had greatness in their blood and that even if they were from rival clans, many of them were brothers with the same blood in their veins.

On previous nights, Silvi's heart had filled with pride, mouthing along with the storyteller the names of her ancestors, starting with Mama and ending with Fippa, witch slayer, spirit of a mother bear, touched by Leapora. The most respected among all the heroes were the heroes of the three Prime Gods—Leapora, goddess of protection and the family; Fradren, god of justice and order; and Klucar, god of war.

But not tonight. Tonight, their first recounting of lineage since the witch's attack, Silvi heard her name called, "Silvi of Clan Spine Mountain." The storyteller had paused for a long moment after calling her name and the people around the circle bowed their heads as if sharing in her shame. After several seconds, the storyteller continued with the next Svekard's lineage.

For a long moment, all Silvi could do was stare at the storyteller with shock. She had never heard of a Svekard being so hated as to be stripped of their lineage. Even Hydol the Childless, who purposely murdered his own infant and was banished, had a lineage. Silvi did not know his lineage personally, but she knew it existed.

Silvi had no power to stop the tears that felt like they were clogging her throat as much as flowing down her face. What would Mama, for whom reputation and image was so important, think if she knew? Silvi refused to think about what Papa would think. She couldn't bear the idea of him being so disappointed in her.

She turned from the group, staring up at the stars, and focused on keeping her sobs silent. Svekards were the most selfless and loyal of people. They came together in a crisis like no other creature Silvi could imagine. To be excluded this way and in every way she had been since the witch's curse was all the harsher for its contradiction to the Svekard approach to life.

There were other clanless Svekards, berserkers who had been touched by the Gods to defeat their enemies. The touch of the Gods was often more than a human mind or body could handle. These berserkers could never reintegrate into their clan and lived the rest of their lives in the service of a clan they could never again be part of.

She had attacked her own people. Silvi wasn't a berserker. There would be no compensation to her family for her service, no home at the edge of any village to call her own, and no knock at her door when she was needed. No one would ever need Silvi. To be useless to the clan was the greatest disgrace for a Svekard. What was it to be detrimental to the clan?

She was without a clan and without a lineage. Was she even a Svekard anymore?

When Slade had finished with the final Svekard in the group's lineage, he turned to the tale of Wygon of Clan Spine Mountain. It was Silvi's second favorite legend after that of Fippa because while Fippa's blood ran in her veins, Silvi had witnessed the Gods mark Wygon. His was the story she drew up in her mind when she prayed to the Gods with her clansfolk. She followed along, trying to let the story console her.

"It was the first true day of winter, when the smell of the air promises snow and the first webs of frost grow across windows," Slade began, and all the Svekards around the circle brought their arms up to act out a collective shiver despite the heat. "When a wise hero rose, a protector of the clan, a chieftain who refused to fall—Wygon of Clan Spine Mountain, hero of Scobata, goddess of knowledge and wisdom."

Silvi drew the symbol of Scobata over her heart along with her people.

"Wygon of Clan Spine Mountain had been the chieftain for many, many winters. Our hero led his people through famine and the coldest winter anyone could remember. He barely had enough gray-white hair to form two braids, and his beard was nothing more than seven long, white wisps. There was a limp to his walk, and the right side of his face always seemed one word behind the left side when he talked. But he knew every member of his clan like they were his children and every law in the Code."

Silvi stroked an invisible beard and swung her shoulder as if walking with a limp, though her legs stayed in their cross-legged position. When Silvi was a child, Wygon was their chieftain and had been since before Silvi's parents were married. Silvi had not known him before the seizure that had slowed him. To her, the man had always been as Slade described: wise, steadfast, and gracious.

"Everyone knew his time as chieftain wouldn't last much longer, but who could replace him? Who could follow such strength of character?" Slade looked around the circle as if challenging any one of them to claim they were up to the task.

"You?" Slade asked, pointing at one of the men who immediately shook his head. "You?" Slade asked the woman on the other side of the circle who uttered a "no" as she shook her head vigorously.

In Svek, it was a moral obligation to unseat a bad leader or prevent a weak leader from taking power. There was pride involved of course, but true Svekards stepped forward because they believed that they could better serve the clan through a place of power. Chieftains fought like mother bears until their last breath in case the Gods needed them to defeat an unworthy challenger. Former chieftains such as those earned a place as advisers to the younger clansfolk who defeated them. Their duty was to fight and to prevent anyone but the best from taking their place, but their duty extended to their successor and their clan after defeat. If they had served long enough to lose the physical luster of youth, their wisdom and knowledge were invaluable.

"Enter Trivel, Son of Jung," Slade announced to the boos of the crowd. Silvi kept her movements small, but shook her fist and booed, nonetheless. Trivel, Son of Jung deserved it. She'd been eight years old the day Trivel had challenged Wygon for the position of chieftain, but she remembered it as vividly as the births of her niece and nephew, moments she held dear.

"He was frustrated by the clan's flagrant underutilization of himself and his virile compatriots to claim more resources and land from other clans." Again, the crowd booed.

"He called for a combat," Slade said.

"His young body rippled with muscles as he paced the combat ground, pawing the dirt like a horse." Around the circle, muscles were clenched and biceps curled. Silvi scrunched up her face in a mockery of the arrogant, thick-headed man she'd seen that day.

"He was anxious for the fight to begin so he could end it and frustrated by the time it took the wise old chieftain, the protector of his clan, Wygon of Clan Spine Mountain, to take up position. Once Wygon of Clan Spine Mountain, father of his clan, and Trivel, Son of Jung, the challenger, had taken their places and the will of the Gods requested, Trivel, Son of Jung leapt from his edge of the circle. Wygon of Clan Spine Mountain, chieftain and five-time Grand Kraun, barely had his guard up when Trivel, Son of Jung's first kick struck him in the gut, knocking him to the ground in a cloud of dust and gasps of shock."

A gasp filled the air, though this moment was a shock to no one. They knew their lines.

"Wygon of Clan Spine Mountain, chieftain without equal in his era, got unsteady feet under himself, dirt sticking to his lips, just in time to receive a punch to the jaw that left it hanging to the right as if to give that side a chance to do more of the talking. Wygon of Clan Spine Mountain, bearer of constant assault, took beating after beating until the crowd was surprised he could even pick himself up." Silvi let her jaw hang, remembering how bad Wygon had looked. She remembered the way she'd gripped Papa's hand, willing it to all stop. It didn't matter that it was Wygon's sacred duty to fight to keep a lesser foe from defeating him. Silvi hated to see anyone hurt, especially someone she admired so greatly.

Slade didn't stop, his voice rose and he sped up as the action grew. "The veins in his temples throbbed, mud caked his chin, hiding the strands of hair. He'd lost the few teeth that had remained, and his face was almost swollen shut. 'Give up, old man,' Trivel, Son of Jung yelled."

The crowd had never booed so loudly. Trivel's words were in clear disrespect of the titles owed to Wygon. Silvi could feel her own anger rising, a muted repeat of the way she had felt. This man cannot be our leader, she had thought, looking to Papa with desperation. Surely someone would do something.

"Trivel, Son of Jung turned to the crowd." Slade extended his arms as if in victory and pivoted on his heels to look the group over with a fiendish look. They glared back at him.

"Whatever Trivel, Son of Jung had intended to say to the crowd, only he ever knew. Behind him, Wygon of Clan Spine Mountain, the hero who would not stay down, rose once more. If you had been there, my friends, the day Wygon of Clan Spine Mountain rose, you would have seen every eye go wide as you watched what you had thought at first was the red glow of exertion and then the smear of blood, become a red aura brighter and deeper than the largest bonfire. You would have seen Wygon of Clan Spine Mountain, chosen of Scobata, radiating the red aura of the Gods. You would have watched in awe as the symbol of Scobata, goddess of knowledge and wisdom, traced itself across Wygon's forehead as if some invisible force was drawing it there in blood."

Silvi closed her eyes and watched the moment replay behind her eyelids. The power of the Gods was too great to fit inside a single human without radiating out and carving itself on the chosen few. For that reason, to see the will of the Gods was rare and breathtaking. The Gods were wary of interference, even though acting through humans was their only way to act out their desires for the world. The Gods' internal squabbles also limited such interactions.

Slade continued, stating what every Svekard knew. "For the Gods to step into this challenge was the strongest possible statement about Trivel, Son of Jung's character and that of Wygon of Clan Spine Mountain, leader by will of the Gods."

"Trivel, Son of Jung, turned to the new hero, his own eyes bulging. The young challenger pulled back his fist in one last desperate act but was too slow. The man who a moment before had been accepting punches because there was nothing else he could do, Wygon of Clan Spine Mountain, swung his first and only blow. The chieftain's elbow came up with a smoothness and strength he had not possessed in twenty years."

Silvi twisted her wrist in against her shoulder just as Papa had taught her to do and thrust her elbow up at the invisible enemy in front of her at the same time as the rest of her people.

"The crowd heard the crunch as the chieftain's elbow connected with Trivel, Son of Jung's chin and the young man fell." Slade announced to the cheers of the crowd. "He did not get up again for several hours. No one carried him from the combat ground and there was a…well," he said with a cheeky grin and long pause, "let's just say there was an influx of livestock that just happened to be herded through the area over the next hour." The crowd's cheers rose, accented by laughter and whoops of joy.

Silvi's clan had witnessed the will of the Gods that day. As Papa had said, if we make ourselves vessels for the Gods, the clan will always triumph. Silvi had never been prouder to be a Svekard and even now, sixteen years later, the story brought tears of pride to her eyes.

Everyone in Silvi's clan knew the name Trivel, Son of Jung, though he had left to seek out a clan for whom his name did not carry a stain of disgrace. Silvi doubted he ever found a place where Wygon's story did not follow and haunt him. Trivel's life would serve as a lesson for generations to come, a life worse than death.

As a chosen of the Gods, the chieftain became a Svekard hero. Wygon of Clan Spine Mountain served his clan for two more years before stepping down, an option reserved only for heroes. Only a hero could be told by the Gods that his or her time of service was done.

The story done, the Svekards rose from their spots on the ground, stretching and mingling in the final minutes before they would settle down for the night into the shared space of a clanbed.

The point of the tightly shared sleeping space of a clanbed wasn't to conserve body heat, but to share strength and willpower. Svekards were the strongest and most resilient people individually, but they were unbreakable because their power was multiplicative, not additive.

The Gods had first created clans before they created individuals. There had been a time when humans had been like ants, each an insignificant piece of a colony made up of many clans. But as the Gods breathed more and more of their own likeness into their favored creation, individuals with personalities like those of the Gods evolved. Recognizing the power they had provided to humans, the Gods dashed the human colony across the land, spreading their strength widely so humans would never see themselves as equal to the Gods. One group of people, Svekards, were left with the concept of the clan. In exchange for their devotion to the Gods, they retained the power to come together as one people and overcome any enemy.

In the face of great struggle or evil, a clanbed was a place to combine all their greatest abilities and call upon the Gods to imbue them with the fortitude to overcome. Only heroes could pray directly to the Gods, but the combined prayers of a clanbed could be carried to the Heavens by the sheer volume of the call.

Silvi's voice would be absent from that call. When every additional person meant a higher chance of the Gods heeding their call, Silvi couldn't imagine a starker statement of her people's distaste and distrust for her.

"Good night and may the Gods watch over us," Slade said before it was echoed by every voice except Silvi's.

Silvi fell asleep to the sound of snoring Svekards. She squeezed her arms against her sides with the rise and fall of the sounds, imitating the press of a body on either side of her. With her face buried in her furs, she pretended to smell the body odor of her companions rather than only her own. With just enough convincing, her body could pretend that she was not alone long enough to sleep through another night. She told herself that tomorrow things would be better. The Gods would answer the prayers of the clanbed, and the sun would rise on a brighter day. The voice in her head was far from convincing.

The next morning brought with it more marching. Though her people would never admit it, the endless days of walking were wearing on them. Their shoulders sagged and their feet dragged, kicking up more dirt to cloud their lungs and make them cough and sneeze.

Throughout the day, Silvi found her gaze drawn time and again over to the witch. The witch had stopped trying to separate her from the protection of her people like a wolf attempting to isolate weak prey from a herd of caribou. Instead, she was busy with her own problems.

As far as Silvi could piece together, two of the Neamairtese women were fighting over who got to walk next to one of the men. The women kept bumping into each other, causing their yokes to bang together and then yelling at each other in the high-pitched, trilling patter of Neamairtese. When they weren't yelling at each other, they appeared to be telling each other off just under their breath. All of this, of course, drew the attention of the Victricites, who had made their position on talking clear.

Silvi watched as the witch tried to silently negotiate between the two, first separating them, then keeping the man by her side to ward off the women, then finally sending the man to the front of the group and walking with one woman on either side of her, holding their hands within their yokes like children. Every time the witch stepped in, the women would nod at whatever she was telling them, as if in reverence of the words, but the moment she moved on, the fighting returned.

Watching the drama play out in front of her, Silvi couldn't help but scoff. How Neamairtese-ish it was to fight amongst themselves over a man while marching into slavery. The pettiness was typical of such savages. More than that, the witch was the weakest leader Silvi had ever seen.

There was no doubt the witch was their leader by the attention she was paid, but she lacked every leadership quality Silvi valued. Any Svekard worth their vegetables would have smacked the women's heads together and told them to shape up. They were harming their people through their self-centeredness.

The witch was indecisive, unsure of herself, and placative. She clearly had powers but power without the will and knowledge to use it effectively was useless. Such a weak leader wouldn't last five minutes in charge of Svekards.

If a chieftain managed to show a tenth of the weakness the witch blatantly displayed, she would be challenged by any one of the Svekards who considered themselves a better fit. That would be any Svekard. The witch would be challenged and defeated instantly. The Gods wouldn't even have to intervene to make sure she lost. Silvi had seen more aggressive, more battle-ready sheep.

More often than not, the winner of a combat was not the biggest and strongest brute, but like Wygon, the one who got struck down and stood back up over and over again. Silvi wasn't sure the witch had it in her to stand up after tripping over her own feet.

Silvi watched the witch become increasingly flustered until finally the tall man who had spent most of the day walking by the witch's side seemed to take charge. By Silvi's estimation, the man was the Svekard equivalent of an oath keeper or judge. He seemed to be advising the witch on her leadership, a task that made him pitiable in Silvi's eyes. Whatever the tall man whispered to the group made the two fighting women disperse, sullen but otherwise non-combative.

It explained a lot, Silvi supposed, of why the Neamairtese were so undisciplined and savage. That man had done what needed to be done and thus should be the leader. If he cared about his group, he would challenge her and end everyone's misery.

A chill worked its way down Silvi's spine, despite the warm sun beating down on her. If anyone challenged the witch, it wouldn't be the witch fighting for her undeserved power—Silvi would be the one fighting to her last breath. She could only hope the Neamairtese allowed themselves to suffer a soggy bread leader, or that whatever gods protected the Neamairtese wouldn't act to dethrone her.

Barra didn't think dusk was ever going to come. She was trapped in some nightmare specifically designed to make every step a reminder of how inadequate she was. Her legs were failing her, she could barely keep her eyes open after not sleeping all night, and she could feel all of their eyes on her, even when no one was looking.

The Lord and Lady were clearly disappointed in her. They had given her a great gift and she was woefully incapable of using it. She was undeserving.

Both nights since the ritual that had marked the Svekard woman as her mate, Barra had called on the Spirits and her magic and found it lacking. Last night, before treating her people's wounds and improving their food, she had gone to the edge of the Neamairtese side of the pen while her magic was untapped for the day and she had attempted a couple of small spells that on a larger scale could facilitate their escape.

She'd tried giving a couple of soldiers food poisoning. She'd tried causing one of the soldiers' fires to flare up and burn them. She'd even tried making one soldier fall asleep. But nothing happened. The Spirits refused to help her, and she didn't have anywhere near the strength yet to do any magic without their assistance. Apparently, they would help her treat her people, but not help her save them.

She'd just finished her attempt and returned to her spot near the line between the Svekard and Neamairtese sides of the camp when three of her people, Redena, Terenesa, and Marsinus, came to speak to her. All three were kindlers.

Kindlers were the most patient, calm, gracious, and encouraging of Neamairtese. It was necessary in order to connect with magic, to coax it into the open, and guide it. That was why there were more female kindlers than male and why male kindlers were so much more desirable mates. In Barra's opinion, it was the reason why Neamairtese were in general such a benevolent people. They were raised to care for each other, to be kind and gentle, not just because it might make the difference between being a kindler and not, but because it was how Neamairtese treated each other.

There were people known as fallen kindlers who had experienced such loss, such tragedy or trials, that they had forsaken the benevolent nature that made the Spirits choose them as kindlers and turned their connection to magic into a link to the dark spirits. These spirits had been banished to the Dark Lands thousands of years ago, and asking for their magic came at a heavy cost. Violent sacrifice was required to draw and keep the attention of these spirits. Someone who made such an offering was no longer welcome amongst the Neamairtese. Choosing dark spirits made a person no longer a chosen of the Lord and Lady and thus they were not a Neamairtese at all. Still, some kindlers chose the path of darkness to reverse the fate of a loved one or themselves. A kindler fell to the seductive lure of the power of the dark spirits every generation or so. Whatever the reason for their choice, fallen kindlers were banished and, as far as anyone knew, wandered into the Dark Lands themselves.

In addition to guiding the Spirits' magic, kindlers could also intensify or help direct the queen's magic, and Redena, Terenesa, and Marsinus came to Barra with an idea to utilize that ability.

"Finding the right rocks, twigs, and thorns won't be too hard. What we can't find in the camp, others can donate out of their hair," Redena said.

"It would be a large ask," Terenesa said. Her own hand went to her hair, her fingers instinctively finding the most precious of items representing her most important memories. "However, no one would say no to the queen, especially if it means a chance at freedom."

"We're getting ahead of ourselves," Marsinus interrupted with a supportive smile and gestured at Redena, an invitation to share what had clearly been her idea.

"Once we have the pieces, including a small bag of salt from Terenesa—" She pointed at Terenesa, who drew a tiny deerskin pouch from her bosom. "The spell all comes down to the correct movements, a stomping kind of dance in a pattern that will awaken the spirit of Earth and ask for her help. With a shaking that will send the Svekards running for the hills, the Earth itself will rise from the ground and ensnare a few of the soldiers."

"With our added efforts, Earth could capture all of the soldiers, giving us the chance to escape," Marsinus said.

Terenesa stepped in, her voice calm yet serious. "It would be a long journey home, with the threat of Victricites following just at the horizon, but it's a chance."

Barra nodded wearily. "It could work," she lied. There was no way she could cast such a spell in her current state. Not without her mate and that wasn't going to happen anytime soon…if ever.

Redena's smile was unaffected by Barra's lackluster response. She pointed at the three kindlers. "Our tribe is one of the easternmost tribes and we learned the spell as a defensive one in case of a Svekard raid. Though it isn't much good without the queen or an independent act of the spirit of Earth, it holds extreme potential in either of those instances."

"We're prepared…" Marsinus began before pausing and looking to Redena.

For a moment, Barra thought it might work. They would know what she was supposed to do and all she would have to do was summon enough strength to put it into the world.

"To do this right, we just need you to show us the steps," Redena finished, wiping away any hope Barra had had.

"I only know my part," Barra lied again. She was the queen; how could she not know her part?

"We'll practice," Redena promised, looking between her companions and brightening at their encouraging nods. "Since the spell is strongest under a hot sun, we can attempt it during tomorrow's marching. It's certainly hot enough under this southern sun."

Barra nodded again and watched them leave, already debating what logic and memory told them about the correct combination of movements. Their debate started out jovial and excited, but it would not remain so.

They returned to their group, their enthusiasm immediately spreading to the people around them. Barra glared from them to her Svekard. She wasn't sure if she was more envious of the kindlers for their ability to instantly lift the spirits of her people in a way she had failed to do or of the people who so easily found comfort from the kindlers when she could find no comfort from anyone. All she knew was that it was easier to blame her Svekard than to layer more self-hatred on herself.

The group-care of her people continued to seem a luxury Barra shouldn't allow herself. She certainly wasn't going to use any of the magic her people needed in order to perform self-care. She was putting all of her energy into improving everyone else's bread and healing their sores, but when it came to her own weeping blisters, she felt there wasn't a drop to spare. A queen improved the lives of her people, and to Barra, if she were truly a good queen, no one would be suffering. Therefore, if anyone was going to suffer, it should be her.

She sat, picking at her bread and telling her mind to stop drifting over to the lonely woman across the pen thrusting her elbow into the air with her people despite the fact that they were ignoring her. Barra needed to focus on remembering anything about the spell she was to cast the next day. The previous queens had cast it several times. She could remember doing it, but the memory was like a shadow. The edges were clear and defined, but there was no color, no expression, no language to it. Like shadows in the late day sun, the memories were distorted by time, and overwhelming fatigue made even the smallest step seem enormous.

No one had expected anything of Barra before. After the death of her mother, she had been without responsibility. She owed no one anything but to carry her own weight on hunts, which had always come so naturally. Now, it seemed she not only couldn't escape the needs of her people, but she couldn't fill them either. She felt hopeless and helpless while at the same time having to portray to her people steadfast certainty in the Spirits.

The next day, the debate on movements was no more resolved than it had been the night before. It spoke to the general attitude of the group that none of the characteristic patience, calm, graciousness, or encouragement was present as the three kindlers attempted to remember and act out the ritual while marching. Within the first hour, Marsinus had given up completely on figuring out the larger picture. He would stand at the front of the group, toward the south, and be the conduit for the spell when the women figured out what the heck they were doing. Redena and Terenesa, on the other hand, spent the whole day arguing. They would agree just long enough to start moving in opposite directions, bump into each other, hitting their yokes together, and then start yelling, at which point the soldiers got involved. Even their quiet chanting drew the soldiers' attention.

Barra tried to intervene, to provide guidance where she had none and suggest formations for Terenesa and Redena near Marsinus or herself and then at opposite sides of the marching party. She hoped to at least get the two women to stop yelling at each other by placing them far apart and perhaps give them the illusion that she had some vague idea of what to do. In the end, Daralan was forced to call it off, accepting the blame for making everyone give up. They reached the next camp, heads hung low.

Barra let them think it was their fault, that their formations were wrong. In reality, it was her fault, and she knew it. She should remember the correct formations from the memories of the queens. They were all there in her memory, but she couldn't focus hard enough to make them materialize.

Her memories were like the deepest lake. Items floated to the surface, but they weren't always the things she needed. With practice, she would learn to draw them to the surface. In the meantime, she tried diving in headfirst as she always had into other aspects of her life. All she found were deep, drowning depths that threatened to pull her deeper and deeper with each memory. Every time she tried, her lungs gasped for air despite the physical absence of any water.

She hadn't even attempted to call on the spirit of Earth. It would have only further damaged her relationship with the spirit when she didn't answer Barra's call.

Even if she could recall every step and word, Barra didn't have the energy to complete the spell. If she tried and the Spirits didn't help, it was possible to use up the last of her magic reserves and then there would be no more, possibly ever.

Magic was a living thing. It had to grow and heal over time. If she cut a branch from a tree, more would grow in its place. If she cut the tree to its stump, the tree would die. The Neamairtese had learned this the hard way. Hundreds of years ago, there hadn't been a queen and her mate, but a king and queen.

At the Council of Neamairt, where the Lord and Lady had first chosen the Neamairtese as their sacred people, the Lord broke a point off one of his antlers and used it to bestow a shard of his magic into the king of his chosen people. The Lady followed suit, providing a wisp of her magic to the queen, causing one of her beautiful locks of red hair to turn gray. Both powers would be passed down upon the deaths of the king and queen to a new pair of soul mates, fated to best guide their people.

This cycle repeated eighteen times before the gift was shattered. The queen of the Neamairtese was dying, her unborn child twisted within her. The infant was quickly passing over into the Summerlands taking its mother with it. In an act of desperation to save the love of his life and her child, the king called out to the Spirits to help him heal her. The Spirits refused. It was her time. She was fated to die at that time and in that way. All three of them would die that day, the king's life inexorably linked to that of his mate as all kings and queens were. The king refused to accept that his mate should die when he had the power to stop it.

Drawing on every ounce of his strength and connection to the magic of the Lord, the king poured his very essence into saving his love's life. The queen woke to a healthy, crying baby and the cold, dead body of her mate. For several days, the Neamairtese were as confused as anything else. If the king was dead, the queen should have died with him. There should have been a new king chosen by the Spirits, but there was none.

In several months' time, the queen fell in love again. She had never expected to find someone who could bring a smile back to her face or a glow to her heart, but she found him without ever looking. Every queen between her and Barra remembered the words spoken by the Lady to that queen and her new mate the moment they exchanged their first kiss, a single echo that went through all of them. "Though the king's magic is gone forever, I will not leave you without the defender and supporter you will need to bear this burden. I have given a piece of your magic to your mate and will do so for every queen to come. Now, you are weaker. So, do not forget your limitations. If you are not prudent, you will leave our chosen people without the defense and support of their queen. All of our magic will be lost to you."

A queen always walked a careful line between fighting for the present and protecting the future. It was better for the queen to die and pass on her gift than to use too much magic and lose it altogether.

More power would come with time and practice, Barra knew, and from having her mate at her side. All this she knew, and yet she'd let Redena and Terenesa fight and draw the attention of the guards just to not look weak. But in the end, she'd still looked weak and been weak.

"It wouldn't have mattered," the now familiar voice told Barra as Daralan approached her from behind.

Barra's hand flashed to her face to wipe away the tears on her cheeks and then smooth up her hair as if nothing was wrong. "What wouldn't have mattered?"

Daralan didn't take a seat next to her as she longed for him to do. He stood next to her, his hand not quite touching her shoulder despite her ache for anyone to do so. "Even if they had remembered the moves, the Victricites have horses. They would have caught us. Without putting anyone in danger, you gave them something to believe in."

Barra couldn't help the blubbery scoff that slipped through her lips. She hadn't done one thing right since becoming queen. What good was it to pretend she had? The fact that he felt the need to build her up, despite her failure, only showed just how needy he thought she was. Plus, the undercurrent was so clear. Daralan was saying it wouldn't have mattered, you're too weak, but I'm too proper to say that to the queen. "Thank you," she said in hopes it would dismiss him.

He stood there for another minute waiting to see if she would seek his guidance before retreating. I don't even know what to ask, Barra thought as she listened to his light footfalls lead him back to the group. All she wanted was to curl into a ball and make it all go away: the marching, the responsibility, the power. The queen wasn't supposed to lean on anyone except her mate, which left Barra with no one.

"If I could give it to someone else, I would," Barra said silently. She'd said it to her Svekard when the woman had demanded she remove the magic. Now, she wished she could give it all away.

She'd felt the woman's eyes on her all day. When she wasn't trying to get her Svekard's attention but was instead hoping no one would look at her, her Svekard was more than willing to pay attention. Barra had caught the woman's expression several times—staggering condemnation. She wondered if the magic told her Svekard how miserable she was. It would explain the expression on the woman's face, like she had grown tired of rolling her eyes and shaking her head. It felt as though she was being picked apart piece by piece and each piece tossed aside, deemed unworthy.

Now, her Svekard sat again with her back to Barra, eating her bread by herself and mimicking the gestures of her people's song. "Yeah, well, nobody likes you either," Barra whispered into the space between them.

Daralan had told her that things with her mate would get better with time, but with every passing day she felt more hated, more deserving of hate, and more biased against the woman the Lady had chosen for her. She wasn't willing to think of her Svekard as chosen by her heart, even if the two were one and the same.

Barra didn't bother to pay enough attention to recognize the footsteps approaching her. "I don't need your advice, Daralan," Barra mumbled, closing her body off even more.

"No," said a feminine voice. "But I think you need mine."

Barra fixed an expression of frustration over her feeling of self-recrimination and looked over her shoulder in feigned skepticism.

Terenesa responded with a smile that only a kindler could manage. Ignoring Barra's attempt at a dismissive look, Terenesa took a seat next to her and stared across the pen. She didn't seem to be looking at anything in particular.

"I remember when I first learned I was a kindler," Terenesa said, not taking her eyes from whatever she was looking at that wasn't there. "At the time, my family was very proud and my friends were ecstatic. You see, my tribe was new and very small. As we didn't have a kindler, there wasn't anyone to teach me, and more importantly, there wasn't anyone to set realistic expectations. Everyone wanted me to make their hunts successful, make the berry bushes have more berries, and tell them where we should go next to find the best game. Despite my abilities, I didn't know how to do any of that, but I thought maybe that was just me. Maybe I wasn't a very good kindler. But I didn't want to tell anyone I couldn't, so I just stopped talking to people so they couldn't ask me to do things."

Terenesa's gaze dropped to her hands, which were folded in her lap. She began to gently rub the calluses at her wrists as she continued, as if to let the current pain drive out the memory of old pain. "One day, my tribe was attacked by wild wolves. All of our hunters were out on a hunt trying to get us food. When you have so few people, it can be very hard and even harder on the eastern edges. Two of the wolves grabbed a young boy and started to drag him away. We were throwing rocks at them and yelling, but everyone who tried to get close was attacked and barely got away with only bleeding gashes. Everyone turned to me and begged me to help."

Barra had a pretty good idea of where this story was going. I saved the boy and everyone liked me again, Barra said silently in a mockery of Terenesa's higher pitched voice. You just have to believe in yourself, she added with a sneer. Terenesa was known not just as a powerful kindler, but also for her work raising wolves. That had been the first thing Terenesa had said when introducing herself the day Barra entered their tribe. She'd raised wolves alongside her baby sons and her wolves were the most loyal and protective Barra had ever seen.

Terenesa wasn't looking at her and didn't see Barra's contempt. A small voice in Barra's head told her that it would be far more damaging to her image as the queen to look so rudely and immaturely at one of her people than it was to look weak.

"I called upon the wind to blow away the wolves. I asked the flame to fly from our central fire and attack the wolves. I pleaded with the ground to swallow up the wolves. I screamed for a storm to drive them away. When nothing happened, the wolves took the boy. I still remember the way he screamed for help as they dragged him away before he went silent somewhere off in the trees." Terenesa's voice fell away. She was back to looking off at the horizon, her eyes glistening with tears.

Barra's heart sank as the moral of the story seeped through the barriers of frustration and feigned emotionlessness she'd put around herself. No one was here to help her learn her powers, yet she was her people's only hope. When they all reached Victricus, they would call out for her and she would fail them.

Pushing away the dread and the shame, Barra desperately tried to rebuild the walls around her heart. Her people needed some kind of a leader; even a weak one was better than a broken one. Believing in herself was beyond her capabilities at the moment. If the Spirits didn't believe in her, how could she believe in herself? However, maybe she could put on the act long enough for her people to believe in her just a little longer.

"I asked too much and too desperately. For the Spirits do not come at our beck and call. Nor can they be persuaded by being yelled at. As a kindler, I asked too much of them and my community asked too much of me. Then and now, I wish more than anything that I had been able to save that boy. But that trauma forced me to tell my tribe I didn't know how to guide the Spirits and to ask for the tribe's help. You see, if you invite the Spirits into a broken home, it's going to be so much harder to draw them in. If you have a loving community around you, that's what will draw in the Spirits."

Terenesa paused again to gently place a hand on Barra's knee. "We have asked too much of you, and I believe you have asked too much of yourself. We are trapped and scared and don't know how to escape. That burden is not yours alone to carry. Though you are the herald of the Spirits and the leader of our community, no one expects you to suddenly know, three days into being queen and weeks into all-day marching, how to free us. A herald doesn't win the battle; a herald leads the charge into battle. What we need is someone to bring us together, not to save us."

Warm tears ran in steady streams down Barra's cheeks, and for the first time since becoming queen, Barra was not ashamed of them. Maybe crying didn't have to be a sign of weakness.

Terenesa rotated in her cross-legged posture to wrap her arms around Barra and pull her into a sideways hug. "The space we have given you was because we thought it was what you wanted. Know that we are Neamairtese and we will take care of you whenever you allow us." At the words, Barra's shoulders slumped, and she surrendered into the hug. She hadn't realized how fiercely she needed human contact and comfort. Ever since losing her mother, she'd considered her independence a strength. Since losing her best friend, Helenda, to a Svekard raid that left her wishing death on all Svekards, she'd considered her lack of bonds a protection. She'd gotten along with her fellow Neamairtese well; she just hadn't needed them. As Terenesa pulled Barra onto her lap and held her close, Barra realized what a lie it had been. Being Neamairtese didn't just mean helping your neighbor, it meant asking them for help in return. Neamairtese were independent to a fault, but they were always there for each other when they were needed.

Barra allowed herself another minute of the tender hold before pulling back from it. Terenesa was right. Her community needed her, and she needed them.

As Barra shifted from Terenesa's embrace, Terenesa pulled her back for a brief and feather-soft kiss on the cheek. They helped each other to their feet and walked back hand in hand to the fire around which their people were gathered, smiling at them.

Why not her? Barra tried to ask her heart, but she knew she was asking the Lady. Terenesa's hand felt good clutched in her own. Would it be so wrong to not let go, to find what privacy they could and see how far they could get? It wasn't the pleasure she really wanted, just to sleep next to someone again, to feel loved, and most of all to feel lovable. But it didn't matter what she wanted. Terenesa wouldn't let anything happen any more than Barra would. The Lady had personally led Barra to her mate. To go against that would be the greatest blaspheme. I'm just lonely, Barra told herself, trust the Lady, trust the Spirits, be with my people.

Barra joined their circle of massages and let her Svekard slip from her mind for the first time in the three nights since becoming queen. She would worry about her later. Now, she was with her people and that was what mattered.

CHAPTER FOUR

A SAVAGE'S COMPASSION

I'll call that one red by-trail-ia," Silvi whispered of the tiny shrub with the cone-shaped red flowers poking out of it like dozens of miniature horns. Since the second day of her isolation, Silvi had started talking to herself. Svekards weren't made to be alone.

At first, she'd simply been mumbling to herself, naming or attempting to identify the natural objects around her. The farther south they got, the fewer of the local flora she could identify. The large leaves of grassland plants had shifted steadily to the thin leaves of hot, dry, scrubland plants. The dust had gotten worse with each day, and she'd almost reached the point where she smelled dirt more than sweat. She told herself that she was being productive in observing the flora, but she was fairly sure she just needed the distraction. If she didn't find something to think about and someone or something to talk to, Silvi was fairly sure her brain was going to go lame and atrophy like an unused, injured limb.

By the middle of the fourth day, Silvi had decided it was probably equally crazy to invent someone to talk to as it was to talk to inanimate objects. More than anything else, Silvi had missed Papa since being taken prisoner, so the choice was easy. As they marched, she pointed out interesting collections of plants and sightings of animals to him and told him of times she had used similar plants or interacted with similar animals. Papa would return the favor, recounting stories in Silvi's mind exactly the way she remembered him doing.

Silvi was close with all the members of her household, both her parents, her sisters and brother-in-law, her niece, and her nephew.

But Papa held a very special place in her heart. Amongst Svekards, fathers played an essential role as caregivers to their children. A man's legacy was his children, and so raising them to be strong, ethical, contributing members of the clan was one of a father's greatest honors. Svekard mothers literally built and shaped their children's bodies and were in charge of their health and well-being, but fathers shaped their minds. While Silvi's sisters were both closer with Mama, for Silvi there wasn't a person more important in her life than Papa.

Despite the fact the soldiers kept the prisoners from talking, none seemed to mind the apparently crazy woman talking to herself. Silvi imagined she looked about as mad as a rabid wolf, pointing to her surroundings and turning her head to talk to nothing but the air. But just like her people, the soldiers did their best to look away when she glanced toward them and otherwise ignored her.

Over the past two days, she'd identified to Papa several of the herbs she grew in a small planter on her inside windowsill. She told him stories about how she had to baby the plants, keeping them warm in the winter and opening the window to cold spring drafts to get them pollinated. Here, in the scrubland, they grew like weeds. Bitter buttons grew like yellow blankets across the open fields. She could de-worm every cow in Clan Spine Mountain with one day's grazing. Along the side of the trail grew enough rosemary to treat bacterial and fungal infections for years.

Silvi found the increase in flora both a welcome distraction and an aggravating frustration. Papa enjoyed her naming the stalks with purple flame-like flower heads "purple scrubbers," for their resemblance to the shape of the cleaning instruments she and her family made from wool wrapped around a stick. However, with each plant's abundance, Silvi was reminded of her people's daily struggles due to the villainy of the Neamairtese. Their constant raids and vile attacks had driven the Svekards deeper into the mountains as far as they could go before being pushed into the Eastern Fjords. Fighting Neamairtese was one of the few times Svekard clans could all agree on something without the direction of an oath keeper or rune reader. Part of Silvi wondered if they could have driven back the Neamairtese generations ago if clans didn't fight amongst each other like jealous distant cousins the same way the Gods argued and fought.

Regardless, without the Neamairtese and their witchcraft, the Svekards would be able to live in the richer lowlands of the mountains where the herbs were plentiful and traders were once common.

The traders that used to live in these lands were only stories now, but at one time Svekard culture had flourished from the trade those outsiders had brought. The stories always said you couldn't trust the traders as far as you could throw them, but things had been easier before the Neamairtese cut her people off from everything except the heights of the mountains. Silvi couldn't help but look at the empty lands and wonder if the Neamairtese had run the people who lived here off as well.

Without the Neamairtese, she and her people could live off the land without the constant threat of starvation. She could have all the herbs she needed to care for the clan's animals. Silvi was proud of her people's heartiness and fortitude, but she wished they didn't have to be so resilient.

Her, and thereby Papa's, favorite plant name so far was for the light red berries that grew on the bushes along the side of the trail which she dubbed slaver's poop. A similar plant grew at home and was called ewe berry for the tendency of sheep to eat it when they had stomachaches as it increased general digestion. She imagined their captors pulling the berries from the stems with only their stupid, barking mouths and then spending the rest of the day abandoning the trail to spend hours in the bushes, ideally poison ivy bushes, evacuating their bowels. The mental image brought Silvi momentary amusement and a long, hearty laugh from her father.

Her amusement ended abruptly as a commotion from the back of the throng drew Silvi's attention. She felt guilty for the thought, but her immediate wish was that it was one of the Neamairtese causing the problem and that it was not the witch. She would rather not have to run to the witch's rescue and could only imagine how bad it would be for her, and potentially all of her people, if she had to defend the witch against the Victricites.

None of the prisoners seemed to be involved as Silvi took in the scene. One of the formerly mounted soldiers was scrambling to his feet and brushing the dust from the cloth paraphernalia of his uniform. His horse lay on its belly, its front legs scrambling to stand. Its back leg on the right was trapped under its body while the one on the left was so swollen that the knee and pastern were barely identifiable. The horse looked as scared as the prisoners, its eyes unnaturally wide to show the whites which had turned a light shade of pink.

The rider drew his sword and approached the horse, yelling at it as it scrambled on two good legs and achieved nothing but throwing more dust into the air. The creature tossed his head, tangling a previously well-tended mane. His lips were pulled back from his large teeth, but he made no noise as he struggled beyond the pained gasps of his breathing.

From the front of the troupe came the Victricite man all the Svekards had easily identified as the leader on their first day as prisoners. He rode back and barked something at the soldier who argued back defensively, pointing his sword at his horse's leg.

Silvi had only a moment to diagnose, but it was long enough. The horse's leg wasn't broken. If it had been, he wouldn't have been able to walk on it long enough to get that swollen. The fact that he'd gotten this far spoke to the level of discipline trained into him and the lack thereof in his rider. It never should have gotten this far. But at this point, the damage was still reversible.

The rider and his superior exchanged several more words, each doing a poor job of hiding their frustration before a decision was made. Silvi was waiting for that moment and hoping against that decision. The rider approached his horse, lifting his sword above his head and letting all of his ire at dirtying himself and looking foolish in front of his leader prepare him for the swing that would end the creature's life. His commander had already turned his horse around to return to the front.

"Wait!" Silvi heard herself yell. She hadn't planned to say it. She'd just been commenting to herself that someone ought to stop the vicious fool, but she'd not planned to be the informed fool that did it.

The entire assembly, well over a hundred people, turned to stare at Silvi, who wished doggedly that she'd just kept her mouth shut. I can help him, Silvi thought, looking past the crowd to the scared stallion who had finally managed to scramble onto three good legs. The desire to run shone brightly in the large brown eye flashing to the humans around him. But just like the rest of the prisoners, he knew he stood no chance of survival if he attempted to flee.

Silvi couldn't help her people, she wasn't even allowed to go near them, but she could help this horse. It was what she did. At home in the Clan of Spine Mountain, Silvi cared for all of the clan's animals. Neighboring clans summoned her to determine if diseased chickens were communicable and she had trained a few apprentices already, both from her own clan and others.

The crowd parted to allow Silvi a broad path as she approached the man with his sword still held high. She felt like the diseased chicken now and perhaps she was. Once she was close enough, heart racing, she acted out her words as best she could with the yoke around her neck. "I can fix that."

Without changing his aggressive stance, the soldier turned to Silvi, but his attention went to his commander, who was quickly returning. The arguing picked up again but far briefer this time. As the commander said his final words, the soldier gave a childish expression of frustration and lowered his sword as if he were going to throw it on the ground.

Don't screw this up, Silvi told herself. She turned her attention to the Victricite leader. He was the one who could give her permission to do the things she needed to and was far more likely to do so than the soldier, whose shame only grew the longer the group stared at his horse.

Silvi pointed off the trail, and back the way they'd come, toward a tall, green plant with long, spikey leaves and a single elongated red cone-shaped flower. "I need that," she told the commander, figuring saying something at the same time she pointed was better than silently miming.

The commander barked orders at his men who all saluted before a gap formed between them to allow first the mounted commander and then Silvi through. Silvi made a beeline for the plant. She didn't look around or deviate one step from the most direct path between her and the plant. When she reached it, the commander removed her yoke, giving her a stern look. Silvi nodded, then broke four of the long, stalk-like leaves off at their base.

This plant didn't grow naturally anywhere in Svek. Many decades ago, the wonderous thing had been traded along with horses to one of the southwestern-most clans by a group of southern nomads in exchange for cod liver oil, honeyed beer, and iron. Just as the horses had been bred and spread throughout the clans, increasing productivity, the Svekards quickly learned how to keep the plant dry and warm throughout the seasons and turn cuttings into additional plants.

Now, it was the most coveted of Svekard plants. Not just because it treated everything from burns and rashes to indigestion and mouth sores, but because the southern nomads hadn't been seen in over a generation. Silvi never would have used four leaves on one horse at home, but then again, she would have had birch oil, holly, and glycerin to add to the mixture.

Silvi returned to the man and held out the plant so he could see what he'd allowed her to retrieve. "Aloe," she said, using the word that had come from the nomads.

The commander nodded. "Aloe," he repeated. Silvi couldn't help her smile. He understood. It wasn't just the word either. He knew what she meant and he approved of her choices. She was surprised by how refreshing it was to be approved of. That single word felt like the most intelligent conversation she'd had in a week.

They returned to the group and Silvi approached the horse slowly, from the front, first placing her hand on its muzzle before running it slowly up the horse's long face to scratch behind the ears. She worked her way down the stallion's neck in massaging circles as she explained to him that she was here to help, and she would make it feel better. Silvi assumed horses knew as much Svekard as the Neamairtese or Victricites did, but as with them, the tone of her voice would communicate what her words could not.

She paused for a long moment at the point where the stallion's neck met his shoulder, rubbing until her fingers turned brown. She'd watched mother horses lick their foals on this spot and knew it as a place of great comfort to them. As a very young child, her own mother had a habit of rubbing her thumb from the bridge of Silvi's nose up her forehead to calm her and she found the gesture comforting to this day.

A grumbling throat clearing drew Silvi's attention back to the soldier who had, in her opinion, caused this entire scene. His expression said far clearer than words could, "Can we just get on with this?"

If this is how you treat your property, Silvi thought, I think I'd rather die out here. As depressing as she had expected the thought to be, there was a power to it. She hadn't yet reached ambivalence, but if she didn't truly fear death, what was there to be afraid of? Silvi gave the man a dismissive look and continued down toward the horse's haunches, pausing momentarily to remove the saddle and saddle blanket.

When she'd reached the stallion's hind leg, she leaned against his hip to push him further off the leg and make her position very clear to him. The last thing she wanted was to surprise him and get kicked. Plus, she would need him to trust her if he was going to let her touch his strained leg.

Silvi squished the gel from inside the aloe leaves and gently began slathering it over the horse's leg, starting above the injury and working down onto the delicate flesh. Silvi received many nervous whinnies, but to his credit, the stallion held still and allowed her to apply the gel. She hoped it felt as soothing to his skin as it felt on her own.

When all of the gel from the four leaves was spread liberally over his swollen limb, Silvi retrieved the saddle blanket she'd removed. It was far too thin of a saddle blanket in her opinion, and she wondered if it was a reasonable change due to the warmer climate or yet another sign of Victricite lack of care. As she took the blanket in her hands and pulled, expecting it to tear like a thin woolen blanket, her hands reached a quick stop. Whatever the blanket was made of, it was incredibly dense and durable. Silvi wrapped her hands closer together and pulled again, but the blanket didn't give any signs of tearing.

Turning to the soldier, Silvi held out the blanket, pointed to the knife on his belt, and indicated for him to cut the blanket. The look she received would have shriveled a bush of slaver's poop. With a sigh she hoped could shrivel a berry, Silvi turned to the rest of the soldiers. Surely one of them could help her. Their commander, who had returned to the front, was allowing her to proceed; why would they stop her?

Silvi picked her man easily from the collection close by, all watching her with feigned disinterest. One man, one of the youngest by Silvi's estimation, was watching more closely than the others. She didn't make a practice of watching the soldiers, but she had never seen this one yell at a prisoner or hit one of them for moving too slowly. The blanket held in front of her, Silvi approached the young man and indicated for him to cut it.

After a few quick looks to his compatriots for an indication of whether he should help and receiving no feedback, the young man drew his knife and made the cuts Silvi asked for. Several long strips in hand, Silvi returned to the horse the same way she had the first time, but pausing only momentarily at each pivotal point.

Within minutes, Silvi had a full sweat wrap swaddling the stallion's leg. Silvi didn't pause. She didn't want any of the men to think she was done. Careful to run her hand along the horse's rump, she moved to the other hind leg, bent it at the knee, lifted it into her lap, and began to wrap it with the remaining strips of cut blanket. In favoring his damaged leg, the stallion would invariably strain his opposite leg and the wrap would help eliminate or at least lessen the chances of reciprocal damage.

Her work done, Silvi returned to the horse's head once more to scratch behind his ears and coo to him. Much as she was anxious to have the entire group stop staring at her, she didn't want this to end. Here, next to this injured animal, Silvi had purpose and meaning. Here, she mattered. Here, someone cared about her.

The soldier was back, but Silvi didn't spare him a glance, at least not at first. The sound of leather slapping fur made her turn to the man once more. He'd thrown the saddle back on the stallion's back and was anchoring it down without any sort of blanket.

"You can't ride him," Silvi said sternly. "He needs to rest his leg. He really shouldn't be walking at all." But surely the soldier knew that and was only resaddling the horse so he didn't have to carry the saddle. He was strong and the horse was weak, but clearly the soldier didn't see it that way. He was exerting his strength by not carrying a burden.

Silvi waited until the soldier began to lift his foot into the stirrup before turning her stern warning into a yell, "No, you can't ride him!" She closed the distance between them and placed both hands on his right shoulder in an attempt to stop him from continuing without at least thinking about how stupid the idea was.

The soldier wasn't interested in thinking. He was interested in regaining control of the situation and getting the appearance of power back. He struck Silvi with the full force of his arm and torso just to the left of her nose.

The pain shot through Silvi's face like fire. She didn't realize she was falling until the wind was being forced out of her lungs by the impact of her chest on the ground. One hand shot to the left side of her face to check for damage and to block the tears flowing freely from her eye. She had no control to stop them no matter how much she insisted to her body that she would not cry.

She scrambled to gain traction under her. She could hear the beat of hooves approaching, and if she wanted any chance at avoiding being trampled, she would need as many working limbs under her as possible.

With her good eye, Silvi locked first onto the soldier who was standing, one foot in the stirrup, the other on the ground and looking down at her with scornful triumph. He was still trying to pull his foot out of the stirrup when his commander's horse stopped inches from the soldier's. With a grace far beyond the skill of the soldier, the commander shifted his weight in the saddle and brought his own fist in a right hook that knocked the soldier onto his back, ribbons of red and gold fluttering down around him. His foot dangled for a few seconds before hitting the ground with a small puff of dust.

The commander didn't waste his breath on the soldier still lying on his back. He took the stallion's reins in his hands and led it slowly around Silvi and to the young man who had helped her cut the blanket. He tossed the young man the reins and said a few brief words before riding to the front of the pack once more and shouting a single word that got everyone moving again.

The young man was looking at the stallion with jubilant awe and petting its face as he coaxed it into a slow gait. Silvi smiled at him, half her face still covered by her hand. He didn't spare Silvi a glance as he walked the horse with the rest of the group.

"He's yours if you treat him well," Silvi whispered from her place on the ground. She imagined the commander's words had been less gracious, but the meaning was clear enough. Good, Silvi thought, the first soldier didn't deserve a horse.

The thought of the soldier and the way his look of triumph had shifted into pained indignation as he fell made her blood run cold. She rolled onto her left too slowly to see the kick coming and took the full brunt of his boot to the right side of her torso, knocking the wind from her once more. She lay sprawled for only half a second before she pulled her knees to her chest and wrapped her arms around her head protectively.

From the corner of her good eye, Silvi saw the Svekards start to surge forward. It was entirely immoral and without honor to strike a person when they were down. Even a person like Silvi would apparently be protected from such a breach. But the Victricites were ready for their response and quickly surrounded the group of Svekards, spears and swords held ready.

Silvi was without her people again. She curled tighter and waited for the next blow to come, wondering if this was how it would end for her.

No blows came.

Silvi slowly unwound from her self-cocoon, wishing she could see what was around her. Her good eye was held just above the ground and the left had swollen shut. All she could make out were several sets of hide boots surrounding her.

A rush of relief eased over Silvi. Somehow, her people must have overcome the barrier of Victricites that barred their way. However, a part of Silvi knew what she was going to find when she rolled over and told herself not to do it. It might be better to stay in the fantasy in which the boots around her were Svekard despite the obvious bone adornments where there should have only been escaping puffs of sheepskin.

Maybe if she rolled back into her ball, the crazy world she'd fallen into would pass her by and she would open both eyes to a world that made sense. But there was someone standing next to Silvi and the survival part of Silvi's mind, and perhaps the pride part as well, overruled the part that told her brain that playing dead was the best option.

Silvi rolled over onto her back and looked up at the witch, not even trying to stifle the groan that worked its way up from her battered abdomen. Surrounding her and the witch was a mob of every Neamairtese prisoner, a wall of people between Silvi and the soldier, but also between Silvi and her own people. Unless the soldier wanted to start attacking all their merchandise, Svekards and Neamairtese alike, to get to one slave, he would have to leave Silvi to whatever the mob planned for her. As far as Silvi could tell by the lack of shouting or hitting, the man had already moved on.

Out of the frying pan and into the fire, Silvi let the words roll through her brain like pushing a piece of refuse into a muddy pond. It was hard to comprehend anything over the pain or the instinctive urge to somehow survive. She would choose to face one Victricite soldier over a horde of Neamairtese any day. Maybe curling into a ball wasn't such a bad plan after all. But the witch had made eye contact with her and was smiling that infuriatingly calm smile at her and holding her yoked hand down as if to offer her assistance to her feet.

"What do you want from me?" Silvi groaned, sliding herself away from the witch. Neamairtese had no more capacity for compassion than the Victricites and certainly none for Svekards. No one without a clan could truly understand selflessness and compassion. Were they simply here to bring her lower? To beat her like a dying horse now that the stallion was safe?

When Silvi pulled away, the witch's smile stayed in its place. It was wickedly soft, inviting, and vexing. For a long moment, Silvi found she couldn't look away, drawn in by the continuing power of the witch's spell. Against her better judgment, she reached out and took the witch's hand, letting herself be pulled to her feet despite the pain shooting through her abdomen.

Silvi looked down at her side, half expecting to see a hole. The broken eye contact was all she needed to restart her brain. She was whole enough to try to save herself from whatever these savages were planning with their knowing, feral smiles.

Breathing came in jagged gasps as Silvi started to stumble away. She needed to escape the mob of strangers around her and get back to her people. The witch was trying to talk to her, but Silvi wasn't going to let herself fall under more spells if she could help it. One hand still gripping her face and the other holding her side as if her guts might suddenly start falling out, Silvi stumbled forward, righted herself, and took several more swaying steps. If she just kept her feet under her, she could surely get away.

Silvi had reached the wall of her Neamairtese captors when she felt a hand wrap itself gingerly over the hand at her side. A cooling blast shot through her hand before she felt it seeping into her side like water over hot coals. In the momentary numbness, Silvi was sure she was dying, the Neamairtese were on all sides finishing her off. But as the panic and numbness melted away, so did the pain in her side.

Silvi looked down at her side and to the hand with tiny red freckles across it covering her own hand. The witch was smiling at her again in her awkward bent over position and partially out of breath. In her other yoked hand, she held the sheaths of aloe that had once been leaves squeezed of their gel. Now they looked like burned husks hanging from the witch's fingers.

More witchcraft, Silvi moaned silently. She had to get away or the witch was going to go for her face next. But the witch had made the mistake of giving her back her ability to run. Silvi let go of her face long enough to shove a hole in the wall of savages and broke into a full run. Her people parted to allow her through before closing like a solid gate between her and her narrowly escaped doom. Even as they parted, they kept their heads hung or tipped back toward the Neamairtese and confused Victricites so as not to make eye contact with Silvi. Only when she had reached the front of the group and had a few dozen Svekards between herself and the witch, did Silvi stop running.

Why can't she leave me alone, Silvi asked silently before looking around her at the Svekards that refused to meet her gaze. And why must *you* ignore me?

With a sigh, Silvi fell into step with them. Part of the problem was that they weren't ignoring her. She would catch them staring at her when they thought she couldn't see. Each night when she got her bread and water, they made sure to separate hers out first, as if to make sure she couldn't contaminate the rest.

Today, she'd saved a horse and seen a human side of the Victricites—intelligent, self-centered, prideful, and excitable. That should be what she was focusing on, not the witch's smile, enticing and fetching as much as enchanting. No matter how hard she tried, she couldn't put the look from her mind. It gave her the feeling of butterflies in her stomach, a vastly improved feeling to the spikes of pain that had told her she was going to die after the soldier kicked her. She helped me, her side seemed to say. And her touch was so soft, almost tender, her hand added.

She used witchcraft on me *again*, Silvi complained to her traitorous body. She surrounded me with savages and cast more spells on me!

Maybe they were trying to protect you from the soldier, Silvi's mind suggested. None of the savages laid a hand on you except the witch to fix you like you fixed the stallion. Now Silvi wasn't even sure who was on her side. Mind, body, and soul seemed to have chosen the witch.

She supposed that while the witch's curse was more than enough to hate and fear the woman for the rest of her life, all she'd done since then was say she couldn't undo it and use further witchcraft to heal Silvi's wounds and offer to heal the injured Svekards. Granted, most of what she was offering to fix had been caused by the witch in the first place.

With a heavy sigh, Silvi admitted that maybe, perhaps, she would see the negative in anything the witch did no matter what her intentions or outcomes. It was possible, however unlikely, that the witch had helped her. Possibly, she'd seen a compassionate side of the savage Neamairtese, however self-fulfilling it might be.

It was long past dusk by the time the group reached the next camp. The prisoners proceeded into the pen with practiced subservience and soon two fires burned, one on either side of the central circle with smaller fires encircling them like tiny echoes of light. After blessing her people's food, Barra found herself once more at the edge of the Neamairtese side trying to get a good look at her Svekard.

In the dim light of the fire blocked by the forms of the other Svekards, Barra could just make out the swelling of her Svekard's face. Barra felt the overwhelming need to know if she was okay. It felt so wrong that her Svekard could protect her, but Barra had no ability to protect her in return. The fact that her Svekard wouldn't let her help made it all the worse. The look of fear on her Svekard's face when she pulled her to her feet made her heart physically hurt.

She'd thought at first that it was just the pain, but her Svekard had run from her. She'd been willing to take the Victricite's kicks like an opossum, but she ran from Barra despite the pain it clearly caused her. Barra almost felt bad for chasing after her and healing her, but she couldn't stand to watch her in such pain. What if her injuries had ended her life without Barra's spell? She couldn't have lived with that choice.

Every day, Barra asked the Lady, why a Svekard? But she realized now the question she should have been asking was why *this* Svekard. The answer was so clear, if only she paused to look closely. Her Svekard wasn't like other Svekards. The other Svekards knew her Svekard wasn't one of them. Why had it taken so long for her to realize it?

None of the other Svekards had the mercy to bat an eye at the struggles of another creature, let alone to risk their life to help a horse. For all of their grunting and posturing, none of the other Svekards would have stood up to the soldier and told him he couldn't ride the horse.

Barra's thoughts went to Terenesa. She was a woman Barra could see herself with—a kindler, a beautiful woman, and a uniquely compassionate human. Perhaps, her Svekard was the Svekard's version of a kindler, but where kindlers were the most valued Neamairtese, it was no surprise that a kindler would be disregarded and scorned by the boorish Svekards. What value could such people give to empathy and tenderness?

Svekards did not understand mercy. When they attacked, they left no one alive; no elder, man, woman, or child was left unslaughtered. Dozens of tribes had been ravaged by the Svekards in the last decade. They killed, burned, and destroyed to the point that there weren't even bodies for half the people who had been killed. Barra couldn't imagine her Svekard doing anything like that, not with the way she had treated that horse.

Barra needed to know that her Svekard was okay. She needed to see her in a way that wouldn't bring out the woman's natural Svekard rage but would still tell Barra whether her Svekard needed healing.

If worse came to worst, she could cross the space herself. The Svekards would flee before her rather than attack, knowing what came for them if they tried to fight. They would abandon her Svekard again if Barra needed to intervene.

All Barra needed was to be able to see farther in the dim light and she knew just the spell. Barra moved her tongue around her mouth to scoop up as much moisture as she could, then spit into her hand. The spell would work better with plain water, but it felt wrong to take her people's rare resource. Spit would do fine.

Next, Barra asked for the spirit of Water's magic, swirling the liquid in her hand with the gentle push of her breath. Barra watched the saliva bubbles pop and disappear before taking on a delicate sheen, like the surface of a lake in the moonlight. Careful not to lose any of the liquid, Barra brought her hand to one eye and then the other, blinking bits of what had been spit into her eyes. With her eyes closed, Barra thanked the spirit of Water.

Casting had grown much easier since rejoining her people, just as Terenesa had said it would. She still lacked the energy, experience, and resources to undertake anything too large. However, by the end of each day, she still had enough reserves left after taking care of her people for a little magic of her own to heal her aching feet and check on her Svekard.

As she opened her eyes, Barra's sight brought the image of her Svekard into sharp relief, as if she were sitting two feet in front of her in the light of a cloudless, noonday sky.

Her Svekard was sitting, her head downturned and tipped to the side, giving a perfect view of the blue and purple swelling across it. Her eyebrow was dark and heavy, falling over her eye. Her cheek was a brighter, shinier bluish-purple color and rose to meet the fallen eyebrow as if in a constant kiss. Her Svekard's eye seemed disregarded in the meeting of the two. Tears slowly dripped from between the layers as if her Svekard were leaking rather than crying. The woman's other eye was focused on her hands, where she was holding her chunk of stale bread and trying to bite off tiny bits of it with the undamaged half of her face. She looked like a sad, lopsided squirrel with an especially hard nut.

Barra wanted to reach out and pet the good side of her Svekard's face and had her hand all the way to her knee before she reminded herself that the woman was not in fact two feet in front of her. Up close, her Svekard didn't seem so uncivilized. Even with half her face swollen and misshapen, there was a beauty in her rounded, smooth features and a depth to her brown eye.

The fact that she was eating, however slowly, encouraged Barra. She wished her Svekard would let her close enough to make the bread soft and warm like she did for her own people. It would make the eating process hurt less and provide much more in the way of nutrients.

Watching her Svekard suffer, Barra couldn't help but hate the woman's people even more. This was her greatest time of need and yet she was being ostracized rather than embraced by her community. "If it were me, I would be there for you," Barra said into the distance between them.

If her Svekard could just let go of her prejudice, she could trade her barbaric brethren for people who would embrace and love her.

CHAPTER FIVE
THE VETERINARIAN

The days blended together until Barra wasn't sure she knew when one ended and the next began. She marked the passage of days by the slow rainbow changes of her Svekard's face as it slowly began to heal. There were still bright splashes of blue mixed with green and yellow across her nose, cheek, and brow. Under both eyes, she had a small black strip as if she had marked herself with charcoal to block the sun on a noonday hunt.

The woman seemed to have settled into her position at the edge of her tribe. She still followed along with their nightly activities from afar, but she no longer seemed so despondent. During the days, she talked to herself, but Barra supposed it was only normal. Barra had Daralan and Terenesa to talk to quietly during the marches, and any of her people were enthusiastic to engage with her on any topic around the fire each night. Without them, she imagined she too would be having lengthy conversations with herself just to have something to do.

As dusk began to settle across the plains around them, Barra found herself scanning the horizon for the next camp. They seemed perfectly evenly spaced. Except for the day her Svekard had saved the horse, they'd always arrived at the next camp at about the same time. A camp should be waiting just at the edge of her vision.

Narrowing her eyes against the dusk darkness creeping onto the landscape, Barra could just make out the beginnings of structures. Whatever camp they were coming up on, it was not like the others. Previous camps had been simple outcroppings or meadows by the side of the road, skirted by a tall fence that got more elaborate as they traveled farther. What Barra saw ahead of her now looked like snowcapped mountains far in the distance.

"Tents," Barra whispered to her companions, inclining her head fractionally. "We must be getting close."

The thought brought a mixture of relief and terror with it. The marching had felt interminable to the point where anything seemed an improvement, but Barra was pretty sure the slavery waiting for them would be far worse. The end of their journey would also mean Barra had failed to change the path before them. Terenesa could say any kind and encouraging words she wanted, but in the end, it was still her responsibility to create a better path.

There was a part of Barra that was intrigued to see what the outer tribes of the Victricites would be like. She felt silly and guilty for her curiosity when she ought to be occupying her mind more effectively, but her inquisitiveness was there all the same.

Since the forest had given way to the plains and scrubland, Barra had been shocked by the complete lack of other people. There had been a time when these plains had been the home of the mounted nomadic Razirgali.

No one amongst the Neamairtese remembered the Razirgali except Barra with her predecessors' memories. As far as she knew, no bands of Razirgali had visited the Neamairtese in a hundred years. But there had been a time when the outer tribes were visited regularly with threats of raids and offers of trade. The Neamairtese did not venture from the protective landscape of the forest, where they felt most connected to the Spirits, but they had once received goods from lands they'd never heard of.

Barra had held a vague hope that their camp might find itself on the receiving end of one of the famous Razirgali raids. Razirgali traveled light. Prisoners would be ransomed back to their people, rather than being enslaved, at least a large group like this. It would be possible to end up with one of the more bloodthirsty bands, but even then Razirgali were a group that could be bargained with, unlike the two cultures surrounding the Neamairtese now.

As the tents on the horizon grew closer, they grew taller. They were not in fact a forest of tents as Barra had first thought, but several large tents with multiple peaks, the canvas of each dipping between six or seven tall tent poles. Perhaps the Victricites were more communal than Barra had thought.

Mounted soldiers rode out to meet the party as they finished their approach. The men greeted each other formally, exchanging very few words as they brought the prisoners the final mile to the encampment.

As Barra looked from her surroundings to her fellow prisoners, several of the Svekards' heads shot up like deer upon hearing the crack of a branch. They breathed deeply, noses high, and furs expanding with the depth of their inhales. If they had been deer, Barra was pretty sure she would have seen their nostrils flair, searching the air for danger.

Barra searched the edge of the nearing tents for danger but saw nothing. Around her, Neamairtese heads began to rise.

"Do you smell that?" came a voice from behind Barra. She turned to see a young man smelling the air in quick gasps. "It smells like fresh meat!"

Barra tipped her nose up, following suit, and felt her mouth water at the now clear smell of cooking meat. She tried to tell her body there was very little chance that the food was meant for them, but she didn't think she'd ever wanted anything so badly.

The group's pace quickened as they reached the first tent. Barra barely noticed anything else about their surroundings as she followed the group to the center of the encampment where above a pit fire, the largest pig Barra had ever seen was slowly roasting. The succulent meat dripped into the fire below it, sending the flames up to lick for more. Barra's tongue flicked out as if she too could savor the fat and flavor as it dripped.

As the prisoners stood transfixed, one of the new soldiers stepped up to the pig, which Barra guessed was about the length of Daralan, but four times the girth. The soldier sliced into the pig with his knife, cutting a chunk from its side and tearing the hunk of meat from the beast, fat dripping down the blade. He laughed and pointed at the faces around him and was soon joined by the other soldiers, new and old alike. Only the soldiers' leader who had helped her Svekard with the horse didn't laugh. After an eye roll, he took his leave of the group, disappearing into one of the tents.

When the soldier with the meat stopped laughing, he said something to the rest of his men before placing the chunk of dripping meat on his sword and holding it out toward the Svekard closest to him. The young man looked at the soldier with wide-eyed skepticism for a moment before darting forward and grabbing the steaming meat from the soldier's blade. The young man gave a slightly pained cry before changing his grip to hold it with only the tips of his fingers. He didn't pause for another second before bringing the meat to his face and taking a hearty bite.

The groan of pleasure that slipped through the young man's lips rippled through the crowd. Every prisoner's eyes went to him for a moment before they all fixed back on the pig ravenously.

The soldier laughed again, but it wasn't the cruel laugh Barra had feared. This man was laughing at them, but their desperation was enough to fuel his amusement, he did not need to truly deny them. He returned his blade to the pig, cutting chunk after chunk and holding it out to the horde of nearly starving people.

The Svekards got the first several servings. The larger brutes pushed their way to the front, but once they'd received and devoured their pieces, they stood guard, silently telling the Neamairtese to stand back.

The Neamairtese had no interest in missing out on their share. Several pushed forward, coming face-to-face with their larger, stockier enemies. There was very little chance that any one of the Neamairtese could win one-on-one, but for a piece of fresh meat, they were willing to risk it.

As both sides balled up their fists, a shout came from next to the roasted pig. "Neamairtese," a new soldier called. His voice was loud and commanding, but without any of the anger or warning the Victricites had used previously to control their captives. Instead, he held out a piece of meat on his own sword toward the Neamairtese who had lumped up on his side of the pig.

He knew this would happen, Barra realized. How many times has he done this before? Barra looked from one serving soldier to the other at the calm precision of their actions and shared eye rolls as every predictable action played out before them. How often did these men host soon-to-be-slaves?

Barra's train of thought stopped there as the man who had rushed forward to take the pork from the second soldier dashed up to her to present the first bite. She would feel a little guilty afterward, but Barra accepted the meat without thanks, grabbing it and thrusting it to her face. Her fingers were burning slightly, and her tongue bristled at the heat, but Barra didn't care. This is what the Summerland will taste like, she thought, taking another bite and savoring the feeling of the juice squishing between her teeth and dripping down her throat. No meat had ever been this tender or juicy, and she didn't think it was just her lack of comparison over the last few weeks.

This hand-cutting and feeding continued until every Svekard and Neamairtese had received a piece and many had returned for seconds. The prisoners were far from done, but the soldiers seemed to have grown tired of the game.

A small gasp brought everyone's attention first to the Neamairtese woman that had made the sound and second to the source of her fright. A new soldier had appeared from one of the tents with an axe the size of a Svekard. Barra ducked and took a handful of dirt into her hands. She wasn't sure what spell might possibly stop the man, but the handful of earth made her feel more prepared.

The group backed away slowly. Unarmed, without mounts, they would all be carved up as easily as their last meal.

Barra picked her spell carefully and was three words in when it became obvious that the man was not headed for the prisoners but for the fire and the roasted pig. She paused to watch the soldiers who had been carving the pig each take one side of the roasting stick and move it to a large wooden slab on the ground near the fire. The man with the axe lifted it above his head and brought it down to cleave the pig in two.

Each man hefted their half of the carcass away from the slab by the wooden rod punched through the creature and now split in two.

The soldier with the front half called out to the Svekards as he dragged the carcass across the ground by the wooden rod. The barbarians trailed after him like pups, their tongues all but hanging out and dripping as they followed the scent of meat. If her own people looked the same as they followed the man with the back half of the pig, Barra ignored it. The smell of pork was too distracting.

The soldier leading the Neamairtese brought them to one of the large tents, a mostly empty room with cots like the ones the Neamairtese slept on at home lining the tent walls. The man deposited the partially carved up carcass into the dirt in the center of the tent and walked away.

Once the soldier left, Barra pushed her way to the center of the crowd. "Wait," she instructed them. They stepped away with only a slight hesitation.

Barra knelt next to the pig, pinching a finger full of dirt off the dead beast. Focusing on Earth's magic, she blew the dirt from her fingertips and watched as every speck of dirt fell from the pig. Her people were not Svekards. They would not eat dirty meat. They would not eat the tarnished brains and eyes that the blonds were almost certainly devouring over in their tent. They were Neamairtese and they would share clean meat, crack the bones and eat the marrow, and place parts of the cleared bones in their hair to remember that even in the darkest times, there were simple pleasures.

When nothing remained of what had been their dinner, the Neamairtese thanked Barra for all the ways and times she had blessed their food, drew the cots into the center of the room, and settled down with a collective sigh. Barra was not amongst the group as they splayed out on the cots, too full to do anything but revel in the feeling. The cot in the center was hers, but Daralan's expressions as he'd caught her eye throughout the feast made it clear she had more to do before she could join them.

"What is it?" Barra tried not to be annoyed. Whatever Daralan had to say would be important and her spirits ought to be high. The problem was that she did feel better than she had in over a week, and she had a distinct feeling Daralan was going to bring her back to reality.

Daralan's eyes flickered to the rest of the group to make sure no one was watching or listening. "Has this been only a prelude? Will they carve us up tomorrow? Like that?" Daralan said. There was no pig left to look at. The fact that his gaze drifted to where Barra's cot now stood sent a shiver down her spine.

Barra bit back the harsh laughter that bubbled up in the back of her throat. There was a part of her that wanted to say she didn't care. If tonight was their last night, then it was a far better way to go than exhausted and beaten. But she did care. These were her people, and they were her responsibility.

"I don't—" Barra stopped. She might not know, but the Spirits did. They knew what was planned and what was fated. She took a deep breath and was thankful for Daralan's characteristic silence. If she listened hard enough as the night breeze worked its way through the flimsy material of the Victricite tents she would be able to hear Air's words, his future-sight.

Eyes closed, Barra listened, pulling words from the whispers at her ears. It took all of her concentration to pull any meaning from the words. The spirit of Earth didn't have much to say but was always straightforward when she did. Air on the other hand was an endless stream of knowledge, and it was often difficult to pull any sense from the hundreds of important messages.

"No," Barra whispered at last. "Something about old friends, or not quite friends, not quite allies, but something like that. Tomorrow will bring greater clarity. There will be pain, but it will be the good kind of pain."

At Daralan's questioning look, Barra shrugged. "I don't know what Air is into." She smiled as she let the innuendo hang. "Sleep, Daralan. Your belly is full. Let your head be less so."

In her dreams, Air continued to whisper into Barra's ear continuous nonsense about friends and enemies, allies and adversaries. Barra strained to understand, but the harder she tried, the faster he spoke until it all blended into one swishing sound like nothing but wind through branches. She woke the next morning, desperately grasping at the words and at the sleep she had lost.

With her eyes closed and her furs draped over her like a blanket, Silvi could almost pretend she was not in a cloth house in the Southern Plains, but at home in bed, thick wooden walls holding in the heat from the hearth. If she didn't move, she couldn't feel the rough texture of the material of her odd folding bed against her uncovered hands and wrists rather than the caress of a bear pelt on top of a straw mattress. Silvi kept her eyes closed and tried to ignore the sounds of other Svekards, an odd cacophony of snoring and waking. She was warm, she was full, and she was not sleeping by herself on the ground.

Last night had been a surprising reprieve, not just from the hunger that had been her constant and only companion besides the memory of Papa. In their fervor for fresh meat, her compatriots had been too distracted to enforce her isolation. She had eaten by their sides, calling out her praises to the Gods as one Svekard voice of gratitude.

At one moment in the night, as the last of the easily grabbed pork was torn away, the group's eyes had turned to her and she'd thought it was all over. They had noticed her presence and would banish her once more. As if by one mind, the group looked from Silvi to the pig's head and back. A man named Keepan, who had taken the place as leader of this makeshift clan, pushed everyone aside. He took the large metal broach that held on his furs, knelt over the pig's head, and looked directly at Silvi. He slammed the broach into the center of the pig's skull. Silvi tried to suppress the involuntary shiver that ran down her spine at the cracking sound that filled the tent.

The threat was clear to Silvi as she scrambled to her feet. Her people would not descend upon her like a horde of savages, but it was a leader's job to protect his community from outsiders. Right now, she was intruding and needed to leave.

Silvi watched transfixed as Keepan turned his attention back to the pig, dug his fingers into the crack he'd created in the skull, and pulled bone chunks aside to reveal the soft, tender brain inside. With the delicacy of a Svekard father toward his newborn child, the man reached two fingers into the cavity and drew out one half of the brain and then the other. He turned to Silvi, still kneeling, and held out the brain cradled in his hands to her.

For a long moment, Silvi only stared from the brain to Keepan and back while the whole room watched her.

The brain was the most coveted part of any animal. Beyond the nutritional value it provided to a people who lived in a cold climate where fruits and vegetables were rare, it was believed that consuming the brain of an animal would bestow on a person great intelligence and wisdom. Bear brains were the greatest of delicacies, but all brains were reserved for leaders, pregnant women, and elders. As an unbetrothed woman, Keepan certainly wouldn't think she was pregnant. Consuming the brain should have been his right, not hers, even if she were pregnant.

If I take it, maybe they will all stop staring at me, Silvi thought and held out cupped hands to accept the offering. Maybe they thought it would break the curse or make her more able to fight it. Now that the offering was in her hands, there was no way she could turn down the honor even if she thought the chances of it affecting the curse were about zero. Silvi bowed her head to Keepan in reverence and gratitude before retreating to one of the folding beds at the outskirts of the tent.

Now, lying on her back, halfway between sleep and wakefulness, she lingered on the memory of that creamy flavor and delicate texture.

She could smell the remnants of the grease rubbed on her chest and brow in the symbol of Garvil, god of thanks and bounty. She smiled and reveled in the feeling of almost being a true Svekard again. Perhaps the clanbed's prayers had been answered after all.

At the call of the soldiers, the Svekards rose from their beds, fixed their hair and furs appropriately, and clustered outside the tent ready to receive their yokes. No yokes were shackled around them. Instead, the group followed the soldiers to a large cloth house in the middle of the encampment.

The house was supported not by strong walls but by timber locked into the ground by blocks of cast stone placed throughout the house to hold up the roof. The area within the house was large enough to hold the entire party of Svekards, Neamairtese, and Victricites, twice over if they crowded.

In the center of the room, in a wicker chair facing the incoming Svekards sat an old woman, watching them through heavy lidded eyes. Her skin was the mottled color of potato skins, with the leathery, wrinkled appearance of the tuber long past its ripeness. Scrawled across every inch of the skin that hung around her face in deep loose wrinkles were black markings faded almost to blue in the shape of runes unknown to Silvi and patterns like the curls of plant stems. The veins of her hands pressed up through the thin flesh to create bluish designs of their own to the point Silvi wasn't sure if they were tattooed as well or the woman's natural anatomy.

The woman wore a scarf wrapped around the top of her head, bits of gray and deep brown hair poking out in thin wisps below it. Her simple brown dress was thin and loose, ideal for this warm climate, but it only made the woman inside look frailer as it billowed around her.

Was this what Victricite women looked like? She looked nothing like the men they had seen, but then again, male and female wrens and ducks had different coloring. Or, perhaps Victricites changed as a matter of aging to explain her appearance. The possibility that this woman was diseased crossed Silvi's mind, but she rejected it. There was too much deliberateness to her markings, and surely the Victricites were smart enough to not crowd people in with a sick woman.

To either side of the woman were two tables filled with small metal objects, pots and bowls of ground substances, and collections of herbs with greater variety than Silvi had ever seen. As the group was pushed toward the woman, she stood, showing her hands to the Svekards in a traditional act of showing she was unarmed and meant no harm.

It was at that moment that the Svekards realized as a group, they were alone. Silvi didn't think she would ever miss the presence of the Neamairtese, but without them, she felt an indescribable sense of unease. She could tell that her clansfolk were feeling it too. They shifted from one foot to the other, scanning the house for people they knew weren't there. On the battlefield it was far more intimidating to not be able to see your enemy than to see their massive numbers. Here, the question in everyone's mind was what had happened to them and would the same happen to her own people?

"If something bad had happened, I would have been compelled to stop it," Silvi coached herself, not entirely sure that it was a comforting statement. Unless the brain really did end the curse, she added, once again unsure if that made her feel better.

They stood silently as the woman scanned them critically, pausing on each Svekard. After a full minute of silence, the woman pointed at Keepan and then to her chair before she stepped to her table to pick up the first of many metal items. Silvi didn't have time to analyze the item the woman had grabbed as two soldiers hurried forward, grabbing Keepan and dragging him to the chair. Keepan's snarls did not faze the guards, one of whom pulled out a knife and held it near Keepan's throat. He raised his eyebrows in challenge first to Keepan and then to the Svekards before relaxing his stance and moving the blade a foot or so from him. He was ready to end Keepan's life if he needed to and would not be disarmed before he could do so, but he did not apparently think it would be necessary.

When Keepan had been sufficiently assuaged, the woman approached. The item in her hand was a small teardrop shape, made of bronze, with a circle of glass wrapped in bronze hanging from it. As the crowd watched in trepidation, the woman brought the glass to her eye and looked into Keepan's eyes at intensely close range. With her other hand, the woman pulled the skin under Keepan's eye down and then pulled his brow up before switching to the other eye and repeating the process.

From Keepan's eye, she moved to his hair, digging into it before stepping away to avoid his violent reaction. To touch a Svekard's hair without permission was a high insult. Only children too young to understand could get away with pulling someone's hair without it being considered a challenge. The threat of the blade pacified Keepan and the woman returned to dig in his hair, turning the braids this way and that as if she was looking to find something in it.

"We're not Neamairtese," Silvi heard one of the men near her grumble.

Whatever the woman had been looking for, she apparently determined it wasn't there because she brought a pot from her table and sprinkled a powder onto his head before working it onto his scalp. When she was done with Keepan's hair, the woman took one of his arms and then the other and rotated it as if helping him wind up to throw a rock. While one hand moved his arm, the other reached under his furs to grip his shoulder. The soldier with the knife gave Keepan another severe look, but as long as the woman didn't try to remove the fur or reach below his woolen clothing, Keepan was unlikely to react. If she decided either was necessary, Leapora, goddess of protection and the family, help them all.

The woman seemed satisfied with what she had achieved and moved next to Keepan's mouth, pulling his lips away from his teeth to show off his already snarling expression. The woman made a clicking noise before returning to her table to retrieve a small metal pick. She placed the pick between two teeth and scraped.

Keepan jerked as he garbled a call of pain around the fingers in his mouth. This time, the woman didn't have a chance to pull back before Keepan could react. He bit down on the finger closest to his teeth and smiled at the woman's cry of pain. She wrenched back, hurrying to her table, her damaged hand cupped in her undamaged one.

While the rest of the room watched the soldiers wrangle Keepan back into submission, Silvi watched the woman first soak her hand in cloudy water before wrapping it in leaves and cloth. Keepan's yelp drew Silvi's attention back to him. The soldier with the knife was cutting a slow shallow line into Keepan's arm, just deep enough to draw a dot of blood every inch or so.

The soldier didn't make it far before the woman called out for them to stop. She seemed more frustrated than anything and spoke without power to enforce her request. She turned to her table, picked out one of the bowls, and brought it to Keepan's side to spread the green contents on his new wound.

"Witchcraft!" the Svekards hissed as one, puffing up and preparing to surge forward.

"She's taking his blood for her ritual," a woman called out.

"She seasoned him and is getting a taste," a man shouted over her. "They're going to eat us!"

Several voices called out that the pig had been to fatten them up. The threat from the other soldiers was clear, but the perceived threat of death was rising with every yell of "witch" and "cannibals!" The Svekards weren't scared, they were angry and that made them far more dangerous.

The woman was backing away. She had abandoned her instruments and was shuffling toward the back exit of the house. Somehow, she hadn't expected such a violent reaction from the crowd.

Silvi's mind was churning as her gaze swept from the crowd of her clansfolk to the soldiers, across the table to the woman still watching them all as she slunk away. The idea didn't make sense. There was a familiarity Silvi couldn't put her finger on, but it didn't make her scared. The table's contents and the woman's actions made her feel more at home than she had since leaving her village.

"She's a vet!" Silvi screamed, her voice managing to carry over the cacophony of fear without intensifying it.

The silence that followed made Silvi's ears burn. Everyone was staring at her, but this time, she needed them to. She also needed them to listen. "She's a veterinarian, but for people, like a healer, but she can't talk to us so she's just looking for what she knows." How did she explain what she had learned to do naturally when presented with a sick animal? "I look in animals' eyes and in their mouths when I don't know what is wrong. She was probably looking for lice in Keepan's hair and checking his joints when she moved his arms around."

The crowd looked at Silvi skeptically, but they were still listening. Silvi thanked the Gods and continued. "Think about it. We're going to be sold as slaves. Maybe they just want to make sure we are healthy enough to be worth keeping." It was a dark way to say it, but maybe dark was what they needed. "Like horses," she added flatly.

The crowd around Silvi, soldiers and Svekard alike, watched Silvi in continued silence. All looks were skeptical as if they were waiting for the hammer to fall and the fighting to begin. Utilizing their paralysis, Silvi approached the woman's table and looked over the metal instruments, many of which were higher quality versions of her own tools at home. She held up the ones she knew one at a time and showed them to the group, explaining their function. The ones she didn't know, the ones that made the hair on the back of her neck stand on end with their sharp blades and long, thin needles, she skipped over as if they didn't exist.

"I don't think she plans to hurt us. I mean, it might hurt a little bit." She looked over at Keepan where he was still being held to the chair, his gums bleeding. "But she's just checking our health and helping keep us healthy."

Though she was fairly sure she was correct, Silvi had no faith that her clansfolk would think so. They were intelligent and keen, but stubborn to change their minds, especially when they had categorized something as evil or dangerous.

The old woman was slowly returning to the center of the house. She was watching Silvi intently and approaching her as if Silvi were a skittish rabbit. Silvi gave her a calm smile, wishing she could speak to the woman and clear up this whole mess. Silence fell over the crowd as everyone waited for the other to act.

It was Keepan who broke the silence. "I am not a horse," he proclaimed. He looked around at the crowd before his gaze landed on Silvi. "I am a Svekard and I can endure torturous pain without flinching. Let this healer do what she must. We will only be stronger and more ready to defeat these Victricite scum when the time comes." He settled back into the chair and centered his gaze on a spot on the far wall. He would not be fazed, no matter what the healer did to him…as long as it wasn't witchcraft, but only medicine.

Around the room, the other Svekards nodded and set their stance, faces impassable. They would endure.

Silvi located the pick the woman had used to scrape Keepan's teeth and swished it in the cloudy water before holding it out to her as if in offering. From the look and smell, Silvi guessed the liquid was salt water which would help clean the pick. Very few people Silvi had met understood the importance of cleaning their tools between patients, let alone with the same patient. Silvi didn't know if this woman did, but either way, it seemed like a good choice. If the woman knew, she would be impressed by Silvi's action, if not, Silvi might have helped decrease Keepan's chances of infection.

The woman took the pick hesitantly before giving Silvi a confused but genuine smile. She returned to Keepan, motioning for the soldiers to stand down, and resumed scraping Keepan's teeth. The healer spent a couple of minutes on Keepan's teeth before she spoke to the soldiers in an accented version of their language and the men let him go, directing him to the far end of the house.

The process continued with each Svekard, the woman inspecting them one by one with Silvi standing close at hand to explain the woman's choices. Silvi had more trouble with the more advanced techniques, guessing several times at the meaning behind the woman's actions. A couple of times, the woman even stopped at Silvi's confused expression and acted out the reason for the current procedure.

The worst were the teeth pullings, of which there were seven. Svekards took good care of their teeth, utilizing chewing sticks to keep their jaws strong and teeth clean. Those that hadn't been as diligent fought back the tears that sprung to their eyes and growled their strength to overcome. The first few times the woman would give a hard yank and jump back, waiting for the Svekard to attempt his or her retribution, but by the third patient, she had learned that no revenge would be sought.

Silvi was the woman's final patient and, except for the powder to stave off lice, she received only the gentlest of teeth scrapings to the back of her front teeth. She made a mental note to pay more attention to that particular sensitive area before realizing she might not ever get the chance. Sure, the Victricites cared about her dental health now, but would they after she was sold?

Silvi joined the rest of her clansfolk as the soldiers finished handing out clay bowls of unsweetened oatmeal. It was the first time they'd received any sort of breakfast, and with sore teeth, the mush was perfect. Otherwise distracted, Silvi took only a few moments to notice the arrival of the Neamairtese. Around her, the corners of a few mouths quirked up as the Svekards settled in to watch the Neamairtese, who were known to run at the first sign of danger and would certainly lack the grit to handle the Victricite healer.

CHAPTER SIX
THE LAST ONE

At the soldiers' direction, the Neamairtese pushed the cots back to the outside walls of the tent and followed the soldiers through camp. The prisoners were relieved for every moment spent out of their yokes, though it was hard to take it as a blessing when it had become the only sure thing in their subordinate condition.

In the bright morning light, Barra could see that, like her own tribe at home, the Victricite camp was built with large, shared tents in the center for meals, social gatherings, and general group functions. The Victricite tents far surpassed the size of even the largest Neamairtese tent, however. Around the central common areas stood the sleeping tents, two large ones for the prisoners surrounded by a collection of smaller tents for the soldiers and guards.

At home, the central tents would be community areas for cooking, eating, and storing ceremonial items valuable enough to travel from one site to the next. The large tents would be common spaces for the children and the elderly during the day and the whole community in the evenings. Council members would share several personal tents closest to the tribe's center followed by Neamairtese couples and their children and, around the outside, the smallest tents each housing a few uncompanioned Neamairtese.

The biggest difference between this settlement and her own home was the permanent nature of everything. The support beams were held in the ground by what looked like rocks shaped perfectly to the hole in the ground. As a tree might grow around a rock to encircle it, the rock seemed to have grown perfectly around the beam, locking it forever in that place. The canvas material that made up the skin of the tents appeared to be one impossibly large sheath as if it had come from the largest animal on Earth. It would be incredibly inefficient and time-consuming to take down, transport, and put back up from one encampment to the next.

Barra knew very little about the culture of the Victricites. The previous queens had never interacted with them directly and had only heard stories of their violent precision from Razirgali traders generations ago. From their stories, she had imagined tribes of Victricites traveling across the southern scrub lands like warrior ants, surrounded by soldiers, all marching in lockstep from toddlers to elderly, consuming everything in their path.

This encampment was not a tribe, Barra thought. There were no toddlers and no elderly, only young and middle-aged men. Barra realized as she looked around at the faces of Victricites in their prime that she'd never even seen a female Victricite. This was not home for these people; it was just an outpost. If they put this level of permanence into their outposts, what did home look like, Barra wondered with renewed apprehension. To hold still like the Svekards, to not travel with the seasons, was unnatural.

The Victricites' central tent was far too large to conserve heat, especially since the top of the tent had no hole for smoke, making a fire inside dangerous. Barra supposed that in this climate, the Victricites didn't need to conserve heat, but it made the space seem uncomfortable and out of place. There was a pungent smell like greenery mixed with strong liquor that burned the inside of her nose.

As the Neamairtese entered the tent, Barra took in the contents of the room in one sweeping glance, her gaze trialing over the ritual materials and herbs laid meticulously out on tables. With the materials provided in this single room, and her growing power, they might actually stand a chance of escape. This outpost might have twice the number of soldiers they'd had on the road, but the potential for Barra's power was about to increase tenfold.

In her eagerness to inventory the materials, Barra almost missed the woman rising from her seat to greet them. "Razirgali!" Barra gasped, looking over the tattooed markings, skin coloring, and head covering. She pushed easily to the front of the group, placed a finger on her forehead, a hand around her groin, and gave a small bow.

The Razirgali woman was halfway to placing two fingers over her heart when Barra's action registered and she stopped to stare, frozen. "Blessings be that the ancestors have brought us together," Barra recited in perfect Razirgali language. The line was a mix of Neamairtese and Razirgali greetings that had been used for centuries between their two peoples. It was typical for the Neamairtese to speak Razirgali when trading, as their own language was much more complex and difficult to learn.

When the woman continued to stare, one of the soldiers approached her, cleared his throat, and gave her a stern look. She nodded and her features set as if she were preparing for the task at hand, but her eyes still shown with wild wonder and confusion.

"We have not seen Razirgali for generations," Barra said, sticking to Razirgali as she spoke. Her people would have no idea what she was saying, but she would be able to translate for them as needed. "Are you brothers with the Victricites?"

The woman thought for a moment, biting the inside of her mouth and drawing out her wrinkles on one side. Barra prepped to parse the truth from what the woman was about to say. The first step when dealing with Razirgali was always to learn what kind of Razirgali they were.

"Me…my Razirgali is no very good. No talk Razirgali in many star cycles." She looked at Barra with clear embarrassment, refusing to meet her eyes. Barra wanted to believe it was true emotion at the loss of her culture, but she reserved her judgment until she knew more.

The soldier who had given her the stern look approached again, this time drawing out a knife and looking at the woman with clear question. Whether he was asking her if he needed to use it on the woman or Barra was unclear. The woman spoke to him briefly in the Victricites' language before turning back to Barra. "I is…I am a slave. I am…" she paused to think through how to best phrase the sentence. "There are very few Razirgali yet. Victricites are not our brothers, they are our slavers and raiders."

In Razirgali, there were two words for raiders. One meant a group of Razirgali that mounted a surprise attack on another group of Razirgali, Neamairtese, or other peoples in order to steal their livestock, resources, and sometimes a few slaves. The other word meant a group of people who attacked a group for the sole purpose of destroying them. These raiders were known for their brutality toward their targets, scalping them alive, after all but destroying them carnally, and then burning anything that remained. The word was considered an affront to all that was holy, let alone the people it was used to describe. The word the woman had used was the latter.

"I need to heal you and them. The Victricite hurt us, if no. We talk too much...uh, more. We talk more while I heal." She pointed to the crowd behind Barra and then at the woven chair in the middle of the room.

Barra nodded her understanding and turned to her people. She had been taking care of the worst of their blisters and cuts along the way, but there was still plenty that could be soothed or treated. "This woman is a Razirgali healer and a slave of the Victricites. She is here to heal us. Aedrican, I will ask you to go first," Barra said. She would have preferred to ask Daralan, but if this Razirgali were not speaking the truth, she would need Daralan safe and healthy by her side. This Razirgali had given no signs of lying yet, but Razirgali never did.

They called it Raiders Tongue, raider coming from the more benign meaning. There were, for the most part, two kinds of Razirgali bands, those that relied on animal husbandry and trading to fulfill their needs and those that relied on raiding and unequal trade to fill their needs and desires. The merchant bands traded with integrity and spoke openly about their wares in order to build long, profitable trading routes and differentiate themselves from the more deceitful bands. Raider bands, on the other hand, did their best to disguise themselves as merchant bands when it suited them because it gave them the best chance of swindling and taking their targets by surprise. Raider Tongue was a manner of speaking to get the most out of an interaction because the one speaking it had no interest in the long-term relationship. A raider lied about anything and everything they felt they could get away with because they did not fear the lie ever catching up with them. Merchant bands did not like raider bands and avoided them when feasible but viewed their way of life as equally valid.

Aedrican nodded to Barra and walked confidently to the chair. Barra had not expected the woman to stare into Aedrican's eyes through an odd piece of metal and glass or after looking at his gums and teeth, to dig in his mouth with her metal items. The only parts that seemed normal were the questions translated through Barra about how he'd felt over the last few months and the part where the Razirgali woman had him stand and pull down his pants and loincloth so she could examine his genitals and rear.

The woman, Ahjva, as she introduced herself, recounted how she had come to be a slave healer of the Victricites as she worked, stumbling through vocabulary and grammar. "Victricites attack my band I was a maiden. I am a healer with my mother. They kill all but young and pretty. His mouth hurt him recently? Pretty and strong become slaves. I bought by soldier. He learn I am a healer and bring me to camps with he. How many poles he see beside the tent entrance? I bought by Victricite raiders to keep slaves healthy. I here long time. So it is. No Neamairtese speak to me before this now. He has trouble with keeping erection recently?"

As Ahjva moved from one patient to the next, she grew more fluent in the language that she had almost lost. She described the systematic destruction of the Razirgali, one band at a time, by the Victricites. They had grown tired of the raiding bands and apparently decided that there being no Razirgali would be preferable to raids. Ahjva's band and those that she knew of hadn't even recognized that they were at war until they had lost. The Razirgali bands had never been known to cooperate well amongst each other, and the Victricites had used that to their advantage. As far as Ahjva knew, no Razirgali bands remained.

Every once in a while, Ahjva would stop in her explanation and questions to examine and treat a concerning sore or other problem. Every few patients, Ahjva would apologize to a patient through Barra before retrieving her pliers and yanking a tooth or two from their jaw. The worst were the six patients that were sent outside the tent after their genital checkup.

Ahjva pulled back from the first such patient she would send outside with a disappointed clicking noise and turned to Barra with a sympathetic frown. "He not like this." She pointed to a rash between the man's legs and explained, "He has a disease. It no hurt him much, just itch, but it spread to all he has sex with. The Victricites mark him with hot iron so no Victricite has sex with him or buys him for having sex. So it is."

The first Neamairtese to be told to leave the tent left with trepidation after Barra explained what was going to happen to him.

After the piercing scream that drew every person's attention in the tent except the Victricites', the proceeding Neamairtese identified as "diseased" left with unhidden dread. Pulled teeth were far preferable to being branded on the rear like Victricite cattle. The branded reentered the tent with a slow waddle and ate their oatmeal lying on their stomachs as they recounted the experience to those lucky enough to avoid it and commiserated with the others.

Barra looked to the Svekards that were sitting with their backs toward the Neamairtese in the far corner of the tent. She had noticed them all turn their curious and sadistic gazes away when Aedrican lowered his pants. She had not heard the scream of a Svekard before they arrived at this particular tent, and that sound traveled. Were the gruff Svekards so stalwart that they could withstand branding without more than a grunt?

When Barra turned the question to Ahjva, she laughed. It was the first time Barra had seen a look other than surprise or focused attention on her face, but the look held no joy. "The Victricites have a saying, 'Yellow in the field, red in the bed.' In the Victricite tongue, both rhyme. Yellow, field, red, bed." She repeated the phrase in the Victricite language before continuing. "It does not value the cost to drop a Svekard's pants. They prefer death to naked." She nodded her head side to side in the merchant Razirgali way of saying that the statement wasn't exactly accurate, and she wanted to be transparent about that fact, but the meaning was captured, nonetheless. "Victricites no buy Svekards for the bed. A groin check is no useful. I no check Neamairtese hair for lice for the same reason. I no talk to Neamairtese before you, so it does not value the cost to try. Neamairtese no allow rest of checkup if they fear for their hair. So it is.

"Svekards have hard time for slaves. They fight, no listen. Strong but mean. That one with the bruised face..." Ahjva pointed over her current patient's shoulder at Barra's Svekard. "She do better. I think she is a healer. She tells the Svekards stop and they allow me to do my work. Svekards are always hard. These Svekards are very, very hard. I never see Svekards very, very angry and scared for teeth cleaning. These Svekards are more...agitated."

Barra nodded guiltily. "That is my fault. They are afraid of me. They probably saw your attempts to treat them as magic...witchcraft."

Ahjva gave Barra a skeptical look before stopping to pull another tooth. She turned to Barra and asked over her shoulder as she swished her pliers in reddish water. "Afraid of you?"

Barra wasn't sure it was a good idea to tell Ahjva about her position or her power. Even if she was a merchant Razirgali as Barra was fairly convinced, Barra could not risk the Victricites finding out. "I can perform simple magic," Barra said, figuring a tiny bit of Raider Tongue in the form of a half-truth was fine. "I have been healing my people, and the Svekards are terrified and hateful of magic."

To her surprise, Ahjva nodded. "These Neamairtese have less damage. You are a good healer. My people speak of Neamairtese magic. I no think magic true. Now, I think maybe magic true." She gave Barra her first real smile before indicating the empty half of the tent and then the chair. She had finished with every Neamairtese and now it was Barra's turn.

Barra was the best patient she could be, silently praying to the Spirits, hoping that she did not have a rash or sores that would mark her for branding. She did not evoke their magic, as to do so in front of the soldiers would be dangerous. She hadn't done it for any of her people either, so to do so only for herself was entirely unfair in Barra's opinion.

"I need to pull two teeth," Ahjva informed Barra with a dash more sympathy than she had given the other Neamairtese. She returned to Barra with the pliers and placed them in position around the first tooth. Barra gripped her eyes shut and prepared for the pain. Instead, she heard Ahjva squeal in fright and the pliers go loose in her mouth before they were pulled away. Barra kept her eyes closed half a second longer, wishing she could will away what she knew she would see.

The soldiers were quickly closing in on Barra and her Svekard, who stood over her, holding the pliers. Ahjva was several paces away looking about as ready to intervene as a rabbit watching a wolf tear apart its prey.

"Tell them to stop. She won't hurt me." Barra stood, taking the pliers out of her Svekard's hand, and walked with feigned confidence past the soldiers to Ahjva. A quick glance over her shoulder confirmed that the soldiers had stopped advancing and were waiting to see what would happen. Her Svekard was also waiting with a disappointed, shaken look. Barra swore silently then turned back to Ahjva. "Do you have to pull the teeth?"

"Now, yes, one for minimum." Ahjva didn't look at Barra when she spoke but over her shoulder at Barra's Svekard. "The Victricites see I plan to do it. I must or they think they must force you. They show power. Why she stop me?"

"My magic does not allow her to let you hurt me." Barra shook her head. "It's complicated."

"But I help you. Those teeth are bad, they hurt you. My hurt is short. They hurt more and more with time."

"I know and my guess is that she does too. She told the Svekards to let you do your work and you think she is a healer. She knows, but she can't help it. The magic won't let her. Please come back to the chair with me so the soldiers will stand down. She will not hurt you either."

With clear hesitance, Ahjva followed Barra back to the chair and stood staring at Barra's Svekard expectantly. Barra's Svekard stared at her in turn as if Barra should have any idea how to proceed. "It's okay, she just needs to pull a tooth," Barra said, acting it out with a smile.

Her Svekard raised her eyebrows and nodded like this was the most obvious statement in the world and changed nothing. Barra supposed it didn't.

"What we do now?" Ahjva asked.

For a long moment, they just stared at each other before her Svekard took a deep inhale and turned to the table, a decision clearly made. She wandered around the table for several seconds before stuffing some bark in her mouth and chewing. She located a vase of water and dropped a handful of what looked like salt into it, swishing the contents as she walked back to Barra with an empty pot. Her Svekard placed the pot in Barra's lap, took a swig from the vase and swished it around in her mouth for several seconds. Leaning over Barra's lap, she spit the contents into the pot and held the vase out to Barra.

At this point, the soldiers seemed tired of waiting. The man who had first approached with the knife when Barra and Ahjva began speaking drew close again, speaking to Ahjva who answered first with a shrug and then a shooing motion. The soldier looked none too happy at Ahjva's choice of action, but stepped back, nonetheless.

Barra took the vase and did as she had clearly been told, swishing the salty water around in her mouth until her Svekard nodded that she was allowed to spit it out. With strong yet delicate hands, her Svekard took Barra's jaw in her hand and opened it to inspect. Barra watched her Svekard nod before pulling the chewed, moist hunk of bark out of her mouth. Barra couldn't help grimacing as her Svekard wrapped the hunk of spitty bark around the gums of a tooth on either side of her lower jaw. The reaction earned her an eyeroll. Her Svekard held up her finger with a stern expression before returning to the table. Barra sighed. She supposed it was the mature thing to do not to pull the bark out of her mouth, even if it did make her feel like a baby bird.

Her Svekard returned with a small, corked bottle after uncorking and smelling several different bottles.

"That is very expensive," Ahjva protested raising her hand to stop the Svekard. "I need it for amputations." The glare Ahjva received shut her up more than anything Barra could have said, so Barra let it pass, her mouth hanging open. Her gums were starting to go numb where the spitty bark was mushed against them, and she hoped this whole thing would just be over soon.

Her Svekard approached again, placing the small bottle in her cleavage and reached out to take the pliers from Barra. Barra was glad she had her mouth hanging open for the tooth extraction as her eyes centered on the bottle resting between her Svekard's breasts. It was her first time truly looking at her body, and for a long moment, all Barra could do was stare at the plump, round, gorgeous flesh. How have I not noticed those before, Barra asked herself, mystified. Because I was too busy seeing her as a Svekard to see her as a woman, Barra chided herself as her Svekard leaned forward and placed the pliers around the first tooth.

Barra had planned to close her eyes against the impending pain, but once her Svekard was sure the pliers were in place, she locked eyes with Barra and Barra found she couldn't look away. For the first time, her Svekard didn't look angry. Her expression radiated confidence and calm, not just in herself, but a confidence in safety that she was trying to pass on to Barra. "Don't worry. I've got you," the look said loudly and clearly.

Grip locked, her Svekard pulled and Barra felt the roots of her tooth give way. She released a long, throaty groan at the pain and reached up to massage her jaw, but her Svekard knocked her hand away. She was already locking the pliers around the second tooth. She gave Barra the look again and Barra felt her heart flutter. She wasn't entirely sure if it was the look or the knowledge of the coming pain, but Barra guessed the former.

A second sharp bolt of pain through Barra's jaw brought tears to her eyes. She barely had time to process the ache that was overtaking her face before her Svekard tipped Barra's head back by her forehead and poured more salt water into her mouth. Barra didn't spit the bloody water out so much as open her mouth and let it fall into the pot in her lap, the bark bits tumbling out with it.

Her Svekard gave Barra's mouth a quick scan before tipping it back once more. She uncorked the small bottle and poured in a small stream that made Ahjva groan in disappointment. The liquid was alcohol, Barra realized, though stronger than she'd ever experienced, and it burned as if her Svekard had poured fire directly into her mouth. She tried to cry out, but her Svekard had her hand over Barra's mouth. Barra considered biting it, but the pain was already dying down to a dull sizzle. Instead, Barra dutifully swished the bit of liquid around under her Svekard's stern watch. When she leaned forward to spit, her Svekard grabbed Barra's head and tipped it back farther than she had previously, pinching Barra's nose shut.

Frustrated, Barra smacked at the arm attached to the hand holding her nose and swallowed, wincing at the burning sensation as it flared down her throat and into her stomach. "I'm not an animal," she tried to complain, but it came out more like, "I na ah aahuh."

Her Svekard gave her a small, amused smirk that Barra was sure was her Svekard laughing at her. She took the pot and returned it to the table along with the recorked bottle. She stood at the table like a sentry and motioned to Ahjva.

Ahjva rolled her eyes and inspected the Svekard's work before having Barra stand for her final check. As Barra reached for the edge of her pants, she looked over to the table hoping to watch her Svekard's expression as she revealed herself. As a healer, she had probably seen it all before, but a not insignificant part of Barra hoped she would like what she saw. But her Svekard was gone. Disappointed, Barra turned back to Ahjva hoping her Svekard's retreat would be the worst part of her genital checkup.

Barra barely registered Ahjva tell her she was clean. She was too busy watching the soldiers talking and pointing at her Svekard. "What are they saying?" she asked.

Ahjva paused in cleaning up to listen and the tanned skin of her face took on a grayish color. "They say the Svekard is a better healer. She can speak to Svekards and…tame Neamairtese. They want to keep her, not me. They say she is better than the last one."

"They can't!" Barra burst out.

Ahjva only shook her head. "It is too late. They say find the woman with the bruised face."

Barra had too many spells to cast and not enough time to cast them. Luckily, she had a feast of spell components laid out for her. "Daralan, I need a distraction! Keep them away from the Svekards."

Barra didn't watch Daralan and her people, though the commotion was loud enough to know they were succeeding. Healing her Svekard's face would be the most obvious solution. The Victricites were bound to have the same trouble telling Svekards apart as she had. Without the bruise they wouldn't know which Svekard was their desired healer. But healing her Svekard's face would require Barra to touch her and that would easily identify her and they would be on her before she could blend into the crowd again.

All I have to do is hide it, Barra thought, grabbing an empty pot and beginning to throw materials into it. All she needed was to get the color close and Water's magic could blend the color into her Svekard's skin, hiding the bruise. When the color in the bowl was close enough, Barra sprinkled a pinch of dirt in to evoke Earth's magic as well. Making sure no one but Ahjva was watching her, Barra threw the pot's contents into the air in one slosh and blew on them as hard as she could.

The Victricites missed the floating orb of honey-colored mud as they chased the screaming Neamairtese around the right side of the tent. The Svekards didn't notice it until it was in their midst as they stared at the Neamairtese moaning and rubbing their jaws while dodging soldiers right and left. At that point, the Victricites were too intent on quelling the current crisis to see what was making the Svekards yelp and scatter.

The only three people to watch the orb strike Barra's Svekard in the face were Barra, who gave a sigh of relief; Ahjva, who stared in open-mouthed wonder; and Barra's Svekard, who accepted the magic with nothing more than flashing Barra a hand sign that Barra had to assume was a vulgar gesture. She didn't care; the color was perfect. If the Victricites were as bad at telling Svekards apart as she had been at the beginning, her Svekard was safe for the moment.

"Done," Barra yelled to her people, and just as suddenly as the commotion had begun, it ended. The Neamairtese that had been screaming and flailing about sat or lay down on the cool ground and continued to rub their jaws or bottoms as if nothing had changed. The Victricites, on the other hand, were not so quick to change from chasing panicked prisoners to shepherding docile captives. Several tripped over their now sitting targets while others crashed into each other, ending up on the floor, yelling and reaching for their knives and swords.

"One more spell," Barra coached herself, reaching for a small collection of rooted stems with tiny pale pink flowers. Rubbing the valerian roots between her palms, Barra called on Earth's cool, calming magic and released the spell. In one collective voice, every person in the central tent took a deep breath and let it out. The Victricites picked themselves up as if rising from a good night's sleep and looked down at the Neamairtese who were smiling up at them. The Victricites gave languid smiles in return and waved their prisoners back into an ordered group at the back of the tent.

Their prisoners returned, the Victricites turned dazedly back to the task of finding the bruised Svekard, though they didn't seem to know exactly why they were doing so. Thanks to their enchanted forgetfulness and calm, when they found no bruised Svekard, the Victricites simply shrugged, rounded up their prisoners, and sent them back to their tents to sleep off the pain. Tomorrow would be another day of marching.

"Thank you," Ahjva whispered to Barra as she pretended to help her clean up her tools and materials, hoping to take some for herself. "You save my life. I am in your debt. So it is."

"How far is it to the place where we will be sold?"

"Five days to walk to the wall and another three to walk in Victricus to the slavers' market," Ahjva said.

"Ask the ancestors to light our dreams and comfort our steps," Barra provided the blessing as a request. She trusted that the Lord and Lady and Spirits were with them, but they would need all the help they could get.

Ahjva placed her palm on Barra's forehead and leaned into Barra's return of the gesture. "Go safely." Barra gave Ahjva one last smile before hurrying to join her people before any soldiers decided she needed to be forced.

Barra had barely made it to Terenesa's side when the adrenaline, alcohol, lack of sleep, and exhaustion hit her. She'd never cast two spells in a row before. She could heal many over the course of the night with one ritual, but to complete two large spells in quick succession felt like a night of partying wrapped into a few short minutes.

"Just tired," she mumbled as she fell into Terenesa's outstretched arms and took in Terenesa's expression of valerian-spell-tempered fear. She would have a headache like her worst hangover in the morning, but she could remember many queens before her going through this same process, and she too would come out the other side. She guessed her jaw pain would last a lot longer than the head and body ache that would come with overexertion. She hadn't used the last of her magic reserves, her people and her Svekard were safe, so as far as Barra was concerned, all was well. She happily accepted the strapping young Neamairtese arms that wrapped around her from behind and carried her back to her cot. Eight more days to find us a way out, Barra thought as she fell into a dreamless sleep.

CHAPTER SEVEN

A BARBARIAN'S LONGING

As the group progressed south from the Victricite outpost, Silvi spent most of her wakeful moments discussing with her imaginary father the odd way the Svekards treated her. They refused to make eye contact with her, yet she constantly felt their stares. She was not allowed to eat or sleep next to them. Each night, they cleared a space many paces away from the firepit of any debris for her to sleep apart from them. Ever since receiving the brain of the pig, she took notice of the slightly larger portion than everyone else that she received each night. Papa of course had no great wisdom to share with her, and Silvi once again wished he was actually there to share more than her own confusion.

That first night after the outpost, lying on her back away from her people and staring up at the stars where the great heroes of Svek watched over them, Silvi closed her eyes and brought up the image of Papa as she had seen him the morning she left for the Summer Fish Fry. He'd promised to tend to her sheep while she was gone and hugged her with the same rib-crushing act of love he'd given since she was a child. "Please," Silvi whispered, "send me your wisdom."

The next morning, while brushing her fingers through her hair and re-braiding it, Silvi caught sight of an owl, sitting on the post of the pen's fence. "Hello, handsome," Silvi said. It seemed to Silvi saner to be talking to a bird than to a figment of her imagination. "I welcome your wisdom too."

Owls were the symbol of Scobata, goddess of knowledge and wisdom. Owls held no power and certainly not the ability to speak to Silvi in return, but all were worthy of a Svekard's respect.

As the group set off south, so did the owl.

Throughout the day, Silvi kept an eye on the bird, far above, tracking the group. Several times, she thought the owl had left only to look up an hour later and see it swooping lower or sitting in a tree watching them all pass.

"Why are you even awake?" Silvi asked as she passed the owl for the fourth time. "Are we the most interesting thing you've seen in a while?" Silvi wondered what a bird would make of this odd human migratory pattern.

Silvi was even more confused the next morning to find the owl once again on the post of the prisoners' pen and consistently above or ahead of them throughout their march. By the fourth day, Silvi had made a practice of saving some of her bread to toss crumbs to her owl friend and was talking more to the owl than to her papa.

Most of the way through the Svekard's fifth day of marching since their encounter with the healer, nearly four weeks since their imprisonment had begun, they reached the outskirts of the empire of Victricus.

A giant wall stretched as far as the eye could see, at least six men tall, and manned by soldiers in perfect, shiny uniforms. The noonday sun glinted off them as if they were jewels on the giant necklace around the neck of Victricus.

The sound of a giant horn rang out like a Svekard call to battle and the front gates began opening to allow the party entrance to the empire.

A soft hooting drew Silvi's wide-eyed gaze from the doors. She was the only one to watch as her owl companion flew down to within arm's reach and began to glow a deep reddish hue as if caught in firelight. With one final hoot, the owl flew across the group of prisoners to the witch, circled around her head several times, and then took flight away to the north. Silvi stared after the bird in disbelief and then around at her people. No one was looking at her, Svekard or Neamairtese, nor in the direction of the departed owl. Had she imagined the entire thing?

In her mind, Silvi turned to Papa and asked what she knew was a stupid question. "Did you see that?"

As they walked through the giant gates of the wall, past dozens of sentries who drew to attention, Silvi's father shrugged.

"You aren't real, how would you know if the owl was?" Silvi said with a sigh and turned her attention once more to her surroundings.

The change within the walls was far greater than Silvi had experienced traveling downriver from the highlands to the lowlands or the lowlands to the plains. Now, they marched on cobblestone-paved roads rather than packed dirt. The air smelled of fresh cut hay, and at no moment could Silvi look around and not see a person. Where the lands beyond the wall were barren and natural, every inch of this land was used, whether for living, transporting, selling, or cultivating. Where the sound of their marching had been the only one for miles, now the sounds of country life interrupted the monotony of their pounding footfalls. Giant farms stretched out to the sides of the road, and laborers, most of whom were identifiable as Svekard or Neamairtese slaves, ambled through the rows of plants, tending and harvesting.

Silvi had never seen such extensive and lush fields. In Svek, the healers were lucky to get their herbs to grow in the cold, hard ground during growing season, and the main crops of potatoes, barley, rye, and oats grew sparsely for a few months each year. Based on the Neamairtese prisoners' stares and gawks, this landscape was as foreign to them as to her. She supposed the tricksy Neamairtese moved around too often to have such crops.

Semi-permanent stands sat at the road's edge and sold fresh consumables to the soldiers as they passed. The men exchanged pleasantries with their countrymen. It was as if the soldiers could breathe fully again.

Silvi also got her first view of Victricite women and determined the healer had not been one of them. The wealth of the agrarian society was visible in the Victricite women's richly dyed, flowing clothing. Their hair was pulled back in militant buns, and they smiled with a tightness that spoke of a social obligation to do so. It was a smile Svekards would have usually reserved for uninvited guests who stayed too long.

At dusk, the group turned off the main road and marched a short distance to a permanent slavers' camp. Two large, heavy canvas tents took up the majority of the camp—one for the Svekards and one for the Neamairtese. Within each was a grid of over two hundred cots, unadorned, but they would be better than the ground.

For a long moment, Silvi couldn't place what it was about this place that made her feel so…wrong.

Nature, she realized. There were no sounds or smells of nature. It was as if the Victricites had peeled away the very earth until there was nothing left and then covered the deathly silence with distinctly human noises—metal striking metal, boots on roads, and the constant murmur of conversation. The ground of the camp was scraped flat and covered in a thin layer of tiny stones. Even the streams had been uprooted from the earth to be placed in elevated troughs.

Disturbed, Silvi followed her people into the musty smelling tent and walked slowly to the back to give her people space. There were plenty of cots in here for her people to sleep in one half of the tent and her to sleep in the other. To her left was a small curtained-off room, the same heavy canvas separating a larger cot from the rest of the room. Did the Victricites think that there was some hierarchy within the Svekards whereby some leader would want this honor? If so, they were wrong. Strength came from being together. No one would want this isolation. She knew that firsthand. Perhaps she ought to take this spot, make it so everyone else wouldn't even have to see her. The thought turned Silvi's stomach, and she went instead to the far right back cot and plopped down onto her back with an unsatisfied grunt.

The smell of fresh stew drew Silvi up. Her stomach gave a long, displeased growl, twisting inside her. Except for the pig roast, the group's food of bread, sparse strips of dried meat, and water over the weeks of traveling had not been enough for the constant exertion of walking.

"Shhh," Silvi told her stomach. Last night the Svekards had only received six strips of meat, of which she had been given one. The food had felt hollow in her mouth. Her people were probably all just afraid that she would hurt them if they didn't provide all they could. Even warm stew would taste more like sand than food if she had to feel that crushing guilt again.

She flopped back down onto the cot and closed her eyes instead. Maybe if she just fell asleep, tomorrow would come sooner, and she'd be a day closer to whatever end lay before her. Slaves had neither honor nor dishonor, right?

"Silvi?" the odd voice said, just above a whisper.

Silvi's brow furrowed. The voice was too masculine for a woman but oddly feminine for a man. She opened her eyes to see Eigen standing just out of arm's reach staring at her. He had just finished his coming-of-age ceremony in Clan Spine Mountain, and he'd been accompanying his brother to the Summer Fish Fry when they had been captured by the Victricite slavers. In addition to staring a little slack-jawed, he was holding a bowl of stew slightly out from his body. He seemed to have not decided yet if he should actually offer the food or set it down and run away.

"Eigen," Silvi whispered, unable to express just what it meant to her that he was here. Her stomach spoke for her with a loud growl. The boy gave the smallest of jumps before looking from Silvi to the stew in his hand and holding out the bowl to her with a thrust that threw some of it onto his hand instead. She took the bowl and began to drink the cool, flavorless broth with its chunks of slimy vegetables gratefully. The simple broth and its delivery brought warmth that had nothing to do with the stew's tepid contents.

Eigen stood for several seconds, shifting uneasily from one foot to the other, and watching her in fear, tempered by curiosity. As a child, he would have grown up hearing plenty of stories about the witches of the Neamairtese, but to actually witness witchcraft was both a horror and an excitement. Slowly, he took a seat on the cot opposite her. "Are you still cursed?" he whispered, his voice still strained and higher than she had heard around the campfires at night.

Silvi paused in her eating to give a small sigh. "Yes." When his eyes widened and he glanced quickly over his shoulder in search of potential reinforcements, Silvi added, "Don't worry. I won't hurt you. The spell gives me superhuman strength and speed, durability too, I think, in order to protect the witch that cursed me." She'd had plenty of time to think through exactly how the magic worked and what it meant. "When she's not in danger, I'm just me. Same old Silvi." Except that everyone used to like me and now they're afraid of me, Silvi thought to herself.

"Can you get rid of the curse?" Eigen asked. The excitement behind the question told Silvi he was thinking of the heroes of old—monster killers and witch hunters. She supposed it only followed that a young man would see this entire situation as a chance to hear his own name in the nightly stories, a modern hero honored among the heroes of old.

Silvi shook her head, much as she hated the witch for what she had done, the idea of someone killing the witch turned her stomach so much she wanted to spit back up her stew. "Even she can't get rid of it. I don't think she meant to give it to *me*. I guess I was just the slowest." She gave a sideways smile, trying to chuckle at her own depravity.

Eigen cocked his head to the side and shook it, his brow furrowed. "No, she definitely chose you. I watched her brush past other people, practically pushing them out of her way to get to you."

Silvi frowned as the thought ran through her head for what must have been at least the hundredth time: why me?

"I've upset you," Eigen said, getting to his feet, his fear returning, and looked over Silvi as if watching for any sign that she was going to attack him.

Silvi just shook her head, not bothering to look up at him. She didn't want him to see the tears at the corners of her eyes. "I'm as scared as you."

"Yeah, but I can't throw people hard enough to kill them." At Silvi's flinch, Eigen gave an embarrassed grimace. "Sorry, I just meant…I'm not helping, am I? I'll just go, then."

Before Silvi could beg him not to go, he was running back to the rest of their people, drawing their suspicious gazes toward Silvi without actually reaching her. Silvi looked down at the last few swallows of stew in her bowl and it looked like sand. She would have plenty remaining to draw her rune tonight for Leapora, goddess of protection and the family. It will be easier with broth than bread at least, Silvi told herself, wishing the thought would lift her spirits and finding it didn't.

❖

The Neamairtese were just settling down to sleep, when the tent door flew open and three men stepped in, arguing quietly. The two soldiers were looking at the man between them with the same repulsion they'd used to look at their prisoners, but with an element of loathing reserved for men who are considered closer to equals. He was wearing the bright colors indicative of the Victricite traders but with a greasiness unparalleled by even the prisoners. While the soldiers watched the man, the man's eyes raked over the crowd of Neamairtese with a hungry lust.

The man's gaze stopped and the whole room seemed to realize what was happening at the same time.

Daralan and the man took their first steps at the same time, the man approaching his target and Daralan placing himself between the two. From around the tent, the Neamairtese rose to their feet and quickly placed themselves between the man and Barra.

The man's yell was harsh and snarling. It barely preceded the swinging of his fists, each one striking Neamairtese aside and to the ground as if he were swinging hammers rather than his fists. He bellowed first at the Neamairtese in front of him and then at the soldiers behind him. The two men in armor gave each other a quick look before one drew his sword and pointed it around the crowd. The other followed suit, yelling at the Neamairtese as well, his own voice much more concerned than angry.

"Stop!" Barra called from behind her people. As every eye in the tent turned to her, Barra took a slow and steadying breath. "I don't want anyone to get hurt."

"He's going to…" one of the men standing next to her said as if she didn't understand, as if she couldn't possibly understand and be as calm as she seemed. But his last words died unuttered. "If that's what it takes, we will all die to protect you."

Take their fear with your lack of it. Had it been the spirit of Earth that had told one of the previous queens that? It sounded like a piece of Earth's wisdom, and the Spirits were known to tell wisdom long before it was needed, their sense of time so different from humans.

"You would all suffer, and he would do it to me anyway," Barra said, though her heart was in her throat and sweat was breaking out across her back. She could feel the hair at the base of her neck standing on end, and every nerve prickled painfully. She had never felt uncomfortable in her near nudity around others with only the thinnest of leather wrapped around her breasts and around her loins, but under his lecherous gaze, her attire made her feel an overwhelming sense of vulnerability.

No one had moved. Everyone was still just staring at her, everyone except Daralan. He was shaking his head. "What if he gets everything? Since you haven't bonded with your mate, we don't know what this will do."

Barra shook her head in return. "I don't love him, he doesn't love me. The magic is safe. I will be okay. We will all be okay." The clipped words flowed out of Barra as if someone else had said them, someone who wasn't focusing all her attention on keeping her legs from shaking or her bowels from letting go.

For his part, the man was done waiting. He pushed through the Neamairtese and grabbed Barra by the shoulders. There wasn't any pain in it; she wasn't sure she could feel anything.

If only she had the strength to cast a spell and banish this man. A queen wasn't supposed to be without her mate.

From beside Barra, Terenesa reached out and petted the man's arm in an overacted invitation. He simply placed his hand over her face and pushed her away, never taking his eyes off Barra. The man pulled Barra to her feet with a hand under each armpit and pulled her along by the elbow to the curtained off section of the tent. He tossed her onto the large cot and pointed to the Neamairtese, clearly telling the soldiers to keep the crowd back. The man passed a small handful of coins to one of the soldiers. The other soldier held out his hand expectantly, but the greasy man only chuckled a short bark before pulling the curtain closed.

Barra felt all her strength and all her faked calm drain out of her in one sinking whoosh as the curtain brushed shut across the packed dirt floor, closing her people out. A dreadful whine slipped from her lips as the man approached her, his hands pulling his belt loose. There was a muffled shout from the other side of the curtain followed by a barely audible crunching noise and a pained cry. Barra's ears strained to hear anything over the ragged gasps of her breathing, but it was only her and this man now. Her people couldn't save her. She'd told them not to.

The man's pants were around his knees and he was stroking a huge, throbbing erection. His eyes, like burning lumps of coal, raked over her again and again, playing out all the plans he had for her as a twisted sort of one-sided foreplay. Barra couldn't take her eyes off his stroking hand. She was squished into the corner of the tent as far from the repugnant man as she could manage.

"Please," she begged just above a whisper. It was not a plea to the man, but to the Lord and Lady. "Please no." She could smell his sweat, her fear, his excitement, all mixing into a grotesque cacophony for her nose.

The sound of tearing canvas caught both of them by surprise. Barra would have believed the man had just torn her deerskin clothing off if she had been wearing it. Perhaps her mind was just a little behind reality, time running more quickly in her panic than she could comprehend. But the man seemed as confused as she was. He looked over his shoulder in time to see her Svekard step through the human-height tear in the back wall of the tent.

Before Barra had even registered what was happening, her Svekard was standing beside the man. Her right hand went to the man's temple while her left landed on his neck. Barra didn't see the motion, but she heard it, the sound of the man's neck breaking before he wilted to the floor.

❖

The look the witch gave her made Silvi's heart ache. Silvi didn't think she'd ever seen so much need and raw desperation. More than seeing it, Silvi felt it. The woman's terror, her relief, her anguish.

Silvi looked down at the dead man on the floor and felt her bile rise at the realization that she had just slaughtered a man as if she'd rung a chicken's neck. Her gaze went next up to the witch, smashed into the corner of the tent, her arms wrapped around herself defensively, staring at the man in continued fear. It was the look of someone so completely lost and scared that they had no power of their own.

Silvi needed to get rid of the body for her own safety as well as the witch's mental state, but she didn't want to leave her either. Perhaps she could just throw the man over the encampment wall. A quick glance at the hole she'd ripped in the tent's wall told her it might be possible. No one had seen her slip between the back of the two tents, though she'd moved so fast she didn't think she had seen herself do it. If she stayed in the darkness, she could go unnoticed, the soldiers overly confident in the infallibility of their tall walls.

"I'll be back," Silvi said, trying to say it with her eyes as much as her words. She grabbed the witch's attacker under the armpits and attempted to heft him toward the hole in the wall. A grunt escaped her lips as the man's deadweight shifted a mere few inches. "Oh, come on!" Silvi growled under her breath. "She's still in danger, see?" She looked up into the witch's desperate face again and felt a surge of strength.

If she hurried, she might just be able to get the man out before the magic she hated so much was inert once more. That was how this magic worked apparently.

Once outside in the pitch-black of the night, Silvi laid the man on his back and took a firm hold of his ankles. He was far larger and heavier than the hammers she'd watched her clansfolk and potential suitors throwing at the autumn festivals, but the same technique seemed applicable. Silvi spun, dragging the man across the ground until she gained enough speed and his whole body slowly lifted off the ground to spin at a perpendicular angle from her. At the last second, as she felt the unnatural strength start to slip from her grasp, Silvi swung her arms up over her shoulder and released the man's ankles. The corpse flew up into the air, and for half a second, Silvi was sure she had waited too long. He wasn't going to clear the wall.

The man's shoulder clipped the top edge of the wall, changing his direction ever so slightly and stopping the progression of the top half of his body. His feet kept going, spinning the rest of his body until it landed softly on the top of the wall. Silvi didn't breathe but she did pray fervently. The man's body sat there for a long second until, as if in slow motion, he slipped slowly off the far side of the wall.

Silvi let out a long, gusting breath and ran back to her hole in the wall. Her limbs were aching from that last show of force and her nerve endings tingled with that same aftereffect she'd come to associate with the witch's curse. It made her feel jumpy and jittery.

The witch was sitting curled up in her same spot on the cot, looking impossibly small. She was staring at the opening in the wall, and a tiny gasp left her lips as Silvi stepped through it again. The tears that the woman had clearly been holding back broke from her eyes to stream steadily down her face.

She's just a woman, Silvi realized, her former hatred slipping. She was still a witch; she cast magic and had cursed Silvi to attack her people. But she was also a scared woman who had been about to be violated. A still scared woman who needed comforting, looking dreadfully alone. Caring for the broken and injured is something I know how to do, Silvi told herself.

Feeling the adrenaline slip slowly from her veins left a coppery taste in Silvi's mouth and a clear memory of what she had just done. She too was broken and injured. Ever since the witch's curse and even back to the night she was captured, her need to hold and be held was the greatest constant. She could see that same need in the witch and empathize on a level that was deeply human, and it was something she could act on.

Silvi took a step toward the cot before pausing. Once she took the woman into her arms, she knew she would not let go, either by her own volition or the allowance of the witch. Anything she needed to do, she had to do now. Silvi moved silently to the curtain that separated this cot from the rest of the tent and peaked through the opening. If they were going to have more attackers tonight, she wanted to be prepared.

The room beyond the curtain looked much the same as her own people's tent but with two obvious differences. Two armed soldiers stood to either side of the curtain watching the Neamairtese cautiously and threateningly. Unlike the Svekards who were huddling down for the night, sharing stories, the Neamairtese stood half naked in a small mob staring back at the soldiers. The clear threat of death was the only thing keeping these people from rushing the soldiers. Silvi could hear their collective breathing coming in angry, scared gasps. One man, the oldest in the group by Silvi's estimation, though still clearly in his prime of life, sat at the front of the crowd, his hands holding a bleeding nose, trying to slow and stop the bleeding.

As Silvi took in the scene, the bleeding Neamairtese caught sight of her and visibly relaxed. He spoke quietly to his people, and a few of the less disciplined eyes in the group flitted to where Silvi was hiding her face before retraining on the Victricites.

The whole group seemed to rise and fall in one single sigh of relief. The man spoke a few more words and the mob began to slowly disperse. They went to the end of the tent farthest away from the soldiers and huddled into a group reminiscent of Silvi's own people.

Once the Neamairtese had fully dispersed and lain down for the night, Silvi watched one soldier turn to the other relieved, before both sheathed their swords and left. They clearly weren't concerned enough about the dead man's safety to waste their night standing watch. Presumably, when he was done with the witch, he was expected to show himself out. Silvi supposed he had, just not willfully.

Silvi had been afraid she'd have to hurt more people, and the soldiers within arm's reach had seemed a guarantee of more violence tonight. With them gone, all she wanted to do was comfort, not damage.

No more time needed to be wasted. She hurried to the cot and pulled the witch into her arms. As if every bone in her slim body had turned to mush, the woman collapsed into the hold, shaking and sobbing. Like a giant bird, Silvi opened up her furs like wings and enveloped the thin woman in their warmth and comfort. She could feel the clamminess of the witch's bare skin through her own thin woolen clothing and held her even tighter.

Silvi was slightly thinner than most of her clansfolk. Their heavy furs hid their shape and gave them the intimidating, stocky look they had always associated with Svekard strength and heroics. Even in the hot sun of the south, the Svekards refused to remove their furs for fear of showing their true shape and size to their Neamairtese or Victricite enemies. Now, she was grateful for the layers that would bring warmth back to the witch. Silvi would fight off the witch's fears as she had done her attackers.

What struck Silvi as she sat there, sobs wracking the witch gripping her, was the complete lack of magical compulsion to stay here. Magic had nothing to do with the ache in her heart or the tenderness with which she was cooing to the woman that everything was going to be okay, that she was there and wouldn't let go. Quietly, she began to whisper-sing to her. The words and tune of one of Mama's lullabies flowed out of her without a second thought.

She cared about this woman, she realized as she rocked and sang. It wasn't pity. She knew what that felt like. And it wasn't the curse. She knew that sensation as well. No, she genuinely felt what she could only define as longing. It felt good to hold and comfort her.

The witch's spells controlled how she acted, not how she felt. When she had attacked her people, she had done it against her will, and every moment had been filled with horror and fear at witnessing what she was doing to them. When she had prevented the witch from cutting herself with the rock, she had felt hatred. She could blame her actions on the curse, but the way she was feeling now had nothing to do with it.

For the first time in the last couple of weeks, she felt like she belonged somewhere, and it was right here. The feeling only deepened as the woman's sobs stopped and soft snores took their place. Silvi stretched out on the cot, keeping the witch clutched against her, and settled in for the night.

Feeling the gentle rhythm of their hearts that were now beating in sync, Silvi relaxed into the sensation. What had been fearful clinging was now a comfortable embrace. In the dark, she couldn't see the woman's wild, savage hair, but only smell the pleasant aroma of a cool forest morning. The fresh smell of pine reminded her of home while the injured creature in her arms brought back the sense of being in control and being useful that had been distinctly lacking in her life over the last weeks. She enjoyed the slender body that was impossibly soft beneath her fingers.

Attraction? Was that what this was? Silvi asked herself in momentary shock. She'd never thought about a woman this way before, though she wasn't positive she'd felt this way about anyone before. But it was hard not to with the woman's warm body pressed against her own. She felt a little guilty for the thought considering what she had saved the woman from, but the thoughts came unbidden.

More than anything, she was confused. Were women attracted to each other? She supposed there was no reason they wouldn't be. Did women have sex with each other? Could they even? Silvi supposed there were plenty of old maids who lived together, and it was entirely possible that they were involved sexually, but no one talked about it. Then again, Svekards didn't talk about sex at all.

During the coming-of-age ceremony, the new adults were taken aside by one of the clan's elders and for the most awkward five minutes of their lives were told the basics of sexual intercourse. Questions were discouraged and everyone quickly moved on with the rest of the ceremony. Silvi knew many found it pleasurable and it usually resulted in pregnancy, and that was about it, besides the technical bodily interaction required. Babies were born and so everyone knew sex was happening, but no one talked about it, ever. Sex was private; nakedness was intimate and definitely not shared. If those old maids were closer than friends, no one mentioned it positively or negatively.

After tonight's activities, the press of the witch's body against her own didn't invoke sexual excitement, but she would be lying to herself if she didn't admit that there was something here between her and this beautiful Neamairtese woman. She felt it in her heart.

As a Svekard, her heart was the core of her very being. It was where her soul resided, protected by the Gods to ensure that no force or witchcraft could ever break the compassion of the clan. The fact that her heart ached for this woman, that her pulse raced clutching her closer, told Silvi that the way she felt had nothing to do with the witch's curse or her spells. On the contrary, her feelings for the woman in her arms were strong enough to overcome her fear and hatred to stir something real inside her.

However, Silvi was pretty sure there was still some small part of her that hated this woman for what she had made Silvi do to her own people.

Silvi fell asleep almost an hour later, content that the magic would wake her up if either of them was in danger. It was the best sleep she'd gotten in over two weeks, even if she did wake up in the morning with the arm under the witch numb and asleep.

The sensation of pins and needles shot through her arm as the witch shifted and jostled Silvi awake. The woman smiled at Silvi affectionately, and for a second, Silvi was sure she was going to kiss her. Her breath caught in her throat. When the witch sat up instead, Silvi wasn't sure if she was relieved or disappointed.

The witch said something that Silvi assumed was a thank you and paused as if trying to figure out how to proceed. Silvi had nothing to contribute on that front so she just sat, waiting for the witch to act. Eventually, the woman gave a nod and a smile, a decision made. She pointed at herself and said, "Barra," a good deal of trilling letters in the middle.

"Your name?" Silvi asked and then repeated, "Bara." She blushed as Barra chuckled and shook her head.

"Barra," she repeated slowly, her mouth opening unnaturally to show the movement of her tongue inside her mouth.

"Baharda," Silvi tried again and blushed all the deeper at Barra's full laugh. She gave an embarrassed grin and tried once more. "Barda."

Barra smiled and nodded her head side to side as if this were close enough.

"Silvi," Silvi said, pointing at herself.

"Silvi," Barra repeated. Her "s" was too long, making the name sound like it was meant for a snake and there was the smallest lilt on the last letter, but Silvi figured Barra had done better than she had, so she'd go with it. Not to mention the airiness had a sensual quality that sent a tiny shiver down her back and made Silvi hope Barra would say her name more often.

Silvi immediately got her wish. Barra dragged her out into the main tent area where the Neamairtese were putting on the clothes they'd worn for the past four weeks. Silvi tried futilely to resist. She hadn't redone her braids yet and there were people out there. Those people stopped mid-action to stare at them, though Silvi was pretty sure it wasn't to judge her unkempt hair. Apparently, everyone had wanted to know what was happening behind the curtain, but no one felt it was their place to go check.

Barra said a couple of sentences before pointing at Silvi and introducing her. Around the room, the Neamairtese smiled and placed two fingers over their heart in greeting. Her arms caught up in her furs, Silvi awkwardly fumbled to return the gesture to the general amusement of the room. Silvi got many chances to do better as Barra took her around the room, introducing her to each person in turn. It was entirely unnecessary for Barra to keep repeating Silvi's name to each one, they'd all heard it the first time, but Silvi was glad she did.

Of the more than forty names Silvi was told, she thought she could remember perhaps five, and she definitely could not have said who those five names went to. It didn't seem to matter though. It was the placement of her two fingers over her heart time and again that brought a smile to each person's lips.

The soldiers weren't paying enough attention to notice that Silvi stepped out into the camp yard with the Neamairtese. They had not witnessed her superhuman race between the back of the two tents in the dark last night and likely wouldn't discover the tears in the tents until much later. Silvi would be long gone by then. The soldiers locked the yoke around her without further action and the group set out on the road once more.

CHAPTER EIGHT

THE FEATHER OF A GHOST

Silvi marched with the Neamairtese, next to Barra; a man whose name she thought was something like Dadan, with several more sounds in the middle just like Barra; and a woman with a name like Tare-da-nay-sah. It had taken hearing the name several times before Silvi thought she'd caught all the syllables. She tried to ignore the constant looks she received from her own people, but she was pretty sure they were more directed at Barra than herself. Their expressions matched those they might wear while watching an especially unfit challenger fight a beloved chieftain. They might be afraid of Silvi, but they clearly didn't see Silvi so much as a deserter as they saw Barra as a kidnapper.

The Neamairtese were an entirely different story. Silvi constantly felt their eyes on her, but when she caught them looking, they hid expressions of wonder rather than anger. The Neamairtese all seemed to be walking as slowly as possible without getting themselves into trouble with the soldiers, in order to place themselves behind Silvi and keep staring at her. Eventually, Dadan seemed to point this out to Barra and the four of them moved to the front of the group so the Neamairtese would stop getting berated.

They were marching through more and more crowded urban areas with each passing hour and the increasing smell of food, with random wisps of sewage undertones, told Silvi they likely didn't have much farther to go before they reached the slavers' market. She tried not to imagine it, nor what would happen when they tried to sell Barra.

As they reached the center of the largest city Silvi had ever seen, she felt their journey must surely be coming to an end. But to her surprise, the soldiers continued on, hardly noticing what seemed to be the grand city around them. How large a place must they be headed toward? Silvi could take down an attempted rapist and five of her own people, but she didn't think she stood a chance against an entire market of slavers and Victricites. There wasn't enough magic in the world for one woman to defeat as many armed and armored people as were in this town, let alone where she was headed. Would she have any choice but to die trying?

As the sun began to set, the group reached what Silvi guessed was the last slavers' camp, with its tall walls and two large tents. She followed the Neamairtese to their tent, rather than the Svekards, and stood in line waiting for her yoke to be removed. Her choice drew the attention of not only the prisoners, but the soldiers as well. Several tried to tell her that she should go to the other one, but Silvi just shook her head and pointed the hand next to her face at the Neamairtese tent.

Eventually, the commotion drew the attention of the commander, who seemed to recognize Silvi from the incident with the horse. He gave her an eyebrow raise, which she met unblinkingly. The commander shrugged and waved his hand dismissively. Silvi's yoke was removed and she followed Barra into the tent with a sigh of relief.

If she was honest with herself, Silvi's relief had nothing to do with Barra's safety, though she told herself it was. She just wanted to be with people who wouldn't scowl at her. She wanted to eat next to other people and hear them talk even if she couldn't understand what they were saying. Most of all, she hoped she'd get to sleep next to Barra again, though that seemed a little risqué to do in a room full of people. Her arms itched to hold Barra, and her chest ached every time she looked at her.

Silvi had spent the majority of the day debating whether her continued feelings for Barra were a further dishonor to the Gods, who so hated the Neamairtese. Then again, hers was a religion that taught her to find someone she truly loved and commit to them, to love them deeply and powerfully for the rest of her life. Silvi wasn't ready to say she was in love with Barra—she barely knew her. But it felt like only a matter of time before Barra was the person to whom she wanted to commit her life. That person was not supposed to be a Neamairtese, but her heart seemed to have chosen and was there anything more Svekard than to follow her heart?

Yes, her mind countered, to serve the clan. But she couldn't, not while under a curse, not while ostracized. Perhaps, she could see her act of joining the Neamairtese as taking the witch away from her people. Barra was certainly paying less attention to the rest of the Svekards now. Could she lie to herself convincingly and say she was serving both her heart and her clan?

When the evening's meal was delivered, Silvi received her bowl second. After every Neamairtese washed their hands, a young man delivered two bowls before any others were poured. The first he handed to Barra and the second to Silvi. Silvi attempted to repeat the words Barra had uttered, hoping they were a thank you. The young man tried to hide his smile before hurrying back to help everyone else get their food.

They all moved the cots in the front half of the tent into a circle and took their seats once they had received their evening meal. Silvi sat to Barra's left, with Dadan on Silvi's left. Tare-da-nay-sah had gone to sit elsewhere in the circle but was still identifiable for the welcoming smile she gave Silvi every time their eyes met.

Silvi's bowl was most of the way to her mouth when she heard Dadan clear his throat at her. Apparently, she wasn't supposed to eat yet. Looking around the room, she saw that everyone was looking expectantly at Barra, though she was fairly sure most of them were looking at Silvi out of their peripheral vision.

Barra began to speak, her voice an airy chant, and everyone's eyes snapped to attention on her. Barra's hands moved over her bowl and her eyes rolled back into her head. She gave several odd cooing noises before turning to Silvi and knocking Silvi's bowl with her own.

Silvi stared in transfixed amazement as the broth of her stew darkened in color and the vegetables solidified into identifiable plants. A hearty smell rose out of the bowl that reminded her of blood sausage. Dadan's throat clearing drew her out of her wide-eyed paralysis. He was looking at her expectantly from her other side. She held out the bowl to him, entirely unsure what to do. He gave her a kind smile before knocking his bowl against hers. For a second, he paused to show Silvi the same transformation taking place in his bowl before knocking it against his neighbor's. The magic traveled around the circle and with it the smell and visible steam of improved food. Silvi stared in slack-jawed amazement.

When the last bowl had been knocked on Barra's right-hand side, Barra began to drink her stew, but she was the only one. Everyone's eyes fell on Silvi yet again and she wasn't so sure she'd been wise when she wished to eat next to people who wouldn't ignore her. Dadan cleared his throat again, but this time she didn't have to look at him to understand. I get my food second…because I'm a guest, Silvi questioned. Regardless of why, no one was going to eat until she did, so unless she planned to starve all these people, she figured she ought to go ahead and start eating.

The feeling of hot, flavorful broth washing over her tongue brought a small sigh to Silvi's lips. She closed her eyes, and for a moment she could imagine she was at home. Mama had just made blood sausage and greens soup. She inhaled deeply and she could almost hear the sound of baas from her sheep herd outside and the soft smacking noise of her sister breastfeeding her baby in the other room. It drove Mama crazy that Nita was always late to dinner. Why couldn't she just start earlier, Mama seemed to ask every evening. Silvi wondered what they would be doing now that she was gone.

The sound of foreign voices all around her drew Silvi out of her memory and she was a prisoner once more. But this time she wasn't alone. Language and customs isolated her, but at least physically she was part of a group again and people liked her. Dinner conversations turned into idle chitchat and Silvi watched them, trying to follow the tiniest changes in their tone and demeanor. These savages…people… were so strange and yet so like her own.

As Silvi reached the end of her bowl of stew, she dipped her finger into the small pool of still warm broth and thought hard about which rune she would use tonight. In the other tent, her people would be using their cold stew remnants to draw their own runes. They most likely would use Cargen's rune, the god of constitution, to help them through the final stages of their journey.

Since being cursed, Silvi had drawn Leapora's rune each night, asking for protection. But tonight, she wasn't so sure she needed protection. It felt ironic to have needed Leapora when she was surrounded by her people and not to need her when surrounded by her people's enemy. The irony didn't make it any less true.

Garvil, god of thanks and bounty, crossed her mind, but Silvi still hadn't decided if her feelings about the Neamairtese and Barra in particular were blasphemy.

Ilode, the god of faith! Of the many, many things Silvi felt she needed right now, faith was at the top. Faith in the Gods, faith in the Neamairtese and Barra, and most of all faith in herself. Her rune was in no way a call to Ilode. Only the epic heroes of Svek had the ability or the right to call on the Gods, but the rune had power of its own.

Carefully, Silvi scooped her finger to retain as much of the broth on it as she could and brought the finger to her face to draw the rune across her forehead, nose, and cheeks. She dipped her finger again, tucked her fingers under her furs and woolen clothing, and smeared the last of the remaining broth over her heart. Silvi closed her eyes and said a short, silent chant.

Silvi heard the giggling before she saw it. When she opened her eyes, half the room was staring at her and most of them were laughing. One was even pointing at her and nudging her companions as they all five chattered and chortled like squirrels.

Maybe I should have gone with protection, Silvi thought glumly, her chin sinking almost to the point where the broth on her chin could touch the broth on her chest. She'd been wrong to think she was anything like these people or that she somehow belonged here. Maybe she should just leave.

Sharp words drew Silvi's head up once more. Barra had risen from her seat and was striding across the room at the chortling women. Silvi couldn't see Barra's face, but from the pink blush of her neck and the stiffness of her stride, Silvi was pretty sure she could guess at her anger.

Barra did not stop her approach when the laughing stopped and the room fell silent. She did not stop when she reached the women either. Barra brought her own face within inches of the petrified woman's face. Silvi did not hear Barra's lightly spoken words, but she was pretty sure the entire rest of the room did. Barra spoke more, slightly louder words, as she pointed her entire arm in Silvi's direction, her face still only inches from the tip of the woman's nose.

The five women stood slowly and shuffled across the room toward Silvi, who couldn't seem to move. The lead woman's face was so deeply red that her freckles had completely disappeared. She didn't look angry, but ashamed. She stopped a good three feet in front of Silvi before tucking her own chin against her chest and placing her right palm in front of her face so that the tips of her fingers touched her forehead. She said a few words that were repeated by the other four as they copied the action.

For several seconds, the women stood there, downturned faces blocked by their hands. Silvi was staring at them while the rest of the room stared at her. Silvi wished she could just say that she accepted their apology, and everyone could go back to talking. She appreciated Barra standing up for her more than she thought Barra could ever understand, but now what?

The thought occurred to Silvi in a flash. She placed two fingers over her heart in the only Neamairtese gesture she knew and said in the most heartfelt voice she could muster, "I forgive you." She knew the gesture was one of greeting, but perhaps it had a similar meaning to the Svekard hail which communicated welcome and the promise of protection against harm.

The whole room gave a collective sigh and Silvi thought she could see Dadan looking over at her with approval. The women looked up gratefully, placed their fingers over their hearts, and scurried back to their seats.

From across the room, Barra was smiling at her with what Silvi thought was assuredly affection. Silvi gave an embarrassed smile back, one she hoped conveyed her wish to stop being the center of attention. She hoped it didn't look too much like she just wanted to run away or climb into a hole, something that still seemed like a reasonable plan.

Barra's smile shifted. There was still compassion in the look she gave Silvi, but sympathy as well. She spoke a few more words to her people who nodded before turning to their neighbors and picking up their conversations. The speed with which they resumed their chatter told Silvi that Barra had most likely told them to do so. It was as if Barra saw through the layers while everyone else only skimmed the surface.

When Barra retook her seat, she gave Silvi one last smile that Silvi thought was acceptance and gave one that was meant as gratitude. Before turning back to the conversation on her right, Barra placed her hand on Silvi's thigh, giving it a squeeze before simply leaving it there. For the next hour, it was the most attention Silvi got and she enjoyed every moment of it. No one stared at her, yet whenever Silvi caught anyone's eyes wandering to or by her, they gave a welcoming smile before turning away. Silvi tried to return the smiles and eventually just found herself smiling at the general feeling of being there.

As if by some silent agreement, the conversations came to an end about an hour later and everyone headed to their cots at the same time. Silvi followed at Barra's heels, feeling a bit like a giant, fluffy lamb. She wanted to reserve a spot next to Barra, if that was possible. A part of her was sure they were going to send her to the far end of the room. She'd never really noticed her own odor, but surrounded by these people, she wasn't sure how she'd ever not noticed it.

Barra took a cot near the center of the room and Silvi pointed at the one next to it, smiling questioningly, "May I?" she asked, trying to sound formal and polite.

Barra tipped her head to the side and pointed at the cot she had picked.

"Yeah, I know, you're going to sleep there. I'm asking if I can sleep here." Stupid language barrier. She pointed at herself and then at the cot.

A disheartened look passed over Barra's face, but she nodded. Silvi wasn't about to let that go. Language barrier or not, she didn't want Barra to look at her like that. She tipped her head and shrugged in question.

Barra pointed at herself and then at her cot before giving a coy smile. She pointed at Silvi and then pointed at the same cot. She shrugged in question.

"Oh." Silvi blushed. She nodded, trying to not look too enthusiastic. The blush only deepened when Barra began to remove her clothing. The Neamairtese all around her were doing the same, but their near nakedness didn't matter to her. It was the beautiful body being slowly revealed to her that made her mouth dry up. Barra's creamy skin was sprinkled with small red freckles and looked even softer in the lantern light than Silvi remembered it being the night before. Her deerskin wrap, which looped behind her neck, made an x across her chest before tying in the back, accentuating the curve of her supple, otherwise naked breasts which were quite a bit smaller but naturally perkier than Silvi's. The simple loincloth hid none of Barra's graceful, muscled legs. As Barra stretched onto the tip of her toes to reach toward the tent ceiling, Silvi took in the elegance of Barra's lithe figure, the plane of her flat stomach, and the expression of contented pride. Silvi had seen Barra in this same state of dress last night, but she hadn't really been looking and Barra hadn't been showing off, as she was clearly doing now.

Barra glanced at Silvi, clearly waiting to see if Silvi was going to remove her own clothing. When Silvi didn't, Barra indicated for her to climb on the cot first. It would be a snugger fit than the night before, but Silvi had no problem with that. They certainly hadn't needed all the space they'd had the night before.

Barra climbed onto the cot and snuggled against Silvi's warmth face-to-face as Silvi enveloped her again in the embarrassingly musty furs. She buried her face in Silvi's shoulder and inhaled. For a long second, Silvi was sure Barra was testing the smell and was about to pull away. Maybe it wasn't such a bad idea for Silvi to have her own cot, Barra would say, and Silvi would pretend not to understand for just a few more seconds of holding her. But Barra wasn't pulling away. She was nuzzling closer, wrapping her arms around Silvi to hold Silvi as tightly as she was being held in return.

From across the room, someone blew out the lanterned candles and the room was plunged into darkness. But this time, Silvi felt it wasn't an unwelcome darkness. Much as they would never admit it, Svekards had a tenuous relationship with the dark. Witches and monsters lurked in the dark. But Silvi had a witch held adoringly in her arms. The darkness wasn't so bad.

Barra pulled back from Silvi's shoulder with her hands still wrapped around Silvi's rib cage. Silvi couldn't see her, but she felt Barra's gaze searching for any visible sign of her anyway. Silvi traced featherlight patterns on Barra's cheek and jawline. She wanted to touch her, to be impossibly close to her, to give action to the things she was feeling that she couldn't give voice to.

In the black of the night, the sound of softly snoring Neamairtese all around them, Silvi leaned forward, not entirely sure she knew what she was doing. She didn't need to know. Barra's lips found hers. Silvi's heart hammered in her chest, blocking out the small sounds around her as Barra's soft lips worked against her own. She pulled Barra's beautiful body even tighter against her, massaging up and down her back, arms, and legs, over the prickles of tiny hairs. She wanted to feel every curve, to know what Barra looked like in the complete darkness.

Goose bumps were breaking out all over Silvi's skin as Barra's hands drew similar paths over clothing and buried themselves in her braids. She trembled and gave a barely audible gasp as one of Barra's hands slipped under her shirt and brushed over sensitized skin, the other still in Silvi's hair, pulling her deeper into the kiss.

"Barda." She whispered the only word she knew would translate. What she wanted to say was "I want you." "I need you," would have been just as accurate in this moment. If not for the crowd around them, she was pretty sure she would have slipped her own hands under Barra's undergarments and tried to touch her in all the places that were burning inside Silvi's own body.

❖

Barra pulled back from the kiss, trying not to moan at how good it felt, and smiled at the face she imagined in front of her. She wished she could see it for real. More than that, she wished Silvi would touch her. Sure, her hands were all over her, but they seemed to have hit a wall, a line Silvi didn't want to cross. Barra ached for Silvi to squeeze her clothed breasts that she kept sliding up and down against Silvi's busty chest. She felt on the verge of grabbing Silvi's hand and simply thrusting it inside her underwear. But if Silvi wasn't there yet, Barra wouldn't push it. She would just have to be content falling asleep in Silvi's arms, horny as a nymph, and wait.

She kissed me, Barra reminded herself. And Lord and Lady, had Silvi kissed her. It had been as tender and needy as it was fierce. She felt safe and loved in Silvi's embrace. Maybe Svekards, or at least Silvi, weren't so barbaric after all. But Silvi was more. She was kind and gentle, and Barra got the feeling that even without the magic, Silvi was fiercely protective and loyal. It hadn't been the magic that brought Silvi back last night after disposing of her attacker. The magic had been idle. Coming back had been Silvi's choice and she was fairly sure Silvi knew that as well. Holding her had been an act of transcendent compassion. The fact that she had an amazing body under all those furs was definitely an unexpected benefit in Barra's opinion.

Barra fell asleep feeling desperately needy and deliriously happy at the same time. Silvi, her Svekard, her heart's mate, loved her...or at least she didn't hate her. Every day seemed like a step in the right direction, though based on Ahjva's information, she had the sinking feeling that she didn't have many days left to stop their impending end.

Morning brought with it a far better mood for the Neamairtese than they'd had since before their hunting party had been captured. There was a general spring in the people's step where there had been a resounding drag. Barra was pretty sure she even heard several whistling or humming as they prepared for the day.

As the people lined up to receive their shackles once more, Barra caught Silvi's frantic movements out of the corner of her eye. She looked back to see her sitting on their cot, desperately trying to undo and redo her long blond braids. Silvi had been so focused on helping clean and organize the tent as well as not impeding the Neamairtese morning routine, she seemed to have almost forgotten the one that was clearly very important to her.

Barra tried to hide her prideful smile and hurried over to be of assistance. The Neamairtese never braided their hair, but Barra had to assume it was the same concept as with rope.

As Barra took a seat on the cot next to Silvi and reached out for her hair, Silvi pulled away. For a long silent moment, Silvi and Barra looked at each other embarrassed and not quite sure what to do about it. As much as Barra thought maybe she should back off, she could see in Silvi's eyes that she wanted to allow this act. Whether it was taboo or simply an intimate act to touch Silvi's hair, Barra wasn't sure. She hoped the latter, as Silvi blew out a calming breath and handed one of the unraveled braids to Barra.

Taking the lock in her hands, Barra was pretty sure her own frantic grabs for Silvi's head during their kiss may have been the cause of the haphazard state of her hair. She undid it and wrapped the hair up again before moving to the last of the five braids.

As she worked her way down the last braid, Barra paused. She reached up and pulled a feather from her own hair and, making eye contact with Silvi to make sure it was okay to do so, wove the feather into the braid. There was no way Silvi could understand the importance of the gesture, even her own tribesfolk didn't know the memory attached to this particular feather. This feather had been the only thing left of her best friend and occasional lover, Helenda, in the wreckage of the Svekard raiding party that had killed her and burned her tribe in the eastern reaches just over a year before. To Barra, passing the feather was an act of forgiveness and letting go of old grudges. By custom, to share it with Silvi was a statement of trust and the desire to create memories together. If her people saw it, they would know that aspect if nothing else. Silvi gave Barra a kind and grateful smile before following her to the line.

As Silvi had her yoke shackled back on, one of the already shackled men slunk up to Barra, a sly smile on his face. "How's the fur feel?" he asked, bobbing his eyebrows up and down and throwing a quick glance at Silvi, though his eyes didn't go to the furs wrapped around her shoulders, but clearly to a place at about hip height.

Barra gave him a sideways look of feigned disapproval and rolled her eyes. "When I get there, you'll be able to ask her yourself and if she doesn't punch you, I will." The man just laughed, an airy and hearty laugh before hurrying to catch up with his friends and report back on what Barra had said. She was the queen and demanded respect, but she was not so far removed from her people as to be safe from their good-natured teasing.

The man had barely left before a woman approached Barra from the other side. "Do they kiss as ferociously as they fight?" She was blushing slightly, but her expression held far more curiosity than embarrassment. "It sounded like a good kiss."

Barra just smirked. "Wouldn't you like to know. She's mine." The last statement wasn't one of possession. Everyone knew Silvi was Barra's alone. It was instead a statement of contentment. The road ahead was still a difficult one, but at least they had the first concrete signs that the Lord and Lady really had meant for what was happening to happen. The Spirits were watching out for them.

Barra received her yoke and the group set out for more of the highly exciting marching through crowded cities and the dense farmland between overpopulated centers. Barra was getting a terrible bruise across the back of her neck and her legs ached more and more each night. She'd like to say she was looking forward to it being over, but then again, she wasn't so sure she was.

The day of marching was grueling. The sun scorching down on them reached an almost unbearable heat, magnified by the cobblestone road and buildings that put the entire group on edge. Two of the Svekards had passed out from the heat, which had led the Victricites to attempt to take the odious furs off all of them for their own good. This of course had led to a screaming, shoving fight in the middle of the street.

All action around them had ceased, as the Victricite citizens stopped to stare at them with fascination, tempered with mild concern. While the soldiers on the perimeter held their swords at the ready, the rest moved in swinging short, thick sticks at any and all prisoners they encountered, driving them to the ground, without regard to Neamairtese versus Svekard.

Much to Barra's dismay, Silvi instinctively took all of the hits meant for Barra, and in the process, took far more than her share, as the Victricites attempted to assert dominance over perceived defiance. With each hit, Barra's heart skipped a beat, and she felt all the worse knowing that by doing so, she was causing Silvi's heart rate to do the same.

When the Victricites' show of force seemed sufficient for prisoners and bystanders alike, they waved everyone to their feet and pushed forward, acting as if they had forgotten all about the furs. Barra helped Silvi to her feet, relieved when Silvi took her offered hand without hesitation. She could see the welts and bruises rising on Silvi's arms under her furs and knew there would be many more on the parts of Silvi's body Barra couldn't see.

That night, in a camp uniform to all the others within the walls of Victricus, Barra used one of the waterskins to begin the long process of healing her people. Everyone seemed eager to partake of what magic they could before the meal would begin. Everyone except one. Silvi accepted her bowl of stew with two fingers over her heart before quickly taking her seat away from the healing magic and waiting for Barra to enchant the meal. When the group had fully assembled, she passed the spell to Aedrican without prompting and ate silently, watching the group talk as if she understood anything that was being said.

She's like a well-trained wolf, Barra thought before chastising herself for once again thinking of Silvi as a creature that needed taming. It was a concept she had to consciously reject, or it would be hard to deny her mind the comparisons.

Barra let out a small huff of frustration and turned to Terenesa who was seated on her right. Terenesa rested her hand on the thigh of the man she'd been speaking to and gave it a reassuring squeeze. "I'm sure she knows. From what I've seen and heard, you've been a good mate, and nothing says you won't be again." She gave him a last affirming nod before turning to Barra, her expression inviting whatever question or request Barra had for her.

"Though she needs to be healed, she's afraid of magic," Barra said without providing a clear question. Silvi still felt like her responsibility and Barra felt she ought to know what to do by herself but was willing to at least broach the subject with a kindler. The blue and purple lumpy circles across Silvi's face and arms made Barra's heart ache every time she glanced at her, and little else had captured her attention since their kiss the previous night.

"As your heart's mate, what does your heart feel she needs?" Terenesa asked, her tone unassuming. She was simply a guide to help Barra to her own answers.

Barra felt herself open up to the question. She was allowed to be unsure and to seek answers and she didn't have to do it alone. "Neither does she like being the center of attention, nor does she like being alone." She was thinking about the look on Silvi's face when they were alone together. There was a willing vulnerability in her expression as if she wasn't sure what to do but wasn't embarrassed by it. In a crowd, Silvi seemed to want to slip into her shell like a turtle and observe. It took one-on-one interaction to draw her out.

"She sounds like my winter mate," Terenesa said. "As a dyad, his spirit is most at ease just in the company of one other." She looked past Barra and Barra could read the question in her eyes as clearly as if she had spoken it: will I ever see him again?

It was Barra who took Terenesa's hand this time, giving it a reassuring squeeze. She had no words of encouragement she could justify, but it seemed Terenesa just needed to know that she was supported in return. "Can you perform the nightly ritual without me?" Barra asked. The night's blessing wouldn't require any magic, only a thanks to the Spirits before everyone headed to sleep.

"Of course," Terenesa said.

Barra turned to Silvi, who had just finished swiftly wiping the remnants of her stew under her furs as she scanned the crowd for onlookers. Her cheeks reddened as she caught Barra watching her. Barra smiled and held her hand out to Silvi, pleased when she took it and the color in her cheeks died down. With deliberate slowness, Barra walked to the back of the large tent, one hand holding the nearly empty waterskin and the other holding Silvi's soft hand.

Once they were seated cross-legged in the back corner, opposite the curtained off area that made Barra's stomach churn with uncomfortable visceral memories, Barra pulled out the waterskin and poured a small pool into the palm of her hand. She watched Silvi stare in fascination as Barra cooed over the water until it began to glow like a moonstruck lake. With Barra's free hand, she reached out to Silvi again, waiting until Silvi took her hand, tentatively this time.

Cautiously and gracefully, Barra brought her hand with the glowing water to Silvi's and began the process of healing her. She could already feel the drain of so many scrapes, bruises, and cuts healed before she even reached Silvi. Silvi's bruises were far more plentiful than any of the people Barra had healed so far, and it would likely take the last of her energy for the day to finish the job, but it would be worth it. All her remaining energy should be Silvi's.

As she moved up Silvi's arm, Silvi's other hand came over to halt her progress. "Come on," Barra mumbled, too tired to express even to herself the level of her frustration. She looked up at Silvi through her eyebrows, doing nothing to hide her exasperation.

The look Silvi gave her lacked the animalistic fear Barra had been expecting. There was a bit of concern on her face, but if anything, Silvi looked sympathetic. The look only made Barra more helplessly annoyed. "What?"

Silvi released Barra's hand to delicately dust a fingertip over the sensitive skin under Barra's eyes where Barra knew her skin was sunken and bluish. Her hand went next to a bit of Barra's hair that was beginning to droop from lack of care. These were the visible signs of the weariness Barra had been trying to contain and hide from her people. She didn't know if her people saw them, but Silvi did and she knew that the magic was only making it worse.

"I want to do it," Barra objected, but Silvi had pulled away fully and shook her head. She tapped the ground next to her instead and waited patiently through Barra's brief arguments and harrumphing before tapping the ground again. Barra blew out a puff of air before acquiescing. Sitting next to Silvi was far from being a step backward.

Once Barra was seated, Silvi gave her a pleased look and said something with an intonation that made Barra assume it had meant something along the lines of "there, was that so bad?" It wasn't.

Silvi's hand worked its way around Barra's waist in jolting spurts as if she felt the need to give Barra constant chances to pull away.

Instead, Barra nestled into the sideways hold, bending to rest her head against Silvi's shoulder while her hair lay behind both of their heads.

As her head reached the soft, well-kempt furs on Silvi's shoulders, Barra felt the wave of exhaustion that had been lapping at her ankles for the last week wash over her. Her eyes drifted shut, despite her internal monologue that they would do no such thing. For the first time in a long time, Barra felt safe to just close her eyes and be.

Soft fingers brushed against her cheek, caressing the rises and falls of her face and smoothing her hair out of her face. No, this wasn't so bad at all. She felt Silvi's head turn slowly to glance around the room before a finger looped under Barra's chin and lifted her face. Barra opened her eyes and her breath caught at the look in Silvi's eyes. There was none of the Lady's magic in that look, nothing making her act but the desire to be here, holding, touching, caressing. Without the eyes of the room on them, Silvi tipped Barra's head farther back to place a lingering kiss on her lips.

Silvi pulled back as if embarrassed and scanned the room again, but no one was looking. Barra was sure Terenesa had instructed them to give them space. Silvi gave her another, longer kiss, one that seemed to explore the sensation of their comingled mouths.

Were she not so tired, Barra would have happily showed Silvi far more of what her mouth could do than languid kisses. For now, the gentle kisses moving up her jawline to her hairline were like a lullaby made physical. Her head sank back down to Silvi's shoulder, as her whole body sank into the feeling of being held and petted.

Soft jostling woke Barra sometime later. She was in Silvi's lap, though she didn't know how long she had been there. Barra fought the tiredness still enveloping her, but Silvi shushed her and petted the sides of her eyes as if directing them to stay shut.

Barra felt herself lifted in Silvi's arms. She was surprised by the ease with which Silvi carried her across the room to a cot in the center of her people. She set Barra down and gave her a chance to undress herself groggily. Barra would have much rather Silvi do it and not just because she could barely make her limbs do what she wanted.

All thoughts of disappointment drifted away as Silvi gathered Barra into her arms once more and laid out on the cot, their bodies snuggled together for the night. It was the best sleep Barra could remember.

The following day, Barra walked as she had the day before, near the front, Silvi on her right, Daralan and Terenesa on her left. They had reached urban sprawl and the soldiers seemed to have given up on keeping the prisoners from talking to each other. Their voices blended with the din of passing merchants, mewling livestock, and shouting children.

According to Ahjva, this would be their last day of marching.

Silvi, for one, was taking full advantage of her new ability to talk to Barra, and much as Barra loved the interaction, there wasn't a whole lot of good to it. The yoke prevented acting out their conversation and Barra didn't have the vaguest idea what Silvi's words meant, no matter how slowly Silvi said them. Silvi kept pointing at things and saying individual words and then looking at Barra expectantly. She pointed at a donkey near the side of the road, said her word, and looked at Barra with a mixture of excitement and frustration.

"I don't know what you're saying," Barra said slowly, her own frustration at the situation bleeding through. The yoke kept her from shrugging, so she hoped her tone got the message across. She wanted so desperately to talk to Silvi, to explain what was happening and to get to know the woman she was destined to spend her life with. It wasn't enough to smile adoringly at Silvi or to make sure her people treated Silvi with the utmost respect, or even to kiss her. She wanted Silvi to know that despite everything she was glad to have Silvi by her side.

"Idin noah yerksing," Silvi said, massacring her attempt to repeat what Barra had said, and looked back at the donkey, then at Barra in surprise.

"She wants you to tell her our word for it," Terenesa explained. "She's trying to learn." Silvi was watching them closely, her stare so intense that Barra was glad Svekards didn't have the power to call demons, as some of the oldest folk tales claimed. She was watching their mouths move and trying to understand how they made those sounds.

"But she doesn't need to learn our language as she'll know it soon enough…hopefully tonight," Barra countered, turning her head to smile approvingly at Silvi before turning back to her councilors.

"But since she doesn't know that, right now she just wants to belong," Terenesa said, giving Silvi a similar, but less overacted smile.

From Terenesa's other side, Daralan added wisely, "When our other option is to walk in silence, isn't it better to interact with your heart's mate however you can?"

Barra shrugged at the wisdom and turned to Silvi. "Donkey," she said. The next couple of hours were filled with similar object naming, Silvi dancing around the way Barra imagined a bear would do after an entire winter in a dark cave. Silvi attempted to get anywhere close to the correct pronunciation of each object Barra named, but had about as much success as she'd had with her first attempts at Barra's name. A few times, Barra repeated the word when Silvi's attempt was too terrible, but otherwise she let it pass. It was nice to just see Silvi smile at her own efforts and to know that Silvi wanted to be here with her. Something had changed between them and Barra was ecstatically glad for it. This Silvi would never throw the healing salve and storm away.

They'd walked for close to six hours when a large splash drew Barra's attention from Silvi to a red-haired young slave woman who had been washing clothing. She had dropped her entire load and was staring at Barra.

"Helenda?" Barra called out to her. Her hair had been cut short and she looked thinner than was healthy, but she was easily identifiable to Barra, who had once known every curve of her body.

"Barra!" Helenda yelled and rushed toward the road. She stopped at the edge, clearly knowing the soldiers would stop her if she moved any closer, and hurried alongside the group. The soldiers seemed to consider her behavior the responsibility of her owner and ignored her.

"I—I thought you were killed by Svekards," Barra said through the crowd of soldiers and over the ruckus around them. How could she be alive? How could she be here? Barra desperately wanted to run to her, to embrace her. She would have tried if she hadn't known the move would spell disaster for Silvi when Silvi tried to protect her from the soldiers' wrath.

"No. After burning our shelters, killing those they didn't want, and leaving evidence of Svekard weapons and furs, the Victricites took us. There are thousands of us, Barra, people I thought were killed by Svekard raiding parties just like you thought happened to—" But Helenda was cut off as a meaty hand closed around the scruff of her neck and hauled her away. Her Victricite owner was yelling at her, and she was weeping and nodding subserviently.

Barra called out to her and took a step forward before a hand closed around her upper arm, pulling her back. Barra's anger washed away as she looked into understanding eyes. Silvi just shook her head.

She didn't speak, but her eyes said that no action could help Helenda now. She didn't need to understand what Barra and Helenda had said or their history together to understand what was happening. She wasn't a dancing bear, but a curious woman desperate for human contact.

Barra looked to the feather woven tightly in Silvi's hair—Helenda's feather. She'd been so sure that Svekards had killed her, yet here she was.

Thousands, she'd said. Barra supposed it only made sense, given the size of the slavers' camps and the apparent consistent use of the outcropping camps along the way. But as far as her people knew, Victricite attacks were rare occurrences against hunting parties that traveled out too far, not full raids on the outer villages, killing men, women, and children. There had always been bodies missing, building up the belief that their barbaric enemies were cannibals as well as general abominations. The Svekards hadn't eaten their victims because the Svekards had never been there in the first place. The Victricites purposefully passed the blame for their raids on to the Svekards, something her people were all too willing to accept.

Moving her gaze from the feather to Silvi's sympathetic expression, Barra wondered how many of the Svekard slaves' disappearances were blamed on the Neamairtese as well. Their people had been enemies long before the Victricites expanded far enough north to make their presence known, but the ancient wars between their people that spanned generations were now little more than legends. The Neamairtese had been moving slowly farther west on each cycle's migration in hopes of escaping the barbarians' influence. They were willing to give up the larger game of the foothills for increased safety, but the Svekard raids continued. Or, at least the Victricite raids disguised as Svekard raids had continued. Barra had heard tell that a war party was starting up in the Central Tribe, bound northeast to drive the Svekards back once and for all. It had been a war party Barra would have happily joined, but it wouldn't have done any good. The Svekards were likely as much of victims as her people were.

They used us, Barra realized. The feeling of guilt at her hatred being used against her was as great as her anger. The long war with the Svekards had put her people in danger of being wiped out entirely. A second war with the Svekards, coupled with continued slaving, would have ended the Neamairtese as surely as the Victricites had ended the Razirgali.

Barra reached out and took Silvi's hand in her own, their yokes knocking together softly and startling Silvi slightly. Silvi wasn't her enemy. Silvi had walked next to her for the past two days, but now Barra wanted to make a statement. No more. She was relieved when Silvi's hand squeeze didn't preempt an attempt to pull away but instead a tighter handhold, as if she somehow understood and agreed.

Completely lost in her thoughts of what exactly to do with this knowledge, Barra barely noticed the changing scenery around them. What had been simple roadside stands were now permanent, canopied collections of shops. Where houses had stood, the buildings now sported restaurants and markets, bustling with people. Everywhere, coins were exchanged for goods. Around them, eyes no longer flitted to them in interest but scanned them appraisingly. The din of life had been replaced by the frenetic clamor of business.

They had reached the slavers' market.

The increasing intensity of Silvi's hold brought Barra out of her musings. The soldiers were separating the Neamairtese and the Svekards at the entryway to a large ramp leading underground, but Silvi was shaking her head and holding on to Barra all the tighter.

Barra looked from Silvi's fierce expression to Daralan's frightened one. *Pick the battles you can win.* The spirit of Earth had definitely told her that one. This was not a battle she could win, nor one she wanted Silvi to fight. Before the situation could get out of hand, she needed to get her hand out of Silvi's clutch.

Silvi already had people pulling at her. Barra would need a different response or Silvi would only increase her grip. Instead, she brought her hand, and thereby Silvi's, over to her face as best she could and placed a soft kiss on the part of Silvi's wrist that she could reach before releasing it. At Silvi's confused and disheartened look, Barra simply nodded and stepped back toward the side of the ramp the Neamairtese were being directed to, hoping Silvi would understand. Silvi still looked dispirited but made no efforts to resist the soldiers as they shoved her back to her own people and down into the torch-lit darkness.

Lord and Lady, please let that have been the right decision, Barra prayed silently. The idea that she might have just sent Silvi to her death made her chest ache. Her heart's mate had no special ability to protect herself, only Barra. So, if Silvi was put in danger first, there was nothing Barra could do about it. If she had some flame, perhaps she could cast a spell of protection, but aside from having no fire, casting a spell in the middle of the Victricite slavers' market seemed highly inadvisable. "Be safe, my dear," Barra whispered before turning to the state of her own people's safety. Once again, she felt overwhelmed by a feeling of inadequacy. She was supposed to be the queen. She was supposed to know what to do and protect her people. She couldn't even keep her mate by her side.

Her small group of Neamairtese was met at the bottom of the ramp by seasoned Neamairtese slaves and the light of many torches. They wore thin, brown, cotton garb and looked as if they hadn't eaten properly in a very long time. The smiles they gave them came with a look that tried to convey both sympathy and welcome. The best advice they could give was to do anything the Victricites wanted, predict their desires, and to learn the Victricite language as quickly as possible.

They handed each Neamairtese soap and a razor set firmly into a metal holder, such that the blade could not be used as a weapon, but only to shave. The seasoned slaves explained that the Victricites wanted their new merchandise to be clean and presentable. Their old deerskin clothes would be replaced by fresh, clean, cotton ones that were more suited to the climate. They would be allowed to keep their hair as it was for now, but in the future that would be up to their new masters.

Barra echoed her people's sigh of relief. She'd never needed a bath so badly in her life. The water would soothe her pains, and to be clean and shaven once more would ease her constant feeling of being disgraceful to the Spirits.

The bath turned out to be indoor rain which came from several metal tubes protruding from the walls. Barra had never seen such magic…technology, she supposed. It made keeping her hair dry more difficult, but the rain proved superior in its ability to wash away the dirt and the soap. All around her, the Neamairtese hummed in contentment at the feeling of cleansing and refreshing. Hopefully, Silvi was having the same wonderful experience.

CHAPTER NINE
A HERO'S EMBRACE

The Svekards met their own clansfolk at the dimly lit bottom of the ramp that smelled of stale water and mildew. The seasoned slaves who held out soap to them were entirely women and wore nothing but thin, brown, cotton garb. They looked so small and un-Svekard-like, even in the dimness that blurred their silhouettes. Silvi could see in their eyes and in their stance that they were acting embarrassed of their physical state, not because they actually were embarrassed, but because they knew the new arrivals were embarrassed for them.

Silvi and her fellow prisoners had seen other Svekard slaves on their journey to the market, but they had looked away, trying not to increase their clansfolk's dishonor at being so exposed. The worst part was knowing that the Neamairtese and the Victricites weren't looking away. They could see the unwrapped Svekards, their furs and pelts removed, and their true shapes revealed. They were witnessing the most mortifying and undignified state of a Svekard—weak.

These women did not have the muscles of their rough and rugged people and they had not for some time. What was left of their previous muscles hung in their armpits and around their knees and waists. These slaves did not do hard physical labor, which made their lives both easier and less Svekard-like. At this point, they were used to it, but they knew their company would not be, so they kept to the shadows as they handed out soap and explained what would come next.

The Svekards would be provided falling water to clean their hair, but they would be expected to fully strip and wash their bodies as well.

Their furs would be taken, and their woolen clothing exchanged for thin, unprotecting cotton.

The women only shrugged at the uproar as the new Svekards yelled and argued that the Gods themselves would have to come down and take their furs, wash their bodies, and force them into whatever witch's material cotton was. A healthy layer of dirt was necessary for strength and survival. No one mentioned that they had no intention of stripping naked with anyone else within shouting distance, let alone within view, because the sentiment was generally understood.

"The Gods are not here to force you or protect you," one woman explained. "That is what the Victricites are for." They would have to quickly learn to follow the Victricite directions or they wouldn't live long enough to learn anything else. Victricites liked cleanliness, and anyone they didn't like ended up in the fighting pits. Those weren't so great and valiant either, the women explained. There was no honor in fighting animals and your own kind just to live another few minutes and do it again.

More shouting and arguing was exchanged, the new prisoners unwilling to yield and the old ones wearily providing arguments they must have made a thousand times. It would be a lot easier on everyone if the new Svekards would just do as they were told, the women instructed. But in the end, the women were as unsuccessful as they had clearly expected to be, and it took ten Victricite swordsmen to painfully manhandle the Svekards into their showers and new clothing. Silvi tried not to fight, she'd seen how little good it did, and wondered to herself if the Neamairtese were having such a distinctly horrible time. All she knew was Barra wasn't in direct danger and she was glad for that.

"Every time," Silvi heard one of the women sigh. "It'll be even worse tomorrow morning at the auction."

"Wait." Silvi tried to push through the crowd to get to the women, to ask them what they knew, and to maybe be the slightest bit prepared for what the future held. But she was being shuffled forward with everyone else, pushed roughly forward down yet another ramp. She hadn't understood how there could be so many people in such a small space out on the streets, but apparently the Victricites built houses on top of houses and houses under houses. How could people be packed so densely without being ravaged by disease? How could they live so close and not starve?

At the bottom of the ramp, the Svekards were pushed into one large cell with metal bars for walls. The room beyond was vast, with several more cells and ramps leading up to what Silvi guessed must be the auction. Tomorrow we'll be sold, she reminded herself. She looked to the only other occupied cell, full of Neamairtese in similar brown cotton garb. "Barda?" she called over to the crowd and held her breath. She didn't have to wait long as Barra was let through the horde to press her body against the bars and smile at an equally longing Silvi. How can I see her right there and yet ache so badly to be with her, Silvi wondered.

"Why?" Silvi heard a man's voice ask behind her. She turned to look at a sour-faced Keepan halfway through braiding his beard. "Why do you want to be with them, near that witch?"

Silvi let out a resigned sigh. She'd been stripped of her honor, her lineage, her community, her furs, and her dirt. What more did she have to lose? "Because I love her." There was a power in those four words, and for the first time since being separated from Barra, she felt the smallest ounce of control over her own life.

"You just think that because you're cursed. That's the spell," Keepan said, pointing his finger angrily toward the Neamairtese and Barra who was watching them with concern.

"No. I mean yes, I'm cursed, but it's not because of the curse." She'd had plenty of time to think it through even more thoroughly between bouts of trying to learn the convoluted Neamairtese language, a task that was proving far harder than she'd thought, and that was saying a lot. "I love her for her, okay? The way she makes me feel, needed, desired, liked. She sees me and likes what she sees."

It was more than just that. Silvi felt like a fire that had almost gone out. She'd barely had enough heat to warm herself the night she'd first held Barra. But somehow Barra had breathed life into her, rekindled her flame, and given her what she needed to burn brightly again. "When I'm with her I feel like I...belong."

"You belong with us. We're your people, your clan," Keepan argued.

For a long moment, Silvi just stared at him. "You don't want me," she said at last, trying to keep the anger and desperation out of her voice.

Keepan stared at her in confusion. "Of course we want you."

"Then why did you push me away?" Who did he think he was? Was this some sort of twisted game, some sort of retribution?

It was Eigen who spoke next, stepping forward from the semicircle that had formed around Silvi and Keepan. "An untouched hero comes into their own alone." He said it as if quoting the great storytellers, his cadence slow and melodic.

Silvi's confused stare left Keepan to fix momentarily on Eigen and then sweep the crowd around her. "You think I'm a hero?" she whispered. That was why they had stopped in saying her lineage. Not because she didn't have one, but because they didn't think they needed to go any further to reach a hero. It was why they had left her out of the clanbed; her people thought she could speak to the Gods directly and didn't need their collective strength to do it. She supposed reverence could explain their actions as clearly as repugnance.

No one spoke, they simply nodded, gazing at her as if in wonder. Keepan finally broke the silence. "This is how all the heroes' journeys begin: a curse, a challenge, unbeatable odds. Just because you have not yet been touched by the Gods does not mean you are not a hero. Your time has not yet come, and it is our job to stay out of the Gods' way and yours."

"I'm not a hero," Silvi said. If they thought she didn't need their strength, they were wrong. Never had she felt so weak or so lost…until she'd held Barra in her arms. "I can't save us. I'm the fool in the story that falls in love with the witch and gets eaten. I'm not the monster slayer and definitely not a witch slayer." Again, the thought turned her stomach, but from her own attachment to Barra, not the impulses of the magic.

"Maybe that's exactly what we need," Eigen said. His eyes had drifted from the conversation to Barra, who looked almost as miserable as Silvi. "Super strength, right?" He seemed to be talking more to himself than anyone else, which was good considering no one else seemed to have any idea what he was talking about.

Eigen took the few steps to the bars and reached an arm through to wave at the Neamairtese. "Hey, you!" he called pointing at the man next to Barra and flailed his arms back and forth. "Hey, you, yeah you. Hit her!"

The entire room turned to watch Eigen with suspicious and concerned crinkled brows. But Eigen was far from giving up. He pointed to the man, then pointed to Barra. He grabbed Keepan by the front of his brown shirt, pulled back his fist, and brought it forward stopping inches from Keepan's face.

When no one responded more than raising or lowering their brows in further confusion, Eigen turned to the people who would at least understand his words. "Silvi has to protect the witch. The spell gives her super strength to do it. I saw her tear a hole in our tent the other night. If Silvi thinks the witch is in danger she'll—"

The force of Silvi's fist connecting with Eigen's jaw cut him off. She'd been able to hold back just enough to not cause serious damage, but if he didn't stop trying to incite violence against Barra, Silvi wasn't sure she could hold back for much longer. The magic was already tingling in her veins, making her skin prickle. Soon, she wouldn't be able to control it at all.

Keepan's eyes widened to the point they looked ready to fall out of his head. He turned to the Neamairtese and followed Eigen's example, thrusting his finger through the bars at the man next to Barra and then at Barra before pretending to slug the woman next to him. He got a fist in the back from Silvi for his troubles and went tumbling to the floor, otherwise unharmed.

"Please, stop," Silvi begged. "I don't want to hurt you." But the Svekards were nothing if not determined and willing to take a beating in order to win. As Keepan went down, another man took his place, miming the Svekard plan across the room to the Neamairtese.

As Silvi's fist connected with the third man, she felt the magic spike and turned to see one of the Neamairtese facing Barra. He held Barra's shoulder with one hand and his other was balled into a fist behind his head. He was clearly apologizing to her for what he was about to do and Silvi couldn't let that happen.

The man's fist began to fly forward as Silvi's hands wrapped around the metal bars of her cell and wrenched them apart as if they were made of clay. His fist connected with the space between Barra's shoulder and the top of her breast as Silvi closed the distance between the cells in a single jumping stride and closed her hands around the bars between her and the scattering crowd of Neamairtese. No one wanted to be between the crazed Svekard and Barra. The man had barely pulled his fist back again when Silvi's hand closed around his neck. She carried him the several paces to the wall by his neck, his legs jumping uselessly below him.

"Never hurt her!" Silvi screamed at the choking man. "Never!"

The man was just beginning to turn a dull color of purple when Silvi felt a soft hand stroke up her arm to pry her fingers from the man's neck. The gentleness behind the touch broke Silvi's hold on the magic and thereby her hold on the man. He fell to his feet and then to the floor when his legs refused to support him. It was all Silvi could do to not crumple to the floor with him. More than the display of force, it was exhausting to feel that much rage followed by this much guilt. She'd hurt her people again and Barra's people who had been so kind to her.

But Barra's face held no trace of blame, only understanding. Her hand reached up to stroke Silvi's face as she whispered something Silvi didn't understand. Silvi turned her face into the caress, placing a kiss on Barra's palm and reveling in the feeling of Barra's touch. Oblivious to the people around her, Silvi placed her hands on the front of Barra's shirt. She drew the neckline to the side to reveal the slowly bluing skin where the man's fist had struck fair skin and placed a kiss on it as well. She was about to provide the same treatment to Barra's lips when a familiar man made a familiar throat clearing noise.

Silvi turned an annoyed glare at Dadan before taking in the scene around her. Her people were all out of their cell, having squeezed through the hole she'd pulled from the bars, and the Neamairtese were quickly following suit. Even the man she'd almost choked was successfully scrambling into the wider room.

Despite the fact they'd managed to work together to get this far, the group immediately devolved into a heated, multilingual debate over which ramp to take, if they should take any at all. They wouldn't have fared any better if they had been able to speak to each other rather than jabbing their fingers this way and that. Both groups appeared set on leaving in opposite directions.

We need each other, Silvi thought, grabbing Barra's arm. "What now?"

Barra's eyes flicked across the room before screwing shut like a small child trying to remember complicated directions. When she opened them a moment later, an idea was clearly burning in them, and her jaw was set in confident determination.

With a stride Silvi had only ever seen in seasoned clan chieftains, Barra strode to one of the burning torches, ripped a tiny piece off her threadbare shirt, and instructed one of her people to boost her up. The ensuing stream of hissed words sent the Svekards running like frightened lambs, several even squishing back into the cell to put as much space and structure between themselves and Barra's witchcraft. Silvi had never thought of her own people as weak or stupid, but in that moment, she couldn't help but bedamn their narrow minds.

They'll never follow us now, Silvi thought, barely pausing to realize she had referred to the Neamairtese as "us" and her own people as "they." Well, I'm going with Barra so that makes it us, Silvi told herself.

Orange flame licked up the piece of brown cloth, harmlessly circling around Barra's thin fingers. She finished her incantation and released the small ball of fire to drift slowly toward the floor. When it reached hip height, the ball hovered for a second before wafting off toward the second ramp from the left, its blaze still as bright, despite the lack of fabric to burn. Grateful relief ran through the Neamairtese as they hurried after the light.

From the other side of the room, the Svekards were having the opposite reaction. Silvi was pretty sure even a sleuth of hungry cave bears couldn't chase her people in that direction.

"I'm not a hero," Silvi whispered to herself and turned to follow Barra. She made it three steps before she wouldn't allow herself go any farther. It wasn't their fault they were afraid of witchcraft. They had every right to after the way it had been used against them for hundreds of years. She couldn't leave them anymore than she could abandon a flock of sheep to the wolves. "We have to go with them," she called out to an unresponsive room.

"They are not our enemies. The Victricites are," Silvi said, walking back to the closest Svekard who pulled away from her. "We've been so sure that we weren't safe outside the clan because Neamairtese hunted us. We all left our clans, and we didn't make it to the Summer Fish Fry, not because of the Neamairtese but because of the Victricites. And how many others? Those that disappeared last year or a decade ago, how many of them are here now, how many more died here? We are escaping together."

The crowd appeared more shocked than convinced.

"I know you're scared." Silvi took a deep breath as she searched for something more rallying to say. "Our stories tell us to be afraid, but our stories also tell us that we are strong and brave, we are hearty, and we are survivors. Our ancestors overcame the long winter, they survived the green blight, and they drove back the Neamairtese in the War of Generations." Silvi tried not to cringe at the last example, which was probably not the best choice. But she had their attention, and she wasn't going to lose it. "When we come together, we are unstoppable. We will survive this too, but only if we face our fears and follow our only hope at freedom."

Silvi looked around at the hesitant faces. They might consider Silvi a hero, but she wasn't a leader until she had a follower. Her eyes locked on the only member of the crowd who looked ready to follow her into the frozen wastelands of the underworld, if that's what it took. Eigen had lost his brother when the Victricites took them and had spent each opportunity since then trying to act like the Svekard his brother had taught him to be. "Come with me," she said to Eigen, holding out her hand toward him.

As if she'd breathed a gust of wind into him, Eigen's chest puffed out, filling him like a sail. He took the several steps necessary to take her hand and said in deliberate, reverent words, "I will follow you."

Around the room, heads nodded hesitantly, and people rose to their feet with clearly dubious expressions. "Come with me," Silvi repeated before turning and running off in the direction the Neamairtese had left. She gave a silent exhale of relief as the sound of footfalls trailed her up the ramp. They might hate the Neamairtese and their witchcraft, but to their credit, they followed anyway.

Silvi reached the back of the jogging Neamairtese mob and the crowd split to allow her through, then closed. The Svekards would be stuck at the back, trusting that their leader was somewhere ahead with their best interests at heart. As if sensing her arrival, Barra looked back with a brilliant smile and an extended hand, much like the one Silvi had offered Eigen. They hurried through the halls, hand in hand, following the floating ball of flame as it rounded corner after corner through the maze of tunnels and ramps.

What Silvi could only assume was a curse slipped from Barra's lips as they rounded a final corner. In the distance, the tunnel opened onto the most organized and solidly built set of docks Silvi had ever seen. Presumably, the water down here didn't freeze over in the winter, so permanent docks were a worthwhile use of resources. A few feet before the opening of the tunnel, the ball of flame was finally burning itself out. Between the bit of magic and its creator stood a portcullis of thick, heavy metal.

The look on Barra's face told Silvi everything she needed to know about their chances of simply magic-ing the barrier away. "Not when we're this close," she growled.

Behind her, the crowd was clumping more and more densely as people waited for Barra to figure their way out of their new predicament. For her part, Barra was only getting paler.

"Move!" Silvi heard yelled from behind. She looked back to see Keepan manhandling Neamairtese out of his way to reach the front.

Oh no, Silvi groaned, taking up position between her leader and the woman she loved.

The gentle breeze coming off the sea beyond brought with it the smell of water, but not nearly enough water for a spell. Wind was only going to batter their people and leave the portcullis intact. If Barra could bury her hand in the dirt maybe the spirit of Earth could open up a tunnel around the gate, but she was already feeling weary from the day of marching and her most recent spell. What if there were Victricites on the other side of the gate and she needed to call on the Spirits again and couldn't?

Barra looked up at Silvi, who was looking back at her with the same expectant look that Barra was getting from every Neamairtese around her. She felt the blood run from her face as she realized just how much they were all relying on her and she had no idea what to do. She had let her rashness endanger them all by running forward without any semblance of a plan.

From behind her, a Svekard yelled and began to advance on her and the gate. Think of something, think of something, Barra coached herself, but when nothing came, all she could do was watch Silvi place herself in harm's way once more.

The Svekard barely noticed Silvi as he walked past her and up to the portcullis, squatted in front of it, took a bar in each hand, and gave a throaty growl. There was no way he could lift it, but that didn't seem to have made it through his thick, burly, bearded head. He was lifting with all of his strength, the veins in his arms and across his forehead standing out on weather-beaten skin from the extreme exertion. The man's grunting and growling was getting louder, to the point Barra was afraid they were going to call the Victricites right to them. Her people looked afraid to be anywhere near this brute. They knew the stories of Svekard berserkers who could lose themselves so fully in the strength of their rage as to beat one enemy with the severed limbs of another.

In their trepidation, the Neamairtese were easy to push aside as one by one, more Svekards pushed to the front, took a handful of metal, and growled at the effort of their lifting. When the last vacancy along the portcullis had been filled, the barbarians'—Svekards' tone changed from a growl to a chant that was quickly joined by the Svekards behind them, including Silvi. Barra stared in relieved fascination as with each utterance of the repeated word, the portcullis rose another inch. When the barrier had reached their shoulders, the Svekards turned their bodies to provide space between them for people to pass under the gate.

The remaining Svekards were the first to move, brushing past the still mortified Neamairtese and out into the mouth of the tunnel. As the last Svekard slipped out of the cramped space, Barra and her people realized the new danger to which they'd opened themselves. All the straining Svekards would have to do was step aside, release their hold, and the portcullis would drop between their two peoples permanently.

Barra dropped into a crouch, grabbing a few lose pieces of dirt. If she was fast enough, she might be able to get out a spell to hold the Svekards in place long enough for her own people to make it through. But she'd been too slow in realizing the danger. The Svekards ran from magic and, with all their people on the right side of the gate, the moment she uttered a word, they would be gone.

A few of Barra's people surged forward, the smallest clearly thinking they might be able to make it through before the gate closed completely and perhaps they could be of more use to the whole if they were on the other side. But their dives were unnecessary. The Svekards holding the gate hadn't moved and the Neamairtese easily made it through.

Barking under the strain, the gate holders began yelling at the remaining crowd of Neamairtese. Barra didn't need to be able to understand their language to understand what they were saying. "What are you waiting for? This thing is heavy! Move!"

Barra had every intention of letting her people go ahead of her. It was her responsibility to make sure everyone was free. Her opinion on the matter meant nothing to the woman holding her hand. Silvi moved between two of the Svekards, pulling Barra along with her before Barra could even attempt to convey her responsibility. Barra made her attempt, nonetheless, resisting Silvi for the half second it took for Silvi to understand her reticence and then fully reject it. With a yank that managed to be both fierce and entirely painless, Silvi pulled Barra under the gate, between two grunting Svekards, and tightly against her chest in a full embrace.

For a second, Barra's breath caught in her throat and all thought of responsibility was gone. She was held not just protectively, but possessively against Silvi's chest, her head cradled on top of warm, large breasts. Whatever Silvi was wearing under her thin cotton garment was providing a good deal of support and enhancement, and Barra was far from complaining. She only wished the shirt was gone so she could bury her face in soft flesh.

Silvi was calling back to the Neamairtese with lots of quick summoning movements of her arms, sending a rumbling through her chest and jostling Barra's breathless appreciation. Barra turned her head toward the gate, reality sinking back in.

With great relief, she watched the last Neamairtese slip through the gap before the Svekards gave three grunts in unison and all released the gate at the same time. The spikes of the gate sank into the ground with a muted thunking noise and a cloud of dirt. The crowd once again turned their attention to Barra, Svekards and Neamairtese alike, as Silvi quickly released her with an embarrassed blush.

We never could have done that, Barra admitted to herself before turning to Silvi with a feeling of profound understanding. "We need each other."

The crowd made a path for Barra and Silvi to make their way to the front at the opening of the tunnel. With a deep breath, Barra peeked out around the edge of the tunnel and out onto the docks. She could feel Silvi pressed up behind her and reminded her body that this was far from the right time to be focusing on how well their curves melded together.

The docks spread out before Barra in a wide circle as far as she could see. It was as if the land never ended and the sea never began, but the two simply blended and mated to create something new. She was surrounded by a forest of masts, the smell of fish and human excrement, and touches of torchlight wandering down mazes of wooden platforms. The closest Victricites were barely visible in the moonlight but for their torches. Barra sent a silent thank you to the spirit of Fire for leading them to this particular exit and to the spirit of Air for the direction of wind that had not carried the Svekard chanting toward their enemies. Barra looked out at the ships with great consternation. Such vessels were completely new to her and she once again felt entirely out of her depth.

Barra turned a concerned and confused look on Silvi, hoping to express her uncertainty, without communicating it to the entire group. Silvi met the look knowingly and gave only a simple, reassuring nod before calling over the man who had first attempted to open the portcullis. How can she see me so clearly, Barra wondered as Silvi turned to the burly man.

The two spoke briefly in hushed tones, and Barra watched their mouths, expressions, and body language, trying to apply meaning to the gruff bark of their voices and jabbing of their fingers toward the water. Their voices got louder and harsher until they both cut off entirely with a single nod. Silvi turned to Barra and spoke two words, pointing out toward one of the ships. Her reassuring nod told Barra far more than the words. "That one," Barra echoed.

This time, the Svekard man didn't wait for Barra and Silvi to lead the way. He moved out of the tunnel in a hunched run, confident that his people and Barra's would follow him. His people followed him and if the Neamairtese planned to keep the party together, they would have to follow suit.

The group moved as one crunched up, silent mob. The Neamairtese had no interest in the threat of being left behind again and intermixed with their blond counterparts. They snaked through the forest of masts, their footfalls blending with the slap of the waves against the ships.

The lead Svekard gave the meandering torchlights a berth that seemed to be leading the group past every ship except their target, but Barra wasn't complaining. She'd wander all night in circles to avoid losing their newfound freedom.

As they reached the chosen ship, the Svekards spread out across the deck like squirrels in a tree, immediately taking the necessary steps the Neamairtese could only guess at. Silvi appeared to be the only Svekard giving the Neamairtese a second glance in the flurry of activity and even then, her purpose seemed to only be to get them out of her people's way. She ebbed and flowed with them as naturally as the tide. With each passing hour, Silvi had seemed to grow closer to Barra and the Neamairtese and further from the people who had cast her out. But now that they were free, Barra got the sinking feeling that maybe Silvi didn't need her so much anymore. What would she do if Silvi chose the Svekards now that she appeared to have a choice again?

To distract herself from the creeping feeling that she was losing Silvi, who she supposed had never truly been hers to begin with, Barra focused on watching the docks. If any Victricites noticed their departure, she would need to be ready, the Spirits would need to be ready. Barra would not let anyone stop them, not when they were this close to true freedom.

The ground beneath Barra shuddered as the ship cast off. She barely noticed, her body accessing the queens' memories of similar journeys in order to create muscle memory for sea legs. Barra had never been on a ship before the Victricite slaver's boat that had taken her and her people up the river, but her predecessors had.

Barra watched as the flickering balls of torchlight became pinpricks on the horizon before disappearing altogether. The majority of the Svekards had disappeared below deck to clandestinely guide the ship into the wider ocean, beyond the immediate threat of the Victricites.

With a roar that made the Neamairtese all but jump out of their skins, the Svekards surged from below deck, from above where they had been hanging from the masts, and from the front and back of the ship. They grabbed each other, tears streaming down their faces, and embraced in what looked like bone crushing hugs. They were all free.

The Neamairtese had only to witness a few embraces before the Svekards turned to them or, from the Neamairtese perspective, turned on them. Several tried futilely to escape the grasp of the Svekards surrounding them, but even those that managed the feat were soon grabbed from behind by a different celebratory Svekard. The people seemed drunk on their success and exuberant to share the feeling.

Barra watched in amusement mixed with astonishment. None of the Svekards had made her the target of their enthusiasm, though whether that was due to her clear leadership role in the group, fear of her magic, or because of Silvi's presence by her side, she was unsure. As if her thought had somehow called them to her, the Svekards all turned to Barra and Silvi and surged forward once more. Barra's heart rate jumped as she was lifted off her feet. Dozens of pairs of hands held her above the Svekard heads, tossing her up into the air. From the corner of her eye, she could see Silvi rising and falling, her braids jumping, as she too was thrust into the air over and over again. They weren't just being tossed either. The pair was being passed from one end of the ship to the other, Svekard and Neamairtese hands directing them.

As they reached the back of the main floor of the ship, Barra realized where the group was inadvertently or purposely leading them. She had a feeling the Neamairtese were the ones with a plan this time and the Svekards were simply caught up in the flow. At the end of the sea of hands was an open door and beside it stood Daralan, a distinctly knowing look on his face. Barra had hoped to bond with Silvi tonight, and now, in the glow of freedom and the aftermath of celebration, she and Silvi would finally have a moment just for them.

The remaining Neamairtese hands placed Barra and Silvi on their feet in front of the door and pushed them very unceremoniously forward into the dimly lit room. Barra spun on her heels in the doorway in time to see the Neamairtese closest to her throw her a wink and shoo the Svekards away. The Svekards looked at each other questioningly before they seemed to realize what was happening and quickly moved away, pretending their celebration had never been interrupted.

Barra turned to the only man remaining. "Tomorrow, we'll have important decisions to make, so everyone should get a good night's sleep."

Daralan gave a small, professional nod. "I'll take care of it."

"And if there's alcohol on this ship, keep the Svekards from it. Since we'll need clear heads, tell our people they are not to have any."

Daralan fixed her with a somber expression and nodded again. "I'll take care of it."

"Set a watch just in case the—" Barra began.

"I'll take care of it," Daralan interrupted, placing a steady hand on Barra's shoulder. "Now go. Your woman is waiting." Barra gave an appreciative smile before turning and closing the door behind her. She didn't think her heart rate had been near normal in quite a while.

CHAPTER TEN

A LACK OF BARRIERS

The room, Barra realized with delight, was a large and exquisite bedroom. In the far left corner was a bed, larger and plusher than Barra had ever imagined. Such an object was simply impossible for nomadic people. The far right corner held a wall-sized case of leatherbound manuscripts with glistening symbols on the edge as well as a large metal contraption that looked like two cauldrons stacked on top of each other with a hat that reached the ceiling. The center of the room was dominated by a thick wooden table set with silver dishes and utensils, as if at any moment a celebration for ten was about to be served. A couple of bottles and a small bowl of fruit sat in the center. On the far wall beneath a collection of intricately decorated swords sat another table with drawers covered in maps. Everything was draped in rich reds and brilliant golds over dark leather and wood, lit by dozens of candles that Barra guessed Daralan had ignited during the preceding celebration. The room smelled of warm wood, candle smoke, and fresh salt water.

In the last corner stood Silvi. Her arms were wrapped around her core while her eyes stared fixedly at the floor. She looked small without her furs and very vulnerable. As Barra took in the sight of the woman she had longed to see in less clothing, it wasn't the swell of her chest, the shapeliness of her hips, the broadness of her shoulders, or the strength of her legs that Barra noticed. It was the quake of her knees, the way she seemed to be hiding herself, and the distance between them.

She was scared, Barra realized. But of what? Of being alone with Barra? Of being without her furs? Of the ship, or the darkness, or the decisions tomorrow would bring? There were many things to fear, but Silvi hadn't been afraid before, so what had changed?

She doesn't want me, Barra thought with a sinking feeling that made her want to cry. Whatever Silvi's people had said to her in the standoff in the other cell had changed things. Barra had thought Silvi was hers, but she was theirs.

No, Barra insisted to herself, drawing up the feeling of Silvi's lips against her palm and against the bruise on her upper chest. The emotion in those eyes had been real. Silvi wanted her and she wanted Silvi. So, what was she afraid of?

Barra's eyes widened with understanding as she looked over Silvi's stance once more. Sex, she thought, that's why we hit a wall the other night, why she wouldn't touch me intimately. She's scared.

Much as the idea was entirely foreign to Barra, she supposed there was a logic to a Svekard woman fearing sex. The old stories were full of warnings about the Svekard proclivity for raping, murdering, and pillaging. Of course, that bred a society of people who viewed sex as an act of power and pain.

If only Barra could talk to Silvi and explain. She would never hurt her. On the contrary, she wanted to bring her pleasure and to show her the depth of her feelings for her. She loved Silvi. She wasn't sure how she could be so in love with someone she knew so little about, someone she'd never had a conversation with, but she knew that she was. It wasn't just Silvi's attractive body or because she knew that they were fated to be together either. Silvi made Barra feel like she mattered without her powers of magic, her responsibility as queen, or her acumen as a hunter. Silvi saw her on a deeply personal level that transcended all of that and bridged race and culture to make her simply want to be with her as a person.

The irony that making love to Silvi was the very thing that would allow Barra to explain everything only frustrated her. But she couldn't push Silvi into bed with her. That could do untold damage to the bonding process and more importantly to their long-term relationship. Much as she wanted to simply run to Silvi, jump into her arms, and kiss her until passion swept them up, that seemed the worst thing Barra could do.

You trust her, show her she can trust you. So, the Spirits hadn't left her entirely without wisdom for her relationship.

Barra began her approach as slowly as possible, inching closer until they were only a couple of feet apart. Fighting her urge to touch Silvi, Barra remained where she was, arms at her sides, waiting. *This will take as long as it takes.*

It took several seconds before Silvi's gaze rose from the floor to Barra, who was looking at her with pure affection. Silvi gave her a sheepish look in return, as if apologizing for her reaction. Her back straightened and her knees seemed to settle slightly, but that was all.

"It's okay. We won't do anything you don't want to do," Barra whispered, wondering if Silvi had any experience with sex whatsoever and wishing she could say the phrase in Svekard.

They stood there for a long minute before Barra felt it was time to take the next step. She wouldn't touch Silvi until Silvi was ready for it, but she could show herself to Silvi, fully vulnerable, and invite her touch.

With slow, deliberate movements, keeping constant eye contact, Barra took the hem of her thin shirt between her fingers and pulled it over her head. The pants followed, leaving Barra in the same state of dress Silvi had seen before. Goose bumps had broken out over her arms and legs. She wasn't sure if it was solely wishful thinking, but in the dim glow of the candles, Barra thought she saw the same rising on Silvi's uncovered arms. Barra next went to the tie of her breast wrap and watched Silvi swallow hard. She took a deep breath. *Please let her like what she sees,* Barra thought and removed the wrap, letting it drop onto her discarded shirt and pants. Her loincloth quickly followed.

Silvi was breathing hard, her gaze fixed on Barra's chest, and fingers twitching ever so slightly at her sides. Her brown eyes were glowing, the pupils dilated to the point that the earthy brown barely showed. *She wants to touch me,* Barra couldn't help her sigh of relief at the thought, *thank the Lord and Lady.* Barra could feel her nipples puckering at the anticipation. She didn't think she'd ever been aroused by not being touched.

Somehow, despite the rising burn, she waited for Silvi to act. Barra closed her eyes, allowing herself to be completely at the mercy of the beautiful woman before her. Again, Barra waited, hoping her display of vulnerability would be understood and returned. The soft touch of Silvi's hand cupping her breast brought a soft moan to both of their lips at the sensation. Barra's eyes opened just in time to see Silvi bring her lips to the hard nipple and take it into her mouth.

Silvi's gaze rose from her hand to Barra's face, and suddenly Barra found she couldn't breathe. There was so much in that single look. Lust. Love. Trust. Gratitude. Silvi rose almost to Barra's height, their lips meeting in an impassioned kiss that left both gasping for air. As the kisses continued, Silvi's hands continued their exploration, sweeping over freshly shaven skin in a sensuous dance.

With a quick pivot, Silvi took full control, pushing Barra up against the wood paneled wall. The kiss only lasted for a second before Barra felt herself held in place with a hand against her chest while Silvi pushed away. Barra looked up confused and concerned, only to have her jaw drop at Silvi's sensuous look of passion. Silvi indicated for Barra to hold still so she could also disrobe. Barra would be expected to wait once more, the anticipation only increasing her heat and desire. Barra smirked in realization. She knows what she does to me, and I like that she knows it, Barra thought.

Under Barra's lustful gaze, Silvi took the fraying hem of her shirt in her hands and pulled it over her head, showing the beautiful sight of her cleavage for the first time. The hide bra Silvi wore was grommeted and laced across the front, pulling her ample bosoms high on her chest and accentuating their plush roundness. Barra didn't wait to ask permission but pushed off the wall as Silvi pulled the lacing open. Barra buried her face in Silvi's inviting warmth.

Silvi's answering moan rumbled in her chest as if she were purring. Without taking herself from Barra's eager kisses, Silvi finished removing the garment then pushed down her pants and the cotton panties she'd been provided, bringing her freshly cleaned body up against the silken smoothness of Barra's.

Barra wanted it, wanted all of it. With a deep breath, she stepped back to take in the sight of Silvi.

For a moment, all Barra could do was stare. In contrast to the sun-kissed skin of Silvi's face, the nearly flawless skin of her body looked like it had never seen the light of day. Her body was a beautiful mix of muscle and voluptuous curves. Silvi had the largest breasts Barra had ever seen, and given her experiences at Torchane, including three trips to the central festival, that was saying something. But they fit her naturally in a way they never could have on the lean figure of a

Neamairtese. Her ample bosom was offset by a thin waist and wide hips. Her curves were perfect, and Barra wanted to experience every inch of them. "Beautiful," she whispered, attempting to say the word with her body as much as her voice.

Silvi took Barra's reaching hand and followed her to the bed. As they reached the edge, Silvi surged forward grabbing Barra by the waist and pulling their bodies together to fall in a heap of limbs onto the covers. She giggled nervously and said what Barra guessed was a long stream of apologies as she worked to untangle herself from Barra. The pink blush that had been working its way up her neck since Barra removed her clothing was now turning Silvi's whole face an adorable shade of red.

Barra had no interest in being disentangled. She giggled mirthfully back and pulled Silvi's lips to her own for an exploratory kiss.

Their naked bodies entwined, they kissed each other's lips, necks, chests, and breasts, tongues following each curve. Their bodies swayed against each other, trying to get as much contact and friction as possible, warm, soft skin grinding against its moist, heated counterpart.

Barra rolled Silvi onto her back, before raising herself onto her side, kissing Silvi while she explored Silvi's body. She reveled in the shivers that spread out in waves of pleasure as she caressed lower before rising slowly up the inside of Silvi's thigh. She looked down at Silvi, taking in every detail of Silvi's breathless expression of pleasure as she rose the last few inches into wet heat. She wanted Silvi to know that there were no barriers between them anymore.

Silvi bucked hard at the feeling of being touched for what Barra guessed was the first time. She brought her lips to Silvi's in an equally heated kiss as she continued her strokes of delicate folds.

After recovering from the initial wave of exhilaration that had overtaken Silvi, she reached for Barra, clearly excited to return the lascivious petting. When she made contact, Barra couldn't hold back the buck of her hips nor the gasp that was wrenched from her chest. Never had she been this needy or felt this taken. She wanted to be a part of Silvi. She was done with waiting. She slipped her fingers effortlessly inside, finally entering Silvi with a deep, guttural moan from both of them.

Barra could tell that Silvi was following her examples and was pleased at Silvi's enthusiasm to not only receive but to give as well.

Barra hoped that would remain true as she moved her lips lower. She'd been intrigued by the idea of what a Svekard would taste like since their first night sleeping side by side and, lewd as she might have felt for the thought, she was excited to finally try.

Silvi cried out at the pleasure and Barra felt her own pleasure resonating with it. Barra was far from new to sex, but while she and her partner had always left contented, she had never gained this kind of fulfillment solely from the ecstasy of her lover. She felt on the edge of orgasm simply from Silvi's taste, nutty aroma, and carnal moans. She couldn't imagine how great Silvi's release was going to feel on her own end. Barra didn't have to imagine for long.

Barra could feel Silvi rising closer and closer to orgasm as she worked her tongue and fingers in unison on and inside Silvi's body. She felt as though her own heart were exploding as Silvi's body began to quake and then jump with each stroke of her tongue. Silvi let out an almost silent scream as every muscle in her body seized, then released. Silvi was gasping, her chest rising and falling jaggedly, as the rest of her body twitched with the aftermath. Barra didn't think she'd ever felt so fulfilled emotionally or physically. She felt like a harp reverberating with the sound of a perfect melody.

Silvi took a minute to recover before pulling Barra to her lips and then rolling on top of her. Silvi seemed lost in the kisses, going for whatever skin happened to be in front of her lips. Each kiss came faster in a feverish craze as if Silvi couldn't even see Barra beneath her but only bare skin.

For a moment, Barra feared that she'd broken Silvi. It was her understanding, jaded as it might be, that sometimes Svekards simply broke and went crazy. Kissing wasn't the worst kind of crazy, but Barra wanted *her* Silvi, gentle as well as fierce, protective as well as strong. But Silvi wasn't just missing her mouth, she was purposely working her way lower with a hesitancy that didn't slow her kisses, only her progression.

When Silvi finally reached her target, Barra felt as though her whole body had been devoured and all sensation had moved to this single location. One swipe of Silvi's tongue and Barra felt ready to finish right there. But the intensity of her pleasure only rose, taking over every thought and sensation.

The way she had felt during Silvi's orgasm didn't even compare to the body-wrenching whiteout that made her eyes swim when she was on the receiving end. One moment she was staring down at Silvi's beautiful face between her legs giving her indescribable pleasure, and the next she felt every nerve of her body exploding in pure bliss.

Barra felt as if she was slipping out of a dream as she reconnected with the thrum of her body and the warm press of Silvi against her side. She looked up into adoring brown eyes that were already drooping with exhaustion and gave a smile that radiated through the whole of her body.

"Ne hobnst il," Silvi whispered, pulling the edges of the bed's quilt over them like a giant cocoon and pressing her lips to Barra's one more time.

"Neh hobinst eel," Barra repeated before providing the phrase she hoped was a translation and knew was true regardless. "I love you."

An overwhelming tiredness washed over Barra as she rolled into the crook of Silvi's arm and fell asleep in the pleasant comfort of her welcoming embrace. In the moment before sleep took her, she could feel everything, the afterglow of her orgasm, the burn of the magic bonding her to her mate, and the soft, lulling rock of the ship. Barra wished she could stay in this moment forever.

The feeling of the ship rocking her felt calming to Silvi, the touch of the plush blanket was luxurious, and the warm press of Barra's naked body against her own was truly divine. Barra's impeccably hairless body made her skin impossibly soft and silky, and Silvi couldn't help but bask in every spot of connection.

None of these sensations pulled Silvi from her dream filled sleep. A small object had worked its way to the edge of Barra's hair and was poking Silvi gently but persistently in the forehead.

Leaning back ever so slightly to still keep as much contact as possible with Barra, Silvi removed the object for a brief inspection. The partially completed antler carving of an elongated wolf was no larger than a whetstone and fit perfectly in her closed palm. It had been the last carving Barra's mother had been working on before she became too ill to continue.

Silvi gave the object a reverent squeeze before tucking it back into Barra's pile of hair with a fond smile. The fact that she knew its origin didn't strike her as odd as she did so. Her only thoughts were of Barra and the pleasure she had brought her.

Silvi was embarrassed by the un-Svekard-like fear she had displayed when she'd realized that Barra and her people expected her to have sex. She had heard the hushed mention of Neamairtese sex rituals with demonic results. She'd grown to like and trust Barra, but wasn't that exactly what witches did? They lulled children and fools into a false sense of security, fed them sweets, and cut out their hearts. Quaking like a toddler, Silvi had been scared to death that at any minute the rest of the Neamairtese would barge in and make her a human sacrifice.

But Barra wasn't interested in cutting out her heart. She'd offered her heart to Silvi in exchange for Silvi's and Silvi had accepted wholeheartedly. It had still been intimidating trying to fumble along copying Barra's divine and clearly experienced caresses. She'd never expected a person, let alone a Neamairtese, to treat her with such tenderness or selfless physical passion. How had she once thought of Barra as a savage? How had she questioned her even for a moment?

She didn't think anyone could love her the way she loved Barra. She couldn't even pronounce Barra's name correctly, but she knew how she felt. She would do anything for Barra, and the thought no longer scared her.

But why me, Silvi wondered. The thought that had been her constant companion took on new meaning this morning. What did she possibly have to offer Barra? She couldn't imagine that she'd been very good at pleasuring Barra last night. She'd been an oaf, and despite the success she seemed to have achieved, she could never compare to what Barra could do to her. She knew why she felt the way she did, but what reason could Barra have for liking a smelly, stocky oaf?

Silvi pushed the thought to the back of her mind to ruminate along with all of her other feelings of incapacity. As long as she had Barra, she didn't want to waste the feeling on thinking about if Barra were gone. Silvi cuddled tighter against Barra's back, bringing her lips to the back of Barra's neck to kiss her gingerly.

Barra gave a contented sigh and cuddled back into the hold even further. She was awake but seemed perfectly happy to stay here in Silvi's arms and pretend the rest of the world didn't exist.

"Good morning," Silvi whispered. There was so much more she wished she could say. Given the unreasonable complexity of the Neamairtese language, she guessed it would be a long time before she could. She would get there though. One day, she would tell Barra how she felt.

"Good morning," Barra whispered back.

Silvi had been halfway to placing a kiss on Barra's shoulder when the perfectly pronounced words broke through her blissful stupor. Barra had repeated several phrases to her over the past two days. Her favorite had been last night when Barra had unwittingly told her that she loved her. Silvi was content to pretend Barra had known and meant it. Based on the look she'd given her, like Barra was looking into her very soul, maybe, just maybe she had meant it. However, no phrase had been repeated with such apparent fluency.

At Silvi's withdrawal, Barra rolled over to pet her confused face. "Last night was amazing," Barra whispered. There was sincerity in her voice, but also clear hesitancy as if she knew her words might prompt a negative response.

"You speak Svekard?" Silvi asked, trying to decide if she was relieved or angry that Barra had let her wander in the dark so long.

"Technically yes, but technically right now I'm speaking Neamairtese. You're simply understanding it as if you spoke it natively."

Silvi did nothing to tone down her skeptical look. "I don't understand the Neamairtese language."

Barra sat up and took a deep breath in preparation for her explanation. There was a part of Silvi that had been longing for this moment for weeks, while another part was annoyed by how much she felt like Barra was treating her like a child. It wasn't a new annoyance and that only made it harder to not express the feeling now that she could. There was a last part of her that wished they could just skip the reality of explanations and understanding to instead just cuddle up in the bed together. She didn't think she'd ever experienced anything so wonderful as holding Barra to her naked body.

"Last night, you and I bonded. Through giving and receiving love, we finished the process that started that first night I kissed you and gave you the magic. As part of bonding, you have all my memories and I have all yours. You don't have any of the previous queens' memories like I do, nor will we share the memories we create going forward, but you have all of my memories up to the moment we bonded. In order to not overwhelm you, the memories function the same as your own. They don't come unless called. If you seek a memory or an answer, it'll come to you."

"None of that makes any sense," Silvi said. If she had Barra's memories, wouldn't this all already be in her head?

Barra bit her lower lip for a second thinking, then asked, "What was my mother's name?"

"Lucina," Silvi answered off-handedly. Her eyes widened as her jaw dropped. "How did I know that?"

"What was the last meal I ate before being captured by the Victricites?"

"Venison roasted on a spit," Silvi said. She closed her eyes and drew up the memory. She could taste the warm, juicy meat on her tongue. It wasn't quite like the real thing but tantalizingly close. She could almost smell the meat, hear the crackle of the fire, and feel the crunching leaves beneath Barra where she sat on the cool forest floor. "I remember it."

"Some things, like language or names, you just know without thinking about it. Because you've been doing so since you were a child, you don't have to remember the meaning of each word a person says. If I speak…slowly…enough…you can…think about…each…word. Think about only one of those words and you'll see it's a Neamairtese word, not a Svekard word. If you focus, you'll be able to speak Neamairtese instead of Svekard too."

Silvi wasn't fully convinced. She was a Svekard after all and that meant questioning what she was told and seeking the truth for herself. She focused on the word slowly…sodash. Barra had said "sodash," not slowly, but she'd known what Barra meant.

Seeing that Silvi had completed the task, Barra continued. "Like the name of my mother, some knowledge comes instantly. For example, I know you lost a younger brother who fell through the ice when he was only a boy. Since his life and death are everywhere in your memories, I don't have to remember the specific moment when you saw him fall." Barra paused. "I'm sorry, I should have picked a better example. I didn't mean to make you sad."

"You've lost too," Silvi said, not sure how else to respond. So much for the memories not being overwhelming.

The memory of losing Barra's mother and the feeling of anguish and guilt flowed into the visceral remembrance of finding Helenda's home burned out and her body missing. Her heart was beating faster as she relived Barra's body-wracking scream and the way she had sworn to avenge her friend and lover. Silvi tried to pull back as she fell into the next memory of Barra's last night with Helenda, the feel of her tongue, the sound of her moans, the smell of her excitement. She was lost in the almost tactile sensations and intense emotions that weren't even her own and never had been.

There were more, so many more memories all demanding her attention at the same time and forcing upon her conflicting emotions. She was in bliss and anguish, fear and excitement, pride and guilt.

Real hands cupped Silvi's face while real, pliant lips pushed against her own in a forceful kiss. She opened her eyes to see Barra staring at her as they kissed. Barra released her without losing the intensity of her stare. "Don't do that. Don't wade out into the river. As if you were sitting on the bank, let the memories pass you by. As if it were a twig floating on the surface, snag out what you need. If you have to go deeper, use a tool, don't climb in."

It was a nice analogy, but Silvi found it far from directly useful. How was she supposed to "snag" a memory without entering it?

"With practice, you'll learn to control it. With all the previous queen's memories and their methods for handling it, I have the advantage. Sometimes, my brain kind of feels like Victricite stew, with its indeterminant squishy vegetables and gritty broth." Barra flashed Silvi a lopsided smile as if she were sharing an established inside joke. Silvi tried to give one in return, but her head was aching a little too much to put much effort behind it.

"I've been wanting to talk to you for a while and I'm glad we can now. For what you have had to go through, I am very sorry. My intentions were never to hurt you or any of your people. I remember how lost you felt and angry too. Looking back, I'm glad the Lady led me to you, but I wish you hadn't suffered. At least I had the benefit of knowing you were my heart's mate." Barra gave Silvi another smile that clearly said she wanted Silvi to return it. Silvi wondered if they would ever stop trying to speak with their eyes and facial expressions as much as their words.

"Wait. You think I'm your soul mate?" She loved Barra and nothing this morning had changed that, but perhaps this was getting a little too serious a little too fast.

"Of course. During the ceremony, the Lady led me to my soul mate. How else do you explain me choosing you and everything that has happened since?"

"There's no such thing as soul mates. That implies fate. A million things could have gone differently, and you and I never would have even met. I really like you, Barra, but that doesn't make us soul mates." Fate made people complacent. It took away a person's responsibility for their own actions. Silvi didn't mean to be too dramatic, but in her opinion and that of her clansfolk, belief in fate could destroy an entire society.

"It doesn't just imply fate; soul mates are a product of fate. Despite the fact that they could have, a million things didn't go differently. What is the likelihood that you happened to leave for the Summer Fish Fry at just the right time to be captured at the same time as me? What is the likelihood that my group's first few days of hunting were so lean we decided to lengthen our trip and travel farther southeast? How about the likelihood that the Victricites chose that day to collect slaves and took the same amount of time to work their way south?"

Silvi didn't like this line of reasoning. She didn't like it one bit. "The choices I make matter." There, that was the heart of it. The piece she would never sway on.

"Of course, your choices matter. Fate's existence doesn't mean you don't have a choice. Though you could have chosen not to go as your clan's representative to the fish fry, it would have felt wrong. There are many paths to what fate has set and you can always make another choice."

Silvi made a sour face. She still didn't like it.

"You know, we don't have to agree. What matters to me is that you are here with me and you are choosing to stay." Barra ran the tips of her fingers over Silvi's bare thigh and smiled at the shiver that ran up Silvi's spine.

"I couldn't leave if I wanted to."

"The magic is keeping you here?" Barra asked. The look she fixed Silvi with was full of unease.

"No," Silvi locked gazes with Barra as she spoke. "I never want to leave you."

Barra gave her a brilliant smile that made her whole face glow. "Last night, I meant what I said. I love you."

"I love you too." Silvi pulled Barra first to her lips and then on top of her as she lay back. She'd been excited to repeat all the things they'd done last night since she'd woken up. She'd tried her best to figure out what she was supposed to do based on the things Barra had done to make her body explode with sensation. Silvi was pretty sure she could do better given a second chance.

Silvi had only gotten her hands halfway to Barra's shapely butt when Barra pulled back violently. "You thought I was going to sacrifice you in a sex ritual?" Barra said. Silvi wasn't sure if Barra was about to laugh or yell.

For a moment, all Silvi could do was bob her mouth open and closed. It sounded kind of dumb said like that and in that tone. At a loss, she said the first thing that came to her lust-filled brain. "Neamairtese do stuff like that."

Barra pulled away fully and Silvi felt her body cry out at the departure. "No, we don't! It's Svekards who make sacrifices. To appease your gods, you burn your own children. That's aside from making heroes out of men that go into a raping, killing rampage."

"Now that's just not fair or true. Berserkers are touched by the Gods and prized warriors, but they are clanless. They are not allowed near the homes of normal Svekards. They are outcasts not heroes. Plus, yes, we burn sacrificial sheep, but then we use that burned meat to attract the bears and wolves that we hunt. The Gods give us bounty in exchange for our loyalty. They would never ask for our children and we wouldn't give them. Svekards have a far greater love for their children than Neamairtese. Neamairtese witches are the ones who eat children—specifically Svekard children!"

"Even you know that's not true!" Barra shot back. "Fallen kindlers aren't Neamairtese anymore and they don't eat children."

If Barra would just pause for a moment, surely she could see Silvi's memories of fear and stories of witches killing, maiming, and sacrificing. But clearly, Barra wasn't willing to even give Silvi's view a second glance.

Barra continued, her volume and color rising. "Why do you tell stories to children to frighten them and make them hate us when you adults don't even believe they're true. Just to get children to do what their parents say, you propagate and pass on falsehoods."

"Don't you realize that when you banish a witch, all you are doing is setting them loose on Svekards?" Silvi countered, sounding defensive even to her own ears. Unlike Barra, she was pulling bits of memory out of the stream and throwing the dark refuse at Barra. "Stories are based on fact."

"Sure, the fact that you hate us and want your children to hate us and their children to hate us." Barra's eyes blazed and Silvi pulled back even farther.

How had this devolved so quickly? They'd been so close to intimacy only to now be sitting on opposite ends of the bed yelling at each other. "I don't hate you," Silvi said slowly.

What Barra had said was true. She'd decided a year or two before her own cohort's coming of age ceremony that she didn't believe witches lurked in the shadows waiting for children to disobey their parents so they could steal them away and bake them into pies. If nothing else, it seemed unlikely that witches would take the bad kids rather than the good ones. If the Neamairtese wanted to weaken Svekard society, that just wouldn't be the way to go about it. Yet, despite her doubt, she'd told all those same stories to her young nephew. She'd made sure to cackle in all the right places and even added the explanation that bad children tasted better than good ones because their hearts were blackened. How different were fallen kindlers and berserkers really?

Barra blew out a sigh between tightly held lips. "Our people really don't like each other."

"There's a lot of history there, bad history."

Barra just nodded. She was staring over Silvi's shoulder toward the door that led to the rest of the ship. Beyond it were nearly one hundred Svekards and Neamairtese who had managed to work together to regain their freedom from a common enemy. "Isn't that always the way of it? We can't find common ground but only a common enemy when survival depends on it."

"It wasn't a common enemy that made me fall for you," Silvi said. "That night…Gods, it was only three nights ago…when that man tried to, you know, use you. It had nothing to do with him, but you. He may have brought us together, but it was the look in your eyes that changed the way I felt. I guess I understood for the first time that Neamairtese are humans too. I know it sounds stupid and narrow-minded, but it was the first time I'd really considered it. You weren't scary, you were just scared. It made me notice all the ways I'd been wrong about you and your people."

Barra nodded. "Yesterday, when your people held the gate for us, that's what happened to my people. Everything we know about Svekards said they would close the gate on us, but they didn't."

"Maybe we're not so hopeless as we think," Silvi scooted back to the center of the bed and smiled when Barra did the same. Now that the language barrier was gone, they didn't seem that much better at communicating. Perhaps they could go back to the kind of communication that needed no words to tell Barra how she really felt.

She was halfway to Barra's lips when a thought struck her and Silvi couldn't help but burst out laughing.

"What?" Barra asked, clearly not sure if she should be excited or concerned.

"I was thinking about how witches don't eat children," Silvi said, gasping for air between continued bouts of laughter.

"I'm not sure I like where this is going."

"No, no." Silvi laughed. "It made me think of something I said to Keepan yesterday. I told him I wasn't a hero. I said that I'm the fool that gets eaten by a witch. Well, at the time it wasn't funny. See, in Svekard there is no word for bringing a woman pleasure with your tongue. So, without context, the Neamairtese phrase translates directly as eating. I was right, I *am* the fool who gets eaten by the witch."

Barra gave an amused chuckle. She placed her hand delicately on Silvi's inner thigh cutting off their laughter. "You said 'gets eaten,' not 'got eaten.' Did you realize?"

"And if I did?"

"Then you'd be right." Barra used the force of her kiss to push Silvi onto her back, savoring her lips before moving over the rise of her breasts and lower still until Silvi was crying out all the things she'd longed to say the night before.

CHAPTER ELEVEN
A FISH OUT OF WATER

Barra helped Silvi wrangle her long blond hair back into braids as they'd lost all semblance of order over the course of the night's and the morning's activities. Much as she would like to spend the entire day in this elegantly furnished box with a very naked and enticing Silvi, two groups of people were just on the other side of the door in desperate need of direction—and two people who could speak each other's languages. The claustrophobia that Barra had been ignoring since entering the room was also setting in, and she was looking forward to being able to see the sky again.

Her hours with Silvi had felt freeing. Not only could she finally explain everything to Silvi, but she no longer felt so alone. Silvi was the only person she could tell just how afraid the responsibility of the Spirits made her, and in Silvi she'd finally found someone who understood.

She'd whispered her fears into Silvi's chest after the morning's first round of fun. She hadn't meant to break the mood. If anything, she was riding the emotional high of feeling safe enough and loved enough to speak the words that had lived in the shadows of her heart since becoming queen. Silvi hadn't attempted to console her or tell her that her anxieties were unfounded. She'd simply pulled back enough to kiss her and then listened. Feelings of inadequacy, loneliness, and overwhelming pressure flowed out of Barra with barely a pause for breath.

Daralan was wise and encouraging and Terenesa was empathetic and supportive, but neither ever would have responded to her fears with a simple sighed, "yeah," as if they really knew what she meant. Barra didn't need to be told the Spirits had chosen her for a reason. She didn't need to be told she had a community around her to support her. She didn't even need to be told what to do. What she truly needed was Silvi's hand squeezing her own, bottomless brown eyes looking deeply into her own, and that one word—"yeah."

Barra was almost embarrassed by the giant tears that had followed, but Silvi had only held her close, pressing kisses to her temple and cheeks until the crying subsided. "Thank you. I needed that," Barra said, wiping her cheeks and attempting to rub the red from her eyes.

"So did I," Silvi said with a rueful smile.

Barra tipped her head to the side. She was so used to acting out her questions or confusion toward Silvi that the action came naturally. Had Silvi needed to see Barra's vulnerability to feel close to her or even to feel like an equal?

Silvi gave a small sigh. "I have felt so lost these last couple of weeks. I guess the only time I really feel in control is when I'm caring for others—people or animals. It's more than just feeling needed. It's also about feeling like I matter. I'm not reveling in your pain or anything. I'm just glad I can be here for you."

"Me too," Barra said with a kiss that sparked the second round of intimacy for the morning, a slower, deeper exploration.

They had reluctantly pulled themselves from the bed. Barra had talked about the immense responsibility sitting on her shoulders—now it was time to act on it. She was a leader, and it was time to lead.

As Barra took the hair for Silvi's final braid, she ran the silken strands between her fingers appreciatively. It was so different from the hair she was used to. The color was that of the brightest daffodils, shinier than wet rocks, and softer than rabbit's fur. The feeling of it on her thighs was enough to drive her wild.

Barra paused as she began to wind the strands. This was the kind of life event that called for sharing a token that would be carried with her in her hair as well as her memory for the rest of her life. She could give Silvi another of her tokens. Silvi had braided Helenda's feather into her hair this morning. But the sentiment wasn't quite right. This wasn't about sharing memories but creating them.

"You've stopped," Silvi said.

"Customarily, among my people, we place trinkets into our hair signifying important milestones and memories. As this is a memory I want to cherish forever, this is the perfect time to share such a trinket. However, traditionally it would be a natural object from nearby. In this room, I'm not sure how to proceed."

Silvi nodded. Barra could see from the flitting of her eyes and squeeze of her lips that she was attempting to skim the surface of her memories for information about the practice. She seemed to be getting much better at the process already. Barra could remember what it was like for the early queens to get lost in cycles of memories and did not envy Silvi that she had to learn it from scratch. It seemed she would always be guilty of making things harder on her.

Barra had only skimmed the very surface of Silvi's memories. With the memories of hundreds of people inside her head, it was hard for her to delve too deeply into any one set of memories without a distinct destination and purpose. She wanted to know Silvi and her culture inside and out, but it would take time to learn everything she wanted to know.

Silvi rose from the bed and walked silently to the table in the middle of the room. She plucked the cluster of grapes from the bowl and brought it back to the bed. Barra smiled and opened her mouth to accept the large green fruit. Grapes at home never grew that large. In Victricus, she had passed rows of latticed wooden towers covered in the familiar vines with fruit that bulged out of the twisting greenery like nipples from the fur of a nursing wolf. Was that what fruit looked like when you tended to it like a pet?

As she closed her teeth down, Barra's mouth filled with a juice sweeter than she had ever experienced. Grapes in the wild were delicious, but they were full of hard, bitter seeds, covered in thick, chalky skins, and barely had enough meat to produce juice. For a moment, juice sliding down her throat, Barra wondered what kind of people could cultivate such treasures and yet be unsatisfied. Victricites had so much, how could they need slaves? Why would they leave their warm climate, their robust fields, their cities of comfort, to wipe out entire peoples and then begin to do it again to two more?

Barra reached out and took another grape from the bunch and popped it in her mouth before pausing to watch Silvi enjoy the delicacy. She loved the look of enjoyment on her face, though she couldn't deny a tiny piece of her that wished Silvi would have fewer grapes so she could have more. Perhaps that was the way for the Victricites as well. They got a taste for riches and couldn't do without them.

Barra plucked another grape from the bunch and placed it delicately between her teeth, tantalizingly close to her tongue. She leaned forward to provide it to Silvi in an open-mouthed kiss. She was not a Victricite. She knew what it was like to work for what she had, to sacrifice for the people she cared for, and to love someone more than herself.

When Barra and Silvi had finished feeding each other the last of the grapes, Silvi offered her the stem. It would harden into the consistency of a twig, which made it perfect as a memento for her hair. Barra tucked it up next to her right temple so it would be most prominent on her mind. "What about for you?"

Silvi shifted uncomfortably on the bed, her hands playing with the tips of her braids nervously. "It's not really something I...I mean, well...Clean, well-kept hair is really important to Svekards...to me. The feather, well, it's important and small and easy to keep in clean hair. But I don't want...I can't keep adding things. I know it's important to you to do so, but I can't."

Barra held in the frustrated sigh that pushed at her lips. She wanted to counter that what Silvi meant was that she didn't want her hair to be a mess like the Neamairtese. Silvi didn't understand. How could a Svekard understand being sentimental, about holding this as sacred?

But Barra knew none of that was really true. She could pull out of her collection of Silvi's memories instance after instance of the items and practices Silvi held sacred. They were simply different from Barra's. Silvi had as much right to her traditions as Barra did.

It wasn't Silvi she was displeased with, but the situation. She accepted that Silvi was her heart's mate; she felt it in every part of her and thus the Lady had led her true. But the truth of their fate and Silvi's right to her culture didn't change the fact that the queen's mate should follow Neamairtese tradition. She should look and act like one of the people. The queen's mate was as much a protector of the people and of the magic as she was of the queen. She had a role in rituals and a place in the tribe's leadership, however ceremonial.

Barra had been so caught up in the clear and present danger of the Victricites, the challenges of her new position, and getting Silvi to like and understand her. She hadn't spared a thought for the long term. There was so much Silvi was supposed to be that she just wasn't.

"I'm sorry," Silvi whispered, her gaze downcast. She looked truly ashamed for her refusal to release that specific custom and yet unwavering in her dedication to it. Barra didn't like it, but she liked Silvi all the more for it.

"No. My wanting it and your not, is not your fault. You aren't asking me to change my hair. Nor would I be willing to if you asked. Certainly, we can find other ways for you to represent and hold memories." She raised Silvi's lips to her own with a finger crooked under her chin. The one good thing about their disagreements and misunderstandings was that it was leading to many extra kisses.

"Maybe you could make me a necklace like yours. I could add items to it like you add them to your hair," Silvi suggested as she pulled back from the newest set of kisses. "We Svekards don't think about holding things in our heads, but in our hearts. Then the memories will be close to my heart always."

Barra didn't try to hold back her grin. Silvi could add items. The future was uncertain, but Silvi wanted to experience it with her. "That sounds like a wonderful idea."

Finding a suitable item proved more difficult than the grape stem had been. While Silvi removed the decorative chain from the scabbard of one of the swords on the room's wall, Barra dug through the room's contents. She returned with a chunk of coal, a string of leather for tying map rolls, a warped cube of wax, and a ring with a large blue stone surrounded by smaller red gemstones like the petals of a flower, all finely inset into the wide golden band.

Silvi plucked the ring delicately from Barra's open palm and examined it closely. "This stone sparkles like your eyes," she whispered reverently, brushing her fingers over it and then the red stones which were a brighter red than Barra's hair, but reminded her of it, nonetheless. She doubted Barra had any idea how rare and valuable of an item she had just found. The idea that she would equate it to the grape twig in her hair would be laughable if Silvi didn't understand the meaning behind it. To Barra, the twig was a priceless memory that would live with her because it was physically present and would slowly become part of her spirit. What were hunks of useless precious metal and gemstones compared to that? Since Silvi would hold it close to her heart as her version of keeping this memory close, the two were equivalent.

"That one caught my eye as well," Barra said, smiling at her own joke. "I stopped after I found it."

Silvi slipped the expensive trinket onto the delicate chain and knotted it several times before slipping it over her neck and settling the ring over her left breast. She gave it one last appreciative look before pulling on and lacing up first her bra and then the thin cotton shirt the Victricites had provided her. She caught Barra giving her breasts the same appreciative look before they were hidden from view.

Without her furs, Silvi still felt naked, but she was finding that naked wasn't so bad either. What kind of a Svekard am I becoming, Silvi asked herself. She wasn't just without her furs and finding it tolerable, she was in love with a Neamairtese, and not just any Neamairtese but the queen. She was far from home, without her clan, her family, or the tools of her trade, all of which had previously defined her. Silvi wondered if she looked in a mirror if she would even see the same woman she knew. Would she see the hero that her people thought she was? Would she see the fierce, graceful, and gentle-spirited woman she found when looking at herself through Barra's memories?

It was surreal to see herself through the memories of another and even more when that image changed with each progressive memory. It wasn't just Barra's feelings that had changed, but the way she saw her. In Barra's memory of their first interaction, she saw a barbarian, stocky features draped in matted rags with brutal strength and blinding speed, her fists dabbled with blood. That night, Barra had seen her closely enough to take in her features, but they were nothing like what Silvi understood of herself. She had bloodshot eyes and large bared teeth. Every feature was filled with vicious hatred and the need to injure, were it not for the magic holding her at bay. But that image of her shifted as the memories progressed. She could see her features soften as she drew up the memory of caring for the stallion and refine from a hunk of Svekard muscle into the sexy, busty curves of a woman in the memories of holding and eventually loving Silvi. If she looked in a mirror now, would she see any of that—aspects she'd never seen in herself before?

Silvi wondered if she could look at this memory, what would she see through Barra's eyes? Certainly not the hesitant, uncertain, weak woman she felt like. Not with the smoldering look Barra was giving her.

She would understand, Silvi realized. If I told her that I don't know who I am anymore, that my people have placed on me a burden I never thought I could carry and I still don't think I can, Barra would get it. But more than that, Barra would still see her as protective, loyal, and beautiful rather than cowardly and feeble. Silvi liked who she was through Barra's eyes.

As Barra finished dressing, under Silvi's prurient ogling, a new and concerning thought occurred to Silvi. "Is everyone going to know that we, you know, did what we did last night…and again this morning.".

"Twice," Barra pointed out, her grin broad and bold. "Yes, my people will know. If the fact that you're now calling me Barra instead of Barda doesn't tip them off, that giant grin will."

Silvi blushed further and tried to lessen her smile but found it immensely difficult. She felt like her entire body was singing. It was like eating warm soup next to a raging fire after coming in out of a desperate cold. Except the warmth was inside her and she didn't think she could hide it, no matter how hard she tried. Maybe that was what she would see if she looked at herself and maybe that could be how she defined herself: a raging fire trying to drive off the cold, kindled by the love of Barra and the faith of her people, even if she thought both might be misplaced.

Dressed, respective hair in its expected state, Barra and Silvi made their way to the door hand in hand, ready to face the people who expected so much of them. As Barra's hand reached the doorknob, Silvi reached out to close her hand loosely around Barra's and prevent her from grasping it. "Wait."

Silvi was getting a better handle on how to sift through the memories, and she needed to address the pattern she was discovering. Barra turned to Silvi expectantly. A small twinkle in her eye asked if Silvi was going to try to drag her back to bed. It appeared that it wouldn't be too hard to convince Barra to delay a little longer despite her claims to the contrary.

"Svekards aren't bad," Silvi said, wishing she had a more eloquent way to say it.

"Okay," Barra said, the extra strong lilt of her voice showing her confusion as to why this seemed so important for Silvi to say.

"No," Silvi said, letting go of Barra's hand to place a hand on each shoulder. "I'm not a 'good' Svekard. Svekards are good. You are about to go out there and ask them to trust you, to follow you, possibly into great danger and risk their lives to save all of ours. You can't do that, you can't ask them to do that if you don't trust them, if you don't truly believe that they are good people."

Barra nodded slowly, clearly fully considering what Silvi had said and trying to rationalize what was in her own memories with what was in Silvi's. Silvi had found with Barra's memories of their encounters it took a concerted effort to blend two memories that contradicted each other. Silvi could remember watching Barra try to get two women to stop fighting over a man and displaying herself as such a terrible leader that Silvi couldn't help but hate her. She could also remember feeling miserable that she was a fraud of a leader while trying to encourage Terenesa and Redena in their efforts to cast a spell against the Victricites. It was hard enough to rationalize having Barra's memories and feelings in her head. Combining those with her own over the same scene gave her a terrible headache. Melding her own values with Barra's was a task she wasn't looking forward to. The strained look on Barra's face told her she'd been right to avoid it so far.

"Svekards are good," Barra repeated. Barra's eyes gave away to Silvi that she was accessing memory after memory in a flood that would have overwhelmed Silvi. "Svekards care very deeply about each other. They would do anything to protect their clan and their family. We are going to need their dedication and selflessness to save both our people."

Silvi felt her lips lift into the giant grin that Barra had referenced, the one she was having trouble containing every time she looked at Barra. She only hoped it would last as she reached down and turned the doorknob, ready to see what had become of their people in their absence.

She'd been braced for fighting, she expected two groups of people sitting sullenly on different ends of the ship swearing at each other in different languages. What Silvi hadn't expected was a miniature caricature of the Svekard Kraunfish festival.

At the end of autumn, the day after the first dusting of snow fell across the lands of Svek every year, Svekards celebrated the coming of winter with a two-day festival of fermenting fish. Fall oats, the last crop to be harvested each year, had been steamed and rolled and any crops not already processed were considered lost to be sewn back into the earth. The Kraunfish festival was a time for drinking the newly made ale, eating fresh baked bread from hearths that would keep the houses warm all winter, and fermenting over ten thousand pounds of fish for the months ahead. All three hundred or so members of the clan were expected to pull their weight, from young children delivering food to their parents and taking dull knives to be sharpened, to the oldest clan members teaching the young what their grandparents had taught them. Everyone served the clan.

Each night after the sun went down and it was too dark to see their work, the clan would celebrate the end of a strong year together by singing, dancing, and playing music. Over the course of both nights, the Svekards competed to win the title of Grand Kraun. There was a competition for the greatest telling of a true story from the past year and another for the best crafted "big fish" story, a story that was just barely too impressive to believe. Another competition was held to determine who could make the most interesting, useful, and often amusing item from the piles of fishbones. Clansfolk competed with their typical level of competitive vigor, but the Grand Kraun was hardly ever the winner of any of the three competitions. The Grand Kraun was selected as the member of the clan who had most greatly served the clan over the past year. They were typically not the person telling the winning story, but more often than not the subject of that story and many others.

The smell of salt and fish hit Silvi in the face, bringing with it instant memories of waking at the crack of dawn to begin scaling, gutting, and deboning fish. She could taste the tang of preserving liquid in her memory as if the air here was full of it rather than just fish, sea air, and olive oil. She remembered laughing with her sister Nita and their older sister, Greta, who had since married a man from another clan, as they raced to finish more fish than each other. None of them could keep up with Mama. From the squeeze of Barra's hand in her own and the half smile lifting the side of her mouth, Silvi was sure Barra was experiencing the same memories.

Spread out across the main deck of the three-masted galley were a dozen or so flopping, gasping fish, larger than Silvi had ever seen. Each fish only managed a few wet slaps on the deck with its large body, before being snatched up and its head cleaved off by one of about twenty Svekards scaling, gutting and deboning the fish. The pile never got below two fish before another netful was dumped onto the deck by one of either of the seven-person netting crews, casting their net off the sides of the ship into the ocean. The last twelve Svekards were manning two giant stoves that they had pulled from the ship's galley onto the main deck for quicker access.

Silvi looked over the industriousness of her people with pride. She watched as one of the cooks loaded a barrel lid with fish, climbed the short ladder to the back of the ship, and held it out to the Neamairtese huddled there. The front-most Neamairtese man's face turned a pinkish shade of green before he ran the short distance to the edge of the ship and puked over the side. The Svekard shrugged, unoffended, placed the barrel lid next to what looked like a previous offering, and returned to the cooks to tell his story and continue his work. A rumbling laugh burst out from the cooks as they continued their furious pace.

"Our people aren't doing well with being on the water," a familiar voice said from his spot next to the door. Daralan, whose name had far too many syllables in Silvi's opinion, looked rather green tinged himself. "It's been hard to keep food down and all the harder with the smell." He winced as a new batch of flopping blue and white fish landed on the deck with a wet smack.

From what Silvi could tell from the body language of the people huddled at the back of the ship, they still hadn't decided if the Svekards would get tired of cutting off fish heads and turn the knives and swords they'd found against them. The fact that the tables had turned, and it was the Neamairtese bunching up like scared sheep, while the Svekards were in their element filled Silvi with gratification. It felt a little petty, but she felt it, nonetheless. Her people were strong and resourceful. They didn't do well chained and threatened, but with a little space to breathe, they always figured out how to thrive.

"They shouldn't be at the back of the boat up high," Silvi commented, though she supposed there wasn't much room for them amongst the mix of live fish and the remains of the old ones.

"They're scared," Barra replied. She opened her mouth to say more, but was interrupted by a shouting, waving Svekard.

"Silvi," Slade, the storyteller, called out to her. Apparently, her hero's time of isolation was over because he was smiling and summoning her over.

Silvi gave Barra's hand a squeeze before releasing it to deal with her people while Barra discussed the Neamairtese with Daralan.

"Have you ever seen fish so large?" Slade asked. "We've lost two nets to fish so large seven men couldn't pull them in."

Next to Slade, a woman named Tana, who was hauling another round of a dozen fish that were at least forty pounds each, gave Slade a distracted glare. Slade only laughed. "If six men and Tana couldn't pull in those fish, there's no way seven men could have!" Tana didn't bother to show Slade her gratified smile, only chuckled as she heaved the fish on board with her team. Slade said, "No one will believe us, but they will make epic stories."

"We have enough." Silvi gestured at the three barrels overflowing with cooked filets set up next to the cooks. They had been placed such that a pyramid of additional fish as tall as a Neamairtese could be stacked on top of the rotund barrels. "It's time to eat and plan." And stop scaring the last bit of composure out of the Neamairtese, Silvi added to herself.

Slade flashed her a grin that made her heart ache. Only Papa had ever given her such a look of both challenge and belief. It was the look he gave her as a child when she said she couldn't, and he knew she could. "Then call it off," Slade said before rushing back to his rope line on the net to pull in another group of massive, pointy-nosed fish.

Keepan had power as the group's leader and Slade had pull as a revered storyteller, but combined they didn't have the influence Silvi did. Keepan could be challenged and Slade outdone, but her people considered Silvi to be a hero and only an oath keeper or rune reader could or would challenge her authority unless her actions or demands were clearly to the detriment of the clan.

Slade's momentary distraction with the fish gave Silvi a chance to compose herself. This was her new role, whether she liked it or felt she deserved it or not. She still had strong doubts that she was a hero, but just like fate, the only way forward was to act to use her resources and power to best serve her people, whether she was doing it because she was meant to or not.

"Enough," Silvi bellowed, surprising herself with her volume and tone of command. No one else seemed startled by her sudden display. They reeled in their nets, snatched up the last of the fish, and gave Silvi as much of their attention as they could without burning the remaining filets. From the upper deck, a few of the Neamairtese poked their heads up like pine martens to watch her.

Silvi cleared her throat uncomfortably. Why did they all have to look at her? "We have enough fish. Let's eat and plan." Her eyes went to the greenish faces looking at her and she added, "Let's make a clean space here for the Neamairtese. They are not used to the sea."

A general chuckle went up amongst the Svekards, but it was not an unkind one. They too were glad the tables had turned. However, with that pride also came memories of their first times on the sea. Silvi could see in them the same empathy building that she had developed days before.

When it was clear Silvi was done with her announcement, Keepan stepped forward from the edge of the ship and took over, dividing the Svekards into groups to clear the detritus, swab the deck, and finish the meals.

Feeling out of place in the bustle, Silvi returned to Barra's side. Barra immediately retook Silvi's hand in her own as if she had been bereft without it. Silvi sank into the comfort of the small gesture. Barra's gaze was full of love and pride as she said, "I know you don't like everyone looking at you, but leadership looks good on you."

Silvi blushed and tried to think of the warmth as a good thing— her fire flaring up in her cheeks. The heat rose up inside her every time she even looked at Barra. In this warm climate where even the ocean spray was warm and her eye was constantly caught by Barra, giving her memories of their night and morning together, Silvi wasn't sure if she would simply start melting.

"Would you like to invite my people down? For them to hear you speak their language, will be very encouraging and for a Svekard to be inviting them into the group will help put them more at ease with your people," Barra said.

"I, uh, I haven't spoken Neamairtese yet." Silvi picked nervously at her hair. "Do I have to do it the first time in front of everyone?"

"If you like, you could practice with Daralan and me," Barra said. Silvi doubted that Barra had ever been afraid to speak her mind or approach a new group of people. She certainly couldn't remember a time.

"If you are worried about them judging you, you do not need to," Daralan said, putting together the conversation from the half he could understand. "They know this is new for you and will be delighted to hear you try."

Silvi felt an unreasonable rush of annoyance at Daralan. She had listened to him speak to Barra only a few minutes before, and while it had been odd to understand him, it was an increase in her abilities. But to have him participate in their conversation felt like an intrusion. It was hard to wrap her brain around the idea that when she and Barra spoke, they weren't in some bubble of magical connection.

Taking a deep breath, Silvi brought up one of Barra's memories of Daralan. He was helpful, kind, and wise. Barra liked Daralan and so should she. "How?"

"Repeat something you remember me saying."

Silvi took a long moment to find the memory she wanted and then, eyes closed, repeated, "She is my mate, and you will treat her with respect. When none of you could, she protected me, and you laughed at her. Shame on all of you." In her memory, the women who had pointed and laughed when Silvi spread the last of her stew on her face and chest in the symbol of Ilode looked smaller and less intimidating. She could feel Barra's anger, embarrassment, and compassion and knew the women would never again have Barra's respect.

Barra and Daralan both gave her a placating smile that, with Barra's former anger stirring inside her, made Silvi want to yell the line again rather than just saying it.

"Good, now say it in Neamairtese," Barra said.

"What? But I just did."

"No, you remembered the meaning of my words and said their meaning in Svekard. You have to focus on the words themselves. Using my exact words, say them the way I did. "

Silvi held in an exasperated harrumph and set her jaw instead. She was very good at the things she did. Sticking with something until you mastered it was a Svekard way of life. Drawing up the memory again, she spoke slowly, letting the exact words shape her mouth, rather than shaping the words to what she wanted to say.

The difference was immediately noticeable. Where Svekard required full use of Silvi's diaphragm and made the back of her throat rumble, Neamairtese was all in the nose and the front of her mouth. She made sounds that simply didn't exist in Svekard. By changing the sound of a vowel slightly, she could change the entire meaning of a word. In Svekard, such differentiation would simply denote a different clan's accent.

Barra radiated pride. "Now that you've done that—very well, I might add—try saying something in Neamairtese that isn't a memory. It will be much easier now that you have the feel for it." She spoke Svekard to Silvi now that she wouldn't be rubbing her immediate ability to switch languages in Silvi's face quite so much. Silvi could see the differences as much as hear them. Barra's breasts rose and fell with her each word in an enticing way and her jaw shape broadened as she opened her throat.

"I'm not really sure what to say," Silvi admitted, focusing on every word to make sure it wasn't Svekard. She was finding it easier to weed out the Svekard words than to pick the Neamairtese ones. She imagined herself pulling tiny rocks from a tray of fresh cut barley.

"Tell me what you would like to tell them."

Silvi cleared her nose and twitched her mouth like a rabbit. "Okay, what you are experiencing is *seasickness*…ah, sickness from the sea… it will get better with time. You should sit near the center of the ship, not up high. Eat some food. Not a lot, but a little to calm your stomach. Look out at the horizon. Come join us…um, the Svekards that is. The Svekards would like the joining in fellowship…I mean the Svekards would like you to join them in a meal and we can talk about what we're going to do next." Silvi gave Barra a sideways half smile. She had avoided all but a few Svekard words but sounded nothing like a Neamairtese. Her cadence was off and even her sentence structure felt wrong.

Daralan stood slowly with a bit of a wobble from the barrel he was sitting on. "Thank you. To have those tips will be very helpful." He wasn't looking at her, but out at the horizon.

"I'll do better the second time." Silvi said as Barra led her by the hand to the ladder up to the Neamairtese. "You appear to be doing well with the sickness from the sea," she observed, trying to get some more last-minute practice in.

"With all of your latent memories, it's much easier. Plus, I'm not the first queen to sail. My body may not be used to it, but my mind is and knows some of how to compensate."

The whole group of Neamairtese minus Barra and Daralan looked up at Silvi as she stepped out in front of them and froze. She could feel Barra standing silently next to her and felt Barra's hand slip back into her own and give it a squeeze. Silvi had thought maybe if she chickened out, Barra would step in, but everyone seemed willing to wait until Silvi drew up the nerve to address them. I'm a Svekard, Silvi said silently to herself before thinking it in Neamairtese. I can do this.

Silvi's second attempt went much better. The Neamairtese didn't look excited by the prospect of moving, let alone moving into the middle of a Svekard horde, but like the Svekards, they appeared ready to push all of that aside to follow Silvi.

As they trudged past Silvi, swaying with the rock of the ship, Silvi turned to Barra. "You move your tongue around in your mouth so much to speak Neamairtese." She dropped her tone and switched into Svekard to whisper to Barra. "That must be why you're so good in bed." The fact that she'd just said so in front of a whole group of Barra's people made her face burn with embarrassment despite the fact that she had specifically changed to a language they didn't understand.

Barra seemed unfazed by the public nature of their conversation but switched into Svekard as well. "The way you speak is already starting to hurt my throat, but I'm sure I could get used to it. With your way of speaking, I bet you'd be very good at fellatio."

Silvi's eyes widened until they throbbed, and her face burned hotter than it had all morning. "Barra!"

"I'm not saying you should try it," Barra clarified, clearly not sure why this was such a big deal. She seemed oblivious to the fact that fellatio was not a Svekard word and now everyone around them knew they were speaking about sex. "Personally, I'm rather hoping you never test that theory. I'm just saying as far as mouth shapes go—"

"Can we…Let's just change the subject." No one had seemed to take notice of their conversation, either too sick or too polite to react. At Barra's shrug of nonchalance, Silvi slipped into the crowd to help them down the ladder and made a mental note to never bring that particular topic up again.

The Svekards had finished clearing the deck and distributing food by the time the Neamairtese took the place set up for them. No one could say Svekards didn't know hospitality.

Around a mouthful of fish, Keepan turned to Silvi and asked, "What now?"

"We have to go back for our people…for all of our people," Silvi said. If she was going to be treated like a hero, she was going to act like one. If she accepted that the Gods had chosen her, which she still wasn't sure about, then their plan for her was larger than saving fifty Svekards. From what she'd seen, there were as many Svekard slaves in Victricus as Neamairtese or more, which meant thousands of her clansfolk. Whether it was what the Gods intended or not, fighting for their freedom and that of the Neamairtese slaves was the right thing to do.

Chapter Twelve
A Tricksy Bit of Magic

Barra found watching Silvi interact with her people and the Neamairtese fascinating. She could see Silvi's consternation and her self-doubt, and yet once she got started or made a decision, she was able to move forward with myopic determination. Where such singular focus would normally strike Barra as close-minded, especially in a Svekard, it allowed Silvi to block out her uncertainty with herself and the situation and truly embrace a power inside her that had nothing to do with Barra's magic. Silvi wasn't just loyal and compassionate, she was exceedingly strong, even if she did not believe it about herself.

Barra took another bite of her fish and marveled at the meaty flavor. The taste was nothing like the significantly smaller fish her people netted out of the rivers at home. Even the fish Silvi was used to were larger than the trout her people typically used to supplement their hunts. These fish were stronger in flavor too, like she was tasting the ocean covered in savory sweetness. She was finding the food was the only thing she liked about the Victricites.

The largest of the Svekards, Keepan, was sitting on Silvi's other side and talking with a full mouth. With each word, small flecks of white fish fell onto his hands. At the end of every sentence, he stuffed his sizable fingers into his mouth one after the other to lick the flecks off and reach for another filet of fish. Perhaps Silvi had been wrong about them having more than enough fish for everyone...at least if everyone ate like Keepan.

The Neamairtese were picking at their fish like spoiled children. Barra certainly didn't blame them. She was far from feeling comfortable herself.

As they ate, careful to keep her actions small and calls to the Spirits clandestine, Barra began casting magic. The Svekards had handed out cups of water along with the fish and the water seemed the easiest place to disseminate her magic without the Svekards noticing and reacting.

Starting with her own cup, Barra called on the magic of Water. She didn't need much magic, less than she'd provided to their stews the last couple of nights, to add the equivalent of the white powder the Svekards knew as bicarbonate soda and citrus to the water. Once it was bubbling, Barra quietly traded it to Daralan who was ever present at her right hand.

With Daralan's help, Barra slowly circulated the concoction and watched her people's coloring return to a normal red-freckled cream. She didn't like the extra time it took to hide her magic, but she was far more concerned with not creating a scene in front of the Svekards.

"Do you have a plan?" Keepan asked, directing his question at Silvi as he reached for yet another piece of fish.

Unlike Keepan, Silvi waited to swallow before speaking, though Barra had a feeling it was because Silvi wasn't entirely sure what she was going to say. "We are strongest together. We need to get everyone together."

"If we had the horn of Blatadur, we could call everyone to attack at once—Svekards and beasts," Slade said. From his expression, he understood the story was more useful as inspiration than a plan.

"We're too spread out," Tana, a woman who Barra swore had arms the size of Barra's torso, grunted in disagreement.

"We need to give everyone a chance to escape," Silvi said.

"We need some tricksy Neamairtese magic," Eigen said. He stood out to Barra from the others for the lack of beard on his young face. It was a fact he clearly tried to hide by braiding as much of his hair to the front as he could. Even the fuzzy tufts on his chin were more than a Neamairtese man would be willing to grow.

The group paid Eigen no heed as more and more Svekards began to shout answers into the group.

"We could sail the ship into the docks and light all the other ships on fire. We'll fight to the last while the others escape."

"We'll have to go back to Svek and bring an army."

"Can we challenge the Victricite leader?"

"Didn't the Neamairtese paralyze our forces at the Battle of Witches Be Damned?" Eigen asked the storyteller. But Slade was too wrapped up in shouting options to listen.

"The Heroes of Broken Shield fought a force ten times their size of mounted cannibals by forming a tight circle in the center of the battlefield."

"What did you just say?" Barra asked, pushing up to her feet and yelling to be heard over the brouhaha. As the crowd turned to her in astonishment, Barra repeated herself. "Eigen, what did you say?"

"B-B-Battle of Witches Be D-damned." Eigen's eyes were almost the size of his gaping mouth as he stammered.

Clearly taking Barra's words as the precursor to attack, Keepan rose to his feet. He took on the most aggressive defensive stance Barra had ever seen. As he rose, so did Silvi, ready to defend Barra. Daralan was close behind. He and all the Neamairtese had been watching the Svekards yell with trepidation ready for it to explode just like this.

The rest of the Svekards and Neamairtese reached their feet at about the same time, fists clenched. The Neamairtese were nimbler, but the Svekards had a shorter distance to rise and were always ready to defend themselves and their brethren.

Barra needed to say something fast if she was going to cool down nearly one hundred hot heads. Eigen cut in before she could. "How can you speak Svekard?"

"Tricksy Neamairtese magic?" Barra said with a hesitant grin.

"I also speak Neamairtese," Silvi said to the crowd, though they didn't stop staring at Barra.

Barra tried again. "Eigen, you said something before that about Neamairtese paralyzing forces."

"Yeah, in the War of Generations. Witches froze our army and slipped past them into the village."

"They salted the fields so no crops would grow and our people would starve," Slade growled.

"They didn't even have the decency or honor to fight the people willing to sacrifice their lives for their homes and families," Keepan said, his voice a barely contained roar.

"I—They left all of your people alive, just drove you off their hunting grounds. You killed the deer and destroyed the forest. They destroyed your crops." It didn't matter that she knew defending herself was a bad idea. Barra could remember being there. She could remember burning hatred and the desperate need to rectify an unfixable wrong.

The Neamairtese had traveled southwest for the winter on their typical migratory pattern. By the time they returned in the summer, the deer population would have replenished. The deer of the foothills provided enough meat and hide to last them over the winter and the salt springs provided just enough salt to preserve the meat, cover ritual needs for the year, and even a little extra for seasoning.

When her people had returned to their ancient hunting grounds just over two hundred and fifty years ago, they had found the forest clear cut. Where there had been great oaks, stood log houses. Where there had been herds of healthy deer, there were pens of idiotic domesticated beasts. Worse still, their source of salt had become a lounging spot for barbarians who didn't even have the decency to take off their dirt matted clothing before taking a dip. The waters were polluted, the forest was gone, and the deer were dead. Many of her people died that winter.

That had sparked the beginning of what the Svekards called the War of Generations. To the Neamairtese it was nothing so grand. They'd fought for the Lord and Lady's land and creatures for decades, raiding when possible and defending themselves as best they could.

The Neamairtese couldn't win in a face-to-face fight. The Svekards were stronger, with forged metals far beyond the capacity of the Neamairtese. The Neamairtese had only two advantages. First, the Svekards insisted on charging into battle face-first and demanding their enemies do the same. The Neamairtese had no such desires. They relied on ambushes, raids, and taking their enemy by surprise.

The second advantage the Neamairtese had was magic. Barra could remember the three queens over the course of that period of time using any and all magic they could muster to aid their people and their cause. The Spirits didn't like magic being used to kill, even if killing would save the animals, the forest, and the Neamairtese themselves. So, Barra's predecessors had used creative solutions to try to drive the Svekards back.

Queens had found every way they could to incapacitate the Svekards rather than killing them. It was a mercy the Svekards never returned.

Svekards left no one alive on the battlefield. Barra now understood that to a Svekard, being crippled rather than killed was incredibly dishonorable not just because they had been denied the chance at a glorious death but also because honorable warriors were turned into a drain on the clan. Barra understood it, but that didn't mean she agreed with it. To her it was simply a weak justification for villainy.

A combination of migrating farther and farther west and making the land unlivable had eventually brought a slow and unsatisfying close to their war. Hostilities had not ended. Winters were harder and salt rarer. At some point in the last hundred and fifty years, what the Neamairtese believed was the inevitable continuation of brutes ravaging their lands and their people had been replaced by Victricites enslaving them, and no one had noticed the difference.

The Svekards were all yelling at her. They apparently took her knowledge of their language as permission to bombard her with it at top volume. They all seemed to have ancestors or ancestors of friends who had somehow been wronged by Neamairtese not killing them directly but leading to their deaths, nonetheless. *And my people?* Barra wanted to scream back.

None of that was important right now, Barra told herself. Her fury and that of all the queens before her were spiraling and that wasn't going to help anyone. Barra focused on the battle or lack thereof Eigen had described. She remembered the queen casting the spell that created a fog to temporarily paralyze the Svekard force headed for the eastern tribes.

"It could work," Barra whispered.

Unlike Neamairtese, who would have fallen silent at the queen's whisper, the Svekards kept yelling. All except one. Silvi, who seemed to spend every moment she could looking at Barra, asked in a tone just above a whisper, "What could work?"

Barra tried to answer, but Silvi held up a hand to stop her. "Shut up!" she screamed at her people who immediately fell silent. "Continue," Silvi said calmly, as if she hadn't just screamed at the top of her lungs.

"What Eigen suggested could work. A cloud that large would require a lot of magic to create, but there must be lots of kindler slaves who could help. To freeze all the Victricite…I couldn't create a cloud that large, but perhaps it would be enough to get us enough Neamairtese and Svekards."

It wouldn't. They had marched for three days to cross Victricus from north to south. Even with kindlers, she couldn't create a cloud more than several miles in diameter. Victricus was just too large. She knew her doubt showed in her face. She closed her eyes and tried to calculate a distance she couldn't quantify compared to a spell she'd never actually cast.

In the background, she could hear Silvi translating the idea to the Neamairtese. It had taken a while, but Silvi was exactly who she needed. Barra wished she could show her gratitude, but besides being rather busy, there was very little she could do that wouldn't make Silvi exceedingly uncomfortable.

"We would help you," Terenesa said, her voice barely above a whisper.

"Yes, we could cover a great distance together," Marsinus said just loud enough to be heard. "We could save many even if we could not save them all."

Silvi translated again, sharing the kindlers' words with the Svekards. The whispers of the Neamairtese were not to keep their comments secret as the Svekards would assume. To speak quietly was to demand silence for words of import.

"That is not enough," Tana objected, her yell drowning out whatever Redena was attempting to say.

"It doesn't need to cover all of Victricus. A raincloud doesn't cover all of Svek at once. It moves," Eigen said.

That could work. Barra felt her excitement rise. She couldn't heal every Neamairtese of seasickness at once, but she could give them a remedy one cup at a time. The cloud could be as wide as her power allowed and could grow with each kindler. "Picking up our people as we go, we could move north together, bringing the cloud with us. Not knowing what was coming, the Victricites ahead of us wouldn't know to prepare and the ones behind wouldn't be able to enter the cloud without being frozen again."

"How long would it last?" Tana interjected, far from ready to celebrate.

"As long as I can stay awake," Barra answered. It wasn't a great answer but the most accurate she could provide.

"It took three days to get from the wall to the city and through it." Silvi said, placing a concerned hand on Barra's shoulder.

"That should be plenty of time to kill the Victricites," Keepan said to the cheers of the Svekards.

"No!" Barra was finding it more effective to shout than whisper. "If you attack, the spell ends. It is of the utmost importance that we cannot fight the frozen Victricites."

The Svekards looked sullen and far from acquiescing. The Neamairtese just rolled their eyes as Silvi translated.

Daralan brushed his hand along Silvi's shoulder, making her cringe. Svekards didn't touch each other unless they were family. She gave him an apologetic smile but took a half step away anyway. He asked, "how will we keep the Svekards we are rescuing from attacking if even these Svekards who know they are not allowed to do so still want to attack?"

"We're going to have to warn everyone that it's coming and what they are supposed to do," Barra interjected. "Svekard and Neamairtese alike. With Air's help, I can manage a spell to contact all of them."

"And then cast a spell to cover Victricus in a paralyzing cloud that you plan to keep active for three days?" Daralan asked skeptically.

Silvi's hand was in Barra's again, protecting as much as supporting her. She repeated Barra's thought from her memory of the night before. "This will take as long as it takes. You can only cast a limited number of times before resting, so we will warn our people and go for them on different days."

Daralan nodded, "And we will reserve your magic for what is needed. With this as the priority, we will get by with no more healing or improved food. Now is our time to support you."

Reluctantly, Barra nodded. She wanted to do all of it. Heal all of them for real, including the Svekards. Cover all of Victricus, the empire, not just the capital city, and save all of the slaves. Communicate her existence back to the Central Tribe where the Neamairtese had gone weeks without a queen and were likely exceedingly scared that they had lost the Lady's magic forever. As queen, she should have gone to the

Central Tribe to take up her duties immediately upon being chosen. She also wanted to take Silvi back into their room and get to know every part of her over and over again while they still had time. Barra felt an impending pressure sitting on her shoulders as if time were slipping through her fingers and when it was gone, she would have nothing left.

"Today, we will solidify and communicate our plan. Tomorrow, we will save our people. Thousands of people we thought were dead, killed by Svekards or Neamairtese, were taken by the Victricites and enslaved. No more." Barra spoke in Neamairtese while Silvi repeated her words in Svekard. The Svekards roared approval while the Neamairtese simply nodded, an expression of unending faith directed at Barra.

Barra spent the rest of the day with Daralan, Terenesa, Redena, and Marsinus reviewing the spell, how it would be performed, and how new kindlers would be brought into the spell as they were freed. Silvi spent her day with Keepan and Tana strategizing with the consistent input of the rest of the Svekards. Slade was especially boisterous, throwing in only slightly helpful examples of the greatest battles and strategies of Svekard history. Barra barely registered their conversation. All she needed to know was that they would not attack until she inevitably failed to continue the spell.

Barra could tell Silvi was trying to present the end of the spell not as an inevitable failure, but a natural completion, when everyone was ready. She subtly implied that there was only a tiny chance Barra would fail them too early, but it was prudent to be prepared, nonetheless. Keepan and Tana had no qualms assuming loudly that Barra would not get them far. They planned battle after battle, from immediate failure at the docks, to the ultimate goal of reaching a day's journey beyond the wall of Victricus, where the Victricites were unlikely to follow them. As far as anyone could tell from what they had seen in their travel through Victricus, the Victricites within the wall liked their wide-brimmed hats that blocked the sun, their glass-windowed houses and their plump grapes. The hope was that the Victricites would only follow so far as they felt safe, which would end at the wall.

The majority of the scenarios took place in the city, surrounded by forces that could not be defeated and dying for their people's honor. Hadrone, god of death, would take their souls into the realm of glory.

Their plans only drove Barra to focus harder and plan more holistically. She didn't want anyone to die, gloriously or otherwise. If they did, it would be because she had failed.

Over dinner, Silvi asked, "What exactly can and can't magic do?" Even with Barra's memories, she wouldn't have a satisfying answer, a fact that Barra knew all too well.

Barra chuckled as she pulled a missed bone from her fish filet and took another bite. She swallowed before answering. "You've spoken Neamairtese for one day and managed to ask the central unanswerable question of Neamairtese religion. The truth is we have no idea. Magic is kind of like cooking. Your ancestors pass down recipes that you know have worked in the past, but you can still mess them up. Based on knowing what foods, spices, and methods go well together and achieve what you're looking for, you can also try any combination you want. Some new recipes make sense, others have a high chance of failure. The important thing is, when you fail, you spend a lot of important resources that can never be regained. And you always have to hold in the back of your mind the fear of poisoning your guests and the fact that any fire, big or small, can end up burning the whole village down."

"So, magic can do basically anything, but it may or may not work?" Silvi asked. Perhaps Barra's analogy hadn't been quite as useful as she hoped.

"Anything that uses air, water, earth, and fire in one way or another, yes, essentially. Every spell runs three potential risks," Barra explained, holding up a finger for each one. "One, that the spell fails or does something unintended, which could be minor or catastrophic. Two, that the Spirits refuse to help because I fail to evoke them properly, they don't think the result is worth the amount of energy that would have to be expended to accomplish it, or it is a result they disapprove of and I anger them. Then, I am limited to my own magic's power and they are less likely to help me in the future. Or three, the Spirits refuse to help because of any of the previous reasons or they can't do all that I am asking, and I use all of my magic, all of the queen's magic, to attempt it and lose the magic of the queens forever. If you think of magic like a plant, it'll help you understand. If you can take leaves from many plants, slowly over time, the plants will grow back. But if you ever cut too greedily, or you only have the one plant to pull from, it may never grow back. No more queens. No more magic."

She didn't like to think about the last option, but as she had said, it was a fact she had to keep ever present in her mind with each spell she cast. The truth was she had no idea how deep her well was, so how could she know what would make it run dry? All she had were the previous queens' memories and her own sense of the flow of the Spirits around her.

"If magic is so versatile, why didn't you use a spell to escape while we were marching?" Silvi asked. Barra could tell she was trying to tone it softly without accusation. Yes, the question played to her insecurity, but coming from Silvi it was simply a question for clarification. Silvi wanted to understand.

"To cast a spell long enough, large enough, or powerful enough to do more than run away temporarily and show the Victricites what I could do, I needed you. Ever since the king lost the Lord's magic, a queen is not whole without her mate. That first night I became queen, when I kissed you, I gave you a piece of my magic, the queen's magic. Without you, I am only a piece of the whole." Barra raised Silvi's fingers to her lips for an acceptable display of affection while surrounded by Svekards.

After dinner, Silvi, Barra, and Slade crafted the message that would be sent to all Svekards and Neamairtese. Barra had everything she needed in order to galvanize the Neamairtese slaves, but she would have to take an entirely different approach with the Svekards. If she sounded like a Neamairtese, using a Neamairtese trick, they would not follow her.

She wasn't allowed to "back into her sentences" as Silvi said the Neamairtese did when speaking. Her accent had to be strong and gruff, and she needed to reference all the right gods and heroes. Barra practiced until her throat hurt and beyond until even Keepan was satisfied.

The sun was setting over the blue horizon when Barra sat down with her spell materials to cast the spell. Silvi sat cross-legged across from her, the pink of the sky reflecting off her hair so that it almost looked red like Barra's as it fluttered in the gentle breeze off the sea. Barra ran through her script once more, wishing she could access Silvi's memory of it. Unfortunately, that wasn't how the magic worked. It was a one-time bonding, all memories after that were supposed to be created together.

Barra sat waiting for her moment. When the Spirits were ready, they would tell her. With Silvi by her side, she could likely cast the spell without their help, but it would take a significant amount of energy to cast her net that wide and she would need all of her energy for tomorrow. Barra heard the gust of wind before she felt it and let a sigh of relief slip through her lips. Air was ready. For a moment, the ship stilled, and the sound of slapping waves were silent. Water was ready. They would carry her message.

Two piles of items sat before Barra. At her right hand was a large pile of antler pieces, feathers, twigs, rocks, and brambles. These items had been donated to the spell by the Neamairtese. When possible, they'd chosen items that related to people they had lost to what had been assumed to be Svekard raids, or simply gone missing. On the top of the pile sat Helenda's feather. The items would not be consumed in the spell and the Neamairtese would each easily be able to find their treasured items afterward.

In the second, much smaller pile, sat a couple fish filets, a scrap of one of the damaged fish nets, a torn piece of cloth that several of the Svekards had rubbed under their arms, charcoal, and a dusting of hair clippings that Silvi and Eigen had begrudgingly provided. Each pile represented to their respective groups what it meant to be a Neamairtese or a Svekard. They would help Barra to contact all of their people.

Barra took a deep breath, placed a hand on each pile, and began to chant. Her arms tingled and her fingers began to twitch to an ancient pattern deep in her memory. She held the image of her people here on the ship in her mind and then the Svekards who had eaten side by side with her people. She drew back, as if climbing the tallest tree and looking down at them from afar.

Farther and farther, Barra climbed until the people on the ship were ants. But they weren't the only ants. Far off, she could see swarms of ants, Neamairtese and Svekards alike, milling, toiling, and living as best they could. This was how the spirit of Air saw all humans.

With a long, slow exhale, Barra let her mind slip from its solid, singular position looking down on her people. She let the spirit of Air carry her over the spirit of Water until she was with her people, not looking down at them, but looking out through them.

Barra started in Neamairtese, explaining to her people that she was the Lord and Lady's new chosen queen and that she was coming for them. She explained the cloud that would freeze their Victricite masters and the plan to gather and head north together. She warned them not to attack the Victricites and to bring only what they needed most for the journey. She told them that the Svekards would be coming with them and were to be treated as allies. Most of all, she told them to have hope and to be ready. Their people were coming for them.

With a shuddering breath, Barra turned mentally to the Svekards and felt her mouth go dry. She was about to lie to them. Silvi had told Barra that if she wanted to ask the Svekards to trust her, to follow her into danger and risk their lives to save her people and theirs, she would have to trust them. She did, but how could she ask them to trust her if she was about to claim to be someone other than who she was?

Barra licked her lips and opened her mouth, but nothing came out. It wasn't just some moral belief stopping her. It was fear. She couldn't speak Svekard without conviction and heart. She couldn't speak with either when it was a beautifully crafted lie. The Svekards would know she was a Neamairtese using tricksy Neamairtese magic to manipulate them. They would rebel against her plan. What would happen if they warned the Victricites? What if they attacked either the Victricites or the Neamairtese? All would be lost.

Faintly, Barra felt Silvi take her hand from the pile of Neamairtese treasures and hold it between both of hers. Barra could just make out Silvi's words. "My name is Barra, and I am a Neamairtese," Silvi said in Svekard. "I'm here with my sister, Silvi of Clan Spine Mountain." Silvi used the Svekard word that had no direct translation to Neamairtese except honorary sister. To give someone the title of family member was the greatest statement of kinship and love. "She is a Gods-chosen hero with a message for you and I will use my magic to share it with you."

Barra gave Silvi's hand a grateful squeeze and repeated her words with all the conviction and strength she had in her. It wasn't just faith in the Svekards, their plan, or even herself. The root of her strength was her mate. The foundation of her faith was Silvi. Where Silvi had faltered on "Gods-chosen" Barra did not. Whether or not she had been chosen by Svekard gods, she had been chosen by the Lady and she had been the right choice.

Barra finished the speech as they had written it, her hand never leaving Silvi's. She spoke of heroes and rising above during dark times.

She spoke of self-restraint and the taste of victory and freedom. Most of all, she spoke of the Svekard will to survive and thrive.

Their plan and the rules of their plan were woven into the speech, but were not the topic, as they had been for the Neamairtese version. Svekards didn't like to be told what to do. They liked to be told why. As Barra ended the speech, she added one last direct plea to not attack a single Victricite—for their people, their clans, their families.

Barra let the spell go, releasing her connection to Air and Water, and centering on her connection to Silvi. She opened her eyes to the most gorgeous, tender expression she thought she'd ever see in her life. Silvi reached out to pet her cheek before closing the distance for a chaste kiss. They drew back at the sound of boots on the deck.

"That was beautiful," Tana said, brushing her eyes to stop a tear from slipping down her cheek. Hers were the driest eyes amongst the group of nearly fifty Svekards. They had heard the speech not from Barra's lips, but in their heads. They'd risen and fallen with her cadence and become steadfast with her calls to action. "They will follow you both anywhere."

"Thank you," Barra said, allowing Silvi to pull her to her feet. The spell had been substantial, but she'd taken her time. Barra was tired, but not so tired as to ignore the soft, warm feel of Silvi's hand in her own, the heat radiating off both of their bodies, and the ache in her heart. She'd never felt so loved, and all she wanted right now was to take Silvi to bed and show her how she made Barra feel. The Svekard response to being so deeply moved might be tears, but the Neamairtese responded much more sensuously. "I must rest for tomorrow. As everyone knows their role, I will see you in the morning. May your gods be with you."

"Our clanbed tonight will pray for our victory," Keepan assured them as they turned and returned to the captain's quarters where the bed was calling to Barra.

Barra gave the group a nod before looking up to the back of the ship where the Neamairtese were gathered for the night. They had adapted well to the sea, given Barra's earlier remedy, and that area of the ship provided the best place to sleep together under the stars. Her people gave her a nod in return before placing two fingers over their hearts and tipping their heads down. Barra and Silvi returned the gesture before closing the door behind them.

As the door clicked shut, Silvi took Barra into her arms. "You were amazing."

Barra accepted and deepened Silvi's kiss, working her hands up under Silvi's shirt. "I couldn't have done that without you," she said as she pulled Silvi's shirt over her head and nuzzled into Silvi's warm chest. Silvi smelled like salt, olive oil, and cooked fish where she'd drawn Ilode's symbol on her chest after each meal. Under that was the musk that was uniquely Silvi. It smelled like a late spring hunt— the smokiness of fire, the tang of sweat, and the earthiness of arousal. She unlaced her bra and buried her face in Silvi's ample cleavage. Barra loved the way Silvi's pounding heart matched her own heart's rhythm.

"You are my strength," Barra whispered as Silvi removed Barra's top and breast wrap. She moaned at Silvi's kisses and gentle bites.

"You are my everything," Silvi whispered back, her breath dancing over Barra's bare stomach. She removed Barra's pants and underwear, her entire focus between Barra's legs.

This was supposed to be me showing her how much I love her, Barra thought as her legs quivered below her. Every time she was with Silvi she was struck by how near to orgasm she felt just from the lightest of kisses and caresses. The feeling of Silvi's breath against her had her ready to explode with bliss.

Barra's fingernails dug into Silvi's shoulders as Silvi pleasured her. She was going to enjoy this night knowing that whatever came tomorrow and the days after was out of her hands tonight. Silvi, on the other hand, was deliciously in her grasp.

Never in a million lifetimes would she have chosen Silvi as her mate. Now, there was not a doubt in her mind that Silvi was her heart's mate. This was not a relationship of convenience—a random Svekard to bridge the divide between their people. Every time Barra felt herself falter, Silvi was there to steady her. She was a natural leader, and it didn't hurt that she had a gorgeous body. Whatever the next few days held, she would follow where the Spirits and the Lord and Lady guided her, devoutly.

"Take me to the bed," Barra panted, unsure if her legs had the power to carry her there.

"Are you sure we should be…you know, since you need to rest?" Silvi asked, raising almost to Barra's height. Her pupils were dilated with lust. Her expression said I want you, but I want what's best for you more.

"Yes," Barra murmured, her tone almost a growl. This was exactly what she loved about Silvi and it only made her want her more. "I need to be with you tonight. It is how I will have the energy to do what must be done."

Silvi scooped her into her arms effortlessly. She laid Barra out on the bed and disrobed completely except for the ring on the chain around her neck before joining Barra. Barra rose to meet her, their bodies entwining, saying, "If I'm your everything, let me give you everything I've got to give."

CHAPTER THIRTEEN
A TRUE SVEKARD

The distant sound of commotion pulled Silvi from her blissful sleep. Her body told her not to respond, just to let the warmth of Barra's naked body pressed against her own and the heady smell of sex carry her back into dreams of a never-ending summer. The rational part of Silvi's brain would not allow such dishonorable folly. Her people were preparing for a combat they could only guess at, planning for every eventuality even though they had no idea what would stand on the horizon or what might sneak up behind them.

Barra would be at the center of it all and the thought scared Silvi. She had immense power to save Barra, but what if it wasn't enough? What if the spell was more than Barra could handle?

Silvi had been the one to say they had to go back and save all of their people. Now, all she wanted was to hold Barra close and never let her go. Why did saving her people have to put Barra in danger?

"It's time, isn't it?" Barra asked, tipping Silvi's head up from its place on Barra's breast to kiss her.

"The scout ship will be leaving now," Silvi said, unwilling to say yes. "We will set sail soon."

Barra gave her a mirthful smile and said suggestively, "So we have plenty of time for licking the lower lips?" Despite her words, which were doing a number on Silvi's resolve, Barra sat up and began the process of extricating herself from the plushiness of the bed and the warm comfort of Silvi's body. Barra had meant it as a joke, but it only made getting out of bed that much harder.

"Why do you have five terms for the same sexual act? You seem to have at least five terms for every single sexual act," Silvi said, a blush creeping up her neck. She hoped if she asked it would decrease her overwhelming desire to pull Barra back down onto the bed and enact one of those many sexual acts. They really didn't have time.

Barra shrugged, locating her undergarments. "For the same reason you have five ways to say son or daughter of. It makes storytelling flow better and sound more interesting when you have multiple ways to say the things you are going to say most often." Barra tipped her head to the side in momentary confusion as she searched her memories. "Why can't I remember any Svekard smut? There isn't even a direct translation for the word, only 'a story about sex.' Don't your people have stories? Don't they talk about it?"

"No!" Silvi burst out, almost insulted and perhaps repulsed by the idea. She knew Barra was speaking Neamairtese because the word smut definitely didn't exist in her language. "We have so many stories, but never about sex, no sex between anybody."

"Well, that sounds boring," Barra said with a grin. She'd almost finished dressing and was looking at Silvi expectantly.

"But," Silvi stammered. "But sex is so personal. Why would you tell a story about sex? It would only make everyone uncomfortable."

Silvi had been expecting her to simply say, "It's fun," but Barra surprised her with an answer that engaged Svekard values rather than Neamairtese. "For the same reason that mothers tell their daughters stories about raising children, or friends tell each other where to find the best berries or grow the best crops, or even the reason chieftains tell stories about their best bear hunts. Stories are the way we teach each other, the way we brag, and the way we share our lives. How can you value stories so much and not incorporate such a key piece of life into them? You have stories about all aspects of your life except sex, but sex is something that is safest and best when you know what it means and go in with open eyes. I think Svekards do themselves a disservice by not talking about it."

It was Silvi's turn to dress while contemplating Barra's words. She understood the value of what Barra was saying for the Neamairtese, but she wasn't so sure the logic truly applied to the Svekards. Sure, she'd been afraid the first time she'd had sex with Barra, but not because her society hadn't taught her about it. She had been afraid because to

Neamairtese sex wasn't personal or private. Her people didn't demonize sex, they just didn't talk about it. They certainly weren't about to change their minds on that just because they could create great epics about it and teach the younger adults to be better at it. That wasn't really what Barra was saying, but that's how the Svekards would understand it. Just because Silvi could understand both Barra's perspective and that of her own people didn't mean anyone else could.

"I need to prepare for the spell," Barra said, stepping up behind Silvi to help her finish braiding her hair. It was becoming a morning ritual of theirs, and Silvi loved the way Barra's fingers felt petting her hair and massaging her scalp. "Are you going to pray to the Gods?"

It was a question Silvi had been asking herself since breakfast the day before. If she was a hero, she should be asking the Gods to bring them victory. If she wasn't, she supposed the worst thing that could happen was the Gods ignored her. There weren't any stories about Svekards being smote for praying to the Gods when they had no right to do so. Then again, Silvi supposed anyone who brought upon themselves the smite of the Gods wouldn't particularly be able to tell anyone what they had done to deserve it.

If Silvi was honest with herself, it wasn't fear of not being a hero that was making her question praying, it was fear of being a hero and not living up to it. What if one of the Gods touched her and she didn't have the will or strength to withstand it? What if they directed her to do or be something she just couldn't? What if they demanded that she forsake Barra and the Neamairtese? Not asking the Gods seemed better than invoking the wrath of the Gods.

"White liver," Silvi whispered, calling herself a coward before turning to take Barra's hands in her own. "Yes, I'm going to pray. Please don't start the spell without me?" Silvi wasn't sure what the spell would entail, but she wanted to be there if anything went wrong. She suppressed a shudder as she considered again what might happen if Barra put too much of herself into the spell and it failed.

"Never," Barra replied, leaning her head down for a kiss. "I love you...and I believe in you."

Silvi tried to give a self-deprecating laugh, but found she had no space in her chest for it. It was as if her heart was trying to push out all of the negativity and focus on one fact. "I love you too."

Barra gave Silvi one more kiss before slipping out of the room and closing the door behind her.

The captain's quarters seemed unreasonably spacious and dead to Silvi as she stood in the silent room. Now was her moment and she had no one else to wait for or rely on.

Silvi's first problem wasn't just how to pray, but who to pray to. The Gods, much like the clans, didn't much like each other. They were siblings and cousins, and when they needed to, they all had each other's back, just as a Svekard would have any other Svekard's back against an outside threat. That didn't keep them from fighting tooth and nail in the heavens every time it rained. For that reason, Silvi couldn't just pray to "the Gods." Unlike the clanbed, she had to pick one to direct her message to.

For a long moment, Silvi stood, looking from the hearth to the swords hung above the captain's map table. With a deep breath, she nodded. If she was going to be a hero, she was going to do it her way. Leapora, goddess of protection and the family, goddess of Silvi's lineage, was her choice.

Silvi took up position in front of the cast-iron stove, prostrating herself before a hearth and thus a token of Leapora's ever present power in the world. Silvi took several more deep breaths, telling herself at the start of each one that this was the one, after this inhale she'd start. On every exhale, she reminded herself that everyone was counting on her.

Enough long, slow breaths later, and Silvi was pretty sure she was going to make herself pass out from not breathing normally if she didn't stop. Just say something, she coached herself.

"Leapora," Silvi stuttered, then chided herself for a weak call to a powerful goddess. "Leapora," she said again with the dedication owed to the goddess. "Goddess of protection and the family, goddess of my lineage, who brings us heat to fight off the cold, blesses our families with strong children and loving kinship, and serves as our shield in times of need, I call to thee."

Silvi had never heard anyone pray, but she assumed that if her Gods were anything like Barra's gods and Spirits, which of course she knew they weren't, they probably liked to be called and welcomed. Such naming had a long and detailed history in Svekard culture, so Silvi pulled several more epithets from the storytellers' epics when describing Leapora.

When she felt she'd spent about as much time as wouldn't seem boring to a goddess who surely knew her own name and role in the universe, Silvi switched to her ask. "Please, watch over us as we embark on this journey to liberate our people. Be our shield and our fire. Bring us together as a clan of one Svekard family to defeat our enemies and repair our broken homes." The words felt flowery in her own mouth, but it seemed like the thing to do.

"Let me..."

Silvi paused for a moment. Was she allowed to or even supposed to mention herself? What about the Neamairtese? If she was honest about what she wanted and needed, she would ask the Gods to protect them too, but would doing so illegitimize the rest of her prayer and drive away the Gods' help?

Terenesa's words came to her via Barra's memory. "I didn't have anyone to teach me," she had told Barra. Terenesa had closed herself off and offered the Spirits a broken home. If Silvi was going to be a hero, if she even could be, she was going to be honest and clear. This group without the Neamairtese was a broken home, and without Barra her fire couldn't burn. "Let me be a bright flame to fight off the darkness for both our peoples...and please keep Barra safe."

Silvi ended the prayer by carving Leapora's symbol into the room's wooden floor with a wide, sturdy dagger Barra had found in the map table drawers when looking for her memory trinket. She thanked Leapora for all that was her life.

"See, that wasn't so bad," Silvi said under her breath, hoping that if Leapora had been listening she wasn't listening to that comment or the second prayer she was about to give. She could only send a prayer to one god at a time, but she hoped she could pray to more than one by doing so separately. What if Leapora wasn't her patron god? She was almost assuredly headed into battle. It might not happen today or even tomorrow, but what if Klucar was the one preening her to lead her people to freedom and victory?

Silvi turned her back to the stove and the symbol she'd drawn and took one of the swords off the wall. It was the weapon from which she had pulled the chain that rested around her neck. She drew the sword from its scabbard, letting the soft noise of metal on metal fill the room for a moment, before stabbing the tip of the sword into the floor.

"Klucar," Silvi announced, her stance wide and unshakable. She was glad she had left Klucar for second. If she had addressed him with a warble in her voice, she might as well have abandoned the prayer right there. "God of war, bringer of victory, slayer of the enemies of Svek, and father of true honor. God of blood and rage, progenitor of berserkers, who fights for Svekard life, culture, and dominance. Bringer of strength and destroyer of weakness. I call thee."

Silvi felt like she was getting the hang of the calling part of praying. These were titles and descriptions she'd heard since before she could remember. Crafting an ask that was equally tailored was not as easy. What she wanted wasn't really to slaughter the Victricites. If Keepan were the one praying, maybe. If Barra were the one praying, never. What she definitely didn't want was an army of a thousand berserkers that might turn on the Neamairtese the moment the last Victricite was down…if not sooner.

"Be our sword against the enemy that seeks to enslave and dishonor us. Lead us to victory and freedom so all Svekards can live an honorable life as true Svekards. Let me be the commander that our people need and let the battle only begin when we can win it." Silvi carved Klucar's symbol with the dagger, leaving the sword planted in the middle of the mark.

Lastly, Silvi turned to the bookcase. "Fradren, god of justice and order." Silvi kept her tone calm and smooth, telling her heart to stop pounding in her chest. "Father of oath keepers, writer of the bond which holds all Svekards in covenant with the Gods, and final judge of all Svekard souls. I call thee."

If any of the Gods didn't need pomp and circumstance, it was Fradren.

"Help us to right the wrongs that have befallen our people and strengthen our alliances." Silvi wasn't entirely sure how to say what she needed to express with flashy words, but she hoped it wasn't entirely necessary or this prayer was about to stop being much of a prayer. "It is really important that everyone follows instructions, and no one attacks the Victricites inside the fog cloud. Also, please help the Svekards keep their covenant with the Neamairtese and not attack them either. We really need them."

Silvi gave a smile that she hoped would serve as an apology if she'd overstepped and carefully carved Fradren's symbol. While her request to him had lacked showiness, he of all the Gods would appreciate the time devoted to doing an intricate task correctly. She gave the room with its three symbols etched into the floor one more look before pulling the door open and marching out onto the deck.

The dawn-lit deck was completely absent of Svekards as Silvi stepped out into the early morning mist. The Svekards were all either above her in the rigging or below deck, manning the oars. With the wind at their backs and Svekards rowing, they would reach Victricus in no time.

It was time to start the spell.

Barra sat at the center of the lower deck, surrounded by Neamairtese all seeming to be trying to find a balance between being actively attentive to Barra's every need and providing her the space she needed in order to work. Next to Barra sat her three kindlers. Behind her, Marsinus held a bucket of water between his legs, whispering to it as if it were a cat curled up in his lap. To her left, Redena had her hands cupped in front of her face and was similarly whispering to a handful of salt. She looked like at any moment she might take a deep breath and blow it across the deck. To her right, Terenesa was quietly chanting, twirling her arms in the empty space in front of her face like a dancer acting out the prologue to a great epic. Barra was holding a torch that she was coaxing into a small steady flame rather than allowing it to burn itself out prematurely.

As Silvi approached, Barra looked up, her face lit by a gorgeous smile. I make her smile just by existing, Silvi thought, knowing it was true for her as well.

Barra pushed to her feet, careful to keep the torch steady, and beckoned Silvi over. "Your prayers went better than you feared?"

Silvi didn't hold back her chuckle. It was odd to have someone besides Papa, who had observed her all her life, understand her so well. She didn't doubt that relief was written into her features but that didn't make the ability to read it any less impressive to Silvi. She nodded. "They did...I think. I guess we shall see."

The statement made her think about the unknown that lay ahead of them. She wished the Svekards would slow down on the oars. She wished the winds would die down. She wished she could just have a little more time.

"It's time," Barra said, holding out the torch to Silvi. "My kindlers will be in charge of engaging with Water, Earth, and Air to strengthen and broaden the spell. You will be in charge of Fire, who will help keep me awake."

"But I don't do magic!" Silvi burst out. She shook her head. How could Barra think this was a good idea? If the plan for Barra staying awake relied on Silvi, their plan was even more doomed than the Svekards feared.

One hundred people, who had specifically been chosen for being in their prime, had walked the length of Victricus City in three days. Pushed forward constantly by soldiers who were used to marching day in and day out, half of whom were mounted, their people had walked a solid ten hours a day. The people they were rescuing would not be able to keep up such a pace. Barra needed her Fire spell to stay awake long enough to lead all of their people to safety. Fire needed someone better than Silvi.

"The spell is cast. What I need isn't for you to know magic or be able to engage with the spirit of Fire. I just need you to keep the torch near me." Barra smiled fondly at the small blaze of the torch the way Silvi might look at her niece or nephew. She continued as if giving directions to a caretaker for her child. "Keep it out of the rain, off the ground, and not burning everything down. All I need is for you to be my literal torchbearer."

Silvi took the torch hesitantly. A large part of her wanted to cradle it rather than simply gripping the bottom. The torch was unreasonably light in her hand, and the moment she took it, she could feel its power. Her whole arm buzzed with the life dancing at the end of the dense stick.

"You can pass it off to someone else to hold when you need to eat and sleep. While it is your job to make sure it is near me, it is not your job to hold it every moment. I expect you to sleep." Barra paused to give Silvi an unwavering stare to make sure she made her point clear. "Much as I would like it to do so, you will not be kept awake by this spell and I will need you rested and at your strongest to protect me and all of us. Do you understand?"

Silvi nodded dutifully. It would be hard to go to sleep knowing Barra couldn't, but there was a clear logic to it.

"One last thing, if you talk to me while I'm in the spell, it will help me to ground myself. Talking back to you won't be possible, but I like to hear your voice and it will help me stay awake too, just having something to listen to." Barra looked sad, as if she were going to miss Silvi while in the spell as much as Silvi was going to miss her.

They would be side by side the whole time. Silvi expected that she would be carrying Barra a good deal of the time. But the distance would feel unbearable. "Too bad I don't know any Svekard smut." She chuckled, wishing she had something moving or heartfelt to say to express how she was feeling.

"Ready?" Barra asked. Her tone said she was ready for anything, but her eyes revealed her true hesitance. She came across bold and brave and Silvi knew she was, but Silvi also knew how much insecurity that bravery and boldness hid.

"No," Silvi whispered in Svekard loud enough for only Barra to hear. She was glad no Svekards were there to watch as she snaked her right arm up around Barra's shoulder. She pulled Barra in as close as she could, dipping her slightly to the right to plant a heated kiss on her lips.

Barra's eyes were glowing, and her lips were lifted into a radiant smile as Silvi pulled back and righted her. Silvi gave an embarrassed smile. "I guess I can be ready now."

Barra just smiled, clearly pleased, and nodded. She returned to her seated spot in the middle of her kindlers and tapped the deck in front of her, indicating for Silvi to sit as well. Barra's eyes were closed as Silvi took her seat. The spell had begun and all Silvi could do was watch and hold the torch that was still vibrating softly in her hand.

Even with Barra's memories, the experience of watching a spell cast still seemed strange to Silvi. The way Barra's eyes rolled concerningly far back in her head, the odd language she muttered, and the crazed animal noises she called made Silvi shudder, despite her attempts to act like this was totally reasonable behavior. It's an ancient form of connecting to the natural world, Silvi told herself. She could remember someone telling Barra that when she was very young, but like Barra, she couldn't remember exactly who.

The Neamairtese around them had gone deathly quiet the moment the spell began. They held hands in ad hoc circles around Barra, heads bowed reverently. The only sound besides that of Barra and her kindlers came from the wind pulling at the rigging and the oars slapping into the water at the sides of the ship.

As the chanting continued, the sound of the oars began to fade and the distinct smell of salt with an overtone of pungent earthy thickness filled the air. Had Silvi not been able to see the wide-open sea around them, she would have sworn she was in a bog.

A chill ran down Silvi's back and the hairs on the back of her neck stood on end. She had the eerie feeling of being stalked as prey and the irrational need to check her blind spot. Silvi turned slowly in her seated position, her eyes shifting first, followed by her head, until she could see the railing at the edge of the ship behind her.

The first cloud of purple-ish fog came over the edge of the ship in a long, spindly thread, like a finger of a giant sea hag. Several more fingers followed suit, spreading out into a thin blanket once they reached the deck. Silvi told herself that this was supposed to happen, but felt the barely controllable urge to run, nonetheless. She turned with frantic speed to see similar fingers bubbling up over the side of the deck in front of her.

She shouldn't rise. She shouldn't run. She was a Svekard and she wasn't scared. She was Barra's mate, and she was not afraid of magic.

Silvi tried to bring up memories from Barra of magic doing good. Instead, she found memory after memory of intense imagery from Svekard tales of witchcraft as a ghastly doom.

The fog would have her in a moment.

Silvi took a deep breath, knowing that it was her last before she would be enveloped by the fog. She could feel the fog pressing in on all sides and not just around her. The fog of panic was blanketing her mind as it had the deck. Run! It shouted, just run!

Silvi's fists clenched around something hard and warm. It was buzzing pleasantly in Silvi's hands like a purring kitten. She was holding Barra's torch, her flame. She, Silvi, was Barra's torchbearer, her flame. The fog was Barra's, and she was Barra's. They would not hurt each other.

She held her breath as she watched the Neamairtese test the air, taking it in small sips and then full deep breaths. Doing her best to copy their approach, Silvi allowed the fog to fill her lungs. There was a stickiness and a girth to it that seemed to move in her lungs as if the fog itself was a living thing. It took several more breaths before Silvi was sure she wasn't going to vomit.

I liked the soup spell better, Silvi thought.

The fog was now encasing the whole of the ship and stretching farther in every direction. As it stretched, it thinned. Where Silvi had barely been able to see the Neamairtese around her, she could now see up to the crow's nest at the top of the ship where an obscured figure was just barely visible, retching into a bucket.

Oh Gods, Silvi thought to herself, imagining the Svekards below her who would have seen the fog bubble in through the oar holes as they rowed. Worse, they would have been forced to breathe it in while it was still dense.

"Stay the oars," came a muffled Svekard call from above them. The call was unnecessary, as the oars had gone still several seconds before, but ship protocol was what kept everyone safe. This ship was much larger than what the Svekards built at home, making clear attention to process necessary.

The figure sliding down the rigging was barely recognizable until she was on the deck a few feet away. Tana approached Silvi cautiously, her gaze flicking to Barra and the kindlers every second or two. "I can't see anything out there," Tana whispered, her tone barely hiding her repressed panic. Her bloodshot eyes told Silvi she was functioning off myopic dedication to her task and now that task was being impeded and she was ready to snap. "I won't know when we've reached the docks until we're smashing into them."

Silvi held out her free arm to Tana, palm up. She wouldn't even consider touching her until her offer was accepted. Tana took Silvi's arm, gripping her forearm as Silvi gripped Tana's arm in a gesture of solidarity. "The fog is thinning," Silvi said, surprising herself with the calmness and steadiness of her voice. "With some time, we should be able to see again. I will check on our oarsfolk. We'll start going again when everyone is ready."

Tana nodded and Silvi could see the red starting to drain from her eyes and return to her cheeks. Tana was still breathing in small gasps, but she was no longer exhaling as if she was vomiting from her lungs each time.

Silvi gave Tana's arm one last assuring squeeze before they released and parted, Tana heading back to the crow's nest and Silvi heading for the lower decks. Barra needed to focus on the spell and it was Silvi's job, aside from keeping the torch safe, to make sure everything around her went smoothly. The torch would keep Barra awake, but there was no reason for Barra to be tired yet, meaning Silvi was needed more below decks. She wasn't looking forward to what she would find. She gave Barra one last glance to make sure she would be okay in Silvi's absence before heading to the stairs, torch in hand.

The acrid smell of the lower deck reached Silvi before she'd even put her first foot on the stairs. The Svekard whose job was to relay messages from outlooks like Tana gave Silvi a tight-lipped, half-smile and nod as she passed.

The fog was just starting to thin in the rowing area and was snaking up the steps. What Silvi saw as she came down far enough to take in the room filled her heart with pride.

Five Svekards were on hands and knees scrubbing up the partially digested remains of the Svekard breakfasts, while two Svekards swapped their dirty water buckets for fresh buckets of sea water. The remaining thirty Svekards sat, backs straight, feet anchored, hands gripping the oars, ready at a moment's notice to begin rowing again. Slade stood on the row master's platform, a small drum in one hand, his expression as stoic and fierce as his clansfolk.

They'd just puked their stomachs empty, but even that couldn't distract them from the task at hand. They were warriors and they were headed to save their people.

"We're ready," Slade said through clenched teeth.

"We're Svekards," Silvi responded, head held high. Her words were met with a rumbling grunt of prideful agreement. No one yelled while on the oars in case directions were needed.

Silvi gave her clansfolk one last nod before returning above deck. The fog had thinned enough for Silvi to see the edges of the ever-widening cloud. It stretched at least a mile and Silvi estimated it would reach another couple of miles in every direction by the time Barra reached her current limit. Once they had more kindlers, they hoped to stretch the cloud wider to cover the whole width of Victricus City.

"On your call," Silvi yelled up to the outlooks on the masts.

"Slow and steady," came Tana's call, echoed by the Svekard at the top of the stairs. Silvi went to the side to watch the water rushing below them and stare out at the endless blue, blanketed in a thin, purple sheen.

Silvi returned to her seated place next to Barra and watched her concentrate. Talk to me, Barra had said. It seemed odd and even rude to do so, especially when all of the Neamairtese were continuing to stand in complete silence around them. But Silvi had to assume that Barra knew what she needed and perhaps a little noise would make the whole scene a little less eerie.

"Have I ever told you about the time," Silvi started in typical Svekard fashion. She reached out and placed her free hand on Barra's knee and squeezed gently. "My little brother Yelt was put in charge of getting all the cats out of the mill. The cats kept out the rats, but in the springtime, at the end of the winter wheat harvest, when we started up the mill, the cats had to be chased out so they wouldn't get in the way. Yelt was six years old at the time, and he had a terrible lisp that my sisters and I found wonderfully hilarious. The three of us stood at the door watching him run around, chasing the cats and listening to him yell, 'Kittieth, kittieth, go on kittieth, kittieth.' We laughed at him and he heard us and got really upset.

"'I can't do it!' he screamed at us and went to pout on top of one of the piles of unmilled winter wheat. Well, the stack was not as steady as it looked, and he went tumbling down. He was unhurt, but it only made him cry harder.

"Greta told him, 'That's what happens when you cry. A true Svekard doesn't cry when they're sad or hurt.' And she and Nita left to go tell our parents. Greta and Nita were always like that, wherever Greta went, Nita followed. When Greta said something was some way, Nita nodded and said, 'Yeah.' Yelt and I were always much closer than I was to either of them."

Silvi remembered how much it hurt to see Nita and Greta run off together without her when she was too young and the way she'd bonded to Yelt. He had needed her, and she had needed to be needed.

"I went to comfort him and help him stop crying. He wasn't a baby anymore and he wasn't supposed to cry, but making fun of him was only making things worse. 'I jutht wanned to be good add it, Thilvi,' he told me." Silvi mimicked Yelt's lisp as best she could. She'd always found it endearing, if amusing.

"I wrapped my arms around him and asked him why the cats would want to leave the nice warm mill and go out into the cold spring air. 'Becauthe we need to thtart the mill. They could get cruthed,' Yelt answered. 'Well, they don't know that,' I told him. 'Why would they want to leave?'

"Yelt just shrugged, so I told him to run to the barn and get some milk and put it in a bowl. When he returned with the bowl, we placed it outside the barn, and soon all the cats were there pushing to get a bit before their brothers and sisters finished it off. Yelt closed the door while the cats drank, and when Greta and Nita returned with our parents to show them that Yelt was crying, instead they found the swarm of cats all outside, Yelt standing triumphantly amongst them.

"The look he gave me over Papa's shoulder as he reveled in Papa's hug told me this was what I wanted to do for the rest of my life. He used to bring me birds with broken wings and cats with bleeding scratches and bite wounds. One day he told me that he thought Greta and Nita were wrong. Crying or not crying was not what determined if you were a true Svekard. Helping or not helping was what determined if you were a true Svekard. He said that when he wanted to act like a true Svekard, he tried to act like me."

Silvi let go of Barra's hand to brush at her eyes and stop the tears that threatened to well up. She hadn't felt like a true Svekard since the day Yelt had fallen through the ice and she hadn't been able to help him. Not until today. It was why she'd picked this story in particular to tell Barra. She was proud of her people, and she wanted to be proud of herself. Looking out at the blue and purple horizon, she knew that this, leading her clan to save their people, was what Yelt had meant.

CHAPTER FOURTEEN
A LASTING FLAME

Barra was in someone's arms, but all she knew was that it wasn't Silvi holding her. A part of Barra wanted to open her eyes to understand who, why, where. The thin, male frame holding her was most likely Daralan.

Barra mentally slapped herself. She didn't have time to focus on who had replaced the warm, soft comfort of her lover with a bony shoulder. If she was being carried, they'd reached the docks and that meant she needed to reshape the fog cloud. Rather than being a circle, which was easiest to maintain, she needed an oval that would stretch as wide as possible.

They didn't need to worry about the Victricites ahead of them, who had no idea what was causing the haze coming for them. Nor did they need to be overly concerned with the Victricites unfreezing behind them as they would have no way to enter the cloud without becoming refrozen. What they did need to worry about were the slaves they might miss on the sides and the risk of the Victricites behind them warning the Victricites in front of them. If that happened, the Neamairtese and Svekard slaves could be targeted and Barra couldn't allow that.

Barra was barely into the process of reshaping when she felt her carrier reach stable ground. The sensation was relieving, but nothing compared to the feeling a moment later when whoever was carrying her handed her off and she felt herself placed on Silvi's back. She could feel her warmth, smell her musk, and if she held very still, she could sense the bond that held their hearts in sync.

Silvi was holding Barra's left arm over her shoulder and Barra's right leg at her hip. Barra could faintly feel the buzz of the torch against her ankle. It was silly for Silvi to be carrying her and the torch at the same time, but Barra was infinitely grateful that she was.

"I've got you." Silvi's whisper barely made it through the fog that lived and swirled in Barra's brain. It was all Barra needed to let go and focus solely on the spell. Silvi would take care of everything else.

Time meant nothing to Barra.

At some point, she'd been moved from Silvi's back to a cart, but Silvi was still by her side and that was all that mattered to Barra. Her kindlers were somewhere nearby, likely also on carts. Their group had obtained two more kindlers, and Barra could feel their efforts combining with Terenesa's, Redena's, and Marsinus's. She was having to put more of her energy into controlling the cloud and less into maintaining it.

Barra marked the passage of the day by the addition of new kindlers and the beginning of new stories, as Silvi told her one after another. Barra didn't have the mental space to follow the majority of Silvi's stories, but every once in a while, enough key words would float through and would trigger one of Silvi's memories inside Barra's head. She'd get the gist of the story before letting it wash over her.

The stories weren't the important part. Hearing Silvi's voice was what mattered.

It was very late by Barra's estimation when Silvi stopped her constant narration.

Barra's first reaction was to check the stability of the cloud. Surely, she wasn't losing it already! What had interrupted Silvi?

The soft press of Silvi's lips to her forehead cast aside her fears. "I'm going to sleep, but I'll be right here," Silvi said. "Eigen is going to keep telling you stories tonight, and he'll hold the torch right here, so you won't get tired." After another second, Barra felt Silvi's lips press a gentle kiss to her temple. "I love you," Silvi whispered in her ear.

In her cross-legged position on the cart, Barra could feel Silvi curl up behind her. The last thing Silvi did before falling asleep was drape her arm over Barra's leg protectively. How does she always know, Barra asked herself.

Eigen was no storyteller, though Barra could see the seedlings of skill in his creatively depicted stories. He had amazing word choice, though every few sentences he'd overreach for a word that wasn't quite the one he'd meant to use. His cadence had promise, if not for the constant halting stops when he realized that he hadn't given all the necessary information or wanted to go back and change the way he'd worded something earlier for greater effect.

Barra didn't mind. It was his enthusiasm and continued effort that kept her focused. With the torch by her side, she didn't feel the least bit sleepy, and with Silvi curled around her, she didn't feel the least bit tired. It was only the first night after all.

❖

Their group was growing faster than Silvi could track. Throughout the first day of the journey, they'd moved like dark syrup in the middle of winter. Her people, Svekards and Neamairtese alike, had spread out to the far reaches of the cloud to make sure no slave was left behind. They'd broken gates, doors, and locks. Where necessary, Svekards had grabbed what weapons they could and embarked outside the cloud to retrieve those outside the early limitations of the cloud.

They'd gained hundreds of people that first day. It was nothing compared to the second day.

With more kindlers, the cloud stretched farther to each side of Barra than the distance between clans. With more and more people, there were plenty to check every house and structure they passed without slowing the pace of Barra and Silvi's cart.

The cart was a four-wheeled wagon with several long wooden planks making a flat bed and a thin wooden fence for protecting goods meant for trade. It was drawn by two mules that were yoked to the wagon. Silvi hadn't thought she would ever want to see a yoke again, but finding the cart at the docks had felt like a godsend.

From her vantage point in the cart, Silvi couldn't see much of the growing crowd around them. Several Svekards and Neamairtese had been stationed in a circle around them to deter interruptions. Silvi didn't like feeling so disconnected from the people around her, even if it was to her and Barra's benefit to be isolated.

Based on what Silvi could see, the former Neamairtese and Svekard slaves seemed to get along better than her group had before escaping together. Both groups walked in clumps of their own people but didn't avoid similar clumps of the other group. From time to time,

Silvi even saw Svekards and Neamairtese speaking to each other in the Victricite language when they needed to cross paths or communicate important information.

Barra had mentioned that a common enemy brought people together, but Silvi had a feeling that shared struggle was just as effective.

Throughout the days, the former slaves scavenged for people and the resources they would need for the journey home. Late into the night, they found what comfort they could in the Victricite homes, barns, fields, or in the middle of the streets if they had to. That was becoming more and more necessary as their numbers reached in the thousands on the third day. The cloud was wide, but it wasn't deep enough to afford them significant mobility.

Their pace was slow and steady, stopping at night to make sure they didn't leave anyone behind. Few of the slaves were old, but there were plentiful children and even babies. They rode on their parents' backs, in carts, and on the shoulders of strangers. Their individual burden was low, but with stops for food, rest, and relieving themselves, the overall pace of the group couldn't compare to their trip south, even with the constant push to move faster.

Taking care of Barra proved to be both a task Silvi loved and a highly awkward affair. Silvi fed Barra and gave her water throughout the day in a way that reminded her entirely too much of taking care of her infant niece and her nephew when he was a baby. Barra would move her mouth and swallow as necessary but was otherwise senseless. Silvi helped Barra relieve herself with as much privacy as she could find them and carried her whenever they had to leave the cart. At night, Silvi held Barra in whatever ways she could, but found it unsettling to receive no response.

Silvi's mother had once told her that true love was loving someone when they were sick. That was when you knew you didn't love the person for the way they looked or for the nice things they said, but loved them through and through. Silvi would care for Barra as long as it took, and the longer the better as it got them closer to safety. She loved Barra thoroughly, deeply, and passionately. Nevertheless, she was looking forward to having her Barra back.

Silvi had been concerned about her ability to direct the Neamairtese as the queen's mate, manage her people as their hero, assist as the only awake person able to translate between the two, serve as Barra's torchbearer, and care for Barra's needs, all while telling her stories. However, with a few exceptions, neither the Svekards nor the Neamairtese bothered Silvi throughout the trip or even approached her except to deliver food, water, and ask her if she needed anything.

The only people who came to speak to Silvi frequently were Daralan, Keepan, and Tana, a few times each day and Eigen to tend to the torch and Barra while they slept. As the days passed, they fell into a pattern. Tana would formulate the plans and share them with the group. Silvi would make necessary decisions and Daralan and Keepan implemented what she decided amongst their respective people.

"While it is your job to take care of Barra, it is our job to take care of our people," Daralan told Silvi at one of his check-ins. At Silvi's questioning look, Daralan smiled. "He and I point at things and act them out. When we need to, we find a Svekard and Neamairtese who each speak Victricite and translate through the third language. He calls me Dadan, like someone I know used to, though."

"And you two aren't having trouble keeping the Svekards from attacking the Victricites?" Silvi asked. Besides Barra's safety, that had been her greatest concern.

Daralan shook his head hesitantly. "While it has not been an issue, they seem to have found an alternative to attacking in the cloud. As we move northward, we have passed many dead Victricites. It appears some of the former slaves are killing their former masters when they see the cloud approaching and then run into the cloud. Though it is not in the spirit of the rule, the cloud spell does not seem to be weakening because of their actions and it has made the Svekards amenable while in the cloud."

Silvi nodded. She couldn't blame them. A large piece of her wanted to be out there with them, putting an end to the people who had enslaved her brethren. Once again, an upbringing of fighting for glory and one's clan conflicted with her memories of an upbringing viewing killing people as an affront to the Spirits. "Thank you for coordinating the kindlers and leading your people, Daralan...and leading mine."

"Thank you for taking care of our queen," Daralan replied.

He gave her a solemn nod as if to leave. "Wait," Silvi said. "Would you like to have dinner with me?" Her days and nights alone with a nearly unconscious Barra were beginning to feel far too much like her "hero's" isolation.

Daralan looked over his shoulder at the crowd as if he felt this really wasn't his place. As far as Silvi could tell, Barra considered Daralan a trusted advisor and if he was going to be that for Barra, it seemed only fitting that he be that to Silvi as well. "Please?"

Daralan certainly wasn't going to turn Silvi down after that. He climbed into the cart and accepted the piece of ham steak she offered him. The group didn't have the time to stop and cook meals throughout the day, so managed with what they could scavenge. Dinners were by far the best meals, as they were able to take the food planned for Victricite dinners. Silvi had a feeling she was brought the best options the group could find.

Silvi looked around for something to break the silence between them. She hadn't invited him just so someone else could be silently near her. "Is that a skull?" Silvi asked, pointing to a thin strip of bone sticking out of Daralan's mounds of reddish-brown hair. She could just make out what looked like tiny, possibly chipped, needle-shaped teeth coming out of its jaw. "I'm sorry if that was rude to ask. Please ignore the question if it was," Silvi said, realizing she wasn't sure if she was supposed to ask about people's hair tokens. She couldn't remember Barra ever asking anyone.

With incredible delicacy, Daralan reached up and unwound the item from his hair to hold out in front of her. It was indeed a small fish skull, treated to last as long as possible in the jumble of his hair. Even so, Silvi could see the miniscule fractures and places where chunks had broken off.

"When I was a young boy, I added this as a memory from my mother's mate," Daralan said as he tipped it this way and that to take in the tiny details that still remained. "He taught me what he called the art of the single fish. You see, with a net, you can catch many fish, but in many of the rivers where we're from, there aren't a lot of fish, so if you net too many, there aren't enough to spawn and the fish population dies off. Nature provides, if you take only what you need."

"He sounds like a great man," Silvi replied, thinking of Papa.

"He was. His heart was the heart of a kindler. Though he never had any direct connection to the Spirits, I think the Spirits spoke to him in their own way." Daralan gave the item one last gentle stroke with the tip of his finger before tucking it back in his hair. "After he and my mother were no longer mates, we stayed close. It was his wisdom that made me the man I am."

Silvi gave a warm smile of her own. She was thinking about the woman she had apprenticed with as a veterinarian. Bilta had been strong yet gentle, fast enough to catch a horse, but slow enough to approach a bunny. The woman had an aura of calm that could tame a panicked ox. Silvi was a Svekard because of Papa, but she was a healer because of Bilta.

Daralan and Silvi spent the rest of the meal swapping stories about their mentors and the people who had shaped them. Stories, as Silvi had found, were a deeply human way to connect across so many differences.

Using the last piece of her ham, Silvi wiped the small bit of meat over her face and chest in the symbol of Garvil, god of thanks and bounty. It was a thank-you for so many things, from Bilta to Barra to freedom and good food. Not every prayer could be for protection today or victory tomorrow. Sometimes, she had to stop and say thank you for everything that had happened along the way.

"After every meal, why do you spread food over your face and chest?" Daralan asked, "If it's not rude for me to ask."

He'd wondered since the day he hadn't laughed at her when so many of the others did, Silvi realized. She smiled at him to assure him it was okay to ask. "Compared to the Gods, we are little more than chunks of meat. Tonight, we dine on the flesh of beasts, but tomorrow it may very well be the beasts who dine on our flesh," Silvi recited. "This is to remind us of that. It keeps us humble, grateful, watchful, and wary. We draw the symbol of one of the Gods in recognition and prayer."

Daralan nodded at the wisdom in her explanation. "As is my job, I really should get back to checking on everyone, make sure all of the kindlers have received dinner and that we have enough directing and enough sleeping." He hopped out of the cart and gave her another smile. "Thank you for the delightful dinner," he said before disappearing into the crowd to continue doing what he clearly considered his duty.

The clan may be uniquely Svekard, but duty to the clan is not, Silvi thought.

❖

Silvi received one unexpected visitor over the course of the journey north. She'd spotted her peaking around the unofficial guards, as if she were simply looking around for a friend and not trying to get a peek past the guards at Barra and Silvi.

"Helenda?" Silvi called out. She would know her anywhere. Her memories told her every curve of Helenda's body, even if they had changed with years of forced servitude.

Silvi watched Helenda look around, unsure if she should approach or not. Silvi wasn't quite sure either. The sight of Helenda brought with it more emotions than Silvi could process at once. She could feel Barra's love and longing almost as if it were her own, and it stirred a jealousy deep within her that made her grit her teeth to hold back from yelling, "I made Barra orgasm harder than you ever did and that was my first time."

It was a childish and entirely inappropriate thought, but Silvi found herself thinking it, nonetheless.

Helenda pushed through the guards who clearly took Silvi's call as an invitation as much as Helenda had. Helenda approached the cart, her gaze flicking between Barra, who sat cross-legged on the wooden floor of the cart, and Silvi, who had her hand resting possessively on Barra's knee. "Is she okay?" Helenda asked tentatively.

"She's fine," Silvi said. She knew her tone was defensive, but she couldn't help it.

"I just..." Helenda started, then stopped, taking in Silvi's posture and expression fully. She slowed a step to allow the cart to pull farther ahead of her. "She's my best friend," Helenda muttered before turning to leave. "I just wanted to make sure she's okay."

"Wait," Silvi called, not exactly sure why she didn't want Helenda to leave, when she was pretty sure it was exactly what she wanted. She didn't want to see the forlorn look on Helenda's face. She didn't want to feel immense compassion for her nor feel guilt for having put that look on Helenda's face. She really didn't want the twinge of arousal that memories of Barra having sex brought with them. "I'm just jealous," Silvi blurted before blushing deeply.

For a moment, Helenda looked at Silvi with only confusion. "You don't need to be," Helenda said at last. "She's your mate. The only way anything would ever happen between Barra and me is if you both wanted to share your bed with me." She was giving Silvi a look that said she would certainly consider it.

Silvi wasn't sure if Helenda liked what she saw or if it was just the novelty of a Svekard. Either way, the conversation's direction was making her very uncomfortable. Neamairtese might talk openly about sex, but she certainly didn't. "Can we talk about something else?"

"Sure, was there something you wanted to ask me about?" Helenda's innocent look contrasted so completely with the sensual one she'd been giving Silvi only a moment before. She supposed for Helenda the topic had been no more taboo than what she had eaten for dinner.

"Uhhh..." Silvi looked for a safe topic. She could speak Neamairtese, but that apparently didn't mean she knew how to speak to Neamairtese. Silvi's gaze went to Helenda's hair. Asking about a trinket had worked the last time she didn't know what to say. But Helenda's hair was cut short. Any self-respecting Svekard man had a longer beard than Helenda's hair. Anything that had been in it was gone now.

Helenda's hand went to her hair, brushing her fingers through it, clearly conscious of what was missing with each strand she passed. "Since I was first bought, it's been like this. I kept what I could, and I still have the smallest of the items. Once we're home, I'll grow it back out and put them in to remind myself that even when everything seems lost, there's still hope."

"You've been through so much," Silvi said, wondering if she could come out the other end hopeful. She certainly hadn't felt that way when she thought she'd been exiled.

Helenda shrugged, though Silvi could tell there was a great deal more pain beneath the ambivalent smile. She hopped up into the cart without further invitation. Silvi could see so much of Barra's brazenness in Helenda and could see why the two had been friends. "I don't have a child, so I count myself lucky," she said.

Leapora, help them, Silvi thought, drawing the symbol of Leapora over her heart. "What will happen to those children without a father?" Silvi tried to ask, but the last word came out in Svekard. Silvi searched her memory for the word for father but couldn't find it. Barra must have had a father, right? Why couldn't she draw up the man's face? Had he died when Barra was too young to remember him?

"What is a *paaten*?" Helenda asked, trying to use the word Silvi had.

"The man who caused your birth, your mother's mate, the man who raised you," Silvi explained. How could she wrap so many ideas and so many important roles into one?

"As it is with all Neamairtese, their mother's mate will help raise them and love them because he or she loves their mother. Since they have not grown up with our culture, it will take them longer to learn our rituals and customs, but it will be a better life than they have lived here."

For a long moment, Silvi just stared at Helenda. "Neamairtese don't have fathers? The man who birthed you doesn't raise you?"

Helenda smiled at her, as if she were talking to a naive child. "How would I know for sure who is the man who birthed me? Even if I did, what difference would it make? He didn't carry me or birth me himself. Even the king who sacrificed the Lord's magic to save his mate and her child, the king who was monogamous with the queen, loved the child as his mate's child. That love is not any greater or lesser because he doesn't claim the child as his own."

Silvi's first impulse was to blame this for the reason Neamairtese were so savage and backhanded, but she knew it wasn't true. Neamairtese, like Barra, learned to be members of their tribe because they were raised by the tribe.

"From your reaction, I assume that's not how Svekards raise their children? The Victricites kept us apart from the Svekards, which made everyone happier, but I imagine it was actually meant to prevent this." Helenda gestured at the crowd of thousands of escaping slaves.

"No. In Svek, fathers are key to a child's upbringing. Svekards get…" Silvi searched for an equivalent for marriage and came up short. "Svekards mate for life. We have a ceremony where the man and woman swear to be faithful to each other for life. Then they raise their children together, knowing their blood and the blood of their ancestors flow through their children's veins."

"But how do you know the person you pick is the person you are going to want to be with all your life? Only the queen and her mate know for sure that they are hearts' mates. What if the first time you choose incorrectly?" Helenda asked. She seemed more interested than judgmental of this foreign concept.

"Svekards marry late and they marry for love, and then they love that person forever because they swore to do so." How did she explain the concept of true loyalty?

"It sounds like your mother and paaten found each other well. Are all Svekards really like that?" Helenda asked.

"Of course...I mean..." Silvi paused trying to come up with the words to describe all Svekard couples and parents without simply describing her own. Nita and her husband loved each other. Sure, sometimes they fought, and Mama told her to keep down their yelling so the neighbors wouldn't know, but they still loved each other dearly. She had no doubt of that. Silvi's mother didn't want the neighbors to know because all Svekards had the kind of marriage that her parents did and not like Nita and her husband did, right?

A father's number one priority was his children. They were his blood. That was clear from Svekard stories and Svekard values. Didn't that mean all Svekard fathers showed their love as ardently as her own?

Silvi supposed she and Papa had always been closer than he was with either of her sisters. They had always been closer with Mama.

"Yeah," she answered with a distinct lack of Svekard confidence in her voice. Even if they weren't all like hers, everything she'd said was still true. Loyalty and parenthood were central tenets of Svekard culture, even if not everyone was as good at them.

"Hmmm." Helenda grunted, rolling the idea over in her mind. "I don't think I'd want to mate for life. It's one of many reasons Barra and I never would have been mates. Even if she hadn't been chosen as queen and led to her heart's mate, I think she might have done that mating for life thing. I couldn't be who she wanted me to be. I'm glad she has you."

Silvi was taken aback by the sincerity in Helenda's voice. She'd felt jealous and insecure the moment Barra's memory of Helenda had first hit her back on the ship. She supposed deep in her memories, she'd known this. However, Barra had hidden the truth of her longest relationship from herself, making it all the harder for Silvi to see the truth of it.

Helenda gave Barra an appraising look before turning back to Silvi. "Though I suppose she already is, she's going to make a great queen. When she doesn't know the answer, she seeks out those who do. But when she knows, she doesn't care what anybody else thinks, she's going to do what she knows is right. She's highly independent, but what she wants more than anything else is to be loved unconditionally."

Helenda gave Barra one last long look before turning back to Silvi. "I should go. I hope you see you have nothing to be jealous of. Thank you for being everything Barra needs." Helenda slipped off the back of the cart and gave Silvi an impish smile before drifting off into the crowd.

Was this just a Neamairtese thing, talking this openly and then disappearing into the crowd? Silvi wondered if she'd ever truly understand them. She believed that Helenda had meant everything she had said. Neamairtese might be tricksy, but they were excruciatingly honest and open, even when she didn't really want them to be.

❖

For five days, the group traversed the city of Victricus. The fog made everything sticky and moist, and the chafing was rubbing on everyone's last nerve. Even through the fog, the constant clip-clop of boots, wheels, and hooves was infuriatingly tedious, especially as more and more people crowded onto the same strips of road.

By the sixth day, the group had reached the outer edges of Victricus where the fields stretched as far as they could see. The mood of the group had changed markedly with more space to move around and the promise of reaching the wall within a day's travel. Silvi thought perhaps if they pushed the group to camp a little later, they might even be able to spend the night on the other side.

Silvi sat in her cart, feeding Barra lunch and looking out at the fields where a group of Neamairtese children, some with signs of a half-Victricite parentage, were chasing each other through the wheat and laughing. Everyone within earshot seemed to be watching them play and smiling.

Caught up in the mood, Silvi almost didn't notice the change in Barra. Silvi tried to give Barra another bite of sliced cured meat on bread only to find that Barra's mouth was still full. She gave Barra a poke and Barra chewed and swallowed before accepting the next bite. Silvi looked back out at the children, wondering vaguely if Barra might be full and was telling her in the only way she could.

A small thunk brought Silvi's attention back to Barra and the partially chewed piece of food lying on the cart between her folded legs. "Are you full, honey?" Silvi asked, knowing Barra couldn't answer her. Unlike speaking to the figment of Papa, somehow talking to Barra made Silvi feel less crazy.

"Can't," Barra mumbled. Her head was sagging to the side and her shoulders bobbed ever so slightly every couple seconds.

It was the first time Barra had spoken in five and a half days.

"Can't what?" Silvi asked, entirely unsure if she should be encouraging Barra to talk. On the one hand, if it was important enough for Barra to try to express, Silvi ought to probe until she understood. On the other hand, should she really be encouraging Barra out of her trance? If she was supposed to be able to figure it out from that single word, Silvi was at a loss.

Barra's head jerked back up, but her eyes stayed closed. "Can't stay awake," Barra mumbled, her words coming out as a moan.

No! Silvi's mind yelled. Her eyes shot to the torch sitting in her lap where the small flame was still burning. How had she not noticed it getting smaller and smaller over the last two days? Now, taking it in, she could see the difference. "The torch is still burning, Barra."

"I keep dreaming that I'm awake and home and then realizing I'm asleep just in time to not lose the spell. Silvi, I can't." Barra's eyelids were fluttering as if she were trying to find a balance between being awake enough to not fall asleep while also holding on to the spell. "I'm losing it."

"We're so close, Barra. We'll reach the wall by the end of the day," Silvi said. She signaled to the Svekard closest to her to bring her Keepan and Tana before taking both of Barra's hands in her own. She held the torch in Barra's right hand, hoping the closeness and vibrations would make a difference.

"I can't," Barra mumbled again, her head sinking farther before snapping back up to attention. There were dark circles under her eyes and her skin had a grayed look.

"I'll help you," Silvi said, releasing her hand and stroking up and down her left arm and leg.

"Silvi!" Barra's voice broke on the single word. "If I push too hard I could exhaust the magic. I could lose it for everyone. I could end the line of queens." A tear ran down her cheek, and Silvi realized she wasn't just tired, she was scared. Barra hadn't slept in five and a half days, she was about to lose her grasp on the only thing between her people and their death or re-enslavement, and on top of that, she had to consider whether it was worth failing a few thousand people to preserve her entire peoples.

It couldn't end like this. Silvi understood Barra prioritizing the magic over herself, but Silvi never would. Barra was the most important thing in Silvi's world, and her spell was what was keeping her, as well as the rest of them, alive. Silvi would fight to her last breath, but she knew she wouldn't be enough.

She'd been receiving reports of the mob following behind them since the second day. The Victricite masters wanted their property back and had followed them for the last five days to reclaim them. The Victricite soldiers at the wall would be to their front with bows and swords and the mob would be at their back, interspersed with soldiers, mercenaries, and slavers. They would all die.

"You won't lose the magic. The Spirits are with you." Silvi tried to reassure her. They only needed a little bit more time. "Your torch is still burning; the cloud is still going. You told me fate brought us together and it brought us here. The Lady won't let you use the last of the queen's magic. This is our purpose. You can't give up now, please."

Barra gave a nod that was barely distinguishable from the hypnic jerks that were popping her head back up every time it reached her chest. She wanted to hold Barra's head up but was afraid she wouldn't be able to tell if Barra was awake if she did. She supposed she would know when the cloud fell apart around them.

"I'm here with you and I will do everything I can to keep you awake. You just have to hold on a little bit longer. We'll do this together. You aren't alone and you are stronger than you know."

From the corner of her eye, Silvi saw Keepan and Tana approaching quickly. "Is it time?" Tana asked, jumping directly to the point.

"We're going to give you as much time as we can, but we need to move faster. We need to try to reach the wall," Silvi answered, not stopping in her petting of Barra nor her tight grip of Barra's hand around the torch. "Send Daralan and Terenesa."

They gave curt nods before heading off in separate directions.

It only took a couple of minutes to feel and see the change of pace. Where children had been playing as their parents kept them moving forward, now everyone moved with dogged attention to the path ahead of them. They had a lot of ground to cover, but maybe, just maybe, they could.

"Don't fall asleep, Barra, or you won't get to hear about the time my father…" She needed a story, one that Barra wouldn't know, one that would keep her attention. "Saved me from a bear." I'm at the Kraunfish festival, Silvi told herself, and I'm going to tell the best big fish story that has ever been told.

Silvi was only a couple of minutes into her story when Daralan and Terenesa arrived. "So, he sunk his teeth into the bear's claw, holding on with all the strength of his jaw, and just wait until you hear what happened next," Silvi said, giving Barra's shoulders a gentle shake.

Silvi turned to Terenesa, who looked almost as run down as Barra. Her hair sagged and her complexion was pale beneath its collection of bright red freckles. The kindlers had been taking shifts since the second day to allow some to sleep while the others engaged with the Spirits, but they hadn't had the power of the torch to bolster them. From her disheveled look, it was hard to tell if she'd been sleeping when Silvi called for her or just coming off an especially long shift.

Silvi looked from one to the other. From their expressions, they knew exactly what was happening. "Daralan, I need you to help the Svekards get everyone moving, then I need you close for when…well, when I need you." Daralan didn't speak. He only nodded and headed off into the crowd.

"Terenesa, can you help make the torch fire stronger?" Silvi asked.

Terenesa climbed into the cart and wrapped her hand around the torch above Barra's and Silvi's entwined fingers. "Yes," she whispered. With her eyes closed, she looked even more tired, to the point of illness. "But it will burn up the torch in a matter of a couple of hours. If I only make it a little bigger, I might be able to get you a few hours, but it will mean she has to fight harder for every minute between now and then."

"And when it burns out?" Silvi asked.

Terenesa opened her eyes and locked gazes with Silvi. "The torch will go out and she will be asleep."

"Give us a few hours," Silvi replied, before immediately going back to her story. She would be trying to keep both Barra and Terenesa awake now.

Silvi dragged her story out, adding every exciting twist and cliff-hanger she could. She'd gotten used to talking for hours to Barra, but she'd been able to speak Svekard. Focusing on speaking Neamairtese was giving her a slight headache, and Silvi wasn't even sure if she was making a difference. The fog cloud was still stable, and the flame had grown back to its original size, so Silvi had to assume she wasn't doing too poorly.

During the next three hours, Silvi, Tana, Daralan, and Keepan planned. Silvi threw in what she could around her story, highly aware of her competing duties. A Neamairtese scout had been sent ahead to report what they could expect as they neared the wall.

A small cheer interrupted their planning two hours into intense debate. The Svekards and Neamairtese around them had gotten their first view of the wall ahead through the obscuring haze of the fog. The cheering people didn't know that when they reached it, they would face almost one hundred archers, nearly as many armed guards on the ground, and be sandwiched between that and the mob at their backs.

"Even if we can hold the gate, the archers on the wall will take out our people fleeing on the other side," Daralan said, gesturing the death of their people to communicate the idea to the Svekards.

"We will take out their archers first," Tana said, swinging an imaginary sword.

"We will do it before the fog ends if we have to," Keepan added, billowing his hands like a cloud, chopping the air, and then wiggling his cloud fingers outward like a dissipating cloud.

"No," Silvi interrupted. "We will replace their archers." She said it in Svekard and then Neamairtese. "The Neamairtese are archers. They will climb the wall, take out the archers, and fire on the mob at our backs."

"Once everyone is in position, we will all strike at once, Neamairtese on the wall and Svekards on the ground, ending the spell and the guards at the same time," Daralan said, already summoning Neamairtese to him to spread the word. They would need their best archers ready.

The group parted, moving off into the anxious crowd to prepare them for the battle to come.

Silvi turned back to Barra, giving her temple a soft kiss. "We only need to hold out for another hour or so," Silvi said, estimating the time and hoping she was anywhere near accurate. She gave both Barra and Terenesa a quick jostle and continued her story, which had morphed slowly into a tale of a wolf and bear cub duo that had become unlikely friends to defeat a twenty-foot sheep and feed both of their families for the winter.

I wish I was a storyteller rather than a veterinarian, Silvi thought, drawing the symbol of Jinter, scribe of the Gods, on her chest with the last of Barra's uneaten lunch. She wished she was a warrior like Tana, strong like Keepan, creative like Eigen, or wise like Daralan. I have them for that, Silvi told herself. My job is to keep Barra going until we reach the wall.

❖

There was commotion all around her. Barra tried to catch hold of any of the streams of words passing by and around her but couldn't seem to grasp more than a constant rumbling. The people around her might as well be speaking the Victricite language.

Barra's stomach gave a lurch at the thought. Had she failed? Was she waking up in captivity?

No. Barra could feel the cloud of fog still in her mind as if she had a butterfly held gently in her hands, protecting it while carefully not touching the wings. The spell was still active, and it was her job to keep it that way.

Silvi had stopped her odd, yet surprisingly compelling story, though Barra couldn't remember what had happened in any part of the intricate plot. Silvi was still there though. Her voice was easy to pick out of the rumble, though her words still eluded Barra.

Why is my hand so hot? Barra wanted to ask. There had been a buzz there for a while, though Barra didn't know how long. All she knew was that what had felt like the purring of a kitten was now barely a hum.

And it hurt. The heat hurt. It burned.

She tried to let go of it, but there were fingers wrapped around hers keeping her there. Silvi's fingers. Silvi was hurting her.

No. Silvi wouldn't hurt her. She needed the pain. It was keeping her awake and thinking about the spell.

The spell.

Barra needed to focus on the spell, but her hand hurt.

She tried to drop the thing in her hand, but there were fingers wrapped around hers.

Silvi's fingers...
Staying awake...
The spell...
Pain...
Silvi...
The spell...

❖

The pain was excruciating. All Silvi could hope was that her hand covering Barra's was protecting her from the flame that was no more than an inch from her own hand. She could see her own skin working its way from a scarlet red to a disturbing purple, and tiny white blisters were beginning to bubble to the surface.

Just a little longer, Silvi coached herself and Barra. They were maybe fifteen minutes from the wall. Reaching the wall was their only chance.

Their people had been clustering tighter and tighter as they hustled the last distance between them and what they hoped would be their freedom. Silvi could barely see the ground for the sea of intermingled Svekards and Neamairtese around her cart.

Tana, Daralan, and Keepan jogged along with her cart gesturing and ensuring everything was in place to execute their plan, utilizing Silvi's translation help when needed. She appreciated the distraction from her hand, but she couldn't stand to have her attention drawn from Barra for too long.

"Arrows!" came a Svekard roar, sending a wave of panic through the group. They didn't scream. They didn't run. They couldn't. More than four thousand people looked up together to watch a flight of a hundred arrows headed directly toward them.

They were packed in, no shields, no defenses. They were the perfect target.

Silvi watched, the pain in her hand temporarily forgotten. The arrows arced down, struck the cloud of fog, and stopped. They hung in the air as if stuck in an invisible wall.

A thunderous cheer rose up from the crowd. For another few minutes, they were safe. "You're saving them, my love," Silvi told Barra. She tried not to look at her hand; it would only turn her stomach.

She was a Svekard and she could withstand great pain before giving in. Soon, it wouldn't matter, the torch would either be burned out or they would be at the wall.

"Can we beat them?" Silvi asked Tana. Silvi might be a hero and Keepan an honorary chieftain, but Silvi knew Tana would be in charge when it came to the upcoming battle.

"We will try," Tana replied. "I must prepare the forces. We will send everyone else through the wall. Their job will be to run, to get out of arrow range and keep going in case we fail. We must rely on the idea that the Victricites will not follow us beyond the wall. Whether we win or lose, they will be safest as far from here as possible."

"You are expecting a second wave of Victricites?" Silvi asked, looking in the direction of the mob, too far to make out through the fog.

"I do not expect the waves to stop," Tana said. "There are so many of them, and any culture that builds that kind of wall will do anything to defend and keep it." Her statement complete, Tana left. She had more important things to do than explain the likelihood of their demise to Silvi.

Silvi looked from the wall to Barra and back. She needed to stay with Barra, but she needed to help at the wall. Barra's best chance, her only chance, was the front line not breaking. What kind of a hero or mate could Silvi be if she didn't stay and fight for all of their lives? What kind of Svekard would she be?

The Svekards and Neamairtese were organizing as they jogged the last of the distance toward the wall. The wall itself was now in the cloud and the archers and guards had frozen in place, many with their arrows nocked and bows drawn.

"We're going make it," Silvi said, turning to Barra in time to watch Terenesa go limp and fall sideways onto the floor of the cart, asleep. Silvi watched in horror as the torch in her hand extinguished like a blown-out candle. Silvi lurched forward, grabbing Barra as she went limp, "No, Barra, we just need one more minute."

CHAPTER FIFTEEN
THE GODS-CHOSEN

It was too late. Silvi could already feel the cloud coming apart around her. She never thought she would miss the salty, earthy smell of stale sea water or the thickness of the air in her lungs, but she felt her body reaching out for them, nonetheless. "She's asleep!" Silvi yelled unnecessarily.

The whole horde had felt the change. Now it was up to them to get almost five thousand people and dozens of carts of supplies through a gate large enough for ten people to walk abreast and about two men tall, surrounded by armed soldiers.

The wall was six men tall and looked as solid as a mountain. Along the top of it were close to one hundred archers, all arrows nocked and pointed at the soon-to-be vulnerable masses of Neamairtese and Svekards. At the foot of the wall, between the horde and the door were dozens of men in shining armor, ready to kill any who tried to escape. They were frozen in place, a mixture of disgust and distain on their still faces. This was the expression Silvi's mother had always said would freeze on her sister Greta's face if she didn't stop making it while cleaning the sheep enclosure as a child.

The horde broke into a run.

Several dozen Svekard warriors took up position next to their frozen foe guarding the wall and prepared to strike them down. Along the wall, nearly one hundred of the best Neamairtese archers swarmed the ladders leading to the wall's parapet, climbing like squirrels from a wolf. They had planned to have time for a synchronized strike, and they would wait for the call if possible, but they would not let another arrow be loosed before they struck.

On the front line, more than four hundred Svekards took up position at the back of the horde between their people and the Victricite mob. They held what weapons they had been able to scrounge. Silvi watched as a man with a pitchfork pulled his wife and daughter into his arms, kissing them both as if the crowd was not there. "Be safe," he mouthed to them before pushing them toward the gate. Silvi lost him in the crowd of blond warriors spreading out to cover every target.

"Daralan!" Silvi called into the chaos, hoping it was not too late to secure his full attention. He appeared out of the crowd as if he had never left, and Silvi wondered how she ever could have doubted it. "I have to stay and fight. I need you to stay with Barra and protect her." There was so much more Silvi wanted to tell him, things she wanted him to tell Barra if she never got a chance to. "Tell her I love her." Silvi gave Barra's still lips one last kiss before jumping down from the cart with the sword she'd taken from the captain's quarters nearly a week before.

Daralan leapt lithely into the cart as Silvi left it. "I will," he said. It was what Silvi needed to hear, but what she had really wanted him to say was that she would tell Barra herself after they won.

Silvi brought her left hand up to grab the scabbard of the sword and hissed at the intense throbbing pain that shot up her entire arm. She took in the burn damage to her hand fully for the first time. Her skin had discolored to a purplish-red that looked more like old leather that might break at any moment. The skin from the second knuckle of her index finger across to the tip of her thumb had bubbled into one giant white pustule that looked on the edge of bursting. Silvi let out a small curse. She didn't have time for this. She stuck the sheath in her armpit and pulled the sword out with her good hand, letting the sheath fall to the ground.

Silvi watched Barra's cart push toward the front of the crowd. She had to go. She had to fight. She had to protect Barra, magic or not.

Silvi pushed against the river of people all trying to reach the same small destination at the same time. Her place was between them and the enemy. She broke through the surge to the trailing edge of the mass of people fleeing through the gate to see Tana and Keepan to her right. Hundreds of Svekards stood to her right and left, hoes, pitchforks, sabers, hammers, chains, and spears held at the ready. They had thousands of their people behind them and thousands more enemies in front.

"They're moving!" came a Neamairtese scream from above and behind Silvi. She looked up to watch a Victricite archer on the top of the wall release the string of his bow. As if in slow motion, the string began to pull forward, taking the arrow with it. The Neamairtese who had called the warning swiped the arrow out of the air before it was completely free of the bow and planted it in the archer's neck.

Tana and Silvi made momentary eye contact before yelling in unison, one in Svekard and the other in Neamairtese, "Now!"

More than one hundred Neamairtese on the wall, and almost as many Svekards at its base, struck frozen Victricites at that moment, felling the guards along the wall above and below.

"For clan and family," Keepan boomed, as the fog fell to their feet in a single sheet of salty rain.

"For clan and family!" every Svekard, warrior and civilian, roared.

The Victricite mob behind them had seen the fog weakening and formed into ranks for the battle ahead. As the fog dropped, so did the arrows that had stuck in the cloud. They ricocheted off the soldier's waiting shields as if they were nothing but rain.

The Victricites marched as a unit, soldiers in the front rank presenting a shield wall. The people behind the first rank were clearly not soldiers but held themselves with the same degree of discipline. Perhaps Daralan had been right not to tell Silvi that she could tell Barra she loved her herself.

The Svekards stood their ground, baring their teeth at the advancing wall of men.

Silvi took a deep breath in the steeped calm. In a moment, the wall of Victricite soldiers would be on them and they would fight to the last person. She glanced over her shoulder, relieved to not see Barra, but desperately wanting just one more look. Silvi closed her eyes and tried to speak to the magic inside her. She'd convinced it to help her throw Barra's abuser over the encampment wall the night she'd fallen for Barra. Surely, she could convince it now.

"Please," Silvi said silently. She had no idea who the source of her ask was. Was she asking the Spirits who had done so much for them already or even the Lady herself? She didn't have the power or the right to ask any of them, so she directed her request to the magic within her. "Help me to protect her, that's our job. She needs me and I need you."

The familiar buzz started in the pit of Silvi's stomach before radiating out, sizzling through her nerves as it went. It wasn't much, but Silvi hoped it would be enough. She opened her eyes to a world brighter and sharper than the one she'd closed her eyes on. She didn't need purely physical strength to fight any army by herself; she needed the senses, the vision, and the voice to lead an army. She could see the gaps between the shields and the sweat on the faces of the men in the second rank, walking several yards behind the first rank. They were tired and scared too. Most of them were simply men who wanted their slaves back, but they didn't want to die. They just needed to think it wasn't worth fighting, at least long enough for Barra and the others to make it far enough from the wall out of Victricus.

"Archers!" Silvi bellowed, her voice carrying impossibly loudly over the clangor of the escaping people between her and the Neamairtese on the wall. "Fire into the second rank. Fire!"

The soldiers in the first rank with shields and spears were a bigger threat, but the masters that made up the second rank needed to see their own fall.

Bow strings twanged in unison, and as if they were one single entity, the front rank of soldiers raised their shields in reaction to the sound. Dozens of masters in the second rank, unprepared and less armored, fell.

Silvi had been waiting for this moment, when the first rank's impenetrable wall became a ceiling, letting them in. "Forward!" she screamed and ran into the fray, a Svekard on each side.

Silvi's sword struck a Victricite square in the chest with enough force to knock the soldier backward, despite his armor. She pivoted, slicing between the gaps in the armor of the soldier to her right and returned to parry the first soldier's attack. Another volley of arrows passed over her head striking farther back into the mass of Victricites.

The first rank of Victricites surged forward, the front line smashing the Svekards back with shields, re-creating their wall, while the second line's spears stabbed out with deadly force clearing the way for a second surge. Silvi stumbled back, knocking the spear aside that would have otherwise gone straight through her thin cotton garb. The Svekard to her left was not so lucky.

Silvi scrambled to her feet and backtracked to keep herself between the Victricite forces and her people. She struck out but hit only shields. She struck harder, hoping to at least push the soldiers back and swore at the crunching sound of metal as the decorative sword broke from its hilt and fell to the ground, a useless piece of sharp metal.

The second line of Victricites lunged forward with their spears, and a roar of pain echoed across the front line of Svekards. Silvi threw herself to the ground, barely missing the spear's attack. If she didn't regain her feet quickly though, she'd have that same spear driven down into her helpless body.

It was all going too quickly. The Victricites were moving forward faster than the Svekards could move back. The archers were firing as fast as they could into the first rank now, but the armored Victricites seemed endless. Every time a Victricite went down, another took his place, picking up a shield or spear and refilling the line. It was like fighting water, only to have it splash in your face.

The Svekards couldn't get in attack range due to the deadly line of spears. They were simply cut down when they tried. She needed to break up their wall.

The spear was coming for Silvi again. She rolled to the right, the spear tip catching only clothing. There were arms around Silvi hauling her to her feet. Tana pulled both of them back several steps, knocking spears aside with a blacksmith's hammer in each hand. She yelled at Silvi without taking her attention off the enemies in front of her. "We need all the archers to fire on the spearman at the same time as they lunge forward. Can you make them do that?"

Silvi didn't answer. There wasn't time for that. "Archers!" she bellowed in Neamairtese. The ability to yell was apparently one of the skills the magic thought she needed and she was glad of it. "Fire into the second line in three..."

Next to her, Tana bellowed in a tone that tried to match Silvi's, "Lunge and grab for the spears in..."

"Two..."

"One..."

"Fire!" Silvi screamed, dodging to the side as a spearman readied to launch forward.

"Grab!" Tana screamed as the spears that had been primed to thrust went limp.

Unarmed, Silvi slammed her body into the shield in front of her, pushing the soldier back far enough for her to safely wrap her good hand around the wood of the spear at the soldier's side. She got several inches before the spear stopped. A Victricite had grabbed onto the other end and was pulling.

"Mine!" Silvi growled and yanked as hard as she could, pushing off the shield with her shoulder. Silvi lurched backward, the spear in her hand, and was glad there wasn't a Svekard behind her to receive the spear point-first.

Up and down the front line, Svekards were wrestling similarly for the spears. Silvi could see torn clothing and bleeding gashes. The majority of the Svekards pulled back, a spear gripped in both hands, but Silvi watched in horror as for every four successful Svekards, one stumbled back, the spear gripped in his or her chest rather than hands.

"Fortify!" Tana bellowed and as one, the Svekards brought their spears forward, planted in the ground for stability, points toward their enemies. They didn't have anywhere near the discipline of the Victricites who would have reacted without command, but they were a clan and they too could act as one.

Behind them, more than half the Neamairtese and Svekard civilians had funneled through the gate and were running north dragging all the supplies they could. However, more than two thousand still stood pushing and trying to escape the carnage less than fifty feet from them.

They'd destroyed the zone of death, but the Victricites were still slowly advancing. The Neamairtese were continuing their onslaught from above, and Silvi could see through the Victricites in front of her that the second rank of men, mainly masters, had stopped their advance. They had clearly expected the slaves to surrender and were willing to wait until the soldiers dealt out and took the brunt of the damage.

A roar from the base of the wall brought the heads of the Victricites up to watch a small stream of reinforcements arrive. These were the Svekards who had struck down the frozen guards at the wall. They returned now to the front lines, armed with the weapons and helmets of the Victricite guards they'd killed.

They filed in next to their clansfolk with the tall protective shields of the Victricites. These were not the weapons or defenses they were used to using on the front line like the Victricites, so the Svekard shield wall would be the back line, protecting their fleeing people. The backline of Svekard warriors took the spears from their clansfolk and stood ready to take any blow that came. Some of the smaller warriors lunged forward, grabbing the bodies of their battered but still living brethren and dragging them to the protection of the Svekard defensive line.

The Victricite line paused, recalculating based on the changing field. This was the moment the most skilled Svekard warriors had been waiting for. The organized Victricite machine had stopped. All down the line, Svekards launched themselves at the wall of shields before the machine could reach a decision and resume its slaughter.

Keepan, chains wrapped around his hands like long, heavy arms, swung overhanded and no defense could stop the deadly metal from curving over the top of his victim's shield.

Tana lunged forward slamming both hammers into the center of the shield in front of her. Spiderweb cracks ran out from the dent in the center. The shield was unbroken, but the same could not be said for the arm directly behind it. The soldier had no ability to hold up his guard as Tana came in with another hammer strike.

Like water breaking through a weakened dam, the Victricite shield wall went down. They had found the chink in the armor and torn it wide open. Svekards swarmed in. An organized front was where the Victricites exceled, but in the chaos that followed, Svekards reigned supreme.

Silvi stood behind the Svekards' impromptu defensive formation, gripping her spear with her good hand and looking out at the battle from her spot.

The ground was littered with unmoving Svekards. Silvi could see each with unnatural acuity and wished for a moment that the magic hadn't given her the ability to see such carnage in that level of detail.

She felt so useless and weak, one-handed, hiding behind a shield. The shields were a necessary device for protecting their people, but not for protecting her. She could see better, fight harder, and swing stronger. Why was she standing here?

Several feet to her left, Silvi picked out a male body, lying on his back with a dirty pitchfork lying across his bloody, lifeless chest. The man who had kissed his wife and daughter good-bye hadn't even gotten a single strike in.

Silvi barely registered the quickening of her heart or the blurring of her vision at the sides. She could see everything she needed to right in front of her. The Victricites were the enemy and nothing else mattered.

There was a tug at her spear. Someone was trying to take her spear. Silvi whirled on her heels to see Eigen standing next to her. He had one hand wrapped around the spear giving it a light tug and the other held out a Victricite sword to her.

Eigen wasn't supposed to be here. He was supposed to be with the civilians escaping. None of that mattered to Silvi as she released the spear, grabbed the sword, and hurled herself at her enemies.

Silvi was surrounded. Victricites were on all sides pressing in with swords and the broken ends of spears. They were exactly where Silvi wanted them—within arm's reach.

To Silvi they moved with a sluggish pace. The man on her right swiped at her and got only shirt. She turned her dodge into a blow to the man in front of her before parrying the man on her left. She struck with enough force to knock him to the ground where another Svekard's hoe took care of him.

Three men rushed Silvi at the same time. "If I go down, I'm taking you with me," Silvi growled, kicking the man in front of her as she stabbed between the plates of armor of the one on the right. The one on her left fell at her feet, an arrow sticking from his neck.

Silvi looked up for half a second to see Helenda, bow in hand, drawing another arrow. She didn't pause to see if Silvi recognized or thanked her. Her attention was on her next target. She drew back the bowstring and loosed another arrow into a Victricite bearing down on a different Svekard.

Silvi didn't pause either. It didn't matter that she had the eyesight to pick out every detail of Helenda's face nor that she had dozens of memories playing at the back of her mind about her. Silvi's world was made up of only her enemy and the things she would need to defeat them. She could feel the gentle buzz of the magic feeding the fire of rage within her. She could smell the sweat of her enemies, hear the pounding of her heart in her ears, and feel the very air as the battle swirled around her.

Nearly half of the Svekard warriors were down, but each fought with a ferocity beyond any of the Victricites. Silvi moved through the forces like a curving arrow. She broke sword after sword over the shields and armor of her enemies, replacing her broken ones with the swords of her victims.

To her right, Keepan was a blur of chains. Soldiers crumpled around him like wheat in a hailstorm.

The soldiers at the front found themselves trapped rather than protected by their shields as more and more Svekards poured in and caught them from behind.

Arrows rained down as if the Gods themselves were targeting the Victricites. The Neamairtese shot with an accuracy the Svekards had only witnessed on the receiving end. Now, they chose their targets one by one, taking out Victricites in the moments before they would have otherwise killed a fallen Svekard.

Dozens at a time, the Victricite soldiers fell.

As the last Victricite soldier near Silvi fell, she scanned for her next target. Her left hand throbbed and the pounding in her head felt like Tana had been hammering on it for the last ten minutes. Her clothes stuck to her with the warm stickiness of blood, and she knew that not all of it was her enemies'. She hadn't felt the deep gash in her side when she'd been struck, but if she slowed, if she allowed herself to think about it even for a second, she was likely to fall and she wasn't entirely sure she'd be able to get up again.

For one hundred feet, the space in front of the Svekard shield wall was nothing but panting, bleeding Svekards and bodies. For another two hundred feet stood an open road, trampled grass, and the remnants of fields, their crops smashed beneath thousands of fleeing and chasing feet. At the other end were thousands of Victricites, uninjured and fresh.

The two forces stood staring across the space at each other. Every moment the Victricites waited was another moment for the Svekards to catch their breath, but also a moment for the wariness and damage to sink in.

Silvi felt more than saw Tana approach, her right arm hung limply at her side, and she was strongly favoring her right leg. "We bought them time," Tana whispered. "Hadrone will take us and not them."

"No," Silvi replied. She was scanning the enemy, and face after face told her the same thing. These were not soldiers. These were masters. And they were scared.

She could see the sweat beading at their brows, the pull of their jaws as they grit their teeth. She could even see wet streaks running down the legs of several finely crafted linen pants.

These masters could not see that the Svekards were on their last leg. All they saw was their fallen army.

"Stay," Silvi commanded, holding out her good arm. She lifted herself to her full height, ignoring the screaming in her side, and strode forward as if this were just another day herding her sheep.

Every step sent a shot of pain to Silvi's brain. Every breath pulled at the gash in her side. Every moment, she lost a little bit more blood.

Silvi reached the edge of the carnage and locked gazes with the man straight across the no man's land from her. His breath quickened and Silvi watched him swallow compulsively.

Silvi braced her feet, shoulder width apart, took the deepest breath her body would allow, and let it out in one long, bellowing roar. She had a burning flame within her. All Svekards did. What they had just done to the soldiers, they would do to these slave masters.

Behind her, a cacophonous roar rose up to shake the very heavens.

For a slow count of three, the Victricites stood stock-still before crumpling backward as if they had been struck physically by Silvi's roar and it had only taken time to reach them. The forces turned and ran.

The roar of victory lacked the force of the first roar. Silvi turned, almost too tired to smile. They had done it.

"No!" Silvi gasped breathlessly as she felt a surge of magic shoot up her spine.

"Mounted soldiers on the horizon!" Helenda's voice carried over the joyous shouts on the ground to Silvi's pricked ears. Silvi knew what she was going to say before the words left Helenda's mouth. She was already moving toward the ladders. "There's an army riding toward our people!"

Silvi reached the top of the wall and looked out at their people, helplessly running toward a mounted army. The dust cloud from the trotting horses would be just visible on the horizon to Helenda's eyes in the light of early dusk, but Silvi could pick out over three hundred soldiers.

"They must have sent a scout from the wall to warn them," Helenda said. Silvi was no longer looking at the approaching threat, but down at her warriors. The magic could get her to Barra's side in minutes, but that wasn't what Barra needed. She needed all of them.

Silvi thanked the Gods for the Victricite wall. Without it, the Neamairtese archers could not have turned the tide of the battle against the soldiers. Without it, they would not be able to see the approaching army.

The Svekards below her were battered and wounded, exhausted, and most had barely escaped death. They had also been willing to accept that death in order to protect their people. There were just as many Svekards around her who had made that sacrifice.

"The army beyond the wall is headed for our people," Silvi announced and watched the color drain from the faces of her warriors. They had known about the army but had expected it to be at least a five days' ride ahead of them. They were supposed to be hundreds of miles from the road by the time the army heard what had happened. Instead, they would be on their unprotected people faster than the battered warriors could get to them and even pretend to protect them.

Dear Gods, we sent them to their deaths, Silvi swore silently.

"They see it," Helenda told Silvi who was still surveying her warriors. Helenda placed her hand on Silvi's shoulder but drew back at Silvi's unconscious pull away from the touch. She pointed at the crowd of their people who were turning and starting to dash back, their carts and supplies abandoned on the road.

"How long do we have?" Silvi asked, hoping Helenda had a concept of distance and horses that was in no way part of Silvi's knowledge.

"Until the riders reach the wall—about half an hour," said an unfamiliar Neamairtese voice from behind her. Silvi turned to see a tall woman with dark brown hair cut to reach only the tips of her ears. She had a piece of long, black horsehair tied into the strands nearest her right temple and a piece of a feather torn from the fletching of an arrow tucked behind her left ear. "Less to reach our people."

The woman turned away from Silvi to point out at the approaching dust cloud. "When they are five minutes out, they will increase speed and gallop the last of the distance. Even running back, they will reach our people just before they get within arrow range of the wall. It wouldn't matter if they did. They will cut down everything in their path before more than a single volley could reach the *carfistos*."

Silvi had to assume the last word was the Victricite one for mounted soldiers. Neither Svekard nor Neamairtese had a word for such a group. "How long until they reach our people?" Silvi asked again.

"Twenty minutes," the woman answered distractedly. She reached up and touched the horsehair at the side of her temple and whispered, "Good horses serve bad people." Silvi couldn't help but wonder if the horse she had saved would be one of the horses charging at her people, one of the horses she would have to stop.

Silvi turned back to the crowd who was watching her as they triaged injured survivors to determine who they would have to leave behind, who they could carry to safety, and who could fight in the next battle. "We have only a minute or so here. We'll get everyone we can to the other side of the wall and then run to protect our people."

She looked around at the broken people around her. They were running on adrenaline as much as she was, and they were quickly running out. How could they be expected to run and save anyone?

She would do everything in her power to protect Barra, magic or not. She would die for her if that's what it took. But she wasn't enough. She needed them.

"We stayed behind because we were willing to die to save our people," Silvi announced to the group. "You swore to Hadrone at the coming-of-age ceremony that you would live each day for the clan until he took your soul. Hundreds of our clansmen died here to fulfill that promise. Maybe Hadrone spared us because our battle is not over. Our people will not survive without our help. I am injured. I am exhausted. I am alive. I will continue to fight until Hadrone takes me. Will you fight by my side?"

"Aye!" Eigen called from the heart of the battlefield where he was unburying a fallen survivor. They would be leaving many behind when they ran, but they couldn't carry them and reach their people.

"Aye!" Tana shouted, pulling another broken sword from the wreckage around her. Having enough soldiers wouldn't be their only problem.

"Aye!" Keepan growled with a concerning wheeze. He was trying to pull a shield from the arm of a soldier and failing.

"Aye!" roared almost two hundred Svekards. Dozens of them were too weak to stand on their own. They had fallen in the fight, but it would not be their last, if they could help it.

"We will follow you into battle," one of the Neamairtese on the wall called. He didn't need to understand her speech to understand the sentiment.

Silvi looked over her warriors, Svekard and Neamairtese alike, with a mixture of relief and guilt. *I'm not leading them to their deaths,* Silvi coached herself as she climbed down the ladder to help her people pull the dying from the dead. *I'm leading them to save our people. I can be a hero.*

As she stepped off the ladder, Silvi caught sight of her left hand out of the corner of her eye. Partway down the ladder, it had started gripping the wood instinctively, helping balance her. The giant blister was gone and her hand wasn't purple anymore. The damage from the torch was gone, and in its place, her hand looked as if it was encapsulated in flame.

Silvi stumbled back, barely noticing the pain in her side was gone. It seemed reasonable to her mind at that moment that her hand was on fire and she didn't want to set the ladder ablaze. Her right hand came up protectively, adding its own red glow to the light emanating from Silvi's left hand. "I'm...I'm..." Silvi stammered, backing away as if she could escape the phenomenon.

"Gods-chosen," Eigen said from behind her. She hadn't seen him approach. The entire field of Svekards had seen and were staring at the power of the Gods radiating out of her. She stared back at them, lost for a moment in fear, excitement, and shock.

"No," she replied, watching broken men and women push themselves up out of the muck to get a look at her. She had magic and Barra. She had to fight whether she wanted to or not. These people had chosen to sacrifice themselves. They were the Svekard heroes. "*We* are Gods-chosen."

She had asked Leapora to be "our" shield, not "my" shield. Leapora, protector of all Svekards, was with them.

"Leapora, be our shield!" Silvi called, raising her voice and her now uninjured left hand toward the sky.

There was a burning sensation across the back of Silvi's hands that felt like holding her hands just a little too close to the fire on a cold winter night. It was both invigorating and concerning, all the more so because she couldn't pull away. She could smell burning flesh but felt no pain. Across the back of her left hand, the red flame slowly etched the symbol of Leapora. The goddess had marked her hero. Now and for the rest of her life, there would be no question that she was God-chosen.

The red glow engulfing Silvi's hand spread and swirled, crisscrossing itself into the interwoven reeds and boards that made up a typical Svekard round shield. From the metal node in the center of the shield, the red shot out, jumping like lightning from one Svekard to the next, creating shields as it went. Red glowing shield after shield, the spark jumped over and under, touching every Svekard whose soul did not belong to Hadrone.

Silvi stared in wonder as the warriors around the battlefield rose to their feet astonished, bleeding gashes closed, broken bones healed, concussive headaches cleared. We have a chance, Silvi thought.

She looked down at her right hand at the bright red glow roiling there. As far as any Svekard knew and any epic told, Silvi's power should have been done. The Gods did not get along and they certainly did not work together. It had been risky to pray to more than one god and cast her net wide, but it was unreasonable that more than one god would have answered.

Nevertheless, the Gods weren't done, and neither was she.

"Klucar, be our sword!" Silvi thrust her empty, glowing hand toward the heavens and watched in shock as the red first etched Klucar's symbol into the back of her right hand and then boiled up the tips of her fingers and out, leaving a perfectly balanced long sword in its wake. From the tip of her sword, the red glow moved outward, silent and unseen until it reached the next Svekard and erupted into a blade before moving on.

Silvi had one god left, but she wasn't glowing anymore. Was it rude to Fradren to leave him out or rude to Leapora and Klucar to call on another god when they had answered her call?

Silvi looked up at the Neamairtese, who were staring with wide-eyed fascination at the Svekards who had risen from the muck, unharmed. The queen's mate had never had his or her own magic, not since the days of the king. But then again, the queen's mate had never been a Svekard.

The Neamairtese were uninjured, but that didn't mean they hadn't risked their lives by staying. They were headed to save their people as well and willing to run into the fray to do so. It was worth one more call.

"Fradren, strengthen our allies," Silvi called, stretching her shield and sword out in the direction of her allies on the wall.

For a long moment of silence, the group stood waiting for something to happen.

"Damn," Silvi whispered under her breath. "Way to end strong," she said before turning back to her people with a resolute nod. They didn't need to know nothing had happened. Sure, there hadn't been any theatrics and she didn't bear the symbol of Fradren, but Fradren was like that about theatrics, or at least she could hope her people assumed that.

"Svekards," Silvi announced, holding Klucar's sword high. "I called on you to fight back a vicious enemy, and you stood side by side to beat them back. The Gods heard your bravery and they are with us now. We have our people to save. To battle!" Svekards roared and Neamairtese howled as Silvi led them, streaming through the gate.

CHAPTER SIXTEEN
THE REINFORCEMENTS

I'm coming for you, my love," Silvi whispered, looking out at the people running back toward the wall and wishing she was there by Barra's side. She would be soon enough.

The group of warriors with glowing shields and swords raced down the road toward the people running toward them. The setting sun to their left hid the mud and blood caked across their every feature and accentuated the glow of their swords and shields to the point that the warriors appeared to radiate power. Their people gaped at the forces coming to their aid, but didn't slow their departure, only split to allow their defenders to continue forward. The army was almost on them, and their best chance of survival was to continue to put as much space between themselves and the battle.

Mothers, children, young, and old streamed past Silvi, but she barely saw them. She was looking for one man in particular. Her heart was in her throat as more and more people passed by her. Where was Daralan?

Silvi took a deep breath and closed her eyes. She didn't need to see Daralan to know where Barra was. She could feel her. Ahead and left. Silvi opened her eyes and rushed forward, veering slightly left to intercept Daralan as he fell farther and farther behind the crowd. She could just make out the top of his head over the tufts of hair surrounding him. A small gang of Neamairtese ran next to Daralan enclosing him and protecting their queen. She would not be left behind.

Silvi hadn't intended to slow down. She hadn't intended to change course. She had intended to ensure Daralan had Barra and then continue to the front line. The magic inside her had other plans.

The army of glowing Svekards and Neamairtese archers followed Silvi, slowing their approach. Silvi turned to run toward the enemy and tried to take even the first step. Her body refused.

"I can't leave her," Silvi hissed to Keepan who was looking at her expectantly. "I mean I physically can't leave her." She knew her eyes portrayed both her guilt and frustration.

"Protect the witch as she protected us," Keepan said, holding out his left arm to her, palm up.

Silvi took his forearm as he took hers, their shields bumping together. "The Gods are with you," she told him before repeating the line to the multitude.

"Forward," Keepan yelled, leading the warriors willing to follow him into death if that's where the path he set led them.

Silvi watched them go before turning to push her way through the Neamairtese to Barra. She needed to see her, to kiss her, to know she was all right. Tears sprang to her eyes as she looked at the most beautiful thing she thought she'd ever see. Barra lay sound asleep, completely unharmed, her head resting on Daralan's shoulder. Her hair hung forward from the jostling of Daralan's uneven gait, and Silvi could just make out the grape stem poking out of the thicket closest to Barra's temple.

She closed the space between them, jogging beside Daralan and petting Barra's hand where it dangled at her side.

"I've got her," Daralan panted without stopping. He was looking at the glowing shield in her left hand and the glowing sword in her right. "Your place is out there."

"I can't..." But she could. More than that, she felt the magic pushing her forward. "Make up your mind," Silvi muttered to the magic. "Yes," Silvi said the single Neamairtese word to Daralan before leaving the circle of Neamairtese once more to head toward the front line.

Her warriors were many paces ahead of her, closing in on the enemy as the horses raced toward them. Silvi tried to speed up but felt herself slowing. The feeling of total lack of control over her body was disconcerting and highly frustrating. "What now?" Silvi hissed at the magic. Was she supposed to be on the front line defending Barra or not?

Instead, Silvi watched from her place on a small hill, halfway between Barra and her warriors, as the horses closed the last of the distance between themselves and the glowing warriors.

Two volleys of arrows struck the horsemen before they reached the line of Svekards, swarming over them like a wave onto the shore. Silvi could do nothing but watch as the soldiers struck the Svekard line before curving and drawing back as if toward an undertow. The horsemen surged forward and back, using their mobility to strike hard and fast.

But the Svekard line did not go down. As far as Silvi could tell, not a single Svekard was being injured let alone being cut down. It was hard to tell through the haze of red mist around the clashing, swarming horde. All she could tell was that the Svekards were standing firm, taking hit after hit to their shields and striking out with their swords at each wave that attempted to trample and destroy them. Leapora's shield was protecting all of them.

Many yards behind them, the Neamairtese continued to shoot into the fray just past their Svekard allies.

Silvi watched as one Victricite soldier pulled from the rest of the group, drawing away to observe the next wave crash uselessly against the Svekard line. The man looked from the Svekard line to the retreating Svekards and Neamairtese and his eyes narrowed in calculation.

I know him, Silvi realized despite the dying light, as she took in his sharp, clean-cut features. He was the commander who had led the capture of her people and their march to Victricus, the one who had known aloe and struck the soldier who had punched her.

As she watched, the commander rose in his saddle and yelled to his forces. While half of his riders continued to attack the line of Svekards, the other half broke off, circling widely around and heading straight for the Neamairtese archers.

Silvi tried to run to their aid but found once again that she couldn't. She pushed desperately against the magic. These Neamairtese were not just her allies, they had saved her life and the lives of her clansfolk. They were not the faceless red-haired savages she had thought they were less than two weeks prior. She knew them, she trusted them. Helenda was amongst them. Silvi wasn't sure exactly how she felt about Helenda, but Barra loved her—not the way she loved Silvi, but it wasn't a competition. Helenda had made that clear.

Silvi didn't pause to think through her strategy. She finally knew exactly what the magic had in mind for her. While the Neamairtese pivoted to try to defend themselves against the onslaught coming, Silvi ran straight toward the commander. When the horsemen took out the Neamairtese archers, the commander would send them after the civilians and Barra. Rushing the unprotected masses was the only thing that would break the Svekard line. Silvi couldn't allow that. She had to take down the commander before he could give that order.

The commander didn't see Silvi until it was too late. He jerked the reins and kicked his horse into a gallop, but Silvi was fighting for Barra and nothing could outrun her. With a single, perfect slice, Silvi cut the rigging of the saddle. The commander leaned forward, grabbing the horse's mane as the saddle began to slip to the side. He grasped wildly for the reins and managed to pull his horse to a stop in time to not crash to the ground.

Silvi was ready for him. She smashed him in the side with her shield, throwing him from his horse to land in a heap of leather and armor on the ground. The man clambered to his feet, drew his sword, and steadied into a fighting stance.

The sun was setting in the west casting long shadows across the field. They squared off, circling slowly.

Silvi didn't want to fight him. She didn't want to kill him. She wanted him to call off his forces and she wanted to keep him from directing them.

The commander lunged at Silvi, his sword striking for her head. The blade sank into her shield instead. Whether instinct had brought it up in time or Leapora, Silvi couldn't say, all she knew was that his sword was buried deeply in her shield and this was her moment. Klucar's sword flashed out, striking the commander in the calf muscle. He fell to his knee and tried to get up again on one good leg.

Silvi struck again, her blade sinking into the thigh of his good leg. "Just surrender," Silvi said to the kneeling man still trying to rise. She knew he wouldn't understand her but willed him to do so anyway. The Neamairtese archers were falling a handful at a time. Once they all fell, nothing would stand between them and the civilians still running toward the Victricite wall.

A broad smile spread across the commander's face as his fingers stretched out in the grass. It took a second for Silvi to understand. She couldn't feel what he could, but she could hear it—the far-off sound of hoofbeats, hundreds of hoofbeats, barreling toward them.

Turning away from the commander, Silvi looked off to the east in the direction of the coming reinforcements. A full moon was rising, obscuring the horizon with a reddish-orange light. Even with her improved senses, Silvi couldn't make out more than the general width of the army. Hundreds had been an underestimate. There had to be thousands.

Silvi looked from the horizon to the commander and back. Why was she here? What was the point of taking down the commander just to be overrun by reinforcements? She had failed Barra, her people, and the Neamairtese. They would all die or be re-enslaved for nothing.

The thunder of hoofbeats was drowned out as a whooping war cry in the voices of thousands pierced the air. Silvi watched the color drain from the commander's face as his smile fell away. These weren't reinforcements, or at least they weren't his reinforcements. He would have known that if he had been on horseback. He might have had time to order his forces to turn and run. From his spot on the ground, all the commander could do was watch the new arrivals, highlighted by the glow of the moon, sweep across the field eliminating his forces.

Silvi stared in her own amazement at the red glow that seemed to emanate from the hooves of the new arrivals' horses. Unless these new people had a magic all their own, Fradren had heard her call and he had answered, just not with the allies she had been expecting. As if responding to her thought, Silvi felt the intense warmth of fire prickling across her brow, smelled the scent of burning flesh, and saw the red glow emanating from her in the darkness. She couldn't see it but knew exactly what had been etched into her forehead—Fradren's mark. Silvi didn't have time to take in the Victricite commander's horrified expression as flame danced across her brow. She was busy watching to make sure the riders posed no risk to Barra and their people.

It took the newcomers a matter of minutes to clear the battlefield of the Victricites, cutting them down like fire across a field of dry leaves. Their skill and grace swirled across the field in a single coordinated wave of red, flameless fire. The commander kneeling in front of Silvi was the only remaining member of the Victricite army.

The commander gave Silvi a look of resigned defeat before planting his sword in the ground in front of him. He was bleeding from his leg wounds but not enough that he was going to bleed out any time soon.

Silvi stepped forward, taking the sword in a gesture she hoped conveyed her acceptance of his surrender and motioned for him to try to stand. She needed to return to the rest of the group.

The new mounted army had reformed into a giant wave of horses and riders on the eastern side of the battleground, staring at the dilapidated group of Neamairtese and Svekards slowly collecting into a cohesive group, like crustaceans trying to scuttle back into their tide pools in the calm after a storm. The Neamairtese and Svekards were looking around themselves, not just to identify the living from the dead, but in clear search for Silvi. Silvi's enhanced vision was fading, a reassuring sign that the newcomers weren't a danger, but she could still make out the consternation in all faces.

The commander managed two stumbling steps before falling to his knees once more. He looked furious, irate with his own ineptitude. With a suppressed groan, he pushed to his feet again and tried to take a step. Silvi was there to catch him this time as he fell.

She shifted Klucar's sword to her shield hand and imitated using the commander's sword as a cane before holding it out to him. The commander gave his sword an incensed look before accepting it. He drove the point into the ground with a grimace before leaning on it and moving forward slowly, wincing.

As she watched him struggle, Silvi realized why he was reacting as violently to placing the sword in front of him as he was to stepping on his bad legs. His grimaces had nothing to do with real damage. Every time he stuck his sword into the ground, he was repeating the gesture of surrender. In attempting to help him, Silvi had provided the commander with the ultimate form of dishonor.

Silvi looked from the commander to the now blurry figures on the ground amongst the Svekards and Neamairtese. Those were people who would never get up again, because of the commander. Around them were people who had been captured and brought here by the commander. He had allowed her to save a horse and he had punched one of his countrymen for acting against her, but that did not absolve him of his evils. She wouldn't kill him, but humiliation felt more than justified.

Once Silvi was close enough, three Svekards hurried forward to take the commander into their custody, freeing Silvi to greet the people who had saved them.

The riders wore bright yellow silken robes laced with strips of leather and intricately embroidered beading. Their skin was a russet brown and covered in tiny black tattoos in the shape of runes. Their hair was black as night and poured in waves out of the top of silken wraps on top of their heads in thin, dense dreads.

These were Razirgali, like the healer Silvi had identified as a veterinarian for humans. Silvi knew nothing of them personally and had none of the previous queen's memories to pull on to understand, only the knowledge that Barra had identified the woman, Ahjva, as Razirgali and that these must be more of her people.

The lead rider looked at Silvi as she approached, while the rest of the group looked back and forth between her and their lead rider. They acted as though they knew what their leader would do about as much as they knew what Silvi would do.

Silvi didn't need to see their expressions to know this man was not like the others. While the rest of their hair was a natural black, his spouted out of his silken headwraps in every color under the sun as if a rainbow was growing directly out of his head and pouring down his back in thick, colored vines.

The lead rider wore the same silken robes as his people, but while the lower parts of the robes were yellow, the upper part was a collage of colors, stained by whatever he put in his hair to achieve the unnatural colors. Shadows of where his hair had sat on his shoulders stayed there like brightly colored snakes crawling down from his neck. The tattoos on his face were more densely drawn, making his skin appear even darker. He was looking at Silvi expectantly out of large, dark brown eyes.

"Ask the ancestors to light our dreams and comfort our steps," Silvi said slowly in a language she'd never spoken before. She was repeating Barra's words exactly as she remembered them from the encounter with the Razirgali healer. She knew it wasn't quite right. If she understood correctly, the phrase was meant for parting, not meeting and should have been stated as a wish for him, not asking him to bless them. It was the best she could provide. If only Barra was awake, Silvi thought for the millionth time that day.

The Razirgali leader gave Silvi a crazed smile, showing off teeth blackened by charcoal and spoke his language in a high-pitched voice that seemed incongruous with his tall, burly stature. Silvi didn't catch a single word of it. She'd hoped to be able to understand words Barra or Ahjva had spoken. Instead, she just stared at him.

The leader chuckled and spoke again, his high voice raising higher at the end of each sentence in questions. Silvi opened her mouth as if to say something, but when nothing came out, she closed it again and shrugged.

The leader threw back his head, tossing his rainbow of dreads and gave a full body laugh that shook him in his saddle. Around him, the other Razirgali laughed, looking at each other like they weren't exactly sure what he was laughing about, but if it was funny enough for their leader, it was funny enough for them. The leader pointed at himself and boomed in his almost squeaky voice, "Toghoneur."

Silvi nodded, trying not to smile too uneasily. She pointed at herself and said, "Silvi."

"Silvi," Toghoneur boomed before launching himself from his saddle and striding up to her. He slapped both hands onto the sides of her shoulders making her jump and announced again, "Silvi."

Now Silvi knew she radiated discomfort, but there was nothing she could do about it. She could sense Barra near and turned to the crowd with limited hope. She was fairly sure the sensation would be different if Barra was awake. She was relieved to see her nonetheless and similarly relieved to see Helenda by her side, bloody and frazzled, but alive.

Silvi summoned Daralan forward to present the queen of the Neamairtese to their new allies. If they proved to be less of allies than hoped, Silvi trusted the magic to allow her to keep Barra safe. "Barra," she said, pointing to her and making sure to put herself between the Razirgali man and Barra.

Toghoneur gave a curt nod to Barra's sleeping body before turning back to Silvi expectantly.

"She can speak to you," Silvi said, pointing at Barra, moving her hand as if it were a talking mouth and then pointing at Toghoneur. "Once she's awake." Silvi pointed at Barra again and mimed waking up and stretching.

Toghoneur shrugged as if he didn't really understand but wasn't too concerned. He apparently assumed he'd figure it out or they would try again if it was especially important. In the meantime, his attention had drifted from Silvi to the Victricite commander. "Victricite," he growled, hissing his way through the second syllable. He drew his saber and advanced on the restrained and bleeding commander.

"Wait!" Silvi called after him. She knew it was silly to be fine killing all of the commander's people, but to want to spare him, but Silvi had accepted his surrender and it was wrong to attack him now.

Silvi barely got the word out before she felt every muscle in her body go rigid. She watched, as if from outside her body, as four pillars of moonlight centered on her, Toghoneur, Barra, and the commander. She had another second to watch Leapora's shields and Klucar's swords melt from the hands of the Svekards and sizzle across the grass to engulf the four of them before everything went black.

CHAPTER SEVENTEEN
THE SECOND COUNCIL OF NEAMAIRT

Barra felt weightless and completely out of control of her own body. She had the vague feeling that these sensations ought to concern her, but she'd never felt calmer or more right in her life. The absence of physical awareness melted away slowly from the outside in, and Barra felt the subtle sensation of standing on something firm.

The weariness, anxiety, and fear that had plagued her for days was completely gone, and it took effort to even remember what negative emotions felt like with this level of contentment. Barra's heart felt the fullness she only experienced in Silvi's arms, and yet so light she wondered if she could fly.

Barra could feel the dappled sunlight of a midsummer's afternoon on her eyelids. She could vaguely remember that it had been near dawn when she'd closed her eyes and started the spell, but that had been days ago. It had been warm and muggy. The air had smelled like salt and cooked fish.

Now, the air was crisp and clear, with the smell of wind through green, leafy trees, with just a hint of past rain and the sound of birds. This was the way a cloudless sunny day at home smelled.

When she'd eaten the succulent pig weeks ago, she had thought it was what the Summerland would taste like, but she'd been wrong. The Summerland didn't taste like the greasy fulfillment of ravenous hunger. There was clarity of mind and spirit that filled her senses. With her eyes closed, the world even tasted like blissful contentment and the complete lack of need.

Being without Silvi was the only thing that could diminish this bliss. Barra opened her eyes and let out a relieved sigh as she took in the sight of Silvi in her plain, brown, cotton garb, spattered in blood, dirt, and mud. Under the thick coat of muck, Barra thought she could see additional red markings covering her forehead. In the dappled sunlight of the Summerland, Barra didn't think there was anyone in any world more beautiful than her mate.

"Barra," Silvi whispered, crossing the small distance between them in three long strides. She took Barra into her arms, holding her as if nothing else mattered.

"My love," Barra answered, gripping her in return, eyes clenched shut. The idea that they both must have died threatened to shatter Barra's calm, thinking of all the Svekards and Neamairtese that must have fallen alongside them. But it was hard to feel sad when she felt this much at peace and her very soul seemed to be telling her that everything was going to be all right.

"Where are we?" Silvi whispered in her ear.

"The Summerlands," Barra said back. "We are in the place where Neamairtese souls live before being reincarnated."

"Father Sun," called a high-pitched male voice from behind Silvi. "Mother Moon." Barra unburied her face from Silvi's shoulder to look at the ridiculous looking man several paces away. He was definitely not a Neamairtese soul.

The man was in the traditional robed armor of the Razirgali, with his hair dreaded and threaded through his silken turban, but it was the most diverse collection of colors Barra had ever seen. He lay prostrated on the wooden floor, his hands out above his head.

It was then that Barra took in their surroundings for the first time. She, Silvi, the Razirgali, and a Victricite soldier were standing, or lying in the Razirgali's case, on an enormous table meant for giants, far larger than the entirety of the ship that she and almost a hundred people had shared. Around the table were platters of food, each large enough to feed an entire Neamairtese village, and goblets the size of Barra herself.

The decor of the table paled in comparison to the seven giant godly beings seated around the table, watching the four of them with differing levels of dispassionate interest. Barra's eyes went first to the man and woman farthest to her right, to whom the Razirgali was prostrating himself.

The man wore bright yellow robes that looked more like liquid gold than fabric. From his back came pristine white wings in the shape of an eagle's wings. The entire ensemble blazed with golden flame such that Barra couldn't exactly tell where the robes ended and the fire began. The man was bald and flame leapt from every spot on his body. His skin beneath the blaze was the color of the darkest wood while his eyes were a piercing blue. He had a radiance that was hard to look at for longer than half a second, and Barra found it necessary to use her peripheral vision to take in his finer details. His attention and that of the woman next to him were focused on the Razirgali man.

Where the man looked down at the Razirgali, unimpressed, the pale-skinned, black-haired woman at his side was gazing at him with deep affection. She wore a white silken dress that hugged her modest curves, and the wings that Barra could just make out at rest behind her seemed to be in the shape of butterfly wings, but with the wispy translucence of dragonfly wings such that it was hard to tell exactly where they ended. She too seemed to almost blend into the background. The woman's hair was the color of an autumn night sky including the twinkling of small silver dots that looked like stars. She was seated with her body tipped toward the man at her side and appeared to reflect his radiance rather than having any of her own. She looked back and forth between the man at her side and the comparatively tiny man before her with a mixture of reverent love and subservient concern as if at any moment she might have to mediate between the two.

Barra felt her breath catch as the goddess at the other end of the table began to speak, drawing Barra's attention. "Welcome," the Lady said, her voice like a bird's song, "So begins the Second Council of Neamairt." The beauty and the magnificence of her presence filled Barra with a sense of familial love unlike any she had experienced since the death of her mother.

The Lady's bright red hair cascaded down her shoulders over her green dress, and a crown of flowers ringed the top of her head. From root to tip, her hair was filled with flora, except for a strip of hair that looked like all the life had been drained from it until it was a dull gray. Barra's magic and that of the queens before her had come from this piece of the Lady. She was looking down on Barra and Silvi with an expression of great pride and fondness. Barra and Silvi never would have found each other without the Lady, so she had every right, in Barra's opinion, to glory in their bliss.

I'm not just in the Summerlands, Barra realized, I'm in Neamairt, the home of the Lord and Lady. Barra's stare of awe went next to the god on the Lady's right, who sat holding the Lady's hand. The bare-chested Lord, his green, moss-covered antlers rising out of his ruddy-brown hair, sat back in his chair with a stillness that was contradicted by the constant movement of his hair and beard. Barra could see small animals nesting, living, and playing in his hair and well-trimmed beard amongst the foliage that grew there naturally. Barra could see the broken edge of one of the Lord's antler points where he had broken off a piece of himself to provide the Neamairtese with the Lord's magic.

"A special welcome to our guests," the Lady said, sweeping her hand out to indicate the tiny humans on the table. "Barra, queen of the Neamairtese; Silvi, hero of the Svekards; Toghoneur, the rainbow rider and uniter of the bands; and Ausonius, Victricite commander beyond the wall. We are here today to create a new future for our people."

"We are here because the first council failed to achieve what we set out to do," the Razirgali god stated, his flame momentarily enshrouding him in bright white light.

Next to him, the Razirgali goddess sat forward with an overly amenable smile. "Thank you for inviting us into your home again and hosting so we can work on a new agreement." She directed her smile at the Lady before shrinking back into her chair.

The man near the center of the table cleared his throat, drawing Barra to the last three gods seated at the table. Barra knew the three hearty blonds from the memories of thousands of stories and drawings Silvi had heard and seen all her life. The first man wore a horned Svekard helmet, and from under it sprouted enough braided hair and beard that Barra almost couldn't make out the dense bearskin furs he wore from the shoulders down. Klucar, god of war, had piercing red eyes that seemed at every moment to be calculating his next move. Those eyes were turned on Silvi with a look of familial pride.

The woman next to him was also looking at Silvi, but with the kind of protective gaze that made Barra's heart leap when Silvi gave it to her. Leapora, goddess of protection and the family, had perfect blond braids that poured down over her ample bosom and white, wolf pelt furs. She wore a golden tiara inlaid with precious gems, and red lightning crackled between her fingers.

The exactness of Leapora's braids could not compete with the precise spacing, size, and dimensions of the hair and beard braids of the man to her left. Fradren, god of justice and order, sat with a calm and regality absent in the other two who were leaning forward in their chairs, each with one hand gripping a goblet and the other a plate. He wore furs unlike any Barra or Silvi had seen, the short, golden fibers of the fur lying like woven cloth across his shoulders in the shape of a robe. Across his forehead, just visible under the braids that tucked neatly behind his ears, were slowly changing lines of iridescent red runic symbols like living tattoos. His gaze was appraising and steady as he took in the four humans before him.

Where the Razirgali gods were defined by their appearance and the Neamairtese gods held within their hair a representation of the life they protected and grew, the Svekard Prime Gods could almost look human, if not for their size and obvious power. Like their people, their symbols and appearance were less important than their actions.

Next to Barra, Silvi's eyes went wide as she took in the three Prime Gods, all staring at her. Barra knew it wasn't just that such power was looking at Silvi. To have the three of them sitting next to each other, not arguing, was impressive. To be sharing in a meal's fellowship with the Neamairtese gods was an idea so blasphemous no storyteller would consider describing it.

"Before we discuss any new agreements, let us review what was determined at the First Council of Neamairt," Fradren said, pushing his plate out from in front of him. In the plate's place, he placed a stack of exceptionally thin stone tablets.

"Yes," the Lady said. "Then our guests can understand the context as well."

Fradren cleared his throat and began to read in the same legalistic tone in which the text had been written. "In attendance, the Lord and Lady of Neamairt serving as hosts; Father Sun and Mother Moon; Klucar, Leapora, and Fradren, serving as representatives of the Clanned Deities. Whereas, the Great Divine War was brought to a close with the banishment of the dark spirits and the evil gods to the Dark Lands, and whereas minor gods and the human colony pose a threat to the newly created balance, now therefore the human colony will be divided amongst the gods and scattered throughout the world. The minor gods will take their people to the far reaches of the world where they will have neither need nor opportunity to challenge the authority of the superior gods. Those people who remain unchosen will be godless and left to their own devices. The peoples of the superior gods will be kept separate by language and prejudice to prevent their hubris from turning them against their gods. It will be each god's highest duty to protect and serve the people who worship and serve them."

His recitation complete, Fradren placed the tablets inside the right side of his robes and drew out fresh ones from the left. He placed his hand over them as if to carve notes on them simply by willing it to happen.

The Lord gave Fradren an appreciative nod before turning the full weight of his gaze on the Victricite commander in their midst. "For millennia, this agreement has kept peace amongst the gods. What it did not account for, however, was that a group of unchosen who collected together and named themselves Victricites would use their godless, opportunistic society to wage a silent, systematic war against our peoples—a war none of them could win individually."

"A dishonorable war!" Klucar burst out. His red gaze was attempting to burn a hole through the representative of his enemy. The man was lucky to be protected by the magic of Neamairt where Barra knew none of them could physically harm each other. To be that angry in a place of such calm was a testament to his rage.

Father Sun's blaze had gained a blue tinge at its depths as he burned hotter and brighter. "You destroyed my people one band at a time until we had to reach into the dreams of our shamans and send what remained into the eastern scrublands just to avoid their complete elimination."

"You won your war without the clan, without magic, without the guidance of the ancestors," Leapora said, arms crossed over her large chest. "You are still nothing but ants, swarming and biting, completely indifferent to the noble creatures around you being destroyed."

Both of our creation stories are true, Barra realized, looking from Leapora to Silvi. The gods, including those of the Svekards, had broken the human colony like an anthill and chosen their people. The Svekard gods had given their people the power of the clan, while the Lord and Lady had given their chosen people the power of magic and the bounty created by the Spirits. Clearly, the gods of the Razirgali had given them a connection to their ancestors through dreams and shamans.

Meanwhile, the Victricites had remained industrious ants with brutality toward anything outside the colony. It had originally been the human ant colony that had threatened the gods, so Barra supposed it shouldn't be surprising that the ant-like Victricites had risen up to threaten the people of the gods.

The conversation devolved as all but Fradren, the Lord, and the Lady added their own pieces and opinions on the dirty, avaricious people who deserved little more than to be cast into the Dark Lands. Fradren sat calmly throughout, noting the responses of the gods around him. When he had heard enough, he called his peers to order.

The Victricite commander had watched and listened to their accusations, stone-faced, his body held to a strict attention. Now, he stepped forward, drawing all their gazes of ire and damnation. "It appears to me," Ausonius, commander beyond the wall, said, "that after condemning us to an unprotected, godless life, you condemn us once more for using our own devices to overcome the inherent darkness of the world. If I fail my people, as I have done in the battle that brought us here, I do not blame my enemy for my own weakness or vanity. I would expect deities to be better."

For a long moment, the entire room stared at the brazenness displayed. At last, the Lord spoke, smoothly and evenly. "Though there was a time when it was otherwise, the world is not inherently dark anymore. It is humanity which harbors the last pieces of the darkness."

"A rider is responsible for his horse," Father Sun said, sternness overriding his previous rage. "That does not give you permission to beat a horse while his rider is absent."

"Even if that rider is neglectful," Mother Moon added with a hesitant smile.

Leapora thumped her fist on the table, ready to get back to shouting if only everyone else would just join her so she didn't look like the instigator. "We won't allow it anymore."

"No, we won't!" Klucar echoed, thumping both fists on the table. He was more than happy to escalate.

The Lady held up a hand for quiet before proceeding. She turned her gaze on Barra and Silvi as she spoke. "We have kept our people apart because we were afraid they would become more powerful than us. In some ways, we were right. Without the strength and bravery of the Svekards, the spirit and skill of the Neamairtese, and the faith of the

Razirgali, we could not have saved our people from the Victricites. The strength of our arms is nothing without you as our hands."

Next to the Lady, the Svekard gods shifted uncomfortably. Svekards knew they were not as burly as their furs portrayed, but a Svekard would never say so. To point out the weakness of the gods was alarming even if it was being done by a god, perhaps all the more because it was being pointed out by a god.

Whether she noticed the effect of her comments or not, the Lady continued. "In some ways we were wrong, for it was in keeping you weak to prevent rebellion that we made you susceptible to the Victricite plague. I therefore move that we end the agreement of the First Council of Neamairt."

Leapora fixed the Lady with a callous look. "You made that move when you led them to each other," she said, pointing from Barra to Silvi.

"Yes," the Lady answered with a raised eyebrow. "They were already soul mates. After fate led them together, I simply bound them together. Then you, the Clanned gods, answered with Scobata's owl. What was a symbol for Silvi became a message to the Lord and me that you were willing to come back to the table."

"We were willing," Leapora said without further elaboration.

"Fradren brought the Razirgali," Klucar said defensively. Barra wasn't entirely sure which side he was arguing for, considering Leapora's first comment had been to accuse the Lady of acting outside their agreement. "Silvi, hero of the Prime Gods, asked Fradren for help and he delivered it."

"He delivered it?" Father Sun asked. His blue eyes held contempt that softened into a look reminiscent of respect as he turned toward Toghoneur. "Mother Moon gave the Rainbow Rider visions to unite the Razirgali, and the ancestors sent the message through the stars to return to the west. They did not need your invitation, even if you did give speed to their final approach. You think six days was enough time to prepare? We have been waiting for this day and for you all to get your heads out of your respective—"

"Darling," Mother Moon interrupted, "I think we can all agree that bringing the many diverse bands together to form a united rainbow has made Toghoneur, like Barra and Silvi, a most valuable guest at this table."

Fradren interrupted before another round of debating and finger pointing could get too far out of hand. "The Lady has moved to end the agreement of the First Council of Neamairt. All in favor?"

Every godly voice around the table spoke at once. "Aye."

"And what do you propose we put in its place?" Klucar asked. "Shall we call the armies of Svek and the Neamairtese? The Razirgali are already here. Let it be a war to end the Victricite infestation."

Barra couldn't help her grimace. If the Lord and Lady were anything like their people understood them to be, there was no way they would agree to that. The Lady opened her mouth as if to speak, but she was a second too late.

It was Father Sun who spoke. "We could burn them to the ground, but we will not. Because Ausonius here is the most respected commander in the Victricite army and he is going to take a message back to his people." Father Sun turned to the Victricite with a blue hot flame burning in his eyes. "He is going to tell his people that they are to release any remaining slaves in any of their fields, houses, ships, or otherwise from everywhere in their empire. He is going to tell them that if they don't, the combined armies of the Razirgali, Svekards, and Neamairtese and all the power of their gods will make every piece of Victricus burn until there is nothing left."

Klucar looked far too pleased at this idea for Barra's comfort. She could only imagine what the commander was feeling. Though any man who could speak to the gods as Ausonius had couldn't possibly be as fearful as she would be. Barra looked over at him and wondered for the first time if he had a family. Were there people back in Victricus that he fought for or just money, pride, and a sense of duty?

Fradren cleared his throat again to clarify that it was his turn to speak. "The following terms of the Victricus's surrender have been suggested: that they will release all slaves and prisoners back to their people, whether they are Neamairtese, Razirgali, Svekard, or some other people, and if we discover that any slave has been kept or that the empire has taken any new slaves, it will be war."

"Aye," Klucar said. The smile he gave Ausonius said he was hoping the surrender agreements would be broken.

"Aye," echoed the Svekard and Razirgali gods.

There was silence for a moment as the gods looked back and forth between the Lord and Lady and Barra, Silvi, and Toghoneur. "It is you who will wage the war," the Lady explained. "Your vote is as necessary as ours."

"So it is," Toghoneur yipped. "Let their wall hold them in and let us thrive in the northern lands."

"Aye," Silvi added. "We give them a chance to right their wrongs and end them if they cannot live in covenant."

The whole group turned to Barra, who wasn't entirely sure she could say yes. The threat was an excellent one and the terms were to her liking, but how could she agree when if the Victricites broke the agreement she couldn't in good conscience send her people to kill men, women, and children.

"No," Barra said, trying to make her voice carry over the large space. She swallowed nervously and scanned the group until her gaze fell first on the Lady and second on Silvi. The Lady's gaze, a look of loving pride from Barra's deity, didn't ignite her the way Silvi's did. She turned back to the gods ready to speak her mind, knowing that no matter how angry it might make some around the table, the ones that mattered most had her back.

Barra squared her shoulders and addressed the gods. "That is not an agreement. It is an ultimatum and ultimatums do not last. What we need is a new agreement that will hold for millennia. Since we have all suffered by being cut off from each other, why shouldn't the Victricites benefit from coming into covenant as well? What do they gain by adhering to our demands? That we don't kill them all? With an agreement like that, we will only build resentment. For centuries, our three peoples didn't get along, but we prospered anyway because of trade. The Victricites must give up their slaves, but they can trade that luxury for the chance to trade with us. If they swear to us not to capture any of us as slaves or attack us beyond their wall, we swear they will be safe within their wall. Though we have magic, and gods, and ancestors, they are stronger than us individually. Isn't it worth offering them something they want like hides, horses, mead and cod fish oil for a chance to learn what they know?"

As she had anticipated, the Svekard gods looked none too happy with Barra's suggestion. Even Fradren seemed to be calculating the complexity of such an agreement with displeasure. Father Sun was looking at Barra as if she were a silly child with childish ideals of a world of constant rainbows, and Mother Moon's placating look felt just as demeaning.

For a long moment, everyone just stared from Barra to each other, waiting for someone to come up with a better idea or at least to tell Barra that her idea was untenable. Barra wished she had more to say, but anything she could come up with would only play to values and morals that would further divide her gods and the rest of them.

Eventually, it was Ausonius who broke the silence. "We have a breed of pig that grows twice as large as any I've seen in the outskirts of Svek. We get spices from kingdoms and empires too far to reach by any means but ship. We can grow crops year-round and can make steel, which is sharper and more durable than iron. You think we are opportunists, and we are, but that is our strength, and it will be yours because being opportunistic means seizing opportunities when they arise. This is just such an opportunity."

From beside him, Toghoneur gave a snorting, squeaking laugh. "Spoken in true Raider Tongue. I would rather barter for their riches than burn them down. So it is."

From Toghoneur's other side, Silvi took a step forward, turning as she spoke to address the whole group. "It's not just their stuff we can trade for. From what I saw, they are better smiths and sailors. Being as crowded as they are, they must know how to construct and how to heal better than any of the rest of us. They have knowledge and we have labor. They don't get our labor for free anymore, they don't get to keep us as slaves. But there is more to be gained by working with them than by destroying them."

Silvi turned to address her gods directly. "I think Barra's agreement is good. It's what is best for the clans and all Svekards."

The Lady's smile seemed to light the room as she turned to the rest of the gods. "It seems our children have come up with a better solution."

Around the table, the gods nodded. "Aye," Fradren stated. The statement was quickly picked up around the room. There was a note of resignation in their voices, but pride as well.

"I cannot speak for all of my people," Ausonius said. "But I will present your offer faithfully."

Klucar pushed his empty plate aside to lean his head down toward the table and put his eyes at the same level as Ausonius. "Know this,

Victricite, if your people turn down or renege on this agreement, my threat still stands. You have an army at your door and thousands more in waiting. Tell your people that we can create as many heroes as it takes to rain a war of complete destruction down upon your heads. Do you understand me?"

"We will protect our own," Leapora added.

Father Sun burned with a bluish hue, words unnecessary to add his own threat to Klucar's.

"Go tell your people of our offer," Fradren said, lifting his hand from his current tablet. With a flick of his wrist, Ausonius was gone and only Toghoneur, Silvi, and Barra stood before their gods.

The Lord leaned forward, his elbows resting on the table and his bearded chin coming to rest on his interwoven fingers. "You have done well, my children. We have sheltered you too long for fear that you would not need us, and you prove us correct. I could not be prouder. There will come a day when you do not need us at all, when our magic will pale in comparison to what you can achieve without us. There will also come a day when we will fade away, our power poured drop by drop into magic, heroes, and ancestors. It is your job to make sure that the day you do not need us comes before the day we are not there."

The Lord paused to take the Lady's hand in his own and give it a squeeze. He reached up to the antler point exactly opposite the missing one and with a perfect mix of strength and delicateness, broke the point off. He held the piece of himself out to Barra who took it reverently. Within her hands, it shrank from the size of a wolf pup to that of a normal-sized deer antler. "It is clear that you need each other. So, take this. Put a shaving of it into a fire and all who stand within that fire's glow will be able to speak to each other, no matter their natural tongue. Moreover, anyone within that fire's glow will be able to speak to anyone within another fire's glow that has received a shaving. As long as that fire burns, it will have this power."

With a solemn glance down the table, the Lord added, "Like us, eventually, the piece will be gone, so tend to your fires and learn well how to live without them and with each other."

Not one to be outdone, Klucar requested one of Fradren's tablets and broke it on the table, pounding it over and over again with his fist. When he had a sufficient pile of tiny tablet chunks, he scooped them into his hand and laid his other hand on top of them to form a person-sized alcove into which he whispered words of power. For a moment, the chunks glowed a magnificent red. Klucar tore off a piece of his napkin and brushed the crumbs of tablet into the napkin piece and held it out to Silvi. "These runes will help keep your fires burning longer and slower."

Leapora reached out a single finger to Silvi as a parent might hold out for a child to grip. "We will protect you for as long as we are here," she said as Silvi wrapped her hand as far around the finger as she could. "We will protect your children and your children's children and on."

"And we will not go out without a fight!" Klucar added.

"Face each day with your head held high," Father Sun said, leaning back in his seat and crossing his arms across his chest. "Each moment is an opportunity to fail, but you have not failed us yet. So it is."

Toghoneur puffed up with pride at what apparently sounded a lot more encouraging to him than it did to Barra.

"Just look to the sky and know we are watching over you," Mother Moon added.

The Lady raised her hands, poised for a clap, and said the final words. "Remember us and tell our stories. You are so very dear to us."

As the Lady's hands came together, the world went black and Barra experienced a sensation similar to what she had felt her first night as queen around the ceremonial fire as she returned to her body. Barra opened her weary eyes and smiled at the Neamairtese gathered around her. She could just make out Svekards several paces away helping Silvi to her feet.

The Neamairtese around Barra stared in slack-jawed amazement as Barra related what had just happened. She could pick out every few words Silvi was saying as she did the same, broken up every once in a while by a roar of approval. Several yards away, Toghoneur was doing the same for his own people, standing on top of his saddle to be seen by more of his people and proclaiming Father Sun's words and Mother Moon's encouragement.

A healed Ausonius was released to return to his people with the terms of their agreement. The Razirgali, Svekards, and Neamairtese returned to the Victricus wall to claim it as their own until Ausonius returned and a final agreement was formed.

The festivities that night were somber. They had all lost many of their people whether in this battle or the silent war years and decades before. A collective ceremony was held to light the first of the Lord's fires as a lighthouse on top of the wall, surrounded by the Prime Gods' runes. Then, the three groups celebrated their victory, thanked their gods, and memorialized their dead separately.

Even Barra and Silvi spent the evening apart until they left their people to sleep and found a quiet space in the grass to lie together in the quiet ruckus of the night. Barra fell asleep with Silvi's head resting on her chest, the Lord's antler gripped in her hand, and the sound of horses filling her dreams.

Three days later, Ausonius returned. By that point, Barra was fairly sure the Neamairtese, Svekards, and Razirgali were as desperate to reach a conclusion and leave as the Victricites were for them to leave. In the wall's storehouses, they had found enough food and water, but no one was enjoying the process of distributing it fairly. By the time they'd finished rationing out lunch, the front of the line was back for their share of dinner. The hordes of thousands might be allies but they certainly weren't friends, and everyone wanted to make sure their own people were taken care of first and foremost.

Ausonius brought with him two men in red robes with purple trim and gold tassels. The men each wore a thin circlet of gold around their heads and a ring with several jewels on each finger. They looked exceedingly displeased to have traveled from Victricus City to the wall.

For hours, the group debated and negotiated around the Lord's fire. Barra had no experience with such negotiations, but had hundreds of years of queens' memories to draw on. What she found hardest was coordinating not only between four different cultures, but also different measures of time and value.

The four groups did not need to be allies. No one expected them to be. Even the Neamairtese and Razirgali, who were the only two of the groups that had never openly or covertly fought each other, had never considered each other allies. Finding the nuanced balance between trading partners with rules of engagement and unrealistic friendship took the group long into the evening, the full moon lighting their discussion and the sounds of thousands of people settling down for the night reminding them exactly who they were negotiating for.

The sky was just turning a light shade of pink and the stirring of rising people filled the air when Silvi finally drew out scrolls and began to document the aspects of the agreement while Barra continued to lead the discussion. Any remaining slaves would be released by the next full moon and they, as well as the current army of released slaves, would be provided with enough provisions to make the journey home. The Victricites would be allowed free passage during that time to withdraw or reinforce their posts beyond the wall. After that, the Razirgali would reclaim the land of their ancestors, migrating across it as they had done for centuries and serving as the merchant fleet of the plains.

Raiding, as well as armed defense of trade caravans, would be allowed. Toghoneur insisted on the right of his people to kidnap and hold people and cargo for ransom, but that such captives were to be treated humanely and exchanged for a reasonable price. The Victricites demanded the same rights and the ability to kill to defend themselves from such attacks. The Razirgali would not be taken within the Victricite borders nor would the Razirgali assault the defenses of the wall. So too, a border was drawn for Svek and the land of the Neamairtese in which they would be safe from invasion or raids. In the end, aside from securing the freedom of their people and the preservation of this fire, Barra was fairly sure she and Silvi had aided in a truce between the Razirgali and the Victricites, more than secured anything for themselves or their people.

The negotiations between the Neamairtese and the Svekards would be a conversation all its own and Barra guessed it would not take place over one night of intense debate. What Barra had in mind for their peoples wasn't a truce, but a relationship to mend the past. That would take time and the slow building of trust.

Each leader etched their mark into the agreement and gave verbal confirmation of their obligations under it in the glow of the Lord's fire.

"So it is," Toghoneur said, holding the agreement up toward the rising sun. He smiled, flashing his charcoal black teeth before handing the agreement back to Silvi. He leapt up onto the edge of the wall and crowed like a rooster at the top of his lungs down at hordes of people camped below. A thunderous cheer followed from below, as Razirgali, Neamairtese, and Svekards joined the call.

Barra couldn't contain her chuckle. "So it is," she said, taking Silvi's hand in her own.

CHAPTER EIGHTEEN
THE REASON I'M LEAVING

For almost four weeks, the Svekards and Neamairtese traveled north together, escorted by the Razirgali.

Barra and Silvi spent most of their days apart, talking to their people.

Every Svekard, more than two thousand people, wanted to hear Silvi recount her experience at the Second Council of Neamairt firsthand. Barra wished it was her telling the stories over and over again. She loved reliving it, where she knew Silvi had come to dread it. Unfortunately, her own people seemed satiated by the single telling Barra had given them that first night. The exact details of what happened between the queen and the gods was far more private to the Neamairtese.

The Svekards found ways to politely ignore Barra's retellings. Instead, they asked Silvi for details that Silvi admitted to Barra she couldn't even remember.

Barra spent most of her day hearing the stories of her people from their lives in captivity. They each wanted to describe the hair tokens they had lost and prove that they had not lost the memories nor the Neamairtese culture that they had held close in their minds while they were slaves. Her people wanted to be told that they had not disappointed her or the Spirits and that they were still Neamairtese even after years without the customs and rituals that defined them.

Over and over, Barra assured her people one-on-one that the Spirits still considered the former slaves to be in covenant and had not abandoned them. The Lord and Lady had chosen Barra to be queen and Silvi as her mate in order to liberate them, and what could be a greater statement of their devotion and recognition of the Neamairtese slaves' devotion?

Each time, Barra wished it was Silvi hearing their stories. She would know what to say to show she truly heard them, and more importantly, Silvi would actually connect with their stories. By the fifteenth story, Barra was finding it hard to keep track of who was confessing to attempting to poison their former master and who was confessing to starting to harbor feelings of love for their former captor.

Silvi had tried to step in and help, but the Neamairtese had taken her squeamishness about their sexual stories as judgment. Her people wanted Barra and Barra had a spiritual duty to continue to serve as their bridge to the Spirits.

Barra and Silvi spent an hour or so after each dinner together, discussing their day and swapping advice for handling their people. They slept side by side, but the camps of thousands allowed for little privacy for any intimacy. That didn't stop many of the Neamairtese, but it certainly stopped Silvi. Together once more, they took pleasure from the simple intimacy of a shared kiss or chaste caress.

Barra took full advantage of the few nights that their timing worked out to utilize the Victricite slave camps, with their many small, private tents meant for the soldiers. Barra was looking forward to getting home and having Silvi all to herself whenever they wanted.

As the fourth week drew to a close, the group reached the river that ran from the mountains of Svek west, through the lands of the Neamairtese and eventually out to the ocean. This had been the point at which Silvi's group of Svekard captives had been combined with Barra's nine weeks prior. Barra found it hard to believe it had been so long ago and yet marveled that so much had happened in such a short time period. She was queen. Her mate was a Svekard. She had helped save thousands of slaves and built a truce between four warring peoples.

This was the point at which the three groups would part ways, the Svekards heading upriver to the northeast, the Neamairtese going downriver to the west, and the Razirgali back to the south. Keepan and Toghoneur were each given several small shavings from the Lord's antler to start communication fires across their lands. The fires would be a way to build up the relationship between their peoples and a way to begin to share customs and languages as well as to keep an eye on the Victricites to make sure they were adhering to their end of the deal. Lack of communication had allowed the Victricites to overrun them once. They would not allow it to happen again.

As the two groups began to part, a few of the Neamairtese, Svekards, and Razirgali gathered to bid each other farewell. A few relationships, which couldn't quite be called budding friendships, had formed over the last few weeks across the cultures, and in a few cases, their people embraced before wishing each other well in their respective languages or the Victricite language.

Silvi and Barra said good-bye to Toghoneur, who gave them a cheeky smile and a boisterous whoop before riding off ahead of his people.

Silvi turned to Barra, clear hesitation in her movements and an emotion that looked like heartbreak in her eyes. Barra felt herself go cold.

They weren't having this conversation.

She'd let the fact that they hadn't discussed this moment reassure her that everything was fine. They didn't need to talk about the day their people parted ways. They were inseparable.

"I need to go with them," Silvi said, speaking heavily with her eyes.

Barra felt her heart constrict in her chest. Her body felt like it was falling into some depthless pit and she found she couldn't breathe. Silvi was leaving. After everything, after saying "I love you" numerous times on both sides, Silvi was going home with her people.

Barra told herself that she couldn't blame Silvi. She was a hero now and Barra knew the kind of life waiting for her in Svek. How could Barra compete with that? Barra was queen, but the position didn't come with much luxury. To stay with her, Silvi would have to give up everything she knew and all the comforts she would be offered in exchange for a life among strangers. She would have to give up her family and so many aspects of her culture. But Barra had to try something. "No, you don't."

"I need to tell my family I'm okay and try to explain what's happened," Silvi said.

"Your people can do that, can't they?" Barra felt certain that this was her only chance. Together, there was a clear spark between them. If Silvi left, Barra wasn't sure she could ever get her back.

Silvi shook her head. "I need to tell them in person."

There was a lump in Barra's throat and a stinging in her eyes. She told herself she wasn't going to cry. Her people would understand if she cried, but they would pity her enough when she returned home without her mate. She didn't want their pity. She wanted their respect.

Silvi reached out a hand to pet Barra's arm and Barra almost pulled away. Was it pity in Silvi's eyes or simply an apology? Barra didn't want either. She felt anger rising up to try to fill the void in her chest. Silvi could at least say her true reasons for leaving. She wanted to be a Svekard hero.

Silvi clearly saw at least some of Barra's reaction. She pulled her hand away as if from a wolf who had bitten at her. "They're going to have a hard enough time understanding the reason I'm leaving," Silvi said defensively.

"Leaving?" Barra asked. Leaving her or…leaving them?

"I thought…" Silvi trailed off, her gaze losing its hold on Barra to travel down to her own booted feet.

"What?" Barra asked. She wanted to understand everything about Silvi, as a queen was supposed to about her mate. That was the point of sharing memories after all. Yet there was still so much to Silvi she didn't understand.

Before bonding, Barra had understood that Silvi was shy and lonely and that had made sense. She'd expected to understand her more with Silvi's memories, like understanding a meal more when she saw it prepared. But Silvi wasn't a recipe. Where Barra had expected to find a rough, barbaric society to explain the loneliness, she had found a loving family. Where Barra had expected to find sexual violence in Silvi's past, she found a complete lack of interaction. Presented with the exact same options, Barra and Silvi chose differently, acted differently, and most importantly, felt differently. They weren't two pieces of the same meat, prepared differently as she had imagined. They were two different kinds of meat.

Barra fixed Silvi with the most amenable expression she could muster. She just wanted to understand. She wasn't angry or hurt, just confused, or so she told herself to keep the expression in place.

"You're the queen." Silvi spoke haltingly. "You have to go back to your people. If we are going to be together, I have to follow you. I may never see my family again. It'll be very hard for them to understand my choice. But I assumed…I guess I should have asked…if I'm invited to, you know, live with you and your people. Do you want…me?" On the last sentence, Silvi's wandering gaze finally locked with Barra's again. Her eyes were shimmering with repressed tears.

Barra felt the knot in her throat release and was sure she was going to cry. "By the Lord and Lady, of course I want you! You are invited. All of us want you. I want you. I want you to live with me as my mate always. I love you."

Silvi pulled Barra to her, burying her face in Barra's shoulder to hide her tears. "I don't want to leave you," she muttered. "I never want to leave you. But I swear I will come back as soon as I can. I'll probably need to gather the chieftains and explain the agreement and the fires and everything. But as soon as I can, I'll come back to you."

For a long moment, Barra just held Silvi to her. She was relieved and moved, but that didn't make her any less desperate to not let Silvi go. "Is there anything I can say to make you stay?" Barra mumbled into Silvi's hair.

"Yes, so many things," Silvi whispered. "So, please, don't say them. I need to go and if you tell me not to, I don't know that I can do it."

Barra let go enough to pull back from the embrace and brush the tears from Silvi's face as if she were simply petting her. No one watching needed to know that Silvi had let a single tear fall. "Then go, my love. And take a piece of the Lord's antler to light a fire in your clan. Once I have a fire lit in the Central Tribe, we'll be able to speak to each other."

Silvi pulled Barra's lips down to her own for a long kiss. For Silvi to cry, however clandestinely, and to kiss her in public made letting her go all the harder.

"I'm coming back," Silvi said again.

Barra lifted Silvi's fingers to her lips for one last kiss before Silvi turned and hurried to catch up to her people. She'd waited as long as she could.

Barra turned back to her people, gripping the Lord's antler hard enough to turn her knuckles white. No queen had ever had to say good-bye to her mate. It wasn't uncommon for the queen's mate to die a few months or even a few years before the queen, but never for the queen's mate to leave. Barra felt the anger bubbling up inside her, trying to cover the pain and sadness that threatened to envelope her.

"She's coming back," Barra whispered to herself in Svekard as she walked, head held high, back to her people.

"She's coming back," Barra explained before leading her people back home.

"She's coming back," she repeated to herself each night of the journey, sleeping alone.

❖

The trip down the river had only taken the Svekards a few days on the giant raft of the Victricite slavers. Walking upstream took nearly two weeks.

All Silvi could think about was Barra. She would be home already, sitting at her version of the Lord's fire in the Central Tribe, wondering where in the world Silvi was.

Silvi desperately wanted to see her, to hear her, to touch her. She spent her days walking and constantly talking until her voice hurt. She spent her nights thinking constantly of Barra until her heart hurt.

Reaching the edges of Svek was a joyous occasion for the Svekards. Silvi did not join her clansfolk in their cheers, their kisses of the ground, or their dancing. She allowed herself a few tears, masked by the celebration before continuing, knowing that each step took her farther from Barra, but closer to when she could turn around and head back.

None of it felt real. The people who thanked her for saving their lives all blended into one. As the group passed through villages, their numbers grew instead of shrinking. People weren't returning home; they were escorting their hero to her home.

From the first clan they encountered, former slaves she'd helped free, their families, and random Svekards she'd never met brought her presents. Her cotton garb was quickly replaced by the best quality bear and wolf furs. People offered her valuable jewelry and family heirlooms, just wanting their hero and savior to have a token from their family line. She had to constantly turn down food because she was too full.

Silvi couldn't help but look back on her time of hero's isolation with envy. She just wanted to be left alone with her thoughts and regrets, rather than constantly having to put on a hero's mask and pretend to be someone she apparently was but didn't feel like and had never chosen to be.

Silvi didn't truly feel home until she reached the edge of her village. It wasn't the sight of the herd of oxen in Levin's field that she'd tended to several times over the past few years, or the smell of barley being harvested, or even the crunch of the gravel road Clan Spine Mountain was known for. It was the familiar sound of her name.

The crowd ahead of Silvi parted to let Papa through. Someone had run ahead of the group to tell him that Silvi was home and he'd come running.

Papa was almost out of breath as the two collided into a weeping hug. "My Silvi. My Daughter. Is home," he gasped.

"She's the hero of the Prime Gods," Slade said. He'd spent as much time as possible at Silvi's side soaking up every tidbit of story he could glean for the hundreds of times he would retell her story.

"She freed our people from Victricite slavery," Keepan pointed out, trying to make his importance known through the way he stood near Silvi and looked at her with approval as if his opinion of her mattered.

"She brought together the Svekards and the Neamairtese because she and the Neamairtese queen are in love," Eigen announced proudly, and the group fell silent. Silvi could feel the people's stares go cold as they turned disapproving looks on Eigen.

Silvi felt her own happiness chill. Her love, the thing that filled her with joy, made her people uncomfortable. It was the piece of the story they wanted to forget, the piece they wanted to pretend wasn't essential to their freedom. She pulled back from her father's hug, not entirely sure she was ready to see his reaction to such news.

Papa looked as if he hadn't heard a single thing they'd said. He didn't care that she was a hero, or Gods-chosen, or in love with a Neamairtese woman. He cared that she was alive and here in his arms. "My Silvi," he repeated, eyes brimming with tears of love.

Three women pushed through the crowd ahead of Silvi, also calling her name. Silvi didn't think she'd ever seen Mama cry. She'd barely teared up at Greta's and Nita's weddings. They all embraced, Mama holding her as if to protect her from a vicious storm.

Silvi couldn't help feeling guilty. Being held by her family filled an ache that had grown almost unbearable between the day she'd left home and the night she'd bonded with Barra. She loved her family so greatly. How could she come home only to tell them she was leaving again?

The celebration that night in Silvi's honor lasted until dawn, and the last dregs of it were still petering out when Silvi woke the next morning. There were Svekards spread across town like butter across warm bread. People from other clans had heard the news slept in the great rooms of her clansfolk or in barns and pastures. Everyone wanted to share in Svek's greatest story.

Silvi was attempting to enjoy the festivities as much for her family's sake as to make everyone feel like they had sufficiently shown their appreciation. She'd thought maybe, if she allowed the feasts, the storytelling, the dancing, and the accolades to take place, and received it all with gratitude and a smile, that it would all end. She was wrong.

The people continued to flow into Clan Spine Mountain. During the days, Silvi met with the most powerful and well regarded Svekards in all of Svek. It was an odd sensation to know that they paled in comparison to her.

She met with rune readers to describe as best she could every aspect of the Prime Gods, what they had said, and what they wanted out of the deal with the Victricites, Razirgali, and Neamairtese. Silvi did her best to balance the explanation of the Svekard Gods' willingness and even zeal to go to war with the recognition that Barra's plan was also in their best interest. Silvi was fairly sure that it wouldn't matter if she was the hero of all the Gods. If her people thought the deal was against what their Gods wanted, the Svekards wouldn't uphold it.

Chieftains from across Svek came to learn of the new agreement and the ramifications for their clans. There were slaves to reintegrate, marriages to codify or nullify, and widows and a few orphans to find care for. Once all the chieftains had arrived, they divvied up the scrapings of the Lord's antler and Klucar's runes to create fires of their own. The debates were heated, as leaders who had gained power through age and wisdom tried to keep to their ways, while younger leaders argued for a greater share for their clans. Everyone wanted their opinion heard, but everyone listened when Silvi opened her mouth. Not all heroes were blessed with wisdom by the Gods, but when anyone with Fradren's mark on their forehead spoke, everyone listened. They didn't necessarily accept everything she said, but they listened to every word.

Silvi spent the least time with the oath keepers. They scribed their copies of the agreement, clarified the nuances, and listened attentively to a single retelling of the Second Council of Neamairt. When their process was done, the oath keepers respectfully informed Silvi that as a chosen of Fradren, she was invited to remain but was not required to. They would determine which laws and oaths would need to change in order to uphold the Svekard side of the agreement, while holding true to the spirit of the oaths and the will of the Gods.

Silvi did not know the laws and it was not her place to be there overriding those that did just because she was Gods-chosen. However, she did think it was her place to remind them that the will of the Gods was not what it had been. "The Gods told us they didn't like the Neamairtese because they wanted to ensure we didn't band together with the Neamairtese against them, not because they actually despise the Neamairtese. But now they see the danger in keeping us apart and know that we are weaker without the Neamairtese."

"Did they say that?" an older female oath keeper with the symbol of Fradren on her forehead asked. Of the one hundred and fifty or so oath keepers in the room, Silvi was one of three people with the mark of Fradren. No one in that room bore the mark of any other god.

Silvi paused to think through their words as best as she could remember. No, it had been the Lord that explained it all, but the Svekard Gods hadn't contradicted and Klucar would not have given them the runes if he didn't agree. She did her best to explain, but the expressions she got in return didn't fill her with much confidence. It had taken a few days surrounded by Neamairtese, including one she loved, to change some of her views. She supposed she couldn't expect them to change all of theirs based on one conversation.

Three days later, the oath keepers filed out of Clan Spine Mountain's fellowship hall to return to their circuit of clans.

Before leaving, the oath keeper who had questioned Silvi approached her. "You would make an excellent oath keeper if you can let go of your bias toward the Neamairtese. I will train you if it is your will."

The offer took Silvi by surprise. Apprentices were almost always chosen before the coming-of-age ceremony. Years had to be dedicated to learning all of the necessary oaths and laws by heart. The fact that the woman considered Silvi to be the biased one surprised her more. She turned down the offer but left out that she didn't plan to stay in Svek very much longer.

Silvi hadn't told anyone she planned to leave. Everyone simply planned based on the idea that she was now a fixture in the clan as she had always been—as all Svekards were.

Every night, a banquet and celebration were held, whether to light the Lord's first fire in Svek, welcome home the former slaves, honor the Gods, or formalize completion of the oath keepers' work. At every event, Silvi was the guest of honor, her participation expected. She would stay as long as it took for everyone to get drunk enough to not notice her slip off and go sit at the Lord's fire.

The shadow of Barra would be waiting for her every night. They sat side by side, Silvi's hand holding the air where Barra's hand appeared to be. Barra's form was wispy and colorless as if she were made of nothing but smoke. She knew a similar version of herself sat at Barra's fire, her hand being almost held in return. Silvi hated not being able to touch her; her hand passed right through.

Barra and Silvi told each other about their days, swapped advice, and told each other the stories of their lives as they had done during the trip north. Every night, Silvi promised to leave as soon as she could, and every night, she mourned that she still hadn't left, and still didn't know when she would get to.

It took just over two weeks of hinting, attempting to broach the topic, and coaching from Barra before Silvi finally announced she was leaving. She'd been asked to recite her experiences of the Second Council of Neamairt before the whole of the congregated Svekards again. They were celebrating the first harvest of barley, a celebration that usually was reserved for the last harvest of barley, and discussing how every Kraunfish story would be about Silvi that year and Silvi would be the Grand Kraun, without a doubt. She would be the Grand Kraun in every clan. Perhaps, each clan ought to have their Kraunfish festival a few days apart, that way Silvi could attend them all. If they started in a few weeks, the remaining Svekards who were returning from Victricus would be home and they could have all of the Kraunfish festivals done before too far into the winter.

"I can't stay," Silvi announced. Everyone looked at her like this was both a non sequitur and obvious. How was she supposed to go to every Kraunfish festival across Svek if she stayed in Clan Spine Mountain? She would always be Silvi of Clan Spine Mountain, but now she served all Svekards, not just her clan. She belonged to all of Svek and would travel the rest of her life…within Svek.

"I mean, I can't stay in Svek. I need to go to the Neamairtese." Silvi took a deep breath and went into the speech Barra had helped her write. She was going to help build a lasting peace between the Neamairtese and the Svekards. It was what the Gods had chosen her for. She needed to teach and to learn. She, the hero of Svek, and Barra, the queen of the Neamairtese, had been tasked by the Gods with creating a relationship between their peoples to outlast the trials of time and outlive the Gods themselves. This was the path the Gods had placed before her.

For a long moment, the crowd of Svekards stared at Silvi, aghast. "You must stay until the remainder of our people return home," a Svekard woman yelled. There was a general uproar of agreement. Silvi could hear anger and hurt in their voices. They would never tell her outright that they thought she was wrong about what the Gods wanted, but they could try to help her see the err of her interpretation.

Over the next two and a half weeks, her people did everything they could to distract Silvi from her plan to leave. They brought her gifts and showered her in praise and attention. She was brought the finest furs, goose feather pillows, and the best food on the most expensive dishes. She had several men vaguely state their interest to court her, as was the typical Svekard way. The parties continued and Clan Spine Mountain became more and more crowded.

Silvi's opinion was sought on everything from minor disagreements to hunting plans to whether crops were ready to be harvested. A few heroes, especially heroes of one of the Prime Gods, sought her out to help share advice on dealing with the attention and burden of being a hero. By the end of their visits, Silvi was fairly sure all she'd learned was that they all expected her to do what was best for the clan and be the hero her people needed…in Svek.

All Silvi's life, her deepest wish had been to serve her clan and to make Papa proud of the Svekard she had become. She felt torn in two. She spent her days being clandestinely guilted into staying, and at night she would return home early just to sneak out to the Lord's fire and talk to Barra until she couldn't keep her eyes open. With every word, she felt like she was apologizing to someone either because she was leaving or because she hadn't left yet.

The night news reached Clan Spine Mountain that the remaining Victricite slaves, nearly five thousand in total, had reached the edge of Svek, Silvi went home to pack. She was met on her doorstep by the chieftain of Clan Spine Mountain. Bren had been her chieftain for almost a decade but, until recently, she had interacted with him far more in her role as veterinarian of his sheep flock than in his role as chieftain. She held great respect for him.

"Silvi, may I speak with you?" he asked, gesturing toward her sheep pen as if it were a normal place to have a serious conversation. "I have always come to you about the health of my flock and so I come to you now. Not about my sheep flock, but my people flock. You have always been so valuable to your clan, but now…I don't have to tell you that we have never had a Svekard as important as you. Your clan *needs* you, Silvi. And, not just our clan, but every Svekard. All of Svek needs you to stay and be our shepherd. You would never abandon your flock, don't abandon us now."

He had learned over their years together that Silvi didn't react to pomp and circumstance. She liked to feel needed and to help. He rested his hand on one of her sleeping sheep, stroking it gently with a look of fatherly love. "I know you will make the right choice," he said, before taking his leave.

Silvi watched him leave, no longer able to hold back her tears. She fled to her room, throwing herself onto her bed. "Barra," she moaned into the darkness.

A quiet knock at her door caught Silvi by surprise. "Just a moment," Silvi called out, her voice making her current state all too obvious.

Silvi tried to bring her crying under control but found it impossible. She was never going to get to leave. She should stay for her clan. She was Gods-chosen. What right did she have to choose love over duty?

Silvi heard the door click behind her as someone entered and closed the door behind them. She kept her back to the door, trying to hide her shame. She tipped her head away from Papa as he took a seat on the bed next to her and pulled her into one of his crushing hugs.

"Silvi, tell me," he said as he had always done when she was little. It was a demand for honesty, but also a promise that he would listen to her side of the story and believe what she told him.

"I should be with Barra," Silvi sobbed into Papa's shoulder. She'd already failed to hide her un-Svekard-like crying, so there seemed little purpose continuing the futile attempt to stop. "I should stay and be our people's hero. I'm a bad Svekard and a bad mate. I don't know what to do. I'm failing the Gods and I'm failing my love and I'm failing you."

"Silvi," Papa said, pulling back from the hug and looking her directly in the eyes. "The Gods chose you to end thousands of years of hatred between our people and the Neamairtese. Our people want you here. That does not mean they know what is best for the clan. Where do you think you should be? Where does your heart tell you to be?"

"With Barra," Silvi said, feeling guilty all over again for telling her father that her heart told her to leave him.

"I know what it is like to love a woman so much you'd do anything for her," Papa explained, looking over his shoulder toward the door. Beyond it, in their room, was the wife he had loved, married, and raised children with.

He continued. "And I know what it is like to love someone so much that when you are apart from them, it feels like your heart is being torn in two." He reached out a hand and held it cupped an inch away from Silvi's face. He had hugged her without her permission like she was a child, but now he showed her the respect owed to her as an adult by offering the gentle touch and letting her accept by closing the distance.

While Silvi had been marching south talking to a fake image of Papa, he had been here at home, sure she was dead. How could she leave him when he was so clearly telling her that she would tear his heart in two if she left again?

"If your heart tells you to be with Barda, then that is where you need to be," he said matter-of-factly. "The Gods chose your heart. It will not guide you astray."

Silvi gave a small appreciative smile. It was all she could muster. That couldn't be what he truly thought. She waited for the "but."

With a soft sigh, he spoke again. "I would love for you to stay. But it is a father's duty to put his child's happiness before his own. You, Silvi, are a good Svekard and you have always made me so proud. Our clan needs you and the Gods need you, but they don't need you here. They need you out there, doing what the Gods chose you to do. The greatest Svekard hero isn't meant to be Grand Kraun over and over again. She is meant to change everything. That starts when you leave. I wish it wasn't true, but it is."

This time, Silvi didn't try to hide her tears. They were tears of joy and tears of love. She pulled Papa into the tightest hug she could manage.

"Come," Papa said before rising and leading her to the small loafing shed within her sheep pen. He ducked under the thatch roof and made his way to the back before climbing out again, backward, dragging something in front of him.

"A boat," Silvi gasped.

"It's not done. It's not deep enough to be very comfortable and I haven't smoothed it yet, but it'll float. Papa's expression was a mix of pride and embarrassment. He'd worked hard on it, but perhaps it wasn't enough.

Silvi had been proud to call him Papa all her life, but she'd never been so proud or felt more loved. Her father, despite his desire for her to stay, had provided her exactly what she needed in order to go. "We could smooth it together tonight and I could leave at dawn," Silvi suggested, trying to balance her desire to show her appreciation and love with her desire to get to Barra.

Silvi and Papa spent the rest of the night smoothing the dugout in the moonlight. Silvi filled the hours telling her father about Barra. She related story after story of their time together and Barra's life before being captured. She tried to explain the magic and Barra's culture but spent most of her time focusing on the aspects of Barra's life that were deeply human and required no translation to Svekard equivalents.

Just before dawn, Silvi woke Mama and her sisters to say good-bye. Mama cajoled her into a shared breakfast before gripping her to her chest in a hug that almost rivaled those of Papa. She shared similar hugs with her sisters and her brother-in-law.

"Silvi?" A small voice broke the solemn moment. Silvi looked over her sister's shoulder to see her four-year-old nephew standing in the door of his parents' room. "You leave?" he asked, the tears of a child welling up in his eyes.

Silvi hurried forward to scoop him up into her arms. Svekards didn't leave their families. Even Greta only lived a day's journey away. How was she supposed to explain to him that he might not see her again?

The thought occurred to Silvi in a flash, and she would have slapped her hand against her forehead if it hadn't been holding a small boy. "I'll be back," she told him, turning to the rest of her family.

She had been so focused on returning to Barra that she hadn't even considered what was going to happen after she did. "If Barra and

I are going to build trust and an alliance between the Neamairtese and Svekards, we're going to have to come to Svek. We'll start with the Neamairtese because they need her to be their queen, but we can't do everything we need to from there. I'll be back and I'll be bringing Barra with me."

Her family let out a collective breath, as if they had just been told the wolf terrorizing their village had been slain. This wasn't truly good-bye.

Silvi gave them all one last hug before she and Papa slipped out of the house into the dewy morning's dawn. They each carried a large rucksack over one shoulder, filled with food and supplies Silvi would need for her journey as well as the things she most didn't want to live without.

The day had fully bloomed by the time Silvi and Papa reached the river. By the time Papa reached her family home, the whole of the clan would know Silvi was gone. Silvi gave him one last hug, gripping him until he pulled back. She could tell from the look in his eyes that if he held on any longer, he might not ever let go.

"I'll be back, and we can always speak through the fire," Silvi said, climbing into the boat and letting him push her off into the river. He was on the brink of tears and the thought scared her.

"I'm so proud of you," he said, allowing a few tears to fall, his sadness masked by tears of pride.

"I love you," Silvi called back before watching his figure get smaller and smaller on the bank as she traveled away.

Since returning to the Central Tribe, Barra had spent her days engulfed in her duties as queen and her nights trying to pretend Silvi was by her side, rather than hundreds of miles away.

Barra had been too focused on saving her people and returning them home to consider how busy she would be once she returned. Her memories could have told her, but she'd repressed them in hopes of a long, deep sleep.

She'd lost days of sleep during the journey through Victricus, days she'd never caught up during the trip home. Now, she stayed at the Lord's fire later and later each night, trying to beg Silvi to come home to her without layering even more guilt onto her shoulders. Barra was finding it harder and harder to pull herself from her bed each morning and advise the elders on the will of the Spirits and the Lord and Lady.

She constantly heard Air speaking in her ear but was finding it more and more difficult to pick out individual words, let alone meaning as her mind wandered between her desire for Silvi and her desire for sleep. Even when she did sleep, her sleep wasn't restful.

Sitting next to the Lord's fire and waiting for Silvi, Barra couldn't help but repeat the phrase that had plagued her first days as queen. "A queen isn't supposed to be without her mate."

Speaking of which, where was Silvi? It often took her late into the evening to arrive at the fire, but never this late.

A dark, smokey figure appeared at the very edge of the fire's glow. Barra's sigh of relief caught in her throat as the figure approached her. It wasn't Silvi. This wasn't the first time a Svekard's curiosity had brought them to inspect the fire and one Svekard had even had the audacity to seek her out several nights ago to inform her that Silvi was their hero and Barra should stop using her witchcraft to try to steal Silvi away from them.

Barra was much too tired to deal with this crap. "Where's Silvi?" Barra asked bluntly.

Barra recognized the voice coming from the shadow from over two decades of Silvi's memories and regretted her harsh tone. "She left this morning," Silvi's father, Ulgar, said. "I made her a boat."

Barra was pleased and surprised. Silvi would be by her side so much sooner, but based on everything she knew about him, she would have guessed Ulgar would be doing everything in his power to keep her in Clan Spine Mountain. The figure of Ulgar strode to a spot opposite the fire from her and sat down, legs and arms crossed.

"If you were a Svekard, you would be expected to come to me in person. You would tell me about your greatest deeds so far and what the rune readers read in your future," Ulgar said, his voice stern.

Barra picked up where he had paused. "I would attempt to put into words, the extent of my love, which reaches to the highest mountains on which the Clanned Gods sit and to the depths of the deepest fjords and out to the vastness of the ocean beyond. I love your daughter more than I thought it was possible to love someone. I don't feel whole when we're apart. My greatest wish is for her happiness. My greatest joy is in seeing her joy. If I were there, I would swear to protect her and to love her every day for the rest of our lives as much as I love her now or more, if that's even possible."

Ulgar nodded slowly, though it was hard to tell his expression from the wispy edges of the smoke that made up his profile. His voice was just as stern when he spoke again. "If you were a Svekard, you would assure me that your union is of greater benefit to the clan than you are each individually. And you would ask for my blessing."

He paused to take a deep breath, and Barra considered picking up where he left off, but he was clearly not done. "Silvi has told me about your great deeds and what she sees in your future. The Gods themselves have told us that your union is what's best for the clan and for all Svekards. She loves you."

"I love her, and every night, I will come here to tell you of the depths of my love and my dedication, until I have sufficiently proven to you that I will do anything for her and our union and have your blessing." Barra felt like there was more she should be doing. In Svek, this process typically lasted days, in which the suitor would bring gifts of great value or items that he had crafted to show his skill and devotion. Barra could do none of that.

The shadowy figure nodded again. "That will suffice. You should know that being the queen does not mean you are worthy of my daughter. Not until you have proven it."

"I understand and I will," Barra said.

She returned to the fire every night for six nights, spending hours trying to put her feelings into words. Ulgar would sit, his arms and legs crossed and listen before telling her that he would see her the next night.

On the seventh night, when Barra had reached the end of her gushing and she could barely keep her eyes open, Ulgar stood and extended an incorporeal hand to her, palm down. "Barra, queen of the Neamairtese, caller of freedom fog, participant of the Second Council of Neamairt, I grant you my blessing in marrying my daughter Silvi. You are to treat her with the respect owed to her as a woman and as a Svekard hero. You are to love her all the days of your life and in all things put her and the clan before yourself. Do you accept these terms?"

Barra rose to her feet and placed her hand inside the gray, billowy hand in front of her. She was going to dedicate her life to Silvi and to bringing the Neamairtese and Svekards together, and nothing could be more important for the clan. Even the Gods had said so. "I accept. Thank you."

Barra returned to her tent and was asleep by the time her head reached the cot.

She woke in the middle of the night to a throbbing feeling in her heart. "Silvi," Barra gasped into the complete darkness. She could feel someone there, but how many times over the past two months had she woken from just such a dream so sure Silvi was there?

"My love," came Silvi's answer as she pushed into Barra's tent and rushed to her side.

"I'm not dreaming, am I? You're here?" Barra asked, grabbing every part of Silvi she could and pulling Silvi tighter against her. Her heart ached and she could barely breathe as she clung to her, desperate to know that she was really there.

"I'm here," Silvi said. "And I always will be."

They kissed, their kisses fluctuating between furious passion and lingering tenderness. Barra wanted to express in each kiss all that she had told Ulgar of her love. It was depthless and would last over a thousand lifetimes. Their souls were meant to be together.

Silvi reached behind her to pull a soft, cream-colored sack onto the cot. "I brought you a present," she said, still holding Barra tight against her chest. She handed a goose feather pillow to Barra who dropped it onto the cot behind them.

"You are the only present I need," Barra replied, pulling Silvi on top of her and disrobing her. They would rest that night spooned together, heads resting on the pillow, exchanging whispered promises of unending love and a life, side by side.

The next morning, Barra gave Silvi the official tour of the tribe that would become her home. The relief in every Neamairtese face was obvious as they greeted her, two fingers placed over their hearts. Barra guessed that her lethargy and melancholy over the almost two months of Silvi's absence had been obvious to everyone.

The Neamairtese had gone without a queen for months, unsure if they had done something wrong and lost the queen's magic forever. Barra had returned with thousands of their people and helped reintegrate those who were former slaves. However, she had done it as only a piece of the queen she was meant to be. Now, with Silvi there, loving their queen and being loved by their queen, things had the chance of returning to normalcy, strange as it was to have a Svekard in their midst.

Slowly, piece by piece, Silvi adapted to life amongst the Neamairtese. She swapped her woolen clothing and eventually her furs for the hides of the people around her, though she insisted whenever the chance arose that she was a very small Svekard compared to her people. Daily washings became part of her routine, starting as clothed midnight outings when no one would see them and eventually graduating to more secluded areas of the river without clothing.

On one such outing, a good way upriver from the rest of the bathing Neamairtese, Silvi got her first glance of Neamairtese having sex while surrounded by people who could see them plainly. Barra knew Silvi had heard it before, and she had definitely heard Neamairtese talking about their exploits. However, she didn't think she'd ever seen Silvi turn such a dark shade of red.

Silvi swirled around in the water, turning to face against the current and covered her eyes. Barra waded the couple of feet from where she had been shaving her arms to wrap her arms around her from the back. "I just...he was...and she...Barra," Silvi gave a stammering moan.

"I know," Barra said. "But remember, sex is a beautiful thing. An action of passion and romance...and fun."

Silvi just groaned. "I still don't have to like knowing when other people are doing it."

"Torchane is going to be hard for you," Barra admitted, running her soapy hands up and down Silvi's sides and pressing gentle kisses to her shoulders and neck.

"Gods." Silvi groaned again. She was clearly remembering Barra's memories of the event and though Barra could see Silvi's nipples hardening, it didn't keep her from dreading it.

"Don't worry," Barra said, reaching up to gently stroke Silvi's breasts. "We'll tie ribbons around your ankles and wrists and no one but me will touch you."

"But I still have to make you orgasm to start the ceremony...in front of everyone," Silvi whispered, her breathing and heart rate picking up. Barra could feel her own heart rate pick up to match it. In Barra, the increase felt warm and sensuous. She could sense Silvi's anxiety, but she could also feel the arousal pumping beneath it.

"We have months to work up to it," Barra reassured her. She pressed her own naked breasts to Silvi's back and wrapped her legs around Silvi's waist from behind.

"You know," Barra whispered, her lips against Silvi's ear. She could feel the goose bumps rising on Silvi's neck and kissed them. "Torchane is a celebration of fertility for the spirit of Earth. You and Earth have a lot in common."

Barra ran her hands over Silvi's muscled arms. "You're both strong."

She swept forward to cup Silvi's breasts. "You're both beautiful."

Barra brought her hands up to poke soapy water on Silvi's pouting lip. "You're both stubborn."

She sank her hands below the water line to pet up the inside of Silvi's thigh and play gently between her legs, loving the way it made Silvi both jump and moan. "And you both need to be reminded from time to time just how good prurience feels."

"You and your dozens of words that just mean sex," Silvi groaned, her tone making it clear she was trying to convince herself to say stop but desperately didn't want to.

"It's called desensitization," Barra said, raising her fingers higher to stroke Silvi the way she knew drove her crazy. "You just need positive experiences slowly pushing your boundaries. Do you want me to stop?"

Silvi was silent for a moment and Barra was concerned she was going to have to pull away. She gave one last hopeful stroke, feeling Silvi buck against her as she did, and knew there was no way they were stopping.

"No," Silvi said, reaching back to grab Barra and pull her around in the water to her front. "I never want you to stop," she added before exploring Barra's mouth passionately.

Barra vowed to never allow such changes to go by without appreciation for what Silvi was doing for her. At her core, Silvi was still a Svekard and always would be. This was not a journey to make Silvi someone other than who she was. It was a journey to merge their lives and eventually to merge their peoples. Barra loved Silvi for everything that made her exactly who she was, the things she compromised on for love of Barra and the things that would always be a part of her.

About the Author

Jennifer Karter lives in the Washington, DC, area with her spouse, their daughter, and their two cats. When she's not working in international development, reading, or writing, Jennifer enjoys quilting, playing board games (of which she owns over three hundred), and hiking. She is a longtime avid Dungeon Master, but only ever of Dungeons & Dragons, and collects female action figures, which are frustratingly rare.

Jennifer.j.karter@gmail.com

Books Available from Bold Strokes Books

Cold Blood by Genevieve McCluer. Maybe together, Kalila and Dorenia have a chance of taking down the vampires who have eluded them all these years. And maybe, in each other, they can find a love worth living for. (978-1-63679-195-1)

Greener Pastures by Aurora Rey. When city girl and CPA Audrey Adams finds herself tending her aunt's farm, will Rowan Marshall—the charming cider maker next door—turn out to be her saving grace or the bane of her existence? (978-1-63679-116-6)

Grounded by Amanda Radley. For a second chance, Olivia and Emily will need to accept their mistakes, learn to communicate properly, and with a little help from five-year-old Henry, fall madly in love all over again. Sequel to Flight SQA016. (978-1-63679-241-5)

Journey's End by Amanda Radley. In this heartwarming conclusion to the Flight series, Olivia and Emily must finally decide what they want, what they need, and how to follow the dreams of their hearts. (978-1-63679-233-0)

Pursued: Lillian's Story by Felice Picano. Fleeing a disastrous marriage to the Lord Exchequer of England, Lillian of Ravenglass reveals an incident-filled, often bizarre, tale of great wealth and power, perfidy, and betrayal. (978-1-63679-197-5)

Secret Agent by Michelle Larkin. CIA agent Peyton North embarks on a global chase to apprehend rogue agent Zoey Blackwood, but her commitment to the mission is tested as the sparks between them ignite and their sizzling attraction approaches a point of no return. (978-1-63555-753-4)

Something Between Us by Krystina Rivers. A decade after her heart was broken under Don't Ask, Don't Tell, Kirby runs into her first love and has to decide if what's still between them is enough to heal her broken heart. (978-1-63679-135-7)

Sugar Girl by Emma L McGeown. Having traded in traditional romance for the perks of Sugar Dating, Ciara Reilly not only enjoys the no-strings-attached arrangement, she's also a hit with her clients. That is until she meets the beautiful entrepreneur Charlie Keller who makes her want to go sugar-free. (978-1-63679-156-2)

The Business of Pleasure by Ronica Black. Editor in chief Valerie Raffield is quickly becoming smitten by Lennox, the graphic artist she's hired to work remotely. But when Lennox doesn't show for their first face-to-face meeting, Valerie's heart and her business may be in jeopardy. (978-1-63679-134-0)

The Hummingbird Sanctuary by Erin Zak. The Hummingbird Sanctuary, Colorado's hottest resort destination: Come for the mountains, stay for the charm, and enjoy the drama as Olive, Eleanor, and Harriet figure out the meaning of true friendship. (978-1-63679-163-0)

The Witch Queen's Mate by Jennifer Karter. Barra and Silvi must overcome their ingrained hatred and prejudice to use Barra's magic and save both their peoples, not just from slavery, but destruction. (978-1-63679-202-6)

With a Twist by Georgia Beers. Starting over isn't easy for Amelia Martini. When the irritatingly cheerful Kirby Dupress comes into her life will Amelia be brave enough to go after the love she really wants? (978-1-63555-987-3)

Business of the Heart by Claire Forsythe. When a hopeless romantic meets a tough-as-nails cynic, they'll need to overcome the wounds of the past to discover that their hearts are the most important business of all. (978-1-63679-167-8)

Dying for You by Jenny Frame. Can Victorija Dred keep an age-old vow and fight the need to take blood from Daisy Macdougall? (978-1-63679-073-2)

Exclusive by Melissa Brayden. Skylar Ruiz lands the TV reporting job of a lifetime, but is she willing to sacrifice it all for the love of her longtime crush, anchorwoman Carolyn McNamara? (978-1-63679-112-8)

Her Duchess to Desire by Jane Walsh. An up-and-coming interior designer seeks to create a happily ever after with an intriguing duchess, proving that love never goes out of fashion. (978-1-63679-065-7)

Murder on Monte Vista by David S. Pederson. Private Detective Mason Adler's angst at turning fifty is forgotten when his "birthday present," the handsome, young Henry Bowtrickle, turns up dead, and it's up to Mason to figure out who did it, and why. (978-1-63679-124-1)

Take Her Down by Lauren Emily Whalen. Stakes are cutthroat, scheming is creative, and loyalty is ever-changing in this queer, female-driven YA retelling of Shakespeare's Julius Caesar. (978-1-63679-089-3)

The Game by Jan Gayle. Ryan Gibbs is a talented golfer, but her guilt means she may never leave her small town, even if Katherine Reese tempts her with competition and passion. (978-1-63679-126-5)

Whereabouts Unknown by Meredith Doench. While homicide detective Theodora Madsen recovers from a potentially career-ending injury, she scrambles to solve the cases of two missing sixteen-year-old girls from Ohio. (978-1-63555-647-6)

Boy at the Window by Lauren Melissa Ellzey. Daniel Kim struggles to hold onto reality while haunted by both his very-present past and his never-present parents. Jiwon Yoon may be the only one who can break Daniel free. (978-1-63679-092-3)

Deadly Secrets by VK Powell. Corporate criminals want whistleblower Jana Elliott permanently silenced, but Rafe Silva will risk everything to keep the woman she loves safe. (978-1-63679-087-9)

Enchanted Autumn by Ursula Klein. When Elizabeth comes to Salem, Massachusetts, to study the witch trials, she never expects to find love—or an actual witch...and Hazel might just turn out to be both. (978-1-63679-104-3)

Escorted by Renee Roman. When fantasy meets reality, will escort Ryan Lewis be able to walk away from a chance at forever with her new client Dani? (978-1-63679-039-8)

Her Heart's Desire by Anne Shade. Two women. One choice. Will Eve and Lynette be able to overcome their doubts and fears to embrace their deepest desire? (978-1-63679-102-9)

My Secret Valentine by Julie Cannon, Erin Dutton, & Anne Shade. Winning the heart of your secret Valentine? These award-winning authors agree, there is no better way to fall in love. (978-1-63679-071-8)

Perilous Obsession by Carsen Taite. When reporter Macy Moran becomes consumed with solving a cold case, will her quest for the truth bring her closer to Detective Beck Ramsey or will her obsession with finding a murderer rob her of a chance at true love? (978-1-63679-009-1)

Reading Her by Amanda Radley. Lauren and Allegra learn love and happiness are right where they least expect it. There's just one problem: Lauren has a secret she cannot tell anyone, and Allegra knows she's hiding something. (978-1-63679-075-6)

The Willing by Lyn Hemphill. Kitty Wilson doesn't know how, but she can bring people back from the dead as long as someone is willing to take their place and keep the universe in balance. (978-1-63679-083-1)

Three Left Turns to Nowhere by Nathan Burgoine, J. Marshall Freeman, & Jeffrey Ricker. Three strangers heading to a convention in Toronto are stranded in rural Ontario, where a small town with a subtle kind of magic leads each to discover what he's been searching for. (978-1-63679-050-3)

Watching Over Her by Ronica Black. As they face the snowstorm of the century, and the looming threat of a stalker, Riley and Zoey just might find love in the most unexpected of places. (978-1-63679-100-5)

#shedeservedit by Greg Herren. When his gay best friend, and high school football star, is murdered, Alex Wheeler is a suspect and must find the truth to clear himself. (978-1-63555-996-5)

Always by Kris Bryant. When a pushy American private investigator shows up demanding to meet the woman in Camila's artwork, instead of introducing her to her great-grandmother, Camila decides to lead her on a wild goose chase all over Italy. (978-1-63679-027-5)

Exes and O's by Joy Argento. Ali and Madison really only have one thing in common. The girl who broke their heart may be the only one who can put it back together. (978-1-63679-017-6)

One Verse Multi by Sander Santiago. Life was good: promotion, friends, falling in love, discovering that the multi-verse is on a fast track to collision—wait, what? Good thing Martin King works for a company that can fix the problem, right…um…right? (978-1-63679-069-5)

Paris Rules by Jaime Maddox. Carly Becker has been searching for the perfect woman all her life, but no one ever seems to be just right until Paige Waterford checks all her boxes, except the most important one—she's married. (978-1-63679-077-0)

Shadow Dancers by Suzie Clarke. In this third and final book in the Moon Shadow series, Rachel must find a way to become the hunter and not the hunted, and this time she will meet Ehsee Yumiko head-on. (978-1-63555-829-6)

The Kiss by C.A. Popovich. When her wife refuses their divorce and begins to stalk her, threatening her life, Kate realizes to protect her new love, Leslie, she has to let her go, even if it breaks her heart. (978-1-63679-079-4)

The Wedding Setup by Charlotte Greene. When Ryann, a big-time New York executive, goes to Colorado to help out with her best friend's wedding, she never expects to fall for the maid of honor. (978-1-63679-033-6)

Velocity by Gun Brooke. Holly and Claire work toward an uncertain future preparing for an alien space mission, and only one thing is for certain, they will have to risk their lives, and their hearts, to discover the truth. (978-1-63555-983-5)

Wildflower Words by Sam Ledel. Lida Jones treks West with her father in search of a better life on the rapidly developing American frontier, but finds home when she meets Hazel Thompson. (978-1-63679-055-8)

A Fairer Tomorrow by Kathleen Knowles. For Maddie Weeks and Gerry Stern, the Second World War brought them together, but the end of the war might rip them apart. (978-1-63555-874-6)

Holiday Hearts by Diana Day-Admire and Lyn Cole. Opposites attract during Christmastime chaos in Kansas City. (978-1-63679-128-9)

Changing Majors by Ana Hartnett Reichardt. Beyond a love, beyond a coming-out, Bailey Sullivan discovers what lies beyond the shame and self-doubt imposed on her by traditional Southern ideals. (978-1-63679-081-7)

Fresh Grave in Grand Canyon by Lee Patton. The age-old Grand Canyon becomes more and more ominous as a group of volunteers fight to survive alone in nature and uncover a murderer among them. (978-1-63679-047-3)

Highland Whirl by Anna Larner. Opposites attract in the Scottish Highlands, when feisty Alice Campbell falls for city-girl-about-town Roxanne Barns. (978-1-63555-892-0)

Humbug by Amanda Radley. With the corporate Christmas party in jeopardy, CEO Rosalind Caldwell hires Christmas Girl Ellie Pearce as her personal assistant. The only problem is, Ellie isn't a PA, has never planned a party, and develops a ridiculous crush on her totally intimidating new boss. (978-1-63555-965-1)

On the Rocks by Georgia Beers. Schoolteacher Vanessa Martini makes no apologies for her dating checklist, and newly single mom Grace Chapman ticks all Vanessa's Do Not Date boxes. Of course, they're never going to fall in love. (978-1-63555-989-7)

Song of Serenity by Brey Willows. Arguing with the Muse of music and justice is complicated, falling in love with her even more so. (978-1-63679-015-2)

The Christmas Proposal by Lisa Moreau. Stranded together in a Christmas village on a snowy mountain, Grace and Bridget face their past and question their dreams for the future. (978-1-63555-648-3)

The Infinite Summer by Morgan Lee Miller. While spending the summer with her dad in a small beach town, Remi Brenner falls for Harper Hebert and accidentally finds herself tangled up in an intense restaurant rivalry between her famous stepmom and her first love. (978-1-63555-969-9)

Wisdom by Jesse J. Thoma. When Sophia and Reggie are chosen for the governor's new community design team and tasked with tackling substance abuse and mental health issues, battle lines are drawn even as sparks fly. (978-1-63555-886-9)